HIDING

SCARS

sands press
Brockville, Ontario

HIDING SCARS

RICHARD ZARIC

sands press

sands press

A Division of 10361976 Canada Inc.
300 Central Avenue West
Brockville, Ontario
K6V 5V2

Toll Free 1-800-563-0911 or 613-345-2687
http://www.sandspress.com

ISBN 978-1-988281-41-4
Copyright © 2018 Richard Zaric
All Rights Reserved

Cover Design by Kristine Barker and Wendy Treverton
Edited by Katrina Geenevasen
Formatting by Renee Hare
Publisher Kristine Barker

Publisher's Note

For information on bulk purchases of this book or any book published by Sands Press, please call 1-800-563-0911.

1st Printing March 2018
2nd Printing August 2018

To book an author for your live event, please call: 1-800-563-0911

Sands Press is a literary publisher interested in new and established authors wishing to develop and market their product. For more information please visit our website at www.sandspress.com.

For June

Welcome to Winnipeg
July 4, 1913

Marko started to run, but stopped. Where would he go? His suitcase had been right beside him. Gone in one second. It was heavy so the thief could not have gotten very far. He focused on every piece of luggage and package that looked remotely close to his own dark brown suitcase but too many people milled about in front of the train station on Higgins Avenue. Some, like Marko, were new arrivals to Winnipeg. Others were their relatives and friends.

The clothes and shaving kit could be replaced, but what of his other belongings? His mother's books? The tools? The photos? Gone. How could he go to Mike's house with nothing? This was not how he envisioned starting his new life. Thankfully he kept his important papers and money in his jacket pocket.

He slammed his fist into his palm. What a fool he was. Just minutes before, the man at the Immigration Hall building beside the train station told him to be careful. He said all kinds of con men and cheats prowled around Winnipeg. After all, it was a boomtown and boomtowns attracted opportunists from far and wide. The man that introduced himself just outside Immigration Hall called himself Igor. Friendly, he even spoke Ukrainian. He told him about an employment agency where Marko might find a job. He gave Marko some quick directions. They shook hands. When Marko reached down he felt only air. It was a set up.

Frantic, Marko swiveled his head back and forth to scan for his suitcase. Where was it? The lout could not have gotten far. Should he even bother telling the police?

Marko's stomach growled. He couldn't remember the last time he ate. What he would do for a bowl of borscht. He was also thirsty, but a shot of whiskey would go down better than water.

He felt a shot of pain like a needle being pushed through his right temple. Not now. Now here. Marko stood still and closed his eyes. He pressed his index and middle fingers hard against the indentation on his temple. He could hear other train passengers around him. A few brushed against him, but he remained rigid and mobile. If he stayed calm the pain would go away. Slow down. Breathe in. Breathe out. Concentrate on something. Anything. His trip….

The journey to Winnipeg had been arduous. Long train rides on both sides of the Atlantic sandwiched around a steam ship crossing. Close enough to smell each other's odours, all the immigrants crammed within the inner belly of the sea vessel, the conditions made worse when some became seasick. Impatience and close contact resulted in more than one fist fight among the passengers. Pangs of hunger added to the misery. The constant moan of crying infants made sleep impossible.

The boat landed in Quebec City where Marko waited a few days before the train ride to Winnipeg. While there, he overheard two Anglos talking about Winnipeg. His English wasn't the best but could make out that Winnipeg had become the biggest and most important community in Western Canada. It was located where two rivers met, the Red and the Assiniboine.

On the long train ride to Winnipeg, Marko and the other immigrants from Eastern Europe squeezed onto benches. The train car stank of sweat and urine. How he longed for a clean bed and a few hours of peace and quiet. Marko picked out his native Ukrainian easily and recognized conversations in Polish, Russian, Romanian, German and a variety of other dialects.

He opened his eyes. The pain subsided. He took a deep breath and wiped his brow with the back of his hand.

Adjusting his hat, he looked towards Main Street. Was that it? Yes! A man wearing a floppy, newsboy-style brown hat was carrying his suitcase across the street from the Royal Alexandra Hotel near the corner of Higgins and Main. The man turned left and disappeared around the corner down Main Street. Marko found a fresh spark of energy.

Marko bobbed and weaved around the horde of people, clipping a few in the process. One man swore at him in Russian. He turned his head to acknowledge the man, but in the moment he looked away he accidently knocked down a woman wearing a head scarf. Overweight with men's shoes on her feet, she fell to the ground, losing grip of a small sack. He apologized and tried to help her up. A large, dark mole hung just below her lower lip. Her husband, a heavy set man with hairy arms, punched Marko on the side of the head and yelled something that sounded Polish. Marko raised his hands up to appease the new immigrants. The husband and wife both wagged their fingers at him before moving on.

Marko made it to the street corner. The sidewalk was filled with people of all types. Businessmen in clean, well-pressed suits and crisp hats walked alongside slovenly, unshaven tramps in soiled, torn clothes. Although mostly men, a few women in full-length dresses with wide-rimmed summer hats or bonnets also strolled the sidewalk. Some pushed baby carriages. Automobiles and horse-drawn carriages bounced up and down Main Street. Too busy to cross, the street looked to be about as wide as three very large barns. Marko lost sight of the thief for a few seconds when other pedestrians blocked his view. Going at a faster pace, he shortened the gap to a half block.

The criminal glanced back. He saw Marko approach and took off across the street, dodging honking automobiles and skittish horses while limping from the weight of the suitcase. Now running, Marko tried to keep his eye on the man in the brown newsboy hat.

The thief ran down a side street. Marko closed the gap to about fifteen seconds.

But when he turned the corner, there was no sign of the thief. Gone. Where did he go? He certainly could not have gotten far. He must have ducked into a building. Marko peeked through a few windows of shops and hotels. He looked both ways up and down the next street, but there was no sign of the man with the floppy brown hat.

Marko spat on the sidewalk and shook his head. Perhaps it was best to make his way to Mike's.

Mike's House
July 4, 1913

Standing on the corner of Main Street and Selkirk Avenue, Marko looked at his map. He was in the North End of Winnipeg. Hotels and places to drink littered Main Street north of the tracks. It was early in the afternoon but already a few men on Main Street smelled of alcohol. Others had difficulty walking. There was also a butcher, a tailor, small grocers, a hardware store, a locksmith and a variety of other small shops. Pedestrians filled the sidewalk. He noticed many Eastern Europeans and even some Jews although most did not appear wealthy.

Vehicles and carriages cluttered both Selkirk and Main. Streetcar tracks travelled down Selkirk Avenue, a sign of Selkirk's importance. Manitoba Avenue was just two blocks north of Selkirk. Crossing Selkirk, a pack of children, perhaps aged ten to twelve, ran past. Each grasped an apple or an orange. A moment later an overweight shop owner wearing a dirty white apron ran past Marko, huffing and puffing, "Get back here you urchins! If I ever catch any of you, I'll cut off your ears!" Panting, the shop keeper doubled over and muttered to himself. Marko turned west when he got to Manitoba Avenue.

The slight wind was enough to raise some of the dust from the streets and roads, but not enough to remove a hat from a man's head. It smelled clean and fresh with only the smallest hint of horse manure. Father told him that you could tell what a city or village was like by smelling the air when you first entered. If it smelled rotten or diseased, it was best to turn around and head back. Winnipeg smelled fine.

Some of the homes on Manitoba Avenue stood so close together neighbors could shake hands through open windows. How could people live so crammed? Most were two-storeys and likely only had a few rooms on the main floor. Although small, some front yards looked well-kept, with nice lawns, flower beds and a few shrubs. Others were mangy and weed-infested. Many sported fresh paint or showed no signs of decay. They must have been built recently, like everything else in the city. The sidewalk consisted of wooden planks, some of them uneven. While walking in front of one home, Marko could hear the strains of a piano being played. Another wafted the distinctive aroma of garlic and fried meat. The women he saw on porches or in yards looked Eastern European with their high cheekbones, big eyes and slight chins. They went about pulling weeds, knitting or scolding their children. None looked particularly happy. Groups of children played hopscotch and tag on the street and sidewalk. There was very little traffic on the street other than the occasional horse-drawn carriage.

Marko pulled the piece of paper from his pocket to confirm the address. 490 Manitoba Avenue. Mike's house, like the others on the street, was a small, two-storey structure. The front steps up to the house first led to an open-air porch. Dusty windows begged to be washed. The tiny lawn had a smattering of thistles and dandelions. A few flower pots on the porch contained chrysanthemums. Walking up the steps, Marko noticed a small, dusty, water damaged wooden table and two upholstered wooden chairs on the porch. Grey stuffing poked through rips in the material on the seats of the chairs.

Marko took a deep breath and rapped on the door frame. He noticed the screen on the outer door had been pulled and separated from its base revealing a foot-long gap. Obviously any bug could enter the home were it not for the closed main door. An easy repair.

He stood for a minute shifting his weight from foot to foot, swatting mosquitos. Back out on the street a few children asked an ice delivery man for chips of ice. The delivery man's horses snorted and shit on Manitoba Avenue.

At last, from within the door, came a woman's voice in English, "What you sell, we no want."

Marko frowned. "I am not selling nothing," he said in Ukrainian.

"W-what do you want?" The woman switched to Ukrainian.

"My neighbor in Galacia … Marek Perofski … he told me to come here to Mike Sokolowski's house. Does Mike Sokolowski live here?"

"Da," the woman said. She unlatched the wooden door and opened it. "What's your name?" the woman asked through the ripped mess of the screen door. Visibly pregnant, she wore a long, light blue-coloured floral dress that went down to just below her knees. It hung from her shapelessly. Her brown hair was up. Crow's feet wrinkles framed her brown eyes.

"Marko Gobinski."

The woman opened the screen door, motioning for Marko to come inside. "Mike is at work but he'll be home soon. Sit." She pointed to a small living room immediately adjacent to the tiny entrance way. The mismatched furniture included a dull red couch and a lime green high-back chair. The wooden table in front of the couch looked old and worn and only had three legs. Books propped up one corner of the table. The table also featured many gouges and gashes, perhaps made by children with their toys. An upright lamp between both the couch and chair had a solid brass frame but the cracked lampshade looked dusty.

Marko took off his shoes and sat on one end of the couch. "What is your name?"

"Maria. Just a moment…." She left the room and muttered a few orders to children hiding around the corner.

After only a few moments he heard a sound, then a giggle from the doorway. Two heads ducked back behind the corner. A few whispers and giggles later, one of the heads poked out, but once the child's eye came in contact with Marko, it pulled back. Eventually the two children gathered enough courage to stare at him.

He winked at the children, which caused them to hide again, although their giggles were louder. "Come out. I don't bite."

Slowly, the two children, both boys, walked into the living room. The older boy's messy hair looked due for a clip. He seemed to be of school age. The knees on his pants were worn. A few years younger, the other boy was a lighter shade of blonde. Too big for him, his shirt could have been handed down from his older brother.

"What you name?" Marko said in English.

"Nicholas."

"How old are you?"

"Six."

"You are a big boy." Marko turned his head to the other boy. "And you?"

"I'm four," the other boy said, holding up his right hand with four fingers outstretched.

"Your mother and father name you Four? That's a funny name," Marko said. Both children laughed.

"No. That's silly." The boy said. "My name is John." Shy, he dropped his head down.

"That's a nice name."

"Do you have any kids?" Nicholas asked.

"Well, ah…"

Just then, Maria came back into the living room carrying a metal tray. "Nick. John. Please leave our guest alone. Go play." Both children left the room and ran up the stairs.

The tray held a few assorted baked treats along with small bits of cheese. Without asking, Maria poured a cup of coffee and placed it on the table near him. She poured herself a cup and sat on the green chair.

"You do not need—"

"Eat, eat," Maria said.

Marko was hungry, no sense in declining. Each item tasted wonderful.

"You are new to Canada?" Maria asked.

"Yes, last week. I just arrived in Winnipeg."

The sound of the back door opening made Maria cock her head. "Mike is here." She left the room to greet her husband.

Mike Sokolowski entered the living room. Shorter than Marko by a few inches and heavier, a bushy moustache dominated his face. His messy, dark, brown hair and filthy clothes made him look like a vagrant. "So, you are Marko Gobinski," he said in Ukrainian.

"Da." Marko stood up.

He flashed a frown at Marko. "Why are you here?"

"I came from Galicia. My neighbor, your cousin, Marek, he told me to see you about a place to stay."

Mike raised an eyebrow. "I know nothing of this."

Maria crossed her arms and looked down before leaving the room.

"Marek … said he sent letters to you. Letters about me coming to Canada. That you have a room available. I have the address he wrote here." Marko took the piece of paper from his pocket and handed it to Mike.

Mike looked at the note and squinted while shaking his head slowly. "It could be his hand. But I don't know." He lit a cigarette and offered one to Marko.

"No thank you. I don't smoke."

Mike blew smoke out his nostrils and shook his head. "Look. Marek and I … we don't get along. Ever since I came to Canada he asks for everything. He thinks I'm a millionaire." Mike raised his arms. "Do I look like millionaire to you? And Marek is a drunk. He gets these fantastic ideas. Maybe he convinced himself that he mailed letters while he was working on a bottle of vodka.

But I didn't get a letter from him. I think he's jealous of me. I took a chance coming here. It's not easy. The English, they run everything in Winnipeg. Everything. But, we do okay. Times are good. These days I can find work. But it could change, like that." Mike snapped his fingers to emphasize his point.

Marko lowered his head.

"Where are your things, your belongings?" Mike asked.

"My suitcase was stolen outside train station."

Marko reached inside his jacket and pulled out his paper and wallet. "I don't want trouble and I'm sorry for bothering you. Please thank your wife for the coffee and cakes." Marko unfolded his immigration papers and handed them to Mike. He opened his wallet. "Look. I have money to pay for things. I can pay to stay a short time, then I can go somewhere else."

Mike inspected the papers and nodded approvingly.

"Mike," Maria called from the kitchen. "Can you come here one moment?" Mike took a puff of his cigarette and placed it in the ashtray before leaving the room.

Marko strained his ear to listen. "Why did you let him in?" Mike said.

"He knows your cousin. But listen, we could use the extra money. Everyone takes in borders."

"We don't own this house."

"How will the landlord find out? He doesn't care as long as the rent is paid every month."

Marko could not make out the rest of the conversation.

After a few more minutes, Mike re-entered the living room.

"Okay," Mike said. "Me and the wife talked. She thinks you're honest. Here is how we do it. We have an extra room upstairs. It's small, but better than nothing, no?"

Marko nodded, his spirit lifted by the change in fortune.

"You pay five dollars each month for room and board. I expect you to help out with house repairs. No sitting around doing nothing."

Smiling, Marko nodded again.

"I see you have money. You pay two months now. Ten dollars."

Marko reached into his wallet, paid Mike and they shook hands.

"Come," Mike said. "Let's have a shot. You can clean up. Tomorrow you need to buy some clothes."

The Garden Party
July 5, 1913

"Mildred, are you ready?" Gladys said. "You need to leave soon. There's no time to daydream."

Broken from her trance, Mildred glanced at Gladys standing at the doorway with her hands on her hips. Gladys wore her white and black maid's uniform.

"I'm just about ready," Mildred said. She sat at the table in her room staring at the wall on the other side of her large, four-poster bed.

"Very well. Come downstairs when you are." Gladys disappeared from the doorway.

Mildred turned her head slightly to view her left profile in the mirror. She looked stunning in her dainty light blue blouse trimmed with white lace. Even without make-up Mildred's left profile was attractive and free of blemishes. She kept her shiny brown hair down. Although just shoulder length, Mother would prefer it up. She examined her features and sighed. Why did she have to go to the party? At 23 years of age, could she not decide on some things on her own?

She closed her eyes. Slowly she ran her fingers down the right side of her face. She wished for symmetry, but that was a fantasy. From the outside corner of her right eye down to near her mouth ran an enormous, deep, red scar, the kind an old longshoreman or a wind-swept farmer would endure as a mark of courage from some terrifying incident decades before. Although just a year old, she knew the scar would be with her for the rest of her life. How would she ever find a husband?

"Mildred, we must be going," called her mother.

Mildred picked up a pair of white gloves from the table, a smallish pink and white parasol leaning in the corner of the room and her frilly, wide-brimmed hat from the bed. The sun would likely be hot. Today would not be an exception. Since they would be outdoors most of the day hopefully there would not be too many pesky mosquitoes. Perhaps the heat could drive them away.

At the bottom of the stairs stood her father, mother, younger brother and James, the driver. In her mid-40s, Mother always had to look her absolute best. Her short, blonde hair had been expensively styled at the beauty salon this morning. Regardless, it was mainly hidden by a colourful, wide hat which included several exotic bird feathers. She wore a light cream-coloured full-length sleeveless dress brought in at the waist and accented with a beige wrap around the mid-section of her body. Her satin shoes perfectly matched her dress. Around her neck she wore a blue locket surrounded by jewels. Diamonds sparkled from the earrings Father purchased for her last birthday. Her finest and most expensive rings adorned several fingers.

Mother also wore a touch of make-up. If Mildred tried she would be considered a tramp. There seemed to be a faint mark on the side of her mother's face. She must have run into the door again.

Father and Andrew dressed similarly. Both wore suits with long, black jackets. Suspenders held their trousers. Andrew's jacket featured thinner lapels than Father's and the colour of Andrew's suit may have been closer to a navy blue. Both wore white shirts with thick, gold cufflinks. The collars opened up at the top and folded over. Each had a black tie and a rigid, black top hat. The men will eventually discard their jackets and hats. The hot sun and a touch of scotch had a way of doing that.

Even James looked chipper with his red serge covering his round belly and matching driver's hat.

"Finally," Thomas said. "There you are."

"It's just a garden party, not a wedding," Mildred said to her father at the bottom of the stairs. "I'm sure we can be late a minute or two."

Thomas looked to James. "Bring the Packard out."

"Yes sir, Mr. Spencer." James immediately left the front door for the garage at the back of the mansion. While the family patiently waited, a few automobiles and horse-drawn carriages passed in front of their Wellington Crescent estate.

James brought the sputtering automobile around. Idling, he waited for everyone to settle in. The soft red leather of the interior felt luxurious while the exterior sparkled in a lovely shade of burgundy.

"Is the vehicle going to make it?" Thomas asked. "It does not sound promising."

"Let's hope," James said. "It needs to be examined by a mechanic."

James turned on to Wellington Crescent for their trip to the Cavindish estate. Mildred pulled her hat down to prevent it from being blown off. After the accident she didn't like to be seen in public to face stares and pity. While she disregarded going back to being a school teacher, at least working in the office of Father's factory kept her occupied.

The Cavindish estate was a short ride on Roslyn Road. A servant at the fifteen-foot iron gates leading to the sprawling estate allowed their vehicle inside. Like the homes along Wellington Crescent, the lawn looked impeccable, manicured to perfection. Various large shade trees, obviously old growth, dotted the front yard providing islands of relief from the hot sun.

The garden party was already in full swing. Groups of guests played croquet games while over to the side some men tossed horseshoes. Children ran about chasing each other. Most of the young girls wore frilly dresses with white stockings. The boys had suits. The more exuberant boys decorated their clothes with grass stains on their knees. Closer to the mansion, under a canopy, an orchestra played in front of several dozen people sitting in chairs under nearby trees. A long table sheltered by a canopy held fruit, treats and other delights on a bed of quickly melting ice. The pastries and danishes looked to be arranged expertly by an artist. Fresh cut flowers accented the table while rose petals had been sprinkled around each food receptacle.

Women adorned the latest and most luxurious fashions including large, wide-brimmed hats. Some featured fancy ribbon displays. Most of the young girls' hats had ribbons attached that hung down so when they ran it trailed and fluttered behind them.

"James, you can go on to the guest house with the other drivers," Thomas said.

James waddled over to the large brick house to the right of the mansion.

The mansion had to be of the largest in Manitoba. The brick monolith featured a countless number of rooms. It even housed its own ballroom and a two-lane bowling alley. The fine brickwork of the home oozed wealth and status with perhaps a touch of ostentatiousness. The staff opened most of the windows to allow what little draft existed to breathe life into the structure.

Near the base of one of the shade trees Betty Cavindish noticed the Spencers and immediately ran over, arms outstretched. "Gertrude, Thomas, Andrew. It's so wonderful you are here." Betty hugged Gertrude. Mildred sniffed. Betty had on more perfume than was needed.

"Cecil and most of the men are in the back," Mrs. Cavindish said to

Thomas.

"Very good, come Andrew, let's join the others." Thomas and Andrew left the women.

"Hello, Mildred," Mrs. Cavendish said with a cheerful smile. "I … ah … have not seen you since…." She looked away, perhaps too embarrassed to look straight at Mildred. "Don't worry, you could hardly notice it. It's good you are out and about."

Instinctively, Mildred brought her head down and to the right. Mrs. Cavendish meant well, but it would be nice if everyone stopped pretending the scar would get better. It never will.

Mildred sat with her mother for almost an hour watching the live orchestral performance and occasionally chatting with other ladies. During some passages Mother would sit with her eyes closed, listening with passion. A life-long member of the Winnipeg Musical Club of Manitoba, she attended many musical performances with Father or other lady friends. She passed that appreciation down to Mildred.

Mildred could feel perspiration dripping down her back. Sitting in one spot for an extended period of time had become too uncomfortable. "I think I fancy a lemonade," she said before leaving Mother with the other hens.

Twirling her parasol slowly, Mildred ventured to the rear of the mansion. Men and women tended to separate into groups. Most of the men were from Winnipeg's business and social elite, much like Thomas. Successful business owners, bankers, judges, lawyers, accountants, politicians, they represented a wide cross-section of movers and shakers.

Waiters formally dressed in black trousers, crisp white shirts and black ties carefully attended to the guests with hors d'oeuvres or a cool beverage. Each waiter also wore a tight arm band on each sleeve. Instead of being served, Mildred went to the make-shift, fully stocked bar closer to the mansion. There, two servants were happy to provide practically any alcoholic drink in addition to a variety of juices and the lemonade she selected.

Over to one side of the back yard stood a large garage with enough space for several automobiles. Beside that, the livery. All dressed in white, young men played tennis on three full-length tennis courts on the other side of the backyard. The yard ended at the Assiniboine River at the very rear. A few boats had been tied to a wooden dock that jutted out into the lazy river.

Mildred strolled over to where Father stood with Andrew and an older gentleman, James Ashdown, underneath a massive shade tree. Father had a glass of scotch in his hand while Andrew held a lemonade.

"The military, you say?" Ashdown said to Andrew. Grey-haired and in his late 60s, Ashdown dressed impeccably in a brown suit with a red tie and matching handkerchief in his breast pocket.

"I would like to," Andrew said. "A few of my friends have talked about maybe enlisting in the army. I haven't decided yet."

"I reckoned Thomas would have you ready to take over the family business. He's not getting any younger." Ashdown winked.

Thomas raised his glass. "Speak for yourself, you old codger. But it's true, I'd prefer to show him the ropes. The lad's only seventeen and still has another year of high school." He turned slightly to speak to Andrew. "You may want to think about which university you want to attend...."

"You can always show *me* the ropes," Mildred said. She was standing behind Thomas.

All three turned to face Mildred. Mr. Ashdown bowed his head slightly to acknowledge her.

"I've been working in the office at the factory for several months now. I would be more than happy to learn how to run the factory."

Ashdown smiled. "I should be checking on the missus. Good to see you again, Mildred … gentlemen." He strolled toward the mansion.

Thomas shook his head. "It's not that easy."

"Why?" Mildred asked. "If Andrew could do it, could not I?"

"Running a factory or any business is not the job for a woman. There's nothing delicate about it. It requires steadfast resolve and an iron will." Thomas pointed to Ashdown, now thirty yards away. "James Ashdown worked hard to build his hardware empire."

"More like shooting fish in a barrel," Mildred said. "Winnipeg has grown by leaps and bounds since it was incorporated. We taught that to children in school. It went from about 40,000 at the turn of the century to 130 or 140 thousand today. Everywhere you look in the city new buildings are being erected. And that's not including the people living on farms in the country. All those men need hammers and hardware, so I'm sure it was not that difficult for Mr. Ashdown. He was in the right place at the right time."

Thomas looked away and shook his head. "I hardly think so. Be happy with your present arrangement helping Elizabeth in the office. It was your mother who insisted you work in the office, not I."

A waiter arrived with more refreshments on a tray. Thomas grabbed two scotch whiskeys. "Here son." With a wink he handed one to Andrew. "You're old enough to have a real drink. Oh, look, there's Frank Patton and Edgar Dalton. I need to discuss business matters." Father and Andrew walked away.

Continuing to twirl her parasol above her head, Mildred's lips formed a crisp, tight line. She was smarter and better educated than Andrew. He was just a boy. Father never did have any trust in her abilities and never gave her a chance to prove herself. Even then there was the unrealistic expectations. And the constant comparisons to Muriel.

She stopped twirling her parasol. Across the yard Father chatted with the other men. Clinking glasses. Patting backs. Shaking hands. Everything a show. Teaching Andrew how to work a party. She could do that too, if given the chance. But maybe now she was just damaged goods to him? And did Andrew even care? He could hardly crack a faint smile, and even then only when someone engaged him. While Mildred had been physically scarred, Andrew's scars were just as deep, but on the inside. He'd been brooding now for over a year.

Mildred grabbed another lemonade from the tray of a passing waiter. Even with her parasol, the heat of the afternoon sun had become unbearable. Cooling off under a shade tree while watching a performance seemed to be the best option.

On the way to the front Mildred noticed a group of younger men at the horseshoe pits. Loud and brash, all were eligible bachelors and came from well-to-do families. There was a time when Mildred could flash a coy smile and men tripped over themselves for her attention at a gathering such as this. Not anymore.

Mildred looked down to the ground. Worse than an overbearing chaperone, her scar would forever repel potential suitors. Was she destined to be an old maid?

One stood out from the others: William Dalton, the son of Edgar Dalton, one of the men Father was drinking with in the back yard. Outgoing, William seemed to have the ear of the others, laughing and joking with his chums. A powerful chin and hatless, his blonde hair shined in the blazing sun. His strong arms threw the horseshoes with effortless ease. He scored solid, loud ringers on both his throws.

Mildred turned her head and aimed her parasol so it blocked her view from the young men. No sense dreaming unrealistic thoughts.

Eventually shadows lengthened. The temperature eased. Slowly attendees began to notice the mosquitoes. The band stopped playing and put their instruments away. One by one, guests left the party.

Mildred stood with her father and mother at the front of the mansion. She noticed Andrew approaching with a pale face and a vacant look in his eyes. If she didn't know any better, she would swear he was drunk.

Gertrude noticed Andrew and put her hand to her mouth. "We must leave at once." She turned to Thomas. "How many alcoholic drinks did you give him?"

Thomas shrugged. "Just one. And that was hours ago. He must have picked up a few through the day."

"Why didn't you watch him more closely? How many did you have? This is so embarrassing!"

Thomas crossed his arms and frowned. "The boy is almost a man. I cannot watch him every moment…."

Gertrude shook her head. She guided Andrew near a tree away from the party and arranged for James to bring the automobile.

"Will you be able to operate the motor vehicle?"

"Not a problem," James said with a wave of his hand. "I've only had about six or seven drinks all day. In fact, I drive better with a drink or two under my belt. Calms the nerves."

Mr. Spencer climbed into the back seat of the automobile. Andrew went to follow, but his inebriation became more obvious by his incoordination. The boy could hardly step up to the running board without tipping over.

After three attempts, Gertrude and James were finally able to get Andrew up and into the back seat of the Packard. The moment Andrew sat down the excesses of the day took their toll and he vomited on Father's lap.

Almost in shock, Thomas blabbered incoherently. Both Gertrude and James stood at the edge of the vehicle, mouths agape at the scene. Mildred feigned disgust by raising her hand to her mouth, but she was really hiding a smile.

Looking for Work
July 6, 1913

Marko closed his eyes and savoured another piece of sausage in his mouth.

"You like?" Maria said in Ukrainian. Mike and his two children were also seated at the dinner table.

"Very much," Marko said, tapping his belly.

"What are you good at?" Mike said. "What can you do?"

"I fix things," Marko said. "Automobiles. Machinery. Farm equipment. Anything. One day I'd like to have my own repair shop."

"It shouldn't take you long to find a job." Mike stabbed a few slices of cucumber and popped them in his mouth.

"I hope so," Marko said. "What do you do?"

"Whatever is available at the employment agency. Sometimes I'll work at a warehouse moving boxes around. Or I might dig a ditch. The city has been putting down miles of underground water lines. It's always something different."

"What's the pay like?"

"I make $15 or $20 a week. It pays the bills, but that's all. There's not much left over. Still, we're better off than most families. Those with seven, eight, nine kids, I don't know how they manage. It's not the old country, where you need all the kids to help on a farm."

Nicholas dropped his fork on his plate with a crash. "Can I go now?" he said in English. "I'm full."

"You didn't eat your beets…" Maria said but Nicholas was already out the back door.

"Boys will be boys," Mike said.

"I know, but I worry. He gets in all kinds of mischief with those other boys from school. And the fights. Always with the English kids."

The men went to the living room for a few shots of whiskey before Marko went to bed. Mike seemed to have a good supply of booze in the house. Rye, rum, vodka, scotch. Far more than he would have expected for a family having a hard time making ends meet. Mike's cheeks and ears turned red after only two shots. His eyes became glassy and he slurred a word or two.

Marko's room featured a small single bed with an old mattress. The only other furniture was a small wooden table with an old rickety chair. He did not have a wardrobe or even a chest of drawers, not that it mattered considering the circumstances. The dusty window overlooked the backyard beyond which was a back lane. All told, the conditions weren't bad and bigger than the farmhouse back home.

He lay on his bed and stared at the ceiling. Faded pink wallpaper with images of daisies covered the walls. So this was Winnipeg. When he landed in Quebec City, they asked him where he wanted to go. The immigration officer rolled out a map of the country. Everything in Eastern Canada seemed so well developed and littered with cities and towns. But he wanted to go somewhere far. The immigration man suggested Winnipeg.

The two Anglos he overheard in the train station in Quebec City said Winnipeg was formed right where two rivers met. The Assiniboine came from out west. From its source in the United States, the Red River meandered north, through Winnipeg, and spilled into Lake Winnipeg, less than fifty miles north of the city. Indians first populated the area. Those Anglos didn't think too highly of them. Maybe they were like Gypsies? They said Europeans came in the 1700s. First the French, then the English. Scots created the first settlement in the early 1800s. But problems with the Metis — mixed blood descendants of Indians and French — led to fighting and the creation of the province of Manitoba in 1870. Four years later Winnipeg was born.

Galicia seemed like a distant memory. A back water. Besides, the king treated Galicia like a remote outpost of the Austro-Hungarian Empire. Being Ukrainian, there was no attachment to the crown. Marko heard from Marek, his neighbor, that in Canada you can have a better life, a good place to start over.

Ma and Pa always told him it was important to work hard. If you work hard, good things will come to you. He never did say goodbye to Vira and Kateryna. His sisters moved on years ago.

Only one photo of Olena and Anastasiya existed, but now that too was gone along with everything from the stolen suitcase. He closed his eyes tight. He could see the images of his wife and daughter in his mind, clear like the reflection on a still lake. Anastasiya's cute smile brought out her dimples. Her long, blonde, wavy hair hung past her shoulders. Always smiling.

And Olena, his beautiful, happy wife. Her hair, also blonde, was up, but tiny strands hung from the sides by her ears. Her blue eyes, deep as the sea. They were always meant to be together, even when they were children. She lived on the next farm over. He caught glimpses of her hair when he helped his father on the fields. Maybe he was twelve, thirteen years old. She would look back from the fence and smile. He would smile back. A few years later he would see more of her in school, at church, in town. Almost naturally, like the way all rivers flow into a sea, they ended up together to start their own family.

Marko opened his eyes. It was all his fault. The images vanished, blurred through his tears. But they would all be back together again. One day.

******

The next morning, a Monday, Marko spent some time on Selkirk Avenue buying clothes and a new suitcase. Selkirk Avenue seemed like the hub of the North End of Winnipeg. While narrower than Main Street and a fair distance from downtown, Selkirk was certainly more practical. Every few blocks he saw groups of people having a friendly chat, perhaps neighbors or acquaintances. He noticed many churches of various denominations, factories, and other businesses off on the side streets.

With a strong south wind, the faint hint of grease and engine oil drifted over from the rail yards just a few blocks away. Mike told him the massive Canadian Pacific yard was the lifeblood of Winnipeg and one of the reasons Winnipeg grew so fast. There were only two places where the yards could be crossed without going around: the Salter Street Bridge and the Arlington Bridge. Most of the workers lived north of the yard in the North End. The Anglos generally all lived south of the tracks.

Mike said the yard itself employed many men to repair and maintain the train engines and cars. Those shop workers needed to be fed and clothed. An entire sub-industry formed just to support those workers. He almost couldn't believe Mike when he said there were thousands of men in Winnipeg working for or related to the rail yards.

After lunch at Mike's, Marko changed into his new clothes and went to find a job at an employment agency.

Not far from the Higgins underpass, a brownish-red Packard stood at the side of the road. Only someone rich could own an automobile like that. The driver had his sleeves rolled up and struggled trying to take off a flat tire.

Two occupants sat inside the covered automobile in the rear seat, an older man and a younger woman. The older man, wearing a top hat, leaned out the window.

"James, what is taking so long? We have to get to the office." Just from the lilt of his tone, Marko could tell the man in the vehicle was well-schooled and of a different class. Not from the North End.

"I'm trying, sir. This is a little tricky," James said. Overweight with a round, red face, James wore a driver's cap. He tried manipulating a jack under the vehicle, but it kept coming apart.

Marko walked over and bent down to survey the situation.

"Go away," James said, "I can handle this."

But after several more minutes of fiddling, it became clear James could not complete the task. The older man in the vehicle snapped his pocket watch shut. "James, in the name of the Lord cease what you are doing. Let the man give it a go. He certainly seems confident."

"Yes, Mr. Spencer."

Within thirty seconds Marko arranged the components of the jack correctly and the car rose up a few inches at a time.

"That's how it's done. The immigrant knows what he's doing," Mr. Spencer said.

"I know how to change a tire," James said. "The jack was being finicky." He crossed his arms.

Marko completed the change and jacked the car back down. He walked over to the open window. "Finished. It be good, now."

Mr. Spencer slowly nodded in appreciation. Marko noticed Mr. Spencer wore a well-pressed suit. The woman had a light purple dress trimmed with lace. A wide-brimmed white hat with ribbons of multiple colours interwoven into the fabric rested on her head. She had pretty brown eyes but he could not help but be drawn to the enormous scar on her right cheek. Stunning otherwise, the jarring blemish made him pause. The woman dropped her head down and to the right.

"You performed that change rather quickly," Mr. Spencer said. "How good are you at general repairs and mechanics?"

"I fix most things. Machines. Woodwork. Plumbing."

"Do you have employment right now? Are you working anywhere?"

Marko took off his hat. "No, I come to Winnipeg on Friday. I now go to job office." Marko pointed in the general direction of the train station.

"Wait a moment," Spencer said with a raised finger. He turned to the woman. "Mildred, will you give this gentleman the address of the factory? Peter has been looking for a repairman for weeks. This immigrant is worth a look." He reached into his jacket and gave Mildred a pen.

"Here you are, Father," Mildred said, handing the little note to Mr. Spencer. In turn he gave it to Marko through the open window.

Mr. Spencer looked at Marko. "Come by tomorrow. Peter will speak with you. You're a foreigner, but you will do, I suppose."

Without saying another word to Marko, Mr. Spencer looked towards James, by now back in the driver's seat. "Onward. To the factory, please."

Marko said, "Thank you," but the car was already too far away for anyone to hear. He stared at the small piece of paper.

Winnipeg Iron Works
July 8, 1913

Marko stood in front of Winnipeg Iron Works located at 845 Logan Avenue. The building itself didn't look particularly inviting. It occupied an entire city block. Dirty and grimy, the few windows along the first floor of the two-storey building looked like they had not been washed in years. Several rows of smaller square windows lined the top of the building. They almost completely encircled the building and likely provided extra lighting. Marko could not see the service doors. They must be in the back. The front door was at the far corner of the building at the end of a short stone staircase. Detailed and intricate iron work on the handrails of the staircase showcased the skill of the shop workers. The metal WINNIPEG IRON WORKS sign above the two wooden doors had also been made of carefully formed metal. He had difficulty reading the signs posted to the right of the doors. After standing on the corner for about ten minutes, he decided he was early enough to look punctual, but not too early to look desperate.

The distinctive smell of metal fabrication entered his nostrils when he opened the door. He approached the front counter with his hat in his hand. A handful of office workers sat at their desks. A stairway ran upstairs along the right wall.

A secretary wearing a grey blouse saw him. She glanced up with a vacant stare but quickly looked back down and continued on with her work. Marko stood patiently at the counter for a few moments. He cleared his throat, hoping to catch the woman's attention, but she didn't acknowledge him. A few minutes passed. "Excuse. I have meeting here. Nine o'clock."

Not bothering to look up, the woman with the grey blouse pointed to the door. "All general labour reports to the back door. Did you not read the sign posted outside?" Her hair was in a tight bun at the top of her head. The deep lines on her forehead looked like they had been chiselled in granite. "Go to the back of the building. There's a door over there."

Marko frowned. "I no labour. I told to come in this door. I have note here."

"Now see here." The woman finally looked up and wagged her finger at him. "You will not use that tone with me or I can ensure you will not find any employment here. Now turn around and—"

"It's alright, Liz. I recognize this man." A second woman cut her off, the same woman from the car yesterday. Mildred, the daughter of the owner. She must have heard the commotion from the back and came to check.

Liz, the woman in the grey blouse, frowned and crossed her arms. "Mildred, this, this … man … barged in here blabbering about this and that. I told him to go to the back."

"Thank you, Liz," Mildred said. "I'm sorry, what is your name?"

"Marko Gobinski."

"Marko repaired father's automobile on Main Street and he thought Marko should see Peter."

Mildred's poise caught Marko's eye. She handled herself with grace. Approaching the desk it looked like she walked on air. Her long pink skirt barely moved with each step. Buttoned up to her neck, her blue blouse also covered the full extent of her arms. Like Liz, her hair was in a bun. Her brown eyes shone like twinkling stars and her skin appeared healthy and full of colour. All pretty qualities except for the nasty scar that extended from the top of her cheekbone all the way to her jaw line. Jagged and deep, uneven stitch marks marred both sides of the gash.

Mildred tilted her head down and to the right. Marko abruptly looked away. He shouldn't stare. After all, he had seen scars before. But this one didn't seem right. Maybe it was because it was on an otherwise attractive woman.

Liz pressed her lips together so hard they turned white. "Oh," she said. "Perhaps I should talk to Mr. Spencer and see what he says about this matter…?"

"You're welcome, Liz," Mildred said. "He's meeting with some of the other managers presently if you would like to disturb him."

Liz paused for a moment and then threw her hands in the air. "Well, then you take care of this. I have work to do." She stormed away, fuming, and sat back down, pretending to pay no attention.

"I'm sorry about that, Marko," Mildred said. "I'll get Peter, the foreman, to speak with you."

She walked through the factory entrance door at the side. Dark fingerprints stained the edges of the door and near the doorknob. The moment Mildred opened the door the sounds of whirling machines, clanging and other shop-related activity filled the air.

A stocky and slightly overweight man wearing a derby walked into the office followed by Mildred. "…always picking up strays from the street. What are his qualifications? Where's he worked before? Did he just get off the boat? Blimey, can he even speak English?" The sleeves of his shirt were rolled up to his elbows. Dark grime and grit stained his hands and hairy forearms. Grease stains from the past weeks and months covered his button-up shirt and trousers. Years of filth permanently blackened his work boots.

"Father arranged for him to come in," Mildred said. "He fixed Father's tire yesterday—"

"Automobiles are quite different from heavy machinery," Peter said. "Mr. Spencer should know that." Peter grabbed his derby, wiped his sweaty brow with his dirty forearm and replaced his hat. He looked at Marko standing at the counter. "Oi. You there. C'mere."

Marko strode over.

"What kind of experience ya got? What've ya done?"

Marko had difficulty understanding Peter's thick British accent. "I … uh … I fix."

"Fix what, man?"

"I fix … things," Marko said slowly, unable to think of the correct word.

Peter rolled his eyes and gave Mildred a strained look then shot a glance back at Marko. "You fix things. Brilliant. Fantastic. What bloody good are ya to me?"

Marko looked at the ground during the long pause. Maybe it was a bad idea to come here.

"Get outa here. You hunky slugs are a dime a dozen. Go on. Go."

Marko slowly turned around to leave.

"You think that is a good idea, Peter?" Mildred said. "What do you want to tell Father when he asks about the mechanic? You know how he can be…."

"Yer right." Peter looked straight up and exhaled loudly. "Oi, hold on!" Marko stopped at the door and turned. "Yes, C'mon … c'mere. Let's go in the shop. Show me what ya got."

The two walked through the door into the factory. Loud crashes and clanks came from all directions. Employees, individually and in groups, worked on various pieces of metal. Some of the metal pieces came in such an odd shape, Marko had no idea what machine they fit. He saw located throughout the factory several dozen bins filled with materials, some raw, others machined and refined. Along one stretch large steel train wheels were being milled by an extraordinarily large machine. Nearby, what looked like finished axles had been stacked four feet high.

A layer of grime and filth coated the factory floor, blacker than a moonless night. Thousands of little metal shavings dotted the floor where they'd been stepped on repeatedly over the years. Marko noticed one boy, perhaps fifteen years old, with a dirty broom sweeping up loose filings on to a wooden tray and depositing them into a barrel he hauled around. Most factory employees didn't pay attention to the two while they walked through the large shop. A few would glance briefly, but then continue on with their work. Like Peter, all the workers appeared dirty and filthy.

Suddenly a loud metallic sound startled Marko. It came from the right, not far away. Someone had lowered an extremely large piece of shaped metal too quickly using an overhead crane. Peter stopped to face the situation. "Hey, you be careful with those pieces. Each one is worth more than you make in a year."

The man grunted. Short, stocky and wearing loose fitting dirty overalls, his most distinguishing feature was his rather large walrus moustache. It completely hid his lips. Marko noticed a frown as they walked by.

"Don't mind him," Peter said. "Eugene's a bit of a hot head." They continued on their walk through the factory. Marko could see that every employee appeared busy. Some manned milling machines, others a section of grinders. Every so often loud sparks from someone welding added intense flashes of light into the factory amid a shower of fire like some ancient fireworks. Vast batches and containers of seemingly completed metal components lay idle, perhaps waiting for the next phase of manufacturing or, if complete, to be shipped out to some factory for assembly into a machine. Marko recognized some pieces as parts from farm machinery.

Overhead lights illuminated the dingy factory floor. The high, smaller line of windows Marko saw at the top of the building indeed helped brighten the factory with natural lighting, in addition to the larger, unwashed windows along the side. The factory floor divided into several large rooms. Although to call each area a 'room' seemed a bit of a stretch since each connected to the next by large, cavernous openings. Still, the partitions created a type of dark, industrial coziness in each room. Large, thick columns intermittently supported the high factory ceiling. Not every machine was manned. A few looked to be in various stages of disrepair. Some had even been disembowelled of their inner workings, with various sprockets and levers and nuts and bolts strewn about on the factory floor like they had been attacked by some machine-eating beast.

The two walked the entire length of the factory to a large opening which accessed a rail line. The factory was obviously strategically placed so that inputs and outputs could be transported quickly to other parts of Manitoba, Canada or even the United States. A handful of shipping employees were in the process of fastening large chains around pallets and bins of completed items. An overhead crane lifted extremely heavy items onto waiting railcars.

Peter walked Marko all the way to the very corner at the end of the factory where they came to a lathe. Used for precisely grinding smaller metal components, the machine looked to have not been used for some time. Dust and spider webs covered the random parts that lay on the ground around the lathe.

"Here we are," Peter said. "This bleeding lathe hasn't been in operation for some time now. Davey Malone started fixing this thing a few months ago. He took off to Regina one day. This has been sitting like this ever since. We never got around to getting it put together. You fix it, ya got yourself a job. Alright?" Peter pointed to a bench. "There's some tools there. If ya need any others, look around."

Marko nodded in agreement.

"And don't take all day." Peter walked away back into the bowels of the factory.

Marko examined the lathe without touching it. He looked at his clothes. He didn't dress for this type of work and would get grease and grime on his nicest shirt and only jacket. His new trousers would also surely be ruined. But he had to prove himself.

He slipped off his jacket and draped it over a nearby half-filled bin of components. After rolling up his sleeves Marko assessed the situation. He carefully sorted the various parts scattered on the floor beneath the lathe, organizing them by function. It looked like Davey Malone had worked on the lathe in a rush. The parts appeared to have been removed randomly or for no reason, like Davey wasn't sure what he was doing.

While tackling the inner workings of the machine, he heard another loud sound, this time coming from the large shipping and receiving door. Several men yelled and shouted. The area erupted in activity. He ran over to view the situation. A large pallet containing machined metal components came apart while being loaded onto a railway boxcar using the overhead crane. The components, each weighing several hundred pounds, lay scattered at the entrance of the shipping door. An unfortunate employee screamed so loud that the bulging veins in his neck turned purple. His leg was pinned under one of the components.

Already on the scene, Peter directed other employees to lift the component up so two other men could pull the injured man away from under the large piece of metal. "C'mon, c'mon, lads! Hurry!"

Still screaming and thrashing his clenched fists on the dirty factory floor, the man's leg pointed in an awkward direction, obviously broken. Peter knelt down to the man and held his hand firmly. "That's alright, Michael. You're fine now. We got ya."

"Ahhhh! My leg, my leg!"

"We'll get ya to the hospital, Mikey, don't ya worry." Peter looked at another employee. "Bring over the horse buggy."

Peter reached into his pocket and pulled out a small flask. He placed it on Michael's lips. "Here. Take a swig. This'll help." The man gulped the booze. It splashed around his mouth and down around to the back of his neck. Within a few moments the colour vanished from Michael's face and he settled into shock. The employees that had gathered around, about thirty to forty, stood in grim silence. By their soft whispers, it seemed like they had seen this scene play out many times before.

Peter stayed down by Michael's side still firmly grasping the injured man's hand. "You'll be back to work in no time." But everyone knew that was a lie. The leg didn't look good. Marko overheard two employees whispering to each other about one young man who was killed two years ago after being hit on the head from something that fell from an overhead crane.

The distinctive clip-clop of the carriage broke the silence. The driver pulled the rear of the carriage close to the lying man. "Joey, grab two wooden planks from the woodshed, will you lad," Peter said. "A few of ya, gather 'round. We're gonna lift him on the back." Joey arrived with two pieces of lumber about three feet long. Another handed Peter some rope. He and a few others tied the planks to Michael's badly injured leg. Just the slightest movement drove spikes of pain through Michael's body. Peter gave Michael a few more shots of booze.

Peter ordered the clean-up boy to accompany Michael to the hospital. The carriage moved away from the back of the factory with Michael propped up on old rags and blankets. The gathering of employees silently watched the carriage turn off on Logan Avenue on its way to the hospital. In a subdued tone Peter said, "Alright, lads let's get back to work. It's all over here. Clean this mess and get everything loaded. And for Christ sake, fasten everything properly. See what happens when it's not?"

"Oi, you finished with the repair?" Peter said to Marko. Marko immediately walked back to the lathe.

******

Marko wiped his dirty hands on a rag. He finished reassembling the lathe and cleaning the work area when he heard Peter approach.

"Well lad," Peter said. "How was the repair. A might bit difficult, I'll wager?"

"I fix. It work good now."

Peter examined the machine thoroughly, up, down and around. He stood in front of the machine, arms crossed. "Turn it on."

Marko started the lathe and engaged the spindle. "I have job?"

Peter continued to stare dumbfounded at the perfectly operating machine. "I can't believe ya put this all together. It was a bloody mess. And ya did it in just a few hours. Alright … ya got yourself a job. Come back tomorrow with work boots and some work clothes. I'll have you repairing things. All right?"

Marko grabbed Peter's hand and shook it vigorously. "Thank you. I work hard. You see."

Peter pulled back his hand. "Yeah. Yeah. Listen, you're only as good as yer last job. You mess up, and you're gone. Now get outta here before I change me mind."

"Yes, sir. I come tomorrow— "

"Eight o'clock. Go on to the front office. They'll sign you in."

******

Marko re-entered the front office through the same grimy door. Liz sat at her desk near the front counter.

"Peter say I come here. You sign me in, he say."

"Well, I do not have time for you." She looked at Mildred sitting at a nearby desk, "Mildred, please take care of this … gentleman, will you."

"But I thought you wanted me to finish these payroll reports?"

"Do them both. Your father wants you do be exposed to the same day-to-day stresses we have to deal with. This is one of them. Sometimes you have to do two things at once. You just have to work harder. We're not sitting on our back porch sipping lemonade, you know."

Mildred frowned. She gave him a form and a pencil. "Come over to the counter. I need you to complete this."

Marko looked at the paper. So many words. So many lines. He tried to read the heading, EMPLOYMENT APPLICATION FOR WINNIPEG IRON WORKS, but had difficulty. He recognized "NAME" and a few other words from his immigration papers but other questions were more difficult. He froze. Perhaps he would not be given the job if he could not fill out the paper?

After a few minutes he noticed Mildred staring at him so he pretended to write something.

"What's the problem? Can you not read?"

Another wave of shame and embarrassment came over Marko. He should just leave. Run back to Mike's.

Mildred took the application from Marko. He'd only filled a few lines. "This is a sloppy, incomprehensible mess. 'Marko Gobinski'. Is that right?" Marko nodded. "490 … What is it? … Manitoba Avenue?" Marko nodded again. Mildred sighed.

Mildred read the next question: "Date of Birth. When were you born?"

"I born Galicia. I Ukrainian."

"No, no. Not *where*! When?" He looked at Mildred and shook his head. Frowning with her lips drawn together, she looked flustered. "When were you born. Which month, day, and year."

"I born 1887. Month January. Day 28."

The tedious experience went on for another fifteen excruciating minutes. It must have been worse for Mildred. She probably thought it was like pulling teeth. Sure, he could fix anything, but what did it matter if everyone thought he had the brain of an infant? He could hardly read or spell. Why come to Canada if he could not function in society?

"There," Mildred said in a stern tone. "I have all the information I need. You really do need to learn English especially if you fancy a life in Winnipeg." Marko looked down, like a child who was being scolded. "Payday is every second Friday. Show up at eight sharp. If you are one minute late, you will be docked fifteen minutes pay."

"And enter through the rear of the factory," Liz said from her desk.

"Thank you," Marko said. Perhaps the woman with the scar was right? To be accepted he would have to be better at English.

Meeting Krafchenko
July 19, 1913

"Marko, we should go out tonight," Mike said in Ukrainian at the dinner table while raising his index finger in the air. The children had already eaten and been excused from the table. Wearing her frilly apron at the kitchen counter, Maria began to scrub a pot. Marko finished the last bit of the sausages with potatoes and onions.

Maria turned her head and frowned at Mike.

"What?" Mike said, "We are not men? Men can't go out for a few drinks? It's Saturday. There's no work tomorrow."

Maria shook her head. "You know how much I hate those Main Street taverns. Only drunks go there. Bad people. Crooks. Every day there's problems in those places."

"Ah," Mike said, waving his hand dismissively. "There are only problems if you make problems. It's always the same troublemakers. We'll be fine. What about the customers that come to our door at night?" Mike turned his head to Marko. "Get ready."

Maria stood in front of the kitchen sink, hands on her hips. Marko sensed the same scene must have played itself out in the past.

Mike got up and left the room. Maria kept the same pose, but her head followed Mike the entire way.

Marko looked at Maria with a sheepish smile and wondered if it was his fault she had a furrowed brow?

Maria relaxed her pose and sighed. "Ah, what can I do?" She cradled her pregnant belly. "Can you watch him? Make sure he doesn't do anything too crazy? Or spend too much money? Maybe it's good you go. Better he's not by himself."

"I'll watch," Marko said. He rose from his seat. "Thank you for dinner. It was very good."

"At least someone likes it."

******

"Where do we go?" Marko asked. He unbuttoned his suit jacket in the warm evening air.

"Main Street."

Occasionally the pair passed others on the wooden plank sidewalk, but other than a quick nod, no one was overly friendly. Their serious faces told stories. Someone lost a job. Someone's child died of cholera. Someone's husband was cheating with the neighbor's wife. Someone drank their money away. No food in the cupboard. Mice ate the flour. The hole in the roof needs to be fixed before winter. Someone's boy got caught breaking a butcher shop's window. Someone's wife was a nag. Someone's father was on his deathbed.

The two rode a streetcar down Main Street to downtown where they got off just before Higgins Avenue. Pedestrians crammed the sidewalk on both sides of Main Street. Almost all were men, several already staggered from drunkenness, wandering aimlessly. A group with their arms around each other slurred off-key songs at the tops of their lungs.

The stench of urine and stale beer filled the air as they strolled south. About a block into their walk they passed one man sitting against a building, legs spread out revealing to the world the dark stain between his legs. His head tilted slightly to the side, his vacant expression betrayed his pathetic intoxication.

A block later, near Logan Avenue, two police constables used their night sticks to smash down a man just outside a hotel. After several quick blows, the man fell limp. The policemen each grabbed an arm and dragged the wretch away, his toes scraping against the pavement.

Mike watched the scene too closely and accidently brushed shoulders with someone walking the other way. The large, burly man with a bushy moustache smelled of rye whiskey and pushed Mike to the ground. "Watch where ya going, ya twerp."

"So sorry. I no see…" Mike said, but the big man dismissed them with a quick wave and continued up Main Street. Mike and Marko looked at each other. They had to pay attention when on rough and tumble Main Street.

Passing City Hall a short distance later, the two noticed several more police officers arresting a drunk near the centre of the street. The disoriented man's shirt featured a brown stain down the front.

"So, which tavern?" Marko said. They had just crossed William Avenue. By this time they had already walked for about fifteen minutes. Marko had seen enough of Main Street.

"The Woodbine. It's just here," Mike said. He pointed a short distance up ahead on the same side of the street to an unassuming two-storey structure nestled between two larger buildings. Easy to miss were one not paying attention.

They entered the hotel's tavern. The most noticeable aspect of the establishment was the noise, likely due to the level of inebriation of the patrons. "My round? Yer round," one patron yelled to his chum, off to the right. To the left, another shouted, "And so I told him to shove it up where the sun don't shine," to two others listened wide-eyed to his story. The off-key sounds of a piano from the back of the bar added to the boisterous atmosphere.

The stand-up bar stood immediately on the right of the long narrow room. With no tables in the tavern, men stood around to drink and socialize. Like every other drinking hole in Winnipeg, no women were allowed. Off to the side two men argued about something. Another slouched overtop the bar, his head in a puddle of beer.

At the end of the bar two men arm-wrestled. One man sported a bushy black beard and wore a tattered shirt. The other had dressed better, with pressed brown trousers and a brilliant white shirt, but had what looked like a recent wound on his forehead. Although not visibly bleeding, the cut looked like it had only recently congealed. Five or six shots of booze stood at attention beside them. The beet-red faces of the opponents looked about ready to pop, like an overripe tomato. They struggled and strained until at last, one finally succumbed and lost the tussle. The loser slumped back while the winner stretched his arms and shoulders. The loser took a shot and the two had another arm wrestle. This time the scruffy man lost and it was his turn to take a shot.

Marko and Mike walked through to the back the tavern and found a spot to stand near the piano player.

"Nice place," Marko said. "You always find the best taverns?"

Mike put on a wry smile. "Why, thank you. Actually, this place is one of the better bars on Main Street. A little quieter. Not as crazy. You should see other places. All fighting. Here we can chat."

Marko frowned. How, with the loud piano player nearby? He had to strain to hear Mike's words.

A waiter in a white, puffy shirt with armbands approached carrying a circular tray. Suspenders held his black trousers up. A grey, dirty apron hung down to his knees. "What can I get you?"

Mike held up two fingers. "Two shots of rye and two beers." The waiter left immediately. He was only one of two servers in the tavern, the other being the bartender. Judging from the size of the crowd, both would be busy all night. Marko could see the waiter walking throughout the tavern getting orders and picking up empty glasses. How could the waiter get everyone's order straight?

"So Marko, how's your new job? You like it?" Mike said.

"Not so bad. The work is good. My foreman was grouchy at first, but he's good now. He sees I work hard, so he's happy. Other workers, not so much." He leaned forward to talk quieter, difficult with the loud piano present. "They are not friendly. The English ones. They tease. They think they are better. But I know I'm better than almost all of them. But I keep to myself. I also keep my mouth shut." Marko emphasized this by making a locking motion with his hand near his mouth.

"Ah, I should do the same," Mike said, "but I talk too much. Complain too much. It will get me in trouble one day, I know…."

"Here you go, lads." The waiter gave them their order. "Let's see, shots are ten cents each, the beer's five. That will be thirty cents, please." The waiter held out his hand.

Both men motioned to pay the tab. "I'll get this one," Mike waved off Marko. "You get the next round." Mike opened his change purse and handed the waiter the money and a few coppers for a tip.

Mike held up a shot glass. "Na zdorov'ya."

"Na zdorov'ya." They clinked glasses and downed their shots in one fast gulp. The warm infusion of rye warmed Marko's gut and he chased it down with a few sips of beer. Marko bought the next round, followed by Mike, then Marko again. Through that time, the piano player took occasional breaks when he would go to the bar, light up a cigarette and drink a beer. Patrons came and went, some drunker than others.

At one point a foul-smelling, dishevelled patron staggered a short distance away. He appeared to be headed for the stairs, perhaps to the washroom in the basement, but it was difficult to tell because he swayed and stumbled in every direction. He fell against another man. Not amused, that man began kicking the unfortunate drunk. The waiter ran over, and with the help of a few other men, dragged him to the back door and threw him out. This was not before they searched his pockets to see what change he had remaining.

Sometime later, maybe ten or fifteen minutes, two constables came into the tavern. Wearing long blue coats with hats fashioned like British Bobbies, they chatted with the bartender who pointed to the back door. Through the opened door Marko could see the police pick up the poor soul for a trip to the drunk tank.

Marko noticed Mike beginning to slur his words. Square on rounds, they drank enough, but the twirl of Mike's outstretched hand caught the attention of the waiter, signalling another round. Marko shook his head. It was going to be one of those nights. Maria would not be happy.

Mike excused himself for the washroom. Before he did, he gave Marko the money for the round. While waiting for their drinks to arrive, Marko glanced around the bar.

Two men about fifteen feet away stood close together, especially when the piano was being played. Marko could not hear any of their conversation, even if he strained his ears.

Perhaps in his mid-30s, one man had a fair complexion with an average build. Clean-cut and neat, he had his hair parted perfectly in the middle. Squinting, Marko noticed a scar on the man's neck near his right ear.

But the second man drew Marko's attention. Also clean-shaven, he had a strong chin and deep-set blue eyes shielded by heavy, dark eyebrows. His short black hair looked neat. A thick, strong neck and oval face gave the man a European look. Women would find him handsome. The only physical feature of the man that caused Marko to pause was his ears: they seemed pointed, especially when viewed from the front of the man's face. They gave the man a slight devilish quality not apparent in his other features. Although shorter than the other man standing with him, he more than made up for his lack of height with muscle. But the most prominent feature of the man was not anything physical. The man somehow exuded a confidence unlike the rabble in the Woodbine. The man commanded an air of authority. He seemed like a man Marko could trust. The waiter always approached him first when in the area and was attentive whenever the man raised his hand for service. In fact, the waiter made sure to fill his drinking needs even if he had a prior order to fill.

Marko stared vacantly at the handsome man. The man seemed to gesture over, but Marko disregarded it. He must have been referring to someone else. The man gestured again. The other man also turned to look at Marko.

Suddenly aware that he had been staring, Marko looked away. He promised Maria there would be no trouble and here he was getting into it. The last thing you ever want to do in a Main Street tavern is draw attention to yourself, especially in a bad way. The man spoke louder right at Marko, but he could not make out what the man said over the incessant piano.

"Phillip, stop," the man yelled. Instantly the piano player stopped. The loud order caught the attention of each patron standing nearby. All conversation ceased. Everyone's eyes trained on the man. He pointed at Marko. "You," he switched to Ukrainian. "Why are you staring at me? You understand that is considered extremely rude? I have pulled a beating heart from a man's chest for far less."

"I'm so sorry, sir," Marko said in Ukrainian. "I did not mean to offend you, I was just daydream—"

Slowly, a grin formed on the man's face. He burst out laughing, slapping his leg repeatedly. He switched back to perfect English. "That's alright. I was only pulling your leg." The man then nodded to the piano and the player resumed tapping the keys. The tavern patrons laughed and hooted uproariously at the outcome of the tense scene. Within moments the volume of the crowd settled back to its regular level.

Mike returned from his trip to the washroom. The man was still chuckling and Marko must have appeared flustered. "Is everything alright?"

"Of course, of course," the man said. "Come, both of you. Join us. I was just having some fun with your friend." At that moment the waiter arrived with Mike and Marko's order of a shot and a beer each. "Here, I'll pay for their round and bring us another. We will each have a shot of rye with our beer." The man held out several coins for the waiter.

Mike and Marko looked at each other and shrugged. What could they do? The clean-cut man paid for the drinks, they might as well join him and his comrade.

The man extended his hand to Marko. "I'm sorry, my name is John."

Marko immediately noticed the firmness of John's grip. One finger had a ring in the shape of a snake. "Hello … I'm Marko. My friend is Mike."

"Pleased to meet you Mike," John said with a wink. "And this is John Buxton. But you can call him Johnny so you don't mix us up."

John took a sip of beer and then ran his finger along the rim of his mug. "I can tell you are new to this country. Sometimes it's nice to meet friendly people. It can be difficult fitting in when you are not familiar with the local customs or language. Is it not?"

Why was John so friendly? Marko found it interesting that John spoke perfect English, not even a hint of an accent. Many people who originated from the old country decades ago continued to speak in a manner that betrayed their true origin. No wonder John could commend so much attention: he could straddle both sides of the immigrant divide. By voice alone John easily passed for an Englishman.

"Yes, it can be difficult," Marko said. "But, not so bad. You need be careful. If you work hard, everything will be fine." Mike hiccupped while Marko spoke.

"So true, so true," John said. "What do both of you do for a living?"

"I work at Winnipeg Iron Works," Marko said.

"I find what I can," Mike said.

John took a sip of his beer. "I'm a blacksmith by trade."

John did not look like a blacksmith. Sure, he had the body type. He seemed strong and rugged enough and his hands appeared strong, yet his fingernails looked clean and well kept. Marko did not see any burn marks or scars on his hands or wrists.

"I have not worked for some time now," John said. "I had a few problems in Ontario and decided to come back to Manitoba."

The overworked waiter arrived with John's order. Marko looked at his pocket watch. Eleven in the evening. It did not look like Mike would last much longer. John raised his shot glass, "Cheers everyone. New friends." They all clinked glasses and downed their rye. Marko could definitely feel the drink burning harder. It became more difficult to swallow each shot. They would have to leave soon, but first he and Mike would have to buy a round. There is nothing more shameful than not buying a round when it's your turn.

Over the next hour they learned more about each other. John Buxton worked as the sales manager at Northwest Builders' Supply. He came from Fort William, Ontario several years ago when he heard Winnipeg was booming. He tried his hand at real estate, but it didn't work out. The two Johns had known each other for years. Marko couldn't help but wonder how he came upon that horrible scar on his neck, but didn't feel it was appropriate to ask. Maybe another time.

After their next round, which Marko made a point of buying, it was a good time to leave.

"C'mon Marko," Mike said "Just one more drink."

"No. We have to go. You want to end up like man in alley?"

"Ah, you're no fun," Mike waved his hand through the air.

"I should be on my way as well," John said. He held out to shake hands with Marko and Mike.

Walking to the front of the tavern with John, Marko helped steady Mike. The street outside still teemed with pedestrians and automobiles.

"It was nice meeting you," Marko said to John. Mike swayed like a tree in a breeze.

"Where do you live?" John asked.

"On Manitoba Avenue in the North End. I rent a room from Mike."

"Well, get him home safely. The police will throw you in the clink if you are Eastern European and have a hint of alcohol on your breath. Your friend looks like he's been swimming in it."

Marko held out his hand. "I'm sorry, I didn't catch your full name…?"

"John Krafchenko."

In the Alley with Mildred
August 5, 1913

The whistle blew.

Marko had just finished repairing a leaky pipe in the employee quarters in the basement. Satisfied, he gathered his tools and supplies into a long wooden-handled toolbox and cleaned himself in the large community sink only a few steps away. He grabbed his lunch and left the employee area.

He'd worked only a few weeks, but it seemed like he was getting harassed just about every day. The employees who hailed from Eastern Europe did not bother Marko. Indeed, those other Eastern Europeans, be they Ruthanian, Russian, Romanian, or any other Slavic nationality, also faced the same taunts.

Sometimes small scuffles developed, but because the Anglos outnumbered the foreigners, it was not worth the trouble. It didn't help that Peter, the foreman, naturally sided with the Anglos.

Marko tried to not let any of the sly comments get to him. Peter didn't bother him much, especially as Marko always completed his assigned tasks, ranging from a complex production-related machine to a squeaky door or loose window sill.

"Marko, you eat with us?" Vladimir asked, a recent Russian immigrant.

"No, I go outside today. Fresh air, no?"

Vladimir shrugged then went with a group of other Eastern European immigrants to the back of the factory. During lunch break the factory workers typically ate in groups. Sometimes the summer heat made it too hot to sit outside and since the factory lacked a lunch area, workers sat on chairs or makeshift benches inside the shop, usually right beside their machines.

Marko enjoyed his time with the Eastern Europeans but sometimes it felt good to gather his thoughts or otherwise get a break from the factory. He went outside to the back lane near the factory worker entrance.

It had rained heavily the night before so the ruts in the lane remained damp and muddy. Fortunately, the soil along the outer wall of the factory had dried enough for him to sit and enjoy his short lunch break. He found a spot with no thistles and sat crossed-legged. His lunch consisted of two hard-boiled eggs, some cucumber, two pieces of buttered rye bread and a small piece of kolbassa.

Marko could hear the busy sounds of nearby Logan Avenue including the clip-clopping of a horse-drawn carriage or the distinctive sound of a streetcar. Occasionally he had to shoo away a fly attempting to land on his lunch. Wild flowers that looked like daisies caught his attention. A single monarch butterfly floated and bobbed.

He gently stroked the indentation on the side of his head. It had been about a month since arriving to Winnipeg. He had found a place to live and a decent job. A good start to his new life. Sometimes old memories rose up like the layer of fat atop chicken soup left over night. He tried to ignore the past, but it became more difficult to keep it down.

The door opened. Mildred stepped out. Any time the factory workers discussed her it usually led to something lewd involving a paper bag covering her head. Mildred wore a long brown skirt with a black, somewhat frilly blouse including matching black button-up shoes.

She didn't seem to notice him sitting quietly nearby. Once the door closed behind her, she raised her hands to her face. She kept her sobs quiet, so it took a few moments for Marko to notice she was indeed crying. Near her face she tightly held a bright white handkerchief.

Should he say anything? Should he mind his own business? Maybe she had woman issues? She likely wanted some time to herself.

Mildred turned away and leaned against the factory wall. She occasionally blew her nose into the handkerchief.

He cleared his throat.

She didn't hear him. Another half-minute elapsed before Marko finally found the gumption to speak.

"Are you fine?"

But Mildred continued to sob into her handkerchief. Did she not hear or simply chose to ignore him?

"Excuse … are you fine?" Marko said, a little louder.

This time Mildred lowered her handkerchief and turned to face Marko, her face a sloppy mess, all red and blotchy. While her white handkerchief absorbed most of her tears, several escaped. He stared at the ugly scar on her right cheek.

Without saying a work, Mildred quickly waved her hand in a dismissive fashion at Marko. She did this with the hand that held the handkerchief. Unfortunately, she did not hold the cloth tight enough and it escaped her grasp and fluttered, like a butterfly, gently and gracefully, into the middle of a mud puddle in the back lane. Made of quality linen, most of the handkerchief stayed above the puddle, but like an iceberg, it slowly melted into the muddy goo.

Mildred carefully reached down and grabbed the handkerchief from the mud puddle. She looked at it and began to weep again, only more openly.

Marko had only wiped his mouth once on his handkerchief. He stood up and offered it to Mildred. "Pretty woman like you … no should cry. Here. Take."

Mildred frowned when she saw Marko's outstretched hand, still dirty with grime and grease. Despite her messy and wet face, she declined his offer with a casual wave and turned her head away and down.

"Take, take, take." Marko said. "I no need." He demonstrated by wiping his mouth on his soiled arm sleeve.

With a half-smile, she maintained her stance. "No. No, thank you. I'm fine now. I do not need your … handkerchief. You use it." Clear mucus poked out of one nostril and began a slow, snail-like journey down to Mildred's upper lip.

Marko tilted his head slightly and placed his handkerchief in Mildred's hand. "You need more. You dripping. No look good. Yours dirty from mud."

Mildred wiped her nose. She turned around to go back through the side door again with her head tilted down and to the right against her shoulder. Before she walked back into the factory, she stopped and turned to Marko. "Thank you."

The door shut. Marko stood for a moment and contemplated Mildred. Too bad for the scar on her face. It must be difficult for her to find suitors even though she was the owner's daughter. She had very pretty brown eyes, though. Smelled nice, too.

Marko sat back down and finished his lunch. A butterfly gently fluttered beside him.

Silk Stocking
August 12, 1913

The end of another workday, Marko walked out the factory through the employee entrance at the back. The murmur of traffic and horse-drawn carriages spilled from the street on the other side of the building.

After rounding the corner to Logan Avenue, he noticed Thomas Spencer's Packard parked directly in front of the factory steps with its hood up and James bent over the innards of the automobile.

Mr. Spencer and Mildred sat in the back seat. "What is the problem?" Mr. Spencer said, adjusting the end of his shirt sleeve peeking out from his dark, three-piece suit. "We have an evening engagement."

"It's the fan belt, sir." James held up the limp broken belt. "I don't know where we'll get another at this time. The service shops are closed."

"Damn!" Thomas slapped the plush seat in front of him, knocking his top hat askew. He noticed Marko beside the vehicle. "You there. Galician. Repairman. What can you do? Have a look, will you?"

Marko nodded and walked to the front of the vehicle.

"There's not much you can do," James said. He handed the broken fan belt to Marko.

Marko poked his head in to inspect the situation. He looked back at the broken belt, now draped over the side of the car bumper. Eyes narrowed, he examined the location in the engine where the broken belt would have gone. Even with a new replacement part it would take some time to fit the belt on. He would also have to go back into the shop for tools. Automobiles always seemed to be breaking down. It was a wonder why men bothered buying them.

Once again Marko glanced at the broken belt, like a dead snake. He mind raced back to when he was a young boy, perhaps nine or ten years old, standing in a field poking at a dead snake. It had just been stepped on by one of the horses pulling a wagon holding a combine. The machine featured many whirling levers and moving parts. His father always reminded him to stay away from the machine. If he caught his hand in it, he would surely lose a finger or maybe even an entire hand. His uncle lost two fingers a few years before. Marko remembered all the blood from that accident. But the combine had broken and his father needed to fix it. Too far from town, he told Marko to run home and ask Ma for a stocking. She didn't want to give it to him. Stockings were expensive and if she gave him one, what would she do with the other? She relented and gave it to Marko. He remembered Pa standing on the wagon in the distance across the field, arms akimbo, smiling, while waiting for Marko.

"…can you hear me?" James said. Marko snapped from his daydream.

"Da, da. I can fix," Marko said. "I need stocking."

"You need what?"

"Stocking. Woman stocking."

"A woman's stocking? Now where are we going to get that? Eaton's is too far away and closed by now anyway."

Thomas overheard the conversation. "What's that?"

Chuckling, James turned to Thomas. "He says he needs a woman's stocking. I don't know how they repair automobiles in his country, but it's certainly not advanced."

"You can repair this vehicle with a woman's stocking? Is that true?" Thomas asked.

Marko nodded emphatically.

"Mr. Spencer, sir, this is not as simple as a punctured tire. It's preposterous to think the man can repair this vehicle with women's clothing."

Thomas looked at his pocket watch. "We may have to get a carriage." Then he looked at Marko again. After a pause, he folded his arms. "Alright, Galician. You say a stocking will repair this Packard. Where are we going to get a stocking…" Slowly Thomas turned to look at Mildred beside him.

Mildred raised her gloved hand to her mouth. "Certainly you don't think … you cannot be serious…?"

Thomas raised his eyebrows. "Come now, Mildred. We all have to make our sacrifices."

******

Mildred cocked her head to the side, the wide brim of her hat touched her shoulder. It perfectly matched her light beige dress. Marko was trying to embarrass her. Perhaps to make up for that day in the office when she had to complete his job application for him. "Father, I do not think this is appropriate. I am wearing my stockings! You expect me to take off my stockings and give them to *him*?"

Thomas shook his head. "Mildred. Go inside the office into the lavatory and take off your stocking and give it to the repairman. Enough of this foolishness."

"But Father—" Mildred started, but it was useless. Thomas had already leaned over and opened the car door. She lowered her head.

Stepping out of the vehicle, her heel caught the bottom of the door opening. She lost her footing and tumbled out of the automobile, landing hard on her bum on Logan Avenue. A passing vehicle honked and swerved to avoid her. Mildred's right hand felt gooey and slimy. It had imbedded in the middle of a fresh pile of horse manure.

Marko ran around the vehicle to help Mildred up from the street. He pulled out his handkerchief and gave it to her, "Here, take. Your … hand…"

Mildred grabbed Marko's handkerchief without protest, it may have been the same one he had given to her that time in the back alley. She wiped her fingers and the palm of her hand. "I will have to wash this again, I suppose."

Once in the lavatory Mildred cleaned herself then removed her stocking from underneath her dress. She felt like a harlot. How embarrassing. What if someone saw her bare leg? Fixing an automobile with a lady's stocking. Who heard of such a thing? She didn't know if she should be more upset at her father or at Marko.

She looked at the handkerchief. Marko would not want it back. Before she left the washroom she threw his soiled handkerchief in the trash. She turned to leave but paused for a moment to look at the handkerchief. Marko really was just a simple man and likely meant no wrong. She reached into the garbage and grabbed the handkerchief, wrapped it in a clean towel and took it along with her stockings back to the scene outside the factory.

Mildred slowly walked down the stairs and handed her stocking to Marko. "I will keep the other with me, thank you. Unless of course you need it."

******

"Thank you," Marko said. The stocking felt so light and delicate in his hand, like a spider's web. If he were to let go it would float away on the tiniest breeze. With no tears or runs, it must have been expensive and made of the highest quality silk. Only minutes earlier the silk garment had touched Mildred's bare leg. He felt the urge to smell it. Something so nice and delicate belonged on a woman's leg, not in the engine of an automobile. He almost felt bad for what he had to do.

Marko went to work. Holding one end, he twisted the stocking around and around many times while keeping it tight. Eventually it resembled a thin rope. Keeping it taut, Marko positioned the stocking around the bare pulleys where the broken fan belt had originally been positioned. Marko tied the ends together, again, trying to keep it tight.

"I need something to cut. Knife?" Without saying a word, James handed him his pocket knife. Marko cut off the excess silk from both ends of the tight knot he had fashioned. He put the remnants in his trouser pocket.

"Start it and see if it works," Marko said to James. It started immediately and the temporary fix held. He closed the hood and walked over to the driver's side. "My fix will not last long."

"I will have to arrange for a repairman," James said.

"See here, Galician," Thomas said. "I cannot help but be impressed by your repair skills. Good, reliable repairmen are difficult to find. I have also heard your name mentioned positively by Peter regarding your duties and responsibilities in the shop. Would you be interested in some side work? Our home is always in need of general repair."

"I work six days in week. I work on Sunday for you at your house?"

"Of course not," Thomas said. "No one works on the Lord's Day. From time to time, when a repair is required, your duties on that day will shift from the factory to my home. Alright?"

Marko nodded.

"Tomorrow I want you to fix my car properly with the correct part." Thomas turned to his daughter. "Mildred, you make the necessary arrangements and particulars."

She nodded slowly, frowning.

Thomas continued. "You will be paid over and above your normal wage here at the factory to help defray incidental costs and the fare for the streetcar. You and Mildred can decide a fair settlement tomorrow."

Mildred began to protest, however Thomas slowly raised his hand, silencing her. "Mildred, give the man our address. You can wait for him at our home until he arrives."

"But what about the office work? I thought you wanted me more involved with the family business?" Mildred said. "I don't want to wait around for him to finish his work."

"You will do as I say. If I tell you to crawl under this Packard to help this Galician while motor oil splatters on your … face, then so be it." Mildred winced and dropped her head down and to the side.

Marko looked away from the family squabble. After he accepted the address from Mildred, he tipped his hat.

******

As the vehicle lurched forward, Thomas slapped Mildred on the leg. "I almost forgot, you will have a gentleman caller quite soon. I have been in contact with Edgar Dalton. His son, William, has an eye for you."

"Really?"

"Yes. From what I understand, William will soon contact you to make arrangements."

Mildred took a deep breath. It had been some time since she had been entertained by a man. A very long time. But why would William Dalton want to see her when there were so many other eligible women in Winnipeg?

The question bounced around her head, but in the end it did not matter. It was better than nothing.

The Spencer Estate
August 16, 1913

Once the streetcar crossed the Assiniboine River, Marko entered another world. Mike told him about the huge houses, wide streets, large yards and lush greenery. He had seen large mansions before in the old country, but the large grouping of them all together in one place felt humbling. The Assiniboine River to the north naturally secluded and isolated the area from the rest of the city. A separate enclave.

Marko stepped off the streetcar. Along the way to the Spencer residence he noticed a group of children running and playing. A small boy wearing a blue sailor's suit clutched a toy train engine. An older girl, perhaps his sister, in a white dress one would expect at church or some other formal engagement frowned at the boy. "Matthew, come. We'll be late for our trip to the park."

The traffic on Wellington Crescent differed from that in the North End. While Wellington still had tell-tale manure piles on the pavement indicating the presence of horses, most of the traffic was motorized. And even then, nice, luxury vehicles, not unlike Mr. Spencer's Packard.

Just before Marko came to the Spencer residence, he heard the fast trot of a team of horses. A rubber-wheeled wagon from Eaton's, the popular multi-storey department store downtown on Portage Avenue, rolled past, cleaner and sharper-looking than most other delivery wagons. The driver turned into the driveway of a mansion. With a tiny flick on the reins, the well-trained horses came to a stop immediately in front of the stone landing leading to the front door. The driver, dressed in a crisp uniform, grabbed a package and jogged quickly to the front door. A moment later he handed it over to the occupant and jogged back to the wagon.

The immensity of the Spencer mansion made Marko pause for a moment. Situated on the river side of Wellington, a long, tall iron fence ran along the front of the estate with two entrances to the property. Both open, each entrance featured a double-gate. A stylized 'S' adorned the very top of both gate doors of each entrance. A cobblestone path led to the residence. The garage, visible from the side of the mansion, had space for three automobiles. The stable, to the right of the garage, was open but empty. Perhaps someone had taken the horse team out on an errand?

Like every other residence on Wellington, Marko noticed the large and spacious front yard featured a well-tended lawn. Not a single dandelion or thistle could be seen. Extremely large, lush shade trees dotted the yard. Smaller ornamental shrubs were placed strategically. A well-kept assortment of blue, orange and white annual flowers lined the inside of the arc pathway.

Made of red brick, the three-storey mansion appeared like a mighty castle, a symbol of wealth and prestige. A strong, sturdy chimney stood proud on the dark-coloured roof. Marko saw how all the windows, even the smaller ones on the top floor, were so clean that they reflected the sky or the leaves from neighboring trees. Naturally, the handrails for the brick steps leading to the front door featured intricate metal work and looked similar to the handrails that supported the Winnipeg Iron Works factory front steps.

Marko walked up the steps to the front door and rang the doorbell.

A moment later the thick front door opened. A middle-aged woman, a maid dressed in pink with a brilliant white apron, glared at him. Lines of contempt crossed her forehead.

"All deliveries or hired work go to the back door," the maid said and immediately slammed the door. He could have sworn the Eaton's delivery man used the front door at a neighbor's home. Marko turned around and went to the back of the mansion.

Also wide and roomy, the back yard looked like a private park. Marko noticed that the land dropped noticeably at the far end when it reached the banks of the Assiniboine River. Trees and undergrowth along the river bank partially obscured the river itself. Large enough to hold twenty people, a bright blue, raised wooden shelter stood in the centre of the backyard. Just like the front yard, a variety of shrubs, plants and flowers complemented the perfectly trimmed lawn. Several benches located around the yard offered relaxing places to enjoy the scenery.

The mansion featured two entrances in the back. At the centre, a pair of large French doors opened to a sizeable porch. Similar to the steps at the front of the house, fancy metal handrails decorated the steps leading up to the porch.

The other, simpler back entrance stood closer to the corner of the rear of the mansion. Square and smaller, the stone staircase must have been the door the maid mentioned. He walked up and rapped on the door.

The door opened a crack. "Hold on, hold on. I know you're here," the same maid said. "I'm busy preparing pastries. It's not like I can drop everything for you. Now, what do you want? You better not be a salesman."

"I come to fix automobile."

"You must have the wrong address. I was not told of any of the automobiles needing repair."

The door opened wider revealing Mildred. She had her hair down. Her beautiful flowing brown hair brought out her striking brown eyes.

"I'm sorry Gladys, I neglected to mention one of the factory workers was coming here today. This is Marko. He will work on the Packard in the garage. See that he has water to refresh himself."

Gladys snorted and walked away into a wide and spacious kitchen. A few other workers looked to be preparing a dinner.

"The garage is open. You can begin the repair," Mildred said. "James obtained the replacement part. I believe it's on the hood of the automobile. I will come out in a moment to discuss terms."

Marko nodded and Mildred gently closed the door. He raised his eyebrows and sighed. So formal.

He exhaled slowly while marveling the contents of the garage. A beautiful black Abbott-Detroit touring car stood beside the Packard. An empty space beside the Abbott-Detroit was likely for a vehicle already out. Some tools hung from hooks attached to the wall, but an assortment of wrenches, screw drivers and hammers littered the unorganized work bench. How odd. Everything so far about the Spencer residence seemed so immaculate and perfect. The previous handyman left a mess.

The three electric lights inside the garage did not provide enough light for the work he had to do. He opened the large garage door, located the tools he needed and went about his work.

Eventually Gladys came to the garage to provide a decanter of water and a glass. She did not acknowledge his polite thank you.

A half hour later, while lying on the ground under the automobile, Marko heard the door to the mansion open. The lady's black button-up boots peeked from under the long white dress. The woman walked right up to the car.

"Marko?"

Marko shimmied out from under the Packard and appeared right beside

Mildred's feet, still flat on his back. "Oh! There you are," Mildred said, caught off guard. "How is the repair progressing?"

"One hour. Maybe two."

"Very good. Shall we discuss terms?"

He slowly rose to his feet. "I no understand. What is terms?"

"Terms. You know. The amount you will be compensated for your work."

Confused Marko shook his head slightly.

"Compensation … money. We need to discuss how much money you should be given for the work you perform."

"I happy to help. If boss say I come to fix … I fix."

"Nonsense. You need some form of remuneration. It's only fair. Let's see now. You make fifty cents an hour at the factory. For a full day you would be making four dollars. Since you are being taken away from your regular job, you should get at least four dollars, let's say four-fifty to cover the cost to get here. Does that sound fair?"

Marko shrugged his shoulders. "But work here not full day. I almost finished. I only here a few hours. I go back to factory?"

"Perhaps today. But listen … I know my father knows you are very good at general repairs. So like he said yesterday, from time to time, your work day will be here instead of the factory. I know Mother wants to build a few more benches for the back yard and we've had problems with our plumbing recently. It's been difficult finding a good repairman, so perhaps this is something that would interest you?"

Marko nodded. Most of the repairs required at the Spencer residence could not be that difficult. The work environment would certainly be better than the factory. Who knows? Maybe if he made enough money through extra side jobs he'd one day have enough to open that repair shop.

"Very good, then," Mildred said with a curt smile. "When you complete today's repair, come to the door." He examined her stride when she walked back to the house.

After an hour, Marko finished his work in the garage and cleaned his workspace. On the ground he noticed the remnants of Mildred's silk stocking that had been used for the original repair back at the factory. He went to throw the tattered and soiled stocking remnant into the garbage container beside the workbench, but stopped himself. He looked at it again and recalled how upset Mildred had been when her father ordered her to remove it. He certainly could not give it back to her. Almost reluctantly, he placed it carefully back in the garbage and covered it with a dirty rag. Best to bury it.

Mildred answered the door after Marko knocked. "Done for today?"

"Yes. Automobile fixed."

"We have a leaky pipe under the sink you can investigate the next time you visit. If you can purchase the tools or supplies you need, perhaps from Ashdown's, I will reimburse you."

"Rem ... remburtz?"

"You will be paid back for any purchases you make dealing with repairs at this estate."

Marko nodded his head. This Mildred always talked so fancy?

Just then his stomach betrayed him and unleashed a horribly loud growl. He looked away.

"You didn't bring a lunch?"

"No. I not sure how long I stay."

"Well ... wait here." Mildred stepped back into the mansion through the kitchen door. She emerged moments later with a thick beef sandwich wrapped in a white handkerchief. "Take this."

"Thank you." So hungry, he did not attempt to refuse the offering.

"You're welcome. I suppose that's it for today. I will see you at the factory on Monday."

Marko tipped his hat and walked away up the cobblestone path to Wellington Crescent. She didn't have to give him food.

******

Mildred watched Marko leave the front yard. In many respects he was a simple man, but one could not doubt his efficiency and honest work ethic. Not quite like the lazy Galicians Father always complained about.

She noticed the open garage door and peeked inside. Every tool, not just the few tools Marko needed, had been put away leaving the bench clear and free of clutter. She raised her eyebrows and slowly nodded in approval.

Mildred's back stiffened and she raised her hand to her mouth. She forgot to pay the man.

English Lessons
August 20, 1913

"Oi, Marko, you're wanted in the office," Peter said.

Marko walked through the door leading to the office. Liz stood at the counter talking to the postman. Preoccupied with their work, the others in the office didn't pay attention to him. He stood near an empty desk for a few moments, not sure what to do.

He noticed a copy of that day's *Manitoba Free Press* and picked it up. Not that it mattered because he could hardly read. He could figure out the easy words, but not much else.

Mildred noticed him. "Oh, there you are. I wanted to let you know James and my father were impressed with the repair you made to the automobile. Runs like a charm. Can you come to our residence again this coming Saturday? Aside from the plumbing, those benches I mentioned need to be constructed for the backyard. We have some wood and other materials, although we have to send for supplies from Ashdown's if anything additional is required."

Mildred turned to go back to her desk when she stopped herself. "Oh, I almost forgot. I have to reimburse you for your last visit. I have the money at my desk. I'll be right back."

"No, no need. I good."

Mildred frowned. "I thought we agreed to terms? I certainly cannot have you working for free. I have to give you something for the work you do at our residence."

"No money. Only pay for things I buy. I like you help."

"You need my help? How can I help you?"

"No, no. I like you help." Marko meant he liked to help, but had difficulty putting his words together. Mildred got the wrong message.

"Yes, of course. I certainly can help. You clearly need assistance with English." Mildred pointed to the newspaper Marko still held. "Can you read this?"

Marko glanced down at the newspaper for only a moment before he shrugged and averted his eyes. He placed the newspaper back on the desk.

"Alright. How does this sound: You come to the house when we need repairs and such. In exchange, I will help you with your English. I was a teacher before coming to work here."

"Da."

"Yes," Mildred said.

Marko cocked his head slightly.

"Yes," Mildred said again. "The proper reply is 'yes,' not 'da.'

Marko smiled. "Yes."

"Very good. Come on Sunday for your first lesson at two."

Mildred turned again to leave.

"One moment," Marko said.

Marko fished around in the pocket of his dirty work trousers and pulled out a handkerchief. "Here. You hanke…hanke…how you say?"

"Handkerchief?"

"Da, handkerchief. Remember you put sandwich in?" He pressed the cloth into her hand.

She glanced down. It looked clean, but in the process of handing it to her, some grease from Marko's fingers transferred to the handkerchief. And the way she grabbed it, grease transferred from the handkerchief to her hand. She scrunched her nose and held the now offending handkerchief away from her body.

"I sorry. I clean…"

"That's quite alright," Mildred said. She threw the handkerchief in the garbage basket at Liz's desk and walked away.

Before Marko went back into the factory, he reached into the bin and put the handkerchief back in his pocket.

William B. Dalton
August 22, 1913

"Would you care for another tea, ma'am?" The waiter asked in the sitting room of the Royal Alexandra Hotel. Dressed in their best clothes and requisite jewelry, most of the other women in the room sat in pairs. Some were acquaintances enjoying their time together while others looked to be mothers and daughters.

"No, thank you," Mildred replied. Anything more than two cups and she would certainly be excusing herself during the meal. She sat alone waiting for William B. Dalton. They had planned to meet at 6:00 pm. She looked at her tiny bejeweled wrist watch. Twenty-five minutes to seven. She had decided to wear her beautiful floor-length off-white satin gown garnished with a bright, thick red ribbon around the waist.

A lone violinist in the corner of the room added sad ambiance. It didn't surprise her, really. After all, why would anyone want to have dinner with someone that looked grotesque? When she entered the sitting room all the ladies stopped and stared. It was the same everywhere. The lively conversations would be replaced by hushed tones of buzzing whispers. She thought she would get used to the comments, but she hadn't.

William entered the room just before she raised her hand to call over the waiter to pay for her tea. Six feet tall and slender, his short blonde hair was parted neatly in the center but slightly out of place in spots. The finest shop in Winnipeg likely custom tailored his neat, pressed trousers and jacket. Black shoes polished to perfection. His face flushed, he spotted her instantly and smiled.

"I am so sorry for being late," he said. "I was tied up and couldn't leave. I'm helping with my father's business and sometimes those meetings take longer than scheduled."

Mildred slowly stood up and let William take her by the hand. Still annoyed at his tardiness, she only provided a faint smile. Her expectations dropped down a peg. Best to get on with the dinner and move on.

William led her to the hotel's restaurant. "Dalton. Party of two," he said to the maître d' who directed them to their table. About three-quarters full, most of the restaurant's guests dressed in formal attire, having taken the time to prepare for an outing. The others, likely hotel guests, ate at the restaurant for convenience, unprepared for the shock when the bill arrived.

The waiter, dressed in black and white, approached the table. He handed menus and provided recommendations and analysis for most for the entrees. He raved about the duck baked in an expensive French red wine. Mildred went for the veal while William ordered a steak.

"…and make sure it's rare," William said. "I will not accept it unless it is."

The waiter nodded slowly. "Can I offer anything to drink?"

"Yes," William said. "I'll have a dry martini. Hold the olive. Mildred, what would you like?"

Despite being full of tea, Mildred thought it was best to comply. "Mmmm … I'll just have a club soda, please."

"You sure?" William said. His upper lip curled into what looked like a sarcastic smile. "You can have anything you want. You're not at home…."

"No, that's fine. Although, I may fancy some wine later when the meal arrives." The waiter nodded and left to fetch the drinks.

After a long, uncomfortable pause, William tapped the table with his index finger a few times. "So, Mildred. I hear you are a teacher. What subjects do you like to teach?"

"I'm not teaching at the moment, but am fond of the classics. I don't mind arithmetic. I did not care much for the sciences, though. I'm presently working in the front office at Father's factory."

"I see." William seemed distracted, looking away from time to time. Was it the scar? How could he not look away? It was so long and deep and right there.

"And what do you do?" Mildred asked. "You are not in university, are you?" She tried not to stare too intently at his beautiful brown eyes. His hands appeared delicate and soft despite a few scuffs and some bruising on the knuckles of his right hand.

"Oh, no. I gave it a go at the University of Toronto. I studied engineering for a few years, but didn't fancy it, so I came back here to help with my father's business."

"Which is…?"

"Cement and masonry."

Mildred gave William a faint smile. At least he had a good job.

"I'm also involved in some charity work," William added.

"Oh, how so?" Mother involved herself in a variety of charities and causes along with her other lady friends.

"Oh, not much, I … uh … help with the disadvantaged. Children that are not well off. You know, orphanages and such."

The waiter arrived with the drinks. Mildred took a small sip of her club soda while William slurped half his martini.

Their food arrived after an appropriate length of time. "For the lady, veal." The waiter placed the scrumptious looking meal in front of Mildred. "And for you sir, our finest cut." Steam still rose from the massive, bloody steak on William's plate. Noticing William did not look pleased, the waiter paused.

"Is everything to your satisfaction?" the waiter asked.

"I do not believe so," William said. "You overcooked the steak. It looks medium-well to me."

"I can assure you our chef paid extra attention to your cut. It is rare."

William cut the steak with his knife. Blood oozed on to the plate. He ate a small piece. The waiter stood there for several tense moments, waiting for some sign from William. Finally, after he completely chewed and swallowed the piece of meat he looked at the waiter and said, "Ah, it will do, I suppose."

The waiter nodded tentatively and forced a smile. "Very good." He paused slightly before asking, "Can I get you some wine?"

William breathed in and exhaled slowly. "Yes, please do. A fine red, of course."

"Of course." The waiter left the table.

Waiting until the waiter left earshot, Mildred leaned forward slightly. "Is your meal to your satisfaction? My veal is excellent. Your steak looks rare."

"Oh, it's perfect," William said, digging at his steak. "I like to have the servers on their toes. It keeps them honest. Why settle for second best? If they know I'm particular, they'll work harder to please me the next time around. I've made restaurants take back meals that were entirely perfect without taking a bite."

"If something is right, it should be accepted and acknowledged. Should it not?"

"Ah, not always, my dear. Not always."

The waiter arrived with a bottle of red wine, Chateau Mouton Rothschild,

1909. After William tested it the waiter expertly poured the wine, first in Mildred's glass then in William's. He held a cloth underneath the wine bottle to catch any errant drops.

Mildred took a sip. A cascade of flavour erupted inside her mouth. A vivid rhubarb, coffee and tobacco bouquet but predominately red fruit and citrus presented in the French wine. She also detected a hint of caramel. "My, this is absolutely wonderful wine."

The two worked on their meals. Famished, Mildred enjoyed her veal. William's plate soon became a bloody mess. He only ate the meat.

"Why are you not eating your vegetables?" Mildred asked.

"I don't eat vegetables. A waste of time. I get to the heart of the matter. Everything else is just a garnish."

Mildred finished her glass of wine. "Here, have another glass," William said. He got up from his chair and walked right beside Mildred. Pouring the wine, he gently placed his hand along the back of her neck. Although Mildred's dress featured an extremely high neckline – right up to the top of her neck – the back swooped down. His hand touched her bare skin. She arched her back slightly, but did not object. She had not been touched in such a long time. William emptied the bottle in his wine glass and motioned to the waiter a few tables away to bring another.

Mildred's cheeks felt warm after her second glass and she really did not want any more, although she agreed on a third glass. She found herself staring at William and noticing his handsome features. She talked about the things she liked: walks in a park, the sounds of birds, reading a good book and, of course, music. Mildred's mother, she told him, had instilled a fine appreciation of music, study of it practically mandatory in the household. As a young girl Mildred dabbled in ballet and other, more modern forms of dance, but never improved to the level expected by her instructors. Far more gifted, her sister, Muriel, excelled in those respects.

Both finished their meals at about the same time. On cue, the waiter appeared and relieved them of their completed plates. "And how was your meal?"

"Wonderful," Mildred said with a smile.

"Adequate," William said.

Again, the waiter paused before nodding and removing the finished plates. "Can I interest you in some dessert? We have a fine assortment of pies and cake? Perhaps some tea or coffee?"

"We'll be on our way," William said.

The waiter turned away to go prepare the bill.

The two just finished the last bit of wine when a man with a thick moustache approached the table. His hair parted to the side revealed a taller than average forehead. "William! There you are, you devil," he said in an Irish accent.

"Thomas Kelly." William immediately rose and firmly shook Thomas's hand.

William turned to Mildred. "This is Mildred Spencer. The daughter of Thomas Spencer."

Kelly smiled slightly and moved to squeeze Mildred's hand. When he noticed her scar, his expression changed slightly. Fortunately, he had the wherewithal to put his smile back on. "Er, pleased to meet you, ma'am."

Mildred threw him a faint smile. "Hello."

The two men resumed talking to each other. "I got it right here," Kelly said. From his jacket pocket Thomas pulled out a thick envelope and handed it to William. "I trust all will be in order?"

William nodded and accepted the envelope and immediately put it in his inside jacket pocket. What could be in the envelope? Money?

Kelly winked. "Make sure to markup that invoice a wee bit like we discussed."

"You stand to profit handsomely on the transaction," William said.

"It's not all me. This project affects many people. Everyone from the general labourers all the way … all the way to the top, shall we say."

William turned his head towards Mildred. "Mr. Kelly's firm just recently won the bid to construct our new parliament building where our provincial legislature resides. It will be a stunning structure once it is—"

"I know the new building will house our legislative assembly…" Mildred said. She cocked her head with a small, wry frown.

The two men exchanged farewells and Kelly walked out of the restaurant. "Funny," she said, "I do not recall that fellow eating in the restaurant."

"No, he had to give me something," William said. "He knew I would be here. It's all just business." He rubbed his hands together and smiled. "Well, that was a superb meal. Shall we go for a walk in a park?"

"That would be wonderful."

William paid for the meal and soon William's driver chauffeured them off. William held Mildred's hand while they sat in the back seat of his black

Inter-State automobile. She felt a little light-headed. Occasionally she glanced sheepishly at William, smiling softly.

After a twenty minute drive, the chauffeur dropped them off at the pavilion in Assiniboine Park. Built about four or five years ago, the pavilion featured a tower that housed a water tank. She and Muriel used to go dancing in the pavilion. There was never a shortage of men asking for a dance in those days. It seemed so long ago.

William helped Mildred out. "I told him to come back after an hour or so. You don't live too far from here, so we'll drop you off. No need to arrange for a driver."

William led Mildred around the building. Dressed in their finest, a few other couples enjoyed the stroll amid the park's flowers and foliage. Behind the pavilion a lily pond shimmered under a vine-covered pergola. Huge trees provided ample shade, although the sun would soon be setting.

The two walked slowly around the pond. Mildred rested her hand in the crux of William's elbow. Occasionally they stopped to admire the pond. Various birds sang from the trees while a few ducks enjoyed their swim in the pond itself.

The two came upon a bench around the back of the pond where they sat. Somewhat secluded and perhaps due to it being a waning hour, not many other people walked past.

William squeezed Mildred's hand and looked in her eyes. "I enjoyed our dinner tonight. I would also very much like to see you again, perhaps another dinner or maybe a show. I can get good seats for just about any performance in town."

"I think I would very much lick that." She put her gloved hand to her mouth. "Did I just say 'lick?' I meant to say like. I would very much like that."

"I might have to hold you to that." They both burst out laughing.

"Oh, aren't you a bad boy," she said. She playfully slapped William on the shoulder.

"Oh, come now." William pulled Mildred face gently towards his and gave her a quick kiss on the lips. Mildred did not expect it, but didn't recoil. She stared at William. He put his arms around her and the two kissed and embraced for a few minutes. William's lips pressed against hers. For the first time in years Mildred felt excited and aroused. His hands caressed her back while her bosom, despite being hidden in layers of clothing, pressed firmly against his chest.

When they broke their embrace, Mildred felt flushed. Surely red from embarrassment. William gently held her hand while smiling at her. "I suppose we need to get you home."

Mildred nodded. "Y-yes. That would be best." Mildred tried her best to appear prim and proper, but it felt futile. Perhaps she should have played hard-to-get instead of immediately kissing him like some two-bit tramp? Maybe it was a test of her character? The alcohol lowered her inhibitions, but he purchased all the wine. Perhaps that was also a test: to see if she was a lush. And why did he have to be so damn handsome? She got up to her feet and straightened out her clothes. William rose and took her by the hand.

"Are you alright?" he asked. He tilted his head slightly and smiled.

"Uh, yes I am. I believe the wine is getting a little to my head."

The two walked back around the lily pond and continued on to the front of the pavilion where William's automobile's drove them to Mildred's home. William walked her to the front entrance.

"Would you like to come inside for some tea or coffee?" she said. By then the last remnants of the sun glowed from the west.

"No, unfortunately I have another engagement I have to attend. In any other circumstance I would. Thank you."

Mildred looked up. "I hope that … that I could see you again. I'm sorry if I…"

"Nonsense. I'll give you a call. Perhaps in a few days or next week."

"That would be wonderful."

William gave Mildred a quick kiss on her good cheek. "Have a splendid rest of the evening."

Mildred stayed at the door and watched William get back into the rear of the vehicle. After it turned onto the street she paused for a moment to contemplate the significance of the evening. She had just received her first gentleman caller in some time – well over a year – and the first time since her life had changed.

The door barely shut when Mother confronted her. Gertrude wore an evening robe. "So … how did it go? Was William Dalton a gentleman?"

"Everything went fine, Mother. Yes, he was a gentleman and we had a lovely meal. He said he would call me. We may go out again."

Gertrude's face brightened.

Lily
September 6, 1913

Marko sat on his bed. He found himself on many evenings biding time in his own room, staring at nothing. He grabbed a bottle from the floor beside the bed and filled a dirty glass. Some nights he didn't need Mike to encourage him to drink.

Maybe he should go out more. Meet new people. Winnipeg was full of interesting characters. Some were unsavory down-and-outs, but most were like him, just looking for a new beginning.

He ran his hand over the sheets and blankets, thick and coarse. Blankets, life … all rough. It had been a long time since he felt the soft, soothing touch of a woman. Not since Olena, her skin tender and smooth. He closed his eyes and thought back to when she used to rub his back and neck with her strong fingers after a hard day of farm chores. In the old country he honestly felt there would never be another woman in his life. But that was a long time ago. Like any other man, he had urges and needs that needed to be filled.

Who needed a sweetheart? Besides, Winnipeg crawled with men. Many of the few ladies had been spoken for anyway. That's what happens in a frontier town.

He downed his glass. Time to take a trip to Annabella Street.

******

He made his way to Main Street. Before walking down Higgins, he went into the Wolseley Hotel's beverage room to take the edge off. Two shots and two beers.

Emboldened by alcohol, he strolled down Higgins into Point Douglas towards Annabella Street, just a ten-minute walk away. Although he had never been to this part of the Point Douglas district, he had overheard enough from his co-workers at the factory to know what to expect.

Many men frequented what Annabella and the neighboring McFarlane Street had to offer, especially on pay days. One of the oldest districts in Winnipeg, people had lived in Point Douglas even before Winnipeg got its name. It was bound on three sides by the meandering Red River. Well-to-do people used to live there side-by-side with the lower classes, but eventually the rich folk moved away to newer, more exclusive districts.

That night Annabella Street throbbed with activity. He saw several men, alone or in small groups, coming and going from the houses along the street. Two men, with arms around each other, stumbled while trying to remember the words to a song. Marko could not tell which man propped which. A short distance away another man slept against the base of a tree. Someone shouted obscenities a block away. The rumble of another train echoed down the street.

Marko stood in front of 157 Annabella. He took two steps toward the front door, but stopped. Was this the right thing? It didn't feel right. What would Olena think? He thought of Anastasiya and felt dirty. But he'd already come this far.

"Hey handsome, where ya going?"

From the bright red porch light he could see a woman standing by the door, her long, white dress adorned with images of red roses. Form-fitting and low-cut above the waist, the dress revealed an ample bosom. Below her waist the material rippled in the slight breeze exposing a slit that ran half-way up her thigh.

"C'mon, have a drink," the woman said. "Then one of my girls'll make you feel good."

Marko's breathing quickened and he froze.

"What are ya waiting for, buddy?" The woman put her hands on her hips. "You're a shy one, aren'tcha? I ain't never seen you before. Must be new. My name's Minnie and this is my house." She walked over and grabbed Marko by the arm and held him close while leading him toward the entrance. Thick, bright red lipstick, extra dollops of rouge and powder tried to hide the wrinkles around her eyes and mouth that betrayed her age. Minnie radiated sexiness and didn't mind showing it.

She opened the front door of the bordello. Old tables and chairs filled a large room off to the side, just past the foyer. Now a waiting room, when a family lived in the home years before, it was probably a dining room or a living room. Years of foot traffic had worn paths in the dirty linoleum. The deepest ruts ran from the front door to the waiting room and from the waiting room to the stairs leading to the second floor.

Entering the waiting room Marko picked up the stench of body odour mixed with alcohol and a hint of vomit. Minnie sat him down alone at a small table. Years of spilled booze stained the rickety furniture in the room. "Just wait here for your turn. What's yer name?"

"Marko"

"From your accent, I'd say yer from Galicia … am I right?"

"Da."

"That means you'll either drink vodka or whiskey. Which'll it be?"

"Whiskey…."

"Whiskey it is." Minnie turned her head and then yelled in the general direction of the kitchen: "Chang! Get yer yellow ass over here. A man needs some whiskey."

A Chinese boy ran into the waiting room with an empty glass and a bottle of whiskey. Within seconds Marko held a half-filled glass.

"Ice, too," Minnie said.

Chang ran back into the kitchen. In moments he plopped a handful of ice chips into Marko's glass with his bare hand.

"Not many places have ice," Minnie said. "This is a good place. You'll enjoy it. I have a feeling I know what you're looking for."

Marko sat and sipped his whiskey. Not the best quality, but it did the trick.

The clientele matched the surroundings, scruffy and generally unkempt. About seven or eight men waited for their turn to go upstairs. All grasped a drink. A few teetered back and forth. One man had passed out on a table, a knocked-over shot glass beside his hand. Unshaven with ripped trousers, another looked like he just got back from the bush. A man at a corner table was missing his left eye. Another with a bushy black beard with sizable mosquito bites on his arms engaged in an animated conversation with a red-headed fellow. With soot streaked on his forehead, the red-headed man frowned with his arms crossed. Those two didn't seem to be getting along.

Every so often a john would saunter down the stairs and head straight out the front door sporting a satisfied smile. A few minutes later a scantily-clad woman would follow. In each instance, Minnie would point to the man next in line. The girl would smile and walk over, but before taking the man upstairs, Minnie would demand money up front. A few complained, but Minnie explained that she had been taken too many times, not a surprise given the unsavory look of most of the guests. Once paid up, the john would follow the girl up the stairs, sometimes stumbling along the way. During down times Minnie went outside to solicit more business, not unlike what she did with Marko. Chang ran around swilling drinks and keeping things tidy.

Some of the girls would first sit and chat with their trick. Maybe have a drink or a smoke. Others would motion with their index finger to their john and up they went. Several of the women did not look attractive. Their hair plain and drab, a few wore no make-up. Maybe those ladies charged less?

Marko finished his whiskey. He held up his empty glass to be filled again.

"You not pay last time," Chang said. "Two shots. Twenty cents."

Marko threw enough change on the sticky table. When Chang reached down to grab the coins, the bearded man flew into him, knocking him over. Small and thin, Chang flew five feet and fell against the wall of the parlour. The bottle of whiskey he had held smashed on the floor while the coins flew in different directions.

The bearded man had just been walloped by the red-headed man with soot on his forehead. The red-head jumped on the bearded man while he was down and the two traded punches, rolling into chairs and tables.

Marko stood and backed away from the dust-up. Other patrons hooted and hollered. Minnie screamed, "Gus! Gus! Gus!"

Gus, a burly man well over six feet with hairy arms, grabbed the heads of both combatants and smashed them together. The red-headed man fell to the floor unconscious while the bearded man looked to be stunned. The previously loud patrons instantly stopped their encouraging yells. Gus dragged the unconscious man by his crimson hair to the front door. With what seemed like an effortless toss, he hurled the man out of the house. Casually, he grabbed the dazed and disoriented bearded man by the back of man's jacket. Gus held him by the back of the pants and tossed him out, head first.

The patrons waited for Gus to leave the room before they spoke in hushed tones. "Did you see that?" one said. "I'll tell you what … you'll never want to tussle with Gus." Through it all, the man passed out on a table remained motionless, oblivious to the action.

"Sorry about that, gents," Minnie said. "You know how it is sometimes. A free round for everyone." The patrons hooted and hollered. One man joked that if a few more fights broke out, they wouldn't ever have to pay for their booze.

Marko settled back in his chair. Chang collected himself, cleaned up and provided everyone with their free round of alcohol.

Minutes went by. Men came and went. Marko sat silently, fidgeting with his glass. What was he doing? Maybe he could meet a nice woman through a church. But then he'd have to go to church every Sunday. He stared at the various yellowed girlie pictures that adorned the walls amid the peeling, stained wallpaper.

She walked into the room.

Scarlet lips and a powdered face, the woman stared straight at Marko, her head tilted gently to the side. A crooked smile slowly appeared on her face. His turn came up.

Most of the ladies lacked appeal. But not this one. She looked thin. Not deathly skinny, just thin. Most men didn't like that trait because they wanted their women to have some meat on them. But from working at the farm in the old country, Marko knew that the women who worked the hardest were the thinnest and strongest. The plump ones sat around too much.

Blue-eyed with curly hair and a radiant complexion, her high cheek bones reminded him of Olena. Her bare arms revealed a few bruises.

His heart quickened when she slowly ambled toward the table. Her long, flowing blue skirt almost touched the floor. Black, ankle-length button-up shoes poked from underneath only when she walked. Like tent poles, her nipples drew attention to her white, loose, almost paper-thin top. Her hips swayed seductively from side to side.

"May I have a seat?" she asked in Ukrainian.

"Da."

In the process of sitting she bent forward allowing Marko to see all the way down. He could not help it – after all, it was right there.

"How long have you been in Winnipeg?"

"Not that long."

"Long enough," she said. She grabbed Marko index finger and stroked it gently. "More than long enough, I'm sure."

Marko swallowed.

"My name is Lilia. Everyone calls me Lily." She took a cigarette from Chang when he passed by.

Marko tried very hard not to gawk at Lily and on several occasions forced himself to look away at anything else. He could not help but stare at Lily's beautiful face or, like a magnet, be drawn to her poking nipples.

"Am I making you nervous?" Lily asked. She blew a stream of smoke out the side of her mouth. "I'm sorry, it's not supposed to be like that. I can tell this is your first time in a place like this. That's fine." She moved her chair right beside Marko.

Marko swallowed again. He could smell Lily's sweet perfume when she leaned into him and put her arm around his shoulder. Her almost-bare bosom pressed against his arm.

She whispered in his ear. "What would you like me to do, Marko. I can do anything. Anything you like." Then she licked his earlobe gently with the very tip of her tongue.

Marko shifted in his chair to accommodate the stiffening presence in his pants. What should he say? What did he want? Lily seemed so … aggressive. Not like any of the girls he grew up with.

"I … I …."

Lily backed away and smiled. Not a seductive smile, but more carefree. She extinguished her cigarette in the ashtray. "Some men like that approach. I can tell it doesn't work for you. How about we go upstairs and see how things go?"

Marko nodded. Sweat formed on his brow and temples.

He passed Minnie five dollars and followed Lily up the stairs. Her golden blonde hair swayed back and forth but he concentrated instead on her cute, round bum. Oohs and aahs of delight and creaking bed springs oozed from rooms along the second floor hallway.

They entered a bedroom at the end of the hallway. Surprisingly warm, the room would have benefitted with an open window. She closed the door behind them. White sheets and a few grey-blue blankets covered the bed. The top of an old chest of drawers near the entrance featured a variety of cosmetics including lipstick and perfume bottles. A few slinky garments and silk stockings were draped over a beige-coloured changing blind in the corner of the room.

Lily sat on her bed and motioned for Marko to sit beside her. She brought her hands up and massaged his upper back and neck. It felt firm and relaxing, just like Olena used to do it. "So, Marko. Here we are. Five dollars will let you do just about anything. What will it be?"

"I don't know. I've never really…"

Lily cocked her head with a puzzled expression. "You've never been with a woman before?"

"No, no, no. I have." He felt his face reddening. "I was married before."

"But you're not any more…?

"No. She died in the old country."

"I'm sorry to hear that," Lily said. She put her arm around Marko. "It's hard being a widower. How long has it been?"

"A while. I don't want to talk about it, if that's all right."

"You can talk about anything you want with me."

Marko stood up. "I think this is a mistake. I'm sorry for wasting your time."

He took a step towards the door, but Lily grabbed his arm. "Wait. Don't go. You're not wasting my time. After all, it's your money. Besides, I would rather you stay because if you left too soon Minnie would think something went wrong and I don't want to bother explaining it to her. You seem like a nice person. Can you stay for a bit?"

Marko looked down at her. Her expression looked honest and innocent, but maybe she put on an act for all the men. "All right."

"Come, sit. Tell me why you came here and what I can do."

Marko shrugged and sat back down. "I don't know. I suppose I get a little tired of being alone."

"Sure. Who doesn't?"

Marko stared at a wooden wardrobe at the corner of Lily's room. He didn't want to talk about himself. "That's a nice wardrobe you have. The carving on the wood is very fine."

"It's not mine. It came with the room. Although I feel like it's mine since I've used it for years now."

"They don't make furniture like that anymore. The carving along the edges. It would have taken hours to do that. Even the legs. These days everything looks and feels so cheap. There's no craftsmanship."

Marko's gaze remained on the wardrobe. Something built so fine was meant to be admired.

"You know your furniture. Anything else you're good at?"

He could hear Lily shuffling. He turned his head and his eyes widened when he saw Lily's exposed breasts pointed right at him.

Lily undid her long skirt and it fell to the floor. Completely naked, Lily's mouth formed into the same wry smile he saw downstairs. She inched towards Marko.

Still on the bed, Marko wrapped his arms tightly around Lily's naked torso while she grabbed his head and placed it between her breasts. Slowly, Marko eased back on the bed and let her earn the five dollars.

Kraf's Fight

September 13, 1913

Marko opened and closed the front door several times. It still didn't shut properly.

"It's worse in the winter," Maria said in Ukrainian, standing behind him. "Sometimes it gets so frosted up it won't close at all."

He nodded then took the door off its hinges to better examine it.

"The problem is not the door. It's the frame. It's not even. But this is an easy fix. I'll have it working perfectly in no time."

He went downstairs to get the tools he needed to complete the repair. After two months, Marko could tell Maria and Mike grew to appreciate his handyman skills around the house. Plumbing, kitchen cabinets, children's toys … nothing was beyond his abilities. Mike's skills could not match Marko's. But he knew what held Mike back: he was a drunk.

Mike drank almost every night. Heavily, especially since Ann's birth last month. Also, it did not take him long to get drunk. Marko had a cousin in the old country who also tipped the bottle. One shot of vodka, and already his cheeks glowed, just like Mike's. A few shots and Mike's speech slurred. Then he lost his motor skills. Marko could only shake his head. After all, the measure of a man is how well he could hold his booze.

Marko planed and sanded the bottom of the door then attacked the door frame. He ripped away the rotten portions and applied new wood. He hammered everything tight and reattached the door back on the hinges.

"Try it," Marko said to Maria.

The door opened and closed with ease, like it was brand new. "Thank you so much. You would make any woman proud."

Marko offered a little smile, but his heart sank. If that was the case, what about Olena?

He gathered up the tools to put them away. Before he left the room, someone rapped on the outer door. Maria opened it and let in a fat man with a ruddy complexion. Another customer.

"The same Yuri?" Maria asked. "Vodka?"

"Da." Yuri rubbed his red nose.

Maria went into the basement and emerged with a bottle. The man gave her cash and took the bottle.

"See you in a few days," Maria said. Yuri nodded without saying a word and left. Marko had seen the Russian before. He lived just a block away.

Maria put the money in her apron and left the room. Now that Mike worked less, the family had to rely more on Maria's side business. Sometimes at night from his room Marko could hear the arguments between Mike and Maria. She would get after him for drinking away the profits. But if someone was an alcoholic, how could he not drink when dozens of available bottles of hooch sat waiting only a few steps away? Bootlegging brought in extra money, but that very product didn't help Mike.

Shipments always arrived in the middle of the night, sometimes at three or four in the morning and always from the back lane. Maria handled everything herself. But for every case she purchased, at least two or three bottles ended up in Mike's belly.

Frequently, Marko would see Maria with her arms crossed. She frowned upon Mike's heavy drinking, but Mike was the man of the house. What could she do? It seemed like Maria almost wished Marko did not stay in her home because it gave Mike an excuse to drink. And when Mike did, he could get loud and obnoxious.

"I imagine you men will be going out again tonight," Maria said. "It's a Saturday, after all." Just then, Ann started to cry from the bedroom. Maria sighed and left to comfort her daughter.

******

This time they went to a North End tavern, still on Main Street, but located north of downtown where the patrons could be rougher. Marko could see that clientele typically consisted of young, bored working class labourers. In past visits he occasionally saw the police charge the drunk men and haul them off, sometimes using wheelbarrows to transport pickled bar patrons to a holding cell. Like the bars a little farther south on Main Street, the places smelled of stale beer, vomit and urine. Men drank simply to get drunk.

"Why does everyone go to the taverns?" Marko said to Mike, now on their sixth round.

Mike shrugged. "I don't know. Nothing to do. The jobs are drying up. I'm not finding much work these days. I'm sure it's the same for others. Especially construction jobs. Any work on a farm would have already been filled. So if you don't have a job already, you might as well drink. That … and there's not enough women. I'm lucky, I have a woman. But most of the men don't. They're unattached. Remember, Winnipeg is new. Most men arrived here like you, by themselves. But instead of dancing the night away with a cutie, they do a different dance. One with fat lips, black eyes and sore heads."

They clinked glasses, signalling the end of another round. "We should be going…." Marko said.

Mike turned his head. "Look, there's the man we met at the Woodbine."

Marko glanced over and squinted his eyes to pierce the haze of tobacco smoke. John Krafchenko arrived with his friend, the one with the scar on his neck, John Buxton. Krafchenko looked drunker than the first time they met. His stride appeared shaky while his head swayed slightly from side to side. Buxton's red face and glassy eyes betrayed a night of heavy drinking. The two men bellied to the bar where the fat bartender with a noticeable forehead lump just above his left eye immediately served them.

"Let's go talk," Marko said, drawn to the fascinating man.

Marko tapped Krafchenko on the shoulder. Instantly the man twirled around and glared, ready to pounce like a cobra. Marko raised his hands in self-defence. Krafchenko uncoiled once he recognized Marko. "Hello, friend." Krafchenko gave Marko a firm handshake. "And I can see Mike is well on his way with the whiskey."

Mike shrugged and smiled.

"Come over here," Krafchenko said. He put his arm around Marko. "Bartender, another round for these gentlemen."

"Immediately, Kraf," the bartender said while Buxton aimed some gob into a metal spittoon near the foot rail. The drinks arrived and the men toasted.

"So, Marko," Krafchenko said, "you making money?"

Marko nodded.

"Things are good with me also. I'm not just a blacksmith. I dabble in other businesses." Krafchenko winked.

"What kind of businesses?"

"Oh, all sorts of side jobs. Selling merchandise, automobile procurement, obtaining machinery for factories, you name it. If I can make money from the operation, I do it."

"What is this 'procerment?'"

Krafchenko smiled and spoke slowly. "Pro-cure-ment. It means getting items … things. Automobile procurement means finding an automobile to re-sell to someone else. Automobiles are all the rage at the moment. Sure, there are still many horses and buggies on the roads, but you watch, in a few years it will be all automobiles. And if I can make money getting autos or even factory machinery and then selling it, that's more money in my pocket."

Krafchenko lit a cigarette. "You never know," he said. "I might have an opportunity for you."

Marko's eyes widened. Krafchenko looked like a successful, trustworthy businessman, someone he'd like to work with.

On his turn Mike went to the bar to get another round. Red ears and bloodshot eyes, he didn't need another one. The busy barkeep ran around trying to fill orders. He couldn't keep up and could have used the help of another person. Seeing Mike's plight, Krafchenko raised two fingers calmly in the air. At once the bartender walked over to the group. "Another round, Kraf?"

"Yes, and I believe this gentleman will be paying." He pointed to swaying Mike.

After a few more rounds Krafchenko and Buxton left the bar. Good thing, because Mike needed to go home. Any more whiskey and he would be sobering up in the clink rather than his own bed. The man couldn't walk a straight line. In Mike's shape, a streetcar operator would not let them on. Marko put his arm around Mike to help him along for the long walk home. He'd likely fall down a dozen times along the way.

The two didn't take 20 steps when Mike broke free of Marko's grasp and grabbed a pole used for harnessing horses. He stumbled and fell partially into a half-filled, dirty horse trough. Mike rolled on Main Street and struggled to get on his feet. Marko managed to get Mike back up, only for him to fall back down. Then Mike vomited.

Just before Marko tried to get Mike to turn down a side street where they would be less noticeable, he heard some shouting and yelling from across the street. Turning to look, he could see one man on the ground with another being circled by a couple of thugs.

The darkness forced Marko to strain his eyes across the wide street. Krafchenko was the man being circled. Buxton had to be the one on the ground. Standing beside Buxton, Krafchenko protected him like a mother bear would protect her cub. The two other men armed themselves with clubs or batons. Perhaps they snuck up on Krafchenko and Johnny Buxton in a robbery attempt? Buxton likely had received a knock on the head.

Large, burly and unshaven, the two attackers looked like they had been in the bush for a month. The labourers could have drifted to town looking for farm work for the harvest or perhaps were loggers preparing to go out into the Manitoba forests for a long winter of hard labour.

A crowd of men began to gather at the standoff, but no one seemed keen to help Krafchenko. If anything, they viewed the scene like children would a school-yard scrap. Marko felt obliged to help Krafchenko. But what about Mike? Just leave him propped up against a building?

Before he could decide, one of the attackers lunged at Krafchenko with a raised club, but Krafchenko deftly sidestepped out of harm's way. No damage done, the two attackers continued to circle the unarmed Krafchenko.

Like a cornered animal, Krafchenko crouched down low and swiveled his head from side to side carefully watching his adversaries' every movement. Krafchenko's face scrunched into an intense fury. Despite being drunk, unarmed and outnumbered, Krafchenko held the upper hand.

The other attacker came at Krafchenko with his swinging baton. Again, Krafchenko moved aside quickly, but this time grabbed the man's outstretched arm with his right hand and rammed the heel of his left hand upwards into the man's face. Blood exploded from the attacker's broken nose. Hard as nails, this only angered the thug. He quickly regained his composure and continued to circle around Krafchenko with his accomplice despite the stream of blood pouring from his nose. What had started to be a simple robbery now got personal.

Impatient, his comrade again went after Krafchenko, but this time Krafchenko fell to the ground and used his legs to expertly trip the brute. The club dropped from the man's hand and he fell to the ground. Krafchenko quickly grabbed the weapon and cracked it over his attacker's skull. The thug lay motionless while blood oozed from a wound just above his hairline. Krafchenko hit him again. And again.

The goon with the bloodied, broken nose came after Krafchenko. The attacker swung his club down, but Krafchenko raised his new-found weapon upward and with his hands on each end of the baton, blocked the blow. He parried another swing. Then another.

Krafchenko bounced up and now grabbing the baton firmly with his right hand, glared at the brute. The bleeding man breathed heavily and steadied himself. Krafchenko and the man circled, sizing each other up, although Krafchenko remained right beside Buxton the entire time.

Like a chess match, both men tested different advances, but each was parried away or otherwise stopped. Krafchenko's expression changed from anger to a broad, evil grin. He actually seemed to be enjoying the messy fight.

Krafchenko's foe made an advance and their batons locked together high in mid-air. Both men's faces inches from each other, they used raw, brute strength to see who would gain the upper hand. The bloodied villain appeared to slowly push Krafchenko down, not surprising given his larger size and heft. But again, Krafchenko smiled. He toyed with the man. The man's forward movement came to a stop, then inch-by-inch was pushed back by Krafchenko. When he had the man in an awkward position, Krafchenko swung his leg around and knocked the man to the ground. The man fell down helplessly. Krafchenko wrested the man's weapon away. Krafchenko hit the man hard in the face, opening a gash near his eye.

He stood over the beaten man and had him at his mercy while holding both weapons. The bloodied man cowered and tried to slither away while holding up his arms in a defensive position.

By this time a large crowd had gathered around the fight and blocked Marko's view from his position. He leaned Mike up against a building and ran across the street to get a better look. With all the attention across the street, Mike would not be noticed. To his amazement, Krafchenko actually encouraged his beaten foe to get up. He even threw a weapon back to the man.

The man rose, blood poured down his face and dripped from his chin. Only pure adrenaline kept the thug up. Only pure stupidity made him lunge clumsily at Krafchenko. Krafchenko blocked the man's thrust then swung his weapon into the man's mouth, breaking most of his front teeth.

On his knees, the man spit out four of five teeth that would never again chew food. Krafchenko kicked the man on the side of the head. Then he proceeded to kick him in the ribs. He hoofed him six or seven times, certainly breaking a few ribs in the process.

Crying and writhing in pain, the thug rocked back and forth. Krafchenko loomed over his beaten foe. He threw the weapon at the thug and pointed his finger at him. "Don't ever jump me or any of my friends again. Next time you will end up in a pine box."

The crowd began to slowly chant: "Kraf! Kraf! Kraf! Kraf!" Like a favorite gladiator from the Coliseum in Rome, Krafchenko raised his fists in the air, soaking in the splendor.

By this time, a groggy Buxton slowly sat upright. Marko ran to his side and helped him up. Krafchenko strolled over. "Hello, Marko. Just another night in Winnipeg, no?" Krafchenko put his arm around Buxton and helped him walk away while the crowd slowly disbursed. Marko shook his head in disbelief. The two beaten men remained on the sidewalk. Like rats, a few spectators fished through their pockets for any pieces of copper. Before crossing the street back to Mike, Marko walked past two onlookers still conversing about the brutal fight they had just witnessed.

"Excuse," Marko said. "Why no one help Krafchenko at start?"

The two men looked at Marko as if he were a fool. "Help him? Are ya daft? Kraf wins every fight. He's the best. He'd just as soon knock your noggin if ya got in his way." The two men strolled away, still excited about the fight.

Father's Concerns
October 12, 1913

"Why do you like helping stray animals?" William said. "What could he possibly offer you or your father?"

Mildred shrugged and looked down. "It's an arrangement we have. He provides his handyman services and in return, I help him with his English."

William scoffed. "Seems like a waste of time to me."

Both sipped lemonade on a bench in the backyard of Mildred's home. A warm Sunday in October, leaves from the deciduous trees blanketed the yard. One of the house staff raked them into a large pile to be later burned. While some trees were almost bare, fantastic hues of orange, yellow, red and gold painted the leaves that remained on branches. Squirrels ran about, preparing for the long winter.

Mildred changed the subject. "So I will not see you tonight for dinner?"

"No, I'm sorry. I have to go meet Thomas Kelly ... then I have to go to the King George Hospital to make a donation."

Mildred nodded with approval. "That is very commendable."

William downed his lemonade and placed the empty glass on the bench. "In fact," he said, "I should get going now."

"So soon? You just arrived a short time ago."

"Sorry, Milly." William kissed Mildred on her good side. "Busy, busy." He got up and fixed his hat. "Don't work too hard with your pupil," he said before waving goodbye.

Mildred smiled slightly and waved. William looked so handsome and put together in his new black suit. She watched him walk the full length of the back yard and finally disappear around the corner to the front of the house.

They had dated for about two months now. He took her to restaurants, the theatre and other engagements. She felt sure of William's intentions but sometimes he seemed somewhat aloof. Maybe some men were like that. Besides, it's not like she could be picky.

Mildred finished her lemonade and took both glasses back to the mansion.

She went to her bedroom to prepare for her upcoming lesson with Marko.

Obviously skilled and very good at what he did, Marko also worked hard. Not just with his handyman chores around the house or even his regular job back in the factory, but also at his English. While his spoken grammar had not improved much, he could now read and write far more proficiently. How could she not appreciate a student who put out the effort to learn a new task? Kind and thoughtful, his graciousness for the help she provided appeared genuine.

Yet…there was something about him. His hands…the way he held his tools…so artistic, like tiny musical instruments, each playing a role in a concert only he could hear. Just last week he repaired an old chair that had fallen apart. He made it sturdy again. Good as new.

Maybe that was it. He made her feel as good as new.

She gathered her teaching materials and went back downstairs.

Thomas hung up the telephone in the large hall at the front of the house. "I see you have another lesson with the Galician labourer."

"Yes, Marko will be here soon."

"Were there any vehicle repairs required this weekend? I do not recall anything needing repair around the estate…"

Mildred cocked her head slightly. "No … no, there is nothing in immediate need of his attention. But whether he performs a repair or not, we conduct lessons every Sunday."

Thomas smiled at the corner of his mouth. "A pain isn't it?"

"A pain?"

"Isn't it a bother for you to set aside your time with him every Sunday? I mean, there are so many other things, other pursuits, you could be doing instead of wasting it with a foreigner. Don't you think?"

"Oh, I suppose it gets to be a bother from time to time. But I don't mind. That was the agreement. Besides, it allows me to maintain my teaching skills for when—"

"For what? For when you go back to your profession? I was under the impression you gave that up some time ago. You need to spend more quality time with William. That's what I think."

"If you so disapprove my providing instruction to the immigrant, I will stop. I only thought it was a fair arrangement. We're saving money and you have not had any vehicle repair concerns for some time now. That's just good business sense. Besides, did you not one time say a problem with foreigners was that they never even try to learn English? Well, here is an instance where one is. Is that not a good thing?"

From his blank expression Mildred knew Father agreed. He pulled down on the bottom of his jacket to straighten it out. "I suppose," he said. "But be careful, a day will come when William will not approve of you seeing unattached men in your own home." Thomas grabbed a newspaper laying on a bureau beside him and walked away towards his study.

The doorbell rang.

"Hello again." Mildred smiled and let Marko through the front door of the mansion.

Lily's Past
October 20, 1913

Marko gently ran his fingers through Lily's hair. Each golden-blonde strand felt like fine gold. Like something rare and forbidding or an experience only entitled to the rich and privileged.

"How often do you…work?" Marko asked in Ukrainian. Both naked, Lily's head rested on Marko's bare chest while they both laid on her bed. A pillow propped Marko while Lily stared at the ceiling. A messy, tangled mess, the bed sheet exposed their limbs. The refreshing breeze through the bedroom window's three-inch opening broke the stench of hot sweat. The thin, white lace curtain tumbled about.

"Usually every day. Sometimes I get a day off. Minnie is a tough madam, but she takes care of her girls. She knows she can't burn us out too quickly because we make the money. So she lets us relax from time to time. Sometimes when the weather is worse, men like to sit and drink in their own rooms and they don't make it here. When there are less men looking for action, then we have spare time."

"On those nights, do you think we might be able to … go somewhere different?"

"What do you mean? Would you like me to come to your room? I don't normally visit clients in their homes…"

"No, no. Not like that. I mean, maybe you would like to go somewhere. Like a park or a restaurant or the theatre or something."

Lily's bare bosom heaved as she sighed. "I don't know if that would work. I'm a prostitute. A fallen woman, as they like to say. There are places I can't go. You wouldn't enjoy the reaction, especially from the other ladies. It would be uncomfortable. I can't walk the same streets as you."

Marko continued to run his fingers through Lily's luxurious hair and gently messaged her scalp. "That's too bad. How long have you…"

"…opened my legs for every settler west of Rat Portage? About six years."

"I'm sorry. I didn't mean it like that."

Lily curled her lip. "That's okay. I'm just teasing. That's my job, you know."

He loved it when she did that. It made her look confident and sexy.

"How did you get into your trade?"

"What else was I supposed to do? There really wasn't much for me. It wasn't always like that, though. I came to Canada from Galicia when I was a little girl. My parents set up a homestead near Dauphin, a town north and west of here. There are many, many Ukrainian people in that part of Manitoba.

"I remember the cold winters and all the snow. My father had to chop piles and piles of wood in the fall so we would have enough to last through the winter. There were only two rooms in our little shack. No running water. Heh, who had running water in those days? Nobody. The frost was so thick on the windows you couldn't see outside. An inch thick.

"But when the spring came, it was like a rebirth. The hard winters made us appreciate each spring and summer even more. My father and mother, they worked so hard. But they never complained. This was life and they dealt with every challenge along the way. My father tended the field while Mama made sure there was a warm meal each night. All the kids … they had to help with the chores. I remember when the mosquitoes came out in the late spring, Mama would start a smudge. My brothers and sisters, all six of us, we would play around the fire. My hair would smell like smoke for weeks."

"Your hair doesn't smell like smoke anymore…."

"No, those days are over. Now I try to avoid fire and smoke." Lily took a deep breath and continued to stare at the bare light in the centre of the ceiling. "Ever since the fire…"

"Fire?"

"When I was eight years old our homestead caught fire. It was the middle of the night sometime in the early fall. I don't know what started it. Maybe a spark from the stove? We didn't have electricity, only lanterns. Everything was dry and went up very quickly. It caught us by surprise. Most of my brothers and sisters died without ever waking up.

"I don't know what made me get up. I was always a light sleeper, I suppose. I ran to wake Father and Mama. But by that time flames were running up the walls. Father told me to run outside. They tried to get the other children out of the fire. I stood under a large tree in our yard and watched the fire consume our home. They managed to pull two of my sisters from the fire, Dariya and Valentyna, but that was all. My father went in to get another, but never came out. My mother was so badly burned, she died the next day. Dariya wasn't even a year old. Too much smoke went into her body and she died the next week."

"That's horrible," Marko said. He stopped stroking Lily's hair and took hold of her hand.

"Valentyna was not much older than Dariya, but she survived. A large family down the road took her in. But the family already had eleven kids. They could not take me, so they put me on a train for Winnipeg. I lived in an orphanage. It was difficult. I was always hungry and tired. No one was happy. The woman who ran it, she was very, very strict. She would hit you with a wooden spoon if you so much as looked the wrong way. But like my father said, that was life. What else did I have? Nothing.

"One evening when I was fifteen I was in the back yard picking weeds in the garden. It was June, when the sun is out late. I was working near the back lane. A few men walked past me. They looked like they were drunk. They whistled and called out to me. I should have ignored them. But instead I smiled and continued picking weeds. They kept walking and I didn't think anything of it.

"A few minutes later I felt a strong arm around my mouth and neck. The men dragged me behind a woodshed that was covered by trees and shrubs. Two held me down and covered my mouth while the other raped me hard. I bit the hand of the man who was covering my mouth so hard that he had to hit me three times in the head before I let go my grasp. I screamed and screamed, but no one could hear. Or if they did, they didn't care. Each time I screamed a man hit me. When it was over, I was bruised and blood was all over my skirt and legs. I was a virgin until then.

"I lay on the ground for almost a half hour after the men left. I was in pain and cried. I felt sorry for myself and wanted to die right then. But I got up and staggered into the house. The head lady was in the kitchen and dropped a pot of water when she saw me. But instead of helping me, she slapped me in the face and called me a whore. She said I was a disgrace to have relations with a man.

"Of course I got pregnant from the encounter. The head lady said I had to leave the orphanage because they could not have a pregnant girl living there. She said I would be a bad influence on the other girls and would lead them down the wrong path." Lily paused and slowly smiled.

"I remember that was the first time someone called me a fallen woman. It was as if I lost my way. But I never really had a choice. It was like my path was laid out for me the moment I was born.

"So I went to some other place where pregnant girls or unwed women go to have their babies. The nurses were not very good at caring for the sick, but I can tell you they were excellent at preaching from the Bible. Crosses everywhere. God this and God that. Everything 'shame, shame, shame.' If they were trying to get me on the right path, they went about it wrong, that's for sure.

"I was already sixteen by the time my baby was born. The birth was cold and painful. My legs were strapped and they told me to push up. A mean doctor with cold hands kept saying, 'Push harder, push harder. What's the matter with you? You had no problem getting pregnant, now you can't deliver the baby?' Finally the baby came out. A girl."

"What is her name?" Marko asked.

"I don't know. I never had a chance to name her. The moment she was born, they took her away from me. I never even held her in my arms. Some rich bitch too barren to conceive from the southern part of the city probably took her. Then they made it so I could never have any babies ever again." Lily paused for a moment. Tears formed in her eyes. She brought her hand to her face. Marko gave her a hug.

Lily wiped her tears with the bed sheet and continued. "After a week or so, they kicked me out of the facility. All my belongings were in a tiny satchel. I had nothing. No money. Nowhere to go. Nothing."

"Did you ever think about going back to Dauphin? Maybe finding your sister? Or going back to the old country?"

Lily reflected before answering. "No, not really. I didn't have any money to go anywhere. I was more concerned about my next meal. Besides, there was nothing for me in the old country. And I was worried if I went back to Dauphin, my sister wouldn't remember me. It had been, what? Eight years? That's a long time when you are a child. I suppose I was afraid I would be rejected. They never wanted me after the fire, why would they want me when I was sixteen? They would say I should go and get myself married off, anyway.

"So I wondered around for a day or two. It was horrible. I was at the lowest point in my life. But, thank God it was the late summer. I was able to raid gardens for food in the evening. Carrots. Peas. I didn't know where to go or what to do.

"I ended up in the train station on Higgins not far from here. That's where I met Minnie. I don't know if she was looking for recruits, but that's how it turned out. When I first saw her, she looked like a star performer coming for a stage show at that fancy Pantages Theatre. Absolutely beautiful. Rosy cheeks and bright red lipstick. Her hair was done up fancy like in a beauty salon. And her clothes … you should have seen the luxurious gown she wore with ruffles and pleats. She was a complete vision. Like an angel from the heavens. She looked so different than all the other drab immigrants and travellers.

"She noticed me sitting alone on the floor of the train station against a post. She could tell I was hungry and tired. She smiled and asked a few questions. I felt in awe of her and told her everything she asked: where I was from, where I lived – which was nowhere at the time – everything. She was so friendly and nice, I couldn't help but hope she would help me; maybe take me in.

"She leaned forward and kissed me gently on the forehead. Just one smell of her perfume was enough to allow her to take me anywhere. She brought me here to this house on Annabella Street. She fed me. She gave me new clothes. I had a warm, clean bed to sleep in."

"Did you not know this was a brothel?" Marko asked.

"No, I didn't know what this home was. Sure, there were many men and the women were dressed scantily. But everyone was having fun. Music was playing. People danced. They laughed. Every day and night. And what's wrong with that? Nothing. Did I know it was wrong? I knew it was better than the orphanage. After I was raped they cast me aside like garbage.

"Did Minnie trick me to do something I didn't want to do? Not really. It was my choice and I'm glad I made it. It was better than starving or dying in a snow bank in the middle of January.

"Besides, Minnie has always been fair with her girls. When she got me in the business, she took it slow. I knew nothing was for free and I had to work and it was time to pay back for her hospitality. She started me off with the easier tricks, only regulars she knew well who liked young, inexperienced girls. But my experience grew and I was able to establish my own clientele."

"And you are one of them," Lily said. She looked over and winked at Marko.

He smiled back. "Don't you ever want to leave this … trade?"

Lily sat up to animate her points. "Why should I? I make more money than most men. I can buy things for myself. My meals are provided. I have my own bed. If there's a problem with a client, Minnie sics Gus on him. I can knit or crochet in my spare time. I don't do any of the housework.

They have Chang for that. And the sex, you know, usually it's good. Not always, but usually. And best of all, there's always a line-up for more. I know more than one girl that got mixed up with a foreigner at a homestead. They live away from everyone in a tiny little house, maybe even just a sod house. Everything's dirty and dusty. They actually have to work. Real, hard farm work. And it's cold and miserable and boring in the winter. They don't realize it before it's too late. Some of them up and leave their husbands and come back. Others get too old and wither away."

Marko raised his eyebrow and nodded. She seemed to have a compelling argument, but still...

A knock came at the door. "C'mon Lily," Minnie said from the other side of the door. "You have other customers waiting for you."

"Thank you, Minnie," Lily said in English. "We're all done here. I'll be right down." Comfortable in her nakedness, she got up from bed, picked up her clothes and threw them behind the changing blind. "See you in a few days?" She said in Ukrainian while she put on black silk stockings.

"Yes." He had already pulled up his drawers and started buttoning his shirt.

She threw on a mid-length, skimpy, semi-transparent blue dress that more resembled lingerie. After Marko dressed, he gave Lily a ten dollar bill. She shot him a puzzled look. "That's too much."

"Take, take," he said, pressing the money in her hand.

"Yoi, Marko. It's only five dollars for you…"

"Buy something special for yourself."

"Thank you," Lily said. She placed the ten in a tin on her counter and took out a five to give to Minnie.

Marko grabbed his hat and Lily opened the bedroom door. "See you later." She stood up on her tip-toes and kissed him on the cheek and quickly turned around for the bathroom to clean up before her next client.

"Still no underwear?" he said when she walked down the hallway.

"Never," Lily said looking over her shoulder while flipping up the back of her dress to reveal her bare bum.

Marko smiled and shook his head.

Layoffs at the Factory
October 24, 1913

"It's almost 5:00. Here are the paychecks," Liz said.

Seated at her desk, Mildred looked up at the thick bundle of envelopes six inches from her face. "Why don't you hand them out?"

"I have more important things to do. Here you go." Liz kept the envelopes in Mildred's face.

Mildred rolled her eyes and took the bundle. Liz always pushed off the menial tasks to her. There were better things to do than standing in the shop around a group of smelly, dirty labourers and doling out envelopes. She could easily learn the more intricate matters of business. It didn't look that difficult.

Carefully lifting her full length skirt a few inches, she walked onto the factory floor. The bottom of the entrance from the office was always caked with grime. The ever-present smell of engine oils and grease invaded her nostrils. Loud, sharp sounds of the factory floor instantly bombarded her ears: clanging metal, pounding hammers, grinding motors and the occasional loud crash. Peter stood a few feet from the door wearing his trademark dingy derby to match the grease and dirt on the rest of his work clothes. Frowning and red-faced, he closely examined a piece of paper. Some sort of list. With a pencil tucked behind his ear and so absorbed in thought, he didn't notice her.

"Everything fine?" Mildred asked.

"Huh?" Peter tipped up his derby. "Oh, ya, everything's a bucket of roses. More like bleedin' dead roses. I met yer father. He told me to lay off twenty-five."

"It's slowed down that much?"

"Aye. Mr. Spencer says there's a recession. It's all over Canada and the United States. Everything's slowing down. That includes this factory."

"May I see the list?"

Peter gave it to her. Foreigners dominated the list. Not a surprise. Father never liked hiring them in the first place. Young and unattached, Jack and Phillip should be able to manage. Scott was never the same after his hand got crushed by a metal beam a few months ago. Anthony often came to work late. She looked at the last name: Marko Gobinski.

She took a deep breath and gave the list back to Peter. "How are you going to do it?"

He looked at his pocket watch. "I got me an idea. Here, let me distribute those."

Mildred didn't hesitate handing the envelopes to Peter. But in her haste, they bungled the exchange and over a hundred envelopes fell to the floor.

"Bullocks!" Peter said. He and Mildred scrambled to pick them up. The envelopes now out of alphabetical order, Peter hastily shuffled them into a semblance of an organized pile. Mildred stepped away and stood by the factory entrance door. She fidgeted with the hem of her blouse. Nothing she could do. Marko was about to lose his job.

At five the whistle blew and the din of the factory died down as one by one workers shut down their machines. Individually and in small groups, the shop employees including Marko approached the front of the factory. Peter waved the bundle of cheques in the air. "Before ya get your pay cheques, I got something to say."

Mildred looked down at her feet for a moment. Several employees crossed their arms while others spoke to each other in whispers. The workers' grim expressions gave no doubt that they knew what was up.

Peter placed a wooden crate on the ground and stood on it, Eugene beside him. "I know what you're up to, you know." Eugene's bushy moustache twitched. The man had been employed at the factory for several years, but sometimes his temper got in the way.

"I know. Sorry, mate. It's the only way," Peter said to him. He turned his head to the gathering of employees. "Alright … everyone here?" he shouted.

After a silent pause, Peter coughed and cleared his throat. "Here's the situation. It don't take a bloody genius to know things have slowed a wee bit over the past month. We're not getting new orders. The old jobs, well, they're essentially done. Wherever you live, West End, North End, you're seeing half-finished homes and apartments. Money's tight. That's just the way it is right now." Some workers shuffled from side-to-side. Mildred smoothed the lace at the end of her full-length sleeves. How could the economy turn so quickly like that? One day they can't find enough workers and the next they're letting them go.

"Alright. Here's how this'll work. Everyone gets a cheque today. That doesn't change. But as I'm giving it to you, I'll let ya know if we need you to come in on Monday."

"What do you mean?" someone from the crowd yelled.

"I mean some of you are being let go. The company can't keep everyone."

"For how long?" another said.

"I don't know. Could be a week. Could be a month. Could be a year. Hard to say. Those of ya not coming back next week … ya best get on with yer lives. You can come and check from time-to-time to see if we're hiring, but don't hold yer breath."

Peter looked at the first envelope. "Michael Jones." Jones, a skinny man about thirty years old wearing a dirty corduroy jacket, worked his way to the front. Peter handed him his envelope. "See you on Monday." Jones smiled and ran off.

"Valerie Botnikov." A burly Russian with a thick moustache appeared. Peter handed his cheque. "Sorry, we won't be needing your services." Botnikov sighed. The crowd moved aside to let the man pass through. Marko shook Botnikov's hand as he walked by.

And so it went. Most employees left the shop relieved they still had a job come Monday, but for those let go, the sudden bad news devastated them. Some, like Botnikov, dropped their shoulders, took their envelope, and held their heads down. Others marched to Peter, snatched their last pay cheque from his hand, and stormed out of the factory. Some swore loudly. A few muttered something only Peter could hear. It must have been difficult for Peter but he handled the situation admirably. Father trusted him so much.

Eventually, the crowd thinned. It became obvious to everyone that most of the foreign workers were being let go. It got to the point where if Peter called out a foreign-sounding name, everyone knew the worker would be out of a job. Helpless to do anything about it, the remaining foreign workers stared at Peter, most with angry scowls.

On a few occasions Mildred turned her head away, unable to watch the scene. Marko stood off to the side with his floppy black hat scrunched in his hands in front of him, his head down. The colour had left his face. Certainly the poor man must have known that inevitably his name would be called. With the order of the envelopes jumbled, it could come at any time. She decided she would give him a little wave before he walked out of the building. A little goodbye.

But it was not only the foreign workers being let go. Peter had no problem telling Jack and Phillip their time was up. Scott seemed to know he wouldn't be sticking around. With just a few employees left to receive cheques, Peter called Anthony's name and told him the bad news.

Anthony walked over to Peter and took off his hat. "Peter," he said in a soft voice. "Are you sure? Is it my drinking? I can lick that problem. Please. I have three kids. What am I going to say to Veronica?"

"I'm sorry," Peter said. Head down, Anthony pulled his hat down almost covering his eyes and quickly left the factory. Peter looked away and fidgeted with the few remaining envelopes in his hand.

Mildred crossed her arms. Only two employees remained, Marko and Eugene. Did this mean Marko wouldn't be coming over to the house for repairs and lessons anymore?

"You've gotta be fooling, Petey!" Eugene said. "Anthony's a fantastic employee and a great pal. How can you do that?"

"Sorry Eugene, that's how it is," Peter said. "This ain't easy, ya know."

"Oh, and ya reckon it's easy on our side of things?"

"No, I just— "

"Shame on you. Thought you had more loyalty than that."

Peter lowered the two remaining envelopes to his side and pointed a finger directly at Eugene. "Don't you go nattering at me about loyalty. Everyone in this shop knows I stick behind 'em."

"Oh, really? Looks to me like you're no different than Spencer and the other suits."

"I'm warning ya. Don't get me going…."

Eugene pointed to Marko. "Next thing you know you'll be keepin' that bohunk."

Marko frowned and pulled his hands out of his pockets.

Peter scrunched his face into a scowl. "I've had enough of you." Using his free hand, he grabbed Eugene by the shirt. Eugene's face turned red and his moustache twitched. "Here's yer pay packet. I changed me mind. You're gone. I don't want to see yer mug within a block of this factory ever again or so help me I'll ram a red-hot iron up your ass. Ya think you can tell me what to do?" Droplets of spit landed on Eugene's nose.

Sweat dripped down the side of Eugene's face. Both stared at each other in silence. Finally, Peter pushed Eugene back. "Now, out with ya."

With a scowl that could melt an iceberg, Eugene rose, adjusted his shirt and walked away. Just before he stepped out, he turned to Peter. "You'll regret this Petey! Mark my words." Eugene slipped out the exit.

Peter handed Marko his pay cheque. "See ya on Monday." Marko wiped his brow with the back of his hand.

Mildred smiled and opened the door to step back into the office.

Kraf's Plan
November 22, 1913

Stuffed, Marko pushed the plate away from the counter and worked on a piece of apple pie. John Buxton had finished his meal a short time earlier but still picked out the remaining pieces of chicken from his teeth with a toothpick.

"Kraf should be here soon," Buxton said. He looked at his pocket watch.

Marko nodded. It's good Kraf kept him in mind for a job. He could sure use the money.

The door opened. Instinctively both men looked, but someone else came through the door, a man with a few days growth of whiskers on his chin. A small gust of cold wind invaded the small Main Street restaurant. Marko shivered.

"Better bundle up," Buxton said. "Winter's here and will stay until April. The winters are long and cold over here. Not like in Ontario."

"I'll be okay. Winter in old country also cold." Marko finished the last bit of his pie. "Who else coming?"

"Two new guys."

Marko nodded. "How long you know Kraf?"

"Oh, a few years. Bumped into him in a tavern, just like you. We had a few drinks and chatted. He could hold his alcohol better than anyone I know. It's just water to him. That's a sign of a real man you know. Anyway, I got a little too drunk and three thugs tried to work me over in a back lane behind a bar. Just like what you saw on Main Street. Kraf saw and single-handedly gave the brutes such a beating, they had to haul them off in a wagon to the hospital. Like a grizzly bear, he trashed them all. From that moment I've been indebted to him. That's how I got this nasty scar." Buxton pointed to his neck. "One of the thugs had a broken whiskey bottle and was working me over when Kraf jumped in. Thankfully it didn't go too deep or I would've been a goner."

"Where he from?"

"Plum Coulee. It's is a small town south of here towards the American border. He was born somewhere in Europe, probably not far from where you're from. He came over when he was a kid with his folks. I know he speaks a whole pile of languages. He learned them all while living here in Manitoba. His English is perfect, like he's an English professor or something. The man's gotta be a genius. His dad was a blacksmith, so that's how I think Kraf got into that line of work. His mom died when he was young, but he got along great with his step-mom. I think she's German. She lives on Furby. He goes there every so often to visit. Don't you ever bug Kraf about his mom."

Buxton looked around to make sure no one was listening. "Kraf's always had a way about him. He's a leader. People will go to war for him. I know I would. The thing about Kraf is he's very, very loyal. If he identifies you as a friend, it's for life and he'll stick by your side. But if you cross him, watch out.

"But boy, he can be a real ladies man. He's pretty handsome. I've seen women, even the rich ones from southern Winnipeg, swoon when he's got the charm on. I heard he even stole his father's mistress from him when he was just a kid. Imagine that." Buxton leaned forward to whisper to Marko: "Then again, his old man was a bit of a boozer and gambled a lot, so maybe it wasn't so tough."

"He not tall, but he seems strong," Marko said.

"You got that right. He's not the biggest man, but boy, solid as a rock. He's in his early thirties now, but when he was in his twenties I think he was a boxer or a wrestler for a while. But it doesn't look like it. His face is too clean. There ain't no scars or nothing. Unless he was a good fighter, of course. But if he was a good fighter, you'd think he'd still be doing it.

"He's been on the wrong side of the law a few times. He told me that when he was a kid he got nabbed for stealing some watches. He even did some time as a teenager for stealing a bike in Morden. But that kind of stuff's normal. These days kids get in all sorts of mischief. You see them scouring around the North End in gangs. Little criminals, all of them. Then they smarten up."

"But some never do," came from a familiar voice. John Buxton and Marko turned their heads. Krafchenko stood three feet away. "I hope you were not telling our friend any lies, Johnny."

Buxton looked distressed. "Uh, no Kraf. Just the good stuff. I was just telling Marko about where you're from. Nothing bad...."

Krafchenko padded Buxton on the back and smiled. "I know you would never say anything bad about me."

"No, never. I never would," Buxton said. "Uh, I'm not done my coffee. Care for one?"

"Don't mind if I do," Krafchenko said.

Buxton turned around and frantically waved to get the attention of the waitress. "Coffee over here."

Seeing Krafchenko, the waitress trotted over and poured a cup for him.

Krafchenko took a sip. "That's good. Sometimes a man needs a drink that does not have alcohol in it."

Marko nodded.

Krafchenko continued. "All the drinking and debauchery in Winnipeg, drinking to the point of collapse. Maybe playing some pool. Maybe paying for a wench. That's the problem with Winnipeg. There's nothing to do but drink, drink, drink. About ten years ago I was away but decided to come back to Winnipeg. For a time I toured around as a temperance lecturer."

"Tem pence?"

"Temperance," Krafchenko corrected. "That's the anti-booze movement. It's picking up steam. I can't rightly say I believed in any of it, but I put on a convincing show. You have to be a bit of an actor, you know."

"Tell him what happened to you," Buxton said. "The train and all that."

"Alright." Krafchenko paused for a moment, shook his head, but then smiled. "Money was tight," he said. "A few of the cheques I wrote … how shall we say … there were insufficient funds to cover them. It was an honest mistake anyone could make. In Regina the police caught up with me and threw me in jail. Unjustly, I might add. I will admit I handed out bad cheques, but I certainly didn't mean to and I fully intended that they would be honoured. I am not a criminal.

"But the judge didn't see it that way and I was sentenced to Prince Albert Penitentiary for eighteen months. Such a cruel and unfair punishment for what was really a minor mistake. Hardly a crime. Along route to the jail my escort was very mean. He did not like immigrants, especially those from Eastern Europe. While handcuffed he hit me numerous times and abused me verbally. He threatened to kill me on several occasions and was drinking heavily. He got up and smacked me on the side of the head with his sidearm and said that when he came back he would shoot me dead and tell everyone I was trying to escape. He didn't want to waste his time ferrying me to Prince Albert. While the officer was in the washroom relieving himself, I gathered all my strength and fortitude and jumped off the train through a window. I had no choice.

"Unfortunately, they recaptured me soon after. The authorities threw me in the slammer in Prince Albert. I bided my time and became a model inmate. Sometime after, due to my good behavior, they allowed me to organize a crew to paint the outside of the prison. While painting, a belligerent guard, an Anglo and also likely a drunk, kept goading and teasing me. He called me a bohunk. He said I smelled of garlic, that I was an imbecile. An idiot. I could put up with all his taunts, but when he made fun of my mother and accused me of having sexual relations with her, that was too much.

"Like anyone else would have done, I grabbed a paint can and thrashed him. So enraged was I by the injustice of it all, I simply left the penitentiary along with several other inmates. I cannot speak for the others – they were likely advantageous criminals – but as far as I was concerned, I was a free man. I had already more than paid my debt to society.

"But enough about me." Krafchenko lit a cigarette.

What could be made of Krafchenko and his story? Some of the situations seemed so farfetched, like they were taken from a nickel novel. Then again, as they say, sometimes truth was stranger than fiction.

Two men entered the diner and Krafchenko waved them over. "Marko, I'd like you to meet Ben Rolf and Bert Bell."

"Pleased to meet you," Ben said. Clean-cut and wearing a spiffy, pressed, brown suit, the young man parted his short hair slightly off centre. His pudgy face, down turned mouth and round eyebrows displayed a sad, meek quality, like that of a puppy-dog.

A smoke dangling from his mouth, Bert nodded and shook Marko's hand. Slightly taller and dressed more casual than Ben, Bert's receding hairline gave him a long face. He also sported a thin moustache.

"Benny over here drives a cab," Krafchenko said.

"I'm a plasterer by trade," Bert said. "I specialized in ceilings. But these days there's not much work."

"Marko is a real whiz at fixing machinery. He's going to help us out," Krafchenko said. "But let's go to my mother's place where we can chat a bit more privately about our plans."

Ben had parked his taxi, a five-seat Overland with '#350' stenciled on the side, on the street not far from the bar. Marko and the other men bundled up against the cold evening breeze whipping down Main Street. Despite being late November, not much snow had accumulated, just small piles and clumps against buildings. The firm grasp of winter had yet to take hold in Winnipeg. It was that between-time of the year when the ground began to get hard and rigid but not yet completely frozen. Vehicular travel by automobile or horse buggy remained, however buggies would soon have to be exchanged for sleighs once more snow fell and accumulated. Eventually many vehicles would be removed from the road by their owners when some areas could not be traveled.

"This car don't start too good in the winter," Ben said. He wiped his snotty nose on his glove. Judging from the yellow-green crust caked on Ben's leather driving glove, he must have frequently used it as a handkerchief.

Ben pulled out on Main Street to the sound of honks from other motorists and proceeded south. They bumped along while Ben avoided a few horse carriages and the assorted meandering drunk. Although not particularly late – perhaps seven or eight in the evening – the sun had set hours ago. They turned on to Portage Avenue and continued to Furby Street. Ben stopped the automobile in front of house number 500. "I'm staying with my mother at the moment," Krafchenko said to Marko in Ukrainian.

Once inside, the five men sat around a wooden table in the kitchen illuminated by a single naked bulb that hung from a wire directly above. Layers of grime, grease and other signs of oil-laden cooking coated the pale walls. Cigarette smoke hung in the air. Krafchenko's mom, a portly woman, scurried about providing various homemade sweets. She wore a tattered full-length apron and featured more facial hair than most men along with several large dark moles on her cheeks and chin. Marko counted no less than five times that the woman asked Krafchenko if she should prepare a better, heartier meal.

Instead, the men took several shots from the three open bottles of hard alcohol on the table. They toasted to just about anything. Finally, after a half hour, Krafchenko asked his mother to leave the room so the men could talk about important matters.

Krafchenko closed the kitchen door and poured one more shot of whiskey into all the glasses.

"Alright … most of you know what's going on, but for the benefit of some of you," Krafchenko pointed to Marko, "let's review everything. In two weeks on a Wednesday I will make a sizable withdrawal from the Bank of Montreal in Plum Coulee."

"You rob bank?" Marko said.

Silence. All eyes locked on Marko.

"That is correct. We are going to rob the bank. And you are going to help us," Krafchenko said slowly.

Marko took a sip of whiskey and looked straight at Krafchenko's blue eyes. "Is it worth it?"

"How much do you make in a week?" Krafchenko asked. "Twenty dollars?"

"Fifteen."

"Fifteen dollars a week? How about enough money to last a lifetime? Enough that you could live the life of carefree luxury and freedom. No more dirty hands or sweaty brows. No more working like a slave for some pompous English fool from Ontario. No more racing from the streetcar to a bar to cash your little pay cheque in a tavern. Look, this city, how do you think it was created? The rich Anglos came over from Ontario and England and Scotland with their Union Jacks. They planted their flags here thirty, forty years ago. They pushed away the Indians and half-breeds and set up shops to cater to the rush of new immigrants. Have you seen a map?"

Marko slowly nodded.

"North America is the last virgin territory on the Earth," Krafchenko said. "Land, land, and more land. And good soil. Good for farming. The government practically gave away the land to settlers regardless of nationality. Well, where do settlers get their tools? Where do they get their other supplies? From a hardware store, of course. The same goes for clothes on their backs and their pots and pans and whatever else they need. Overnight Winnipeg became the agricultural centre of the West. The population of the city exploded. Warehouses were built to service distribution. Industry developed almost overnight to feed the demand of the railway and the fantastic growth of the city. It sounds good, no?

"But there was a problem, and that problem still exists. Everything in this city is controlled by a small number of wealthy, selfish men. They control all the industry and business. They control City Hall. The police. Everything. You have been to the southern part of the city. You like what you see? Nice, wide boulevards. Beautiful parks. Large yards. What's it like in the North End? Cramped. No space between the houses. Homes do not have adequate plumbing. Planks for sidewalks. Narrow streets. A ghetto. How many Anglos live in the North End? Only a few of the poor ones, that's it. They have their own exclusive clubs of which neither you nor I will ever be a member. They play golf on Sundays while the women sip tea on porches wearing their best summer frocks and hats.

"How do you think those men got their riches? Off our backs. Mine and yours and yours and yours and yours." He pointed to each man in turn. "They get cheap labour and use it until it falls in a grave. Wages are a pittance, barely enough to live on. Yet the products and goods we produce, they sell for massive profits.

"They don't care about us. We are nothing to them. A ripped up, dirty handkerchief to be tossed into a stove without the slightest regard. You think Spencer cares about you? The moment you are not needed, you will be fired. That's a plain fact."

Krafchenko eyes pierced Marko's soul. "It's time to take back what is ours. What's important is I get it back. I need to know if you are in or out." Krafchenko motioned to the others. "It's the same with the rest of you. Are you in or are you out?" Krafchenko tilted his head forward so that his deep blue eyes glared at each man.

Again, silence. The only movement in the room came from the thin tendrils of cigarettes smoke. Each weaved elegantly skyward only to suddenly explode into chaos adding to the haze hovering above the kitchen.

"I'm in," Ben said with a snort. One by one all the others emphatically announced their support. All except Marko, who sat staring at a half-empty rye whiskey bottle.

"Well, Marko," Krafchenko asked in a softer tone. "What say you?"

Marko picked up the bottle and filled his glass three fingers high. He shot back the alcohol and slammed the glass down on the table. "You want us help you. Why? What we get? You keep all the money?" The other men seemed to blindly accept Krafchenko's plan without inquiring about their stake. Why take such a risk to help someone do something illegal, even if, as Krafchenko claimed, somehow he had been slighted?

Krafchenko smiled. "You are a smart one, Marko. Or maybe you hold your alcohol better than the others. Of course you will be handsomely compensated. Probably what you make in six months of hard work. Marko, I want you to be my look-out. Any sign of the authorities or anyone else, you let me know, pronto. And make sure you are dressed nice to fit in. Just a regular, honest man on the street. It will be the easiest five hundred ever in your life. You can sock the money away. Get your own house. Whatever you like."

"If police catch us, we go jail," Marko said.

"There is no chance of that," Krafchenko said. "Plum Coulee is a small, wind-swept town. There are no guards. No police. We will be quick. In and out. We come back to Winnipeg right after. We lay low for a stretch and after a short time everyone will forget about the matter."

"Do you know how the bank is set up?" Buxton asked.

"Benny drove me there three days ago so I got to review the area. I grew up there. I know the town like the back of my hand."

"Why Wednesday? Middle of week?" Marko asked.

"Because it will be quieter. No one will be cashing any pay cheques. The busiest days of the week are at the beginning of the week and the end of the week. Wednesday is perfect," Krafchenko said.

"We work, no?" Marko pointed to the other men seated. "I work on Wednesday. Every Wednesday. If I don't work, I get fired, maybe."

Krafchenko smiled again. "My friend, that is the chance you will have to take. Besides, I'm sure you're a model employee. Have you even missed one day since starting at the factory?"

"No."

"Then you can miss one day without much harm coming to you. I'm talking about hundreds of dollars … so what will it be … in or out?"

Marko breathed deeply and exhaled. Stealing was wrong, even if Krafchenko could justify it, but it would be hard turning away that kind of money. And he would not actually be doing the robbery. Besides, after what happened in the old country, he wasn't an angel. So what difference did it make? He could keep the money hidden for a stretch and when the time was right it could be an initial investment toward that shop he wanted to open.

"I'm in." he said.

Krafchenko smiled and patted Marko on the shoulder with hard slaps. He lit another cigarette and continued pacing in the kitchen. "Here's how it will work. I will go to Plum Coulee a few days ahead." He walked over to the large calendar on the wall and slipped over the page. "December 3rd is the date."

Krafchenko turned to Ben. "You're the driver. Ensure there is enough gasoline in your automobile. The town's south of here and a bit west. It will take three, three-and-a-half, maybe four hours depending on the roads. Come in early in the morning. I'll arrange where we are to meet that morning. I want to do this around lunch time when the bank is quiet. It's very likely only the bank manager will be in the establishment."

"I'll fill her to the top," Ben said.

"I have a friend just outside Plum Coulee. That's where I'll be staying before the job. His name is William Reigie. He'll drive to Winnipeg to find you. When you meet him say, 'I am the man from Gibraltar.' That will be your password. He will give you an envelope which will give you instructions telling you when and where you and Marko need to be."

Ben nodded, although he looked to be confused.

"Bert and Johnny, you guys help me when I get back. I'll need a hideout and some type of disguise. You guys will also have to hide some of the loot. I don't want it in one spot. That way if a stash gets found, I don't lose it all." Bert nodded slowly and took a sip of whiskey.

Krafchenko turned to Marko. "Bring some tools. Automobiles can be finicky, especially in December. If we break down, it's up to you to get us up and running. Can you do that?"

"Da."

"I don't want to take any chances, that's why I want you part of this job. I can fix anything myself, but I'll be busy. But, that's enough talk for tonight. Let's meet again here in two days to finalize plans."

Krafchenko lifted the bottle of rye and filled everyone's glass. "Alright, let's drink on it."

Angry Snake
November 24, 1913

Marko leaned Mike's bike against Kraf's mother's house. His fingers felt numb despite wearing gloves. Thankfully the roads still lacked any measurable snow. It would have taken longer had he walked. He looked at his pocket watch. Fifteen minutes early. No sense standing around outside. He knocked on the door.

"Nein, John not here," his mother said in a thick German accent. "But come, come. He here soon. Sit, sit." Marko entered the home, taking his shoes off at the door. Most of the furniture in the living room appeared dusty and old. A large stain dominated the small wooden table in front of the couch.

Krafchenko's mom brought him a small plate of treats while he waited for Krafchenko and the others to appear. Although not the slightest bit hungry, he ate a few while Krafchenko's mother watched. You can never say 'no' when an older woman offers food.

"Eat, eat," she said before going into the kitchen. She wore the same worn apron from the night a few days ago.

Marko looked at his pocket watch. Where was everyone?

Krafchenko's mother raised her voice from the kitchen, but he could not understand her German. She poked her head into the living room, an outstretched hand held an empty cup. "I no have any sugar. I go to Bernice next door to see if she have sugar. You, okay? Want coffee?"

"No, no. I fine, but can I use washroom?"

"Oh … yes, yes … just down hall."

Marko went into the washroom. He heard the back door close when Krafchenko's mother left the house. He splashed cold water on his face. For several minutes he stared at himself in the mirror, water dripping down his nose and cheeks. What was he doing? He came to Canada to start a new life, not get mixed up in schemes. What if he walked away from the plan? He still had a job. But then again, all that money … it would take care of everything.

That dream of an automobile repair shop would be closer to coming true. Never know, maybe one day he'd be laid off? And Krafchenko seemed so compelling.

He heard a sound. Just before he opened the door into the hallway, he heard two men speaking on the other side of the door, one of them Krafchenko.

"…must be in the washroom," Krafchenko said.

"Do you know whose shoes they are?" the other man said. Marko did not recognize the voice.

"No. We will find out soon enough. Where are the others? Where's my mother? Why is everyone late all the time? If we are off like this on Wednesday, the operation definitely will not go as planned." Krafchenko sounded annoyed.

Instead of walking out, Marko put his head closer to the washroom door to try to make out the conversation.

"Let's have a look inside," Krafchenko said.

Marko could hear the sounds of something being opened. Perhaps a latch? What did they have? Weapons or guns to be used for the robbery?

"Not much here," the other man said. "Mostly clothes. A few pictures and trinkets. Nothing special. You might be able to use a shirt. The trousers are too long, although we could have them brought up at a tailor."

Someone rapped at the front door. "Finally," Krafchenko said. He and the other man walked out of the room towards the front door.

As he passed by, Krafchenko knocked on the bathroom door, "You alive in there? Come on out."

"I'll be right out," Marko said. He looked at himself in the mirror one last time. He dabbed his face with a towel before leaving the washroom.

He could hear voices at the front door. The other men all arrived at the same time. He began to walk down the hall but stopped. Curious, he glanced into the now-unoccupied bedroom across from the washroom.

His stolen suitcase lay open on the bed.

He ran over to it and sifted through the items, all in disarray and picked over. The contents of the wooden box that held photographs and mementoes from his past had been spilled on the bed.

He flipped over a down-turned frame. Olena and Anastasiya.

He felt a sudden, sharp pain in his temple.

*****

He sees his daughter, Anastasiya. The pretty six-year-old girl from the photo is running through a field of golden, ripe wheat. Her long blonde hair bouncing with each stride. Her smile is so large and innocent, an ounce of it would brighten a room for an entire winter. Her dress, a pretty white one fringed with pink lace and a large pink bow on her back flutters and ripples with each stride. She is wearing her good shoes. The ones she could only wear to church or special occasions.

It is the middle of the day, a brilliant blue cloudless sky near the end of summer.

Marko turns his head. His beautiful wife, Olena, is right beside him. Her left hand interlocks with his right. Smiling and laughing, she squeezes his hand with the amount of force only a woman in love can give. Her perfect white teeth glisten. Her full, long blonde hair hangs gently over her shoulder. Like Anastasiya, she too is wearing her best dress, a stunning, flowing white summer dress interlaced with tiny blue beads. Barefoot, Olena holds her shoes in her other hand.

Anastasiya continues to run towards them through the field.

Marko breaks Olena's grasp and puts his arm around her. She does the same. They embrace. Olena stands on tip-toes and they kiss. Anastasiya arrives and hugs them both.

The perfect day.

*****

His eyes shut tight, Marko massaged the sore spot on the side of his head. After a minute he reopened them. Where he felt doubt and uncertainty, there was now complete resolve. Going down the wrong path and falling into the ditch, the photograph, the only one of his family, saved him.

Marko threw the scattered items into the suitcase and snapped it shut. His head high, he marched into the living room where, by now, everyone held a smoke and nursed a drink.

"Ah, there you are," Krafchenko said. "We were wondering what you…" Krafchenko stopped and pointed. "Why are you holding that suitcase?"

Marko tilted his head down to glare at Krafchenko. "Because it is mine. It was taken on the first day I come to Winnipeg."

Krafchenko said nothing. The others in the room – Johnny, Ben, and Bert – silently observed the drama.

A man entered the living room from the kitchen holding a half-filled bottle of whiskey. "I found more booze in the kit—" He stopped short when he saw Marko and the suitcase.

Marko glared at the man, the one who had just spoken with Krafchenko in the bedroom and the same villain who stole his suitcase that day in July in front of the train station.

"You!" Marko yelled, nostrils flared. The man appeared confused at first, but quickly realized the situation, backed into the kitchen and ran out of the house through the back door, still clutching the bottle of rye whiskey.

Marko didn't bother chasing the thief. No way he was leaving his suitcase unattended. He turned and faced the other men. Everyone remained silent and didn't move. Marko tightened his grip on the suitcase. Enough with Krafchenko and his escapades.

"There goes our booze, eh?" Ben said. Bert elbowed him in the ribs.

"That man … he took my suitcase." Marko glared at Krafchenko. "You know that … that thief. He works with Igor to steal suitcases at the train station. You're together with him. Me … I … I trusted you. You betrayed me."

But Marko's harsh words rolled off Krafchenko like dew on a leaf. He casually lit up a cigarette and blew a stream of smoke into the air in Marko's general direction. "Do I know him? Yes, I do. His name is Metro, by the way. Did he take your suitcase from you, yes, he did. Did I tell him to? No, I did not. But that's just what Metro does. He and Igor target the unsuspecting at the train station. If people are too distracted to watch over their things—"

"Igor distracted me!" Marko yelled, cutting off Krafchenko, the pain in his temple intensified. "He acted like a friendly person, distracted me, and your friend … this Metro ... he took my suitcase and ran. They're criminals, both. You're his friend. Now you want to rob a bank. You're a criminal, just like them."

The clouds parted from Marko's mind. In that clarity he saw Krafchenko for what he really was: a fantastic manipulator. A vastly intelligent man with little or no morals. Marko clenched his jaw.

Krafchenko calmly took another long drag of his cigarette and blew more smoke towards Marko.

"Hey, that shirt … the one you're wearing. It's my shirt. You took my shirt."

"Now that you mention it, it just may be." He took another puff and a sip of whiskey. "I honestly did not realize it was your suitcase." He looked down and thumbed the material of the sleeve. "I need a shirt. I'm not wearing what I normally wear to the job on Wednesday. I may not wear this one. I might even dress all in black, like an old Jew. That was the entire reason Metro brought over the suitcase. I don't doubt he has a dozen more in his room, all with similar items within. Besides, you will make enough money from this operation to buy a hundred shirts. What is a shirt between friends? They always say a sign of a friend is if he would take the shirt off his back for his comrade, no?"

Despite his ever increasing headache, Marko continued to glare at Krafchenko. How could he twist the conversation to his advantage? An explanation for everything. Marko figured the other men in the room knew well enough to lay low and remain silent, watching the verbal volley with the same amusement one would get from viewing an automobile accident on Main Street.

"I'm not robbing a bank," Marko said. He stormed toward the front door, suitcase in hand, to put on his shoes.

"See, I told you he would bail out," Buxton said. "He's a little too clean cut."

Krafchenko carefully placed the remainder of his cigarette in an ashtray and his glass on the table, got up and with a steeled determination, slithered to Marko.

He grabbed Marko by his jacket and slammed him against the wall, his iron grasp tighter than a boa constrictor on its prey, firm and unwavering. Krafchenko held Marko aloft against the wall with only his left arm while his right fist remained cocked, ready to drive into Marko's skull with the force of a train engine.

The disgust and anger Marko felt quickly evaporated into cold fear. He was at Krafchenko's absolute mercy and Marko knew it. His right temple pounded.

For several seconds, although it felt considerably longer, Krafchenko stared at him with a mad, intense fury. The reassuring, comfortable smile Marko usually saw from Krafchenko vanished. Instead, Krafchenko's twisted face resembled that of a savage demon. A snake from Hell only moments from claiming its next victim. Surely others who crossed Krafchenko's path faced this fury. This was how Krafchenko controlled the minds of his minions. Pure, absolute evil.

"Are you going to double-cross me?" Krafchenko said through clenched teeth.

Marko shook his head, his fear bubbled up.

"Do I need to make an example of you?"

"N-no. I no mean to…" Marko dripped sweat like he was working outside in the extreme summer heat. For certain Krafchenko's example would be one of the worst experiences of his life. "Listen … I only know you a short time. How can you expect me to rob a bank with you?"

"Ben," Krafchenko said, looking over his shoulder. "How long have you known me?"

"About a week."

"Bert?"

"About the same," Bert said.

Krafchenko turned his head to face Marko and curled his lips into a wicked smile. How could men he knew for only a week be willing to do his bidding? The man had the devil inside him.

Still holding Marko against the wall, Krafchenko reached into his back pocket and pulled out a switch blade. Slowly and carefully, he held it to within an inch of Marko's eye.

"I used this knife before and will use it on you if I have to." He lightly flicked the knife against Marko's earlobe, drawing a drop of blood. "Maybe an ear." He brought it up against Marko's right cheek and gently flicked, again drawing a very tiny drop of blood. "Maybe a nice scar on your face, something to go with that dent by your ear. Or maybe … maybe a finger or an entire hand. It will be pretty hard fixing things if you didn't have a hand, no?"

The tiny cuts hurt no more than mosquito bites, but the fear of what they could lead to mortified Marko.

"L-listen, Kraf … I no want trouble. I no say nothing to nobody. B-but … but …" Marko swallowed and tried to ignore the pain throbbing in his head. "But I no rob bank. It's wrong." Marko closed his eyes in anticipation of some vile act that would scar him for life.

At that moment, Krafchenko's mother called from the kitchen. "I back! Johnny, are you here? I was with Bernice but she talks too much. Blah, blah, blah." Krafchenko still held his knife in front of Marko's face, but the arrival of his mother distracted him.

"Johnny? Are you here? Johnny?" his mom yelled.

Annoyed, Krafchenko finally said, "Yes, I'm here."

"Oh, good. And all your friends? That nice boy, Marko, he come early.

I'm baking now, but have to make a fire. The stove door is stuck again. Come and open for me."

Through all this time, Krafchenko still held Marko aloft against the wall, but lowered the knife and looked away to yell back at his mother. "Not right now, Mommy. We are … we're discussing business."

"You come now. I not wait forever. You like Bernice, all talk, talk, talk. It only takes a moment…" By now, the other men shuffled and fidgeted, almost as embarrassed by the situation as was Krafchenko.

"I bring coffee for you and friends," Krafchenko's mother said.

"No wait, I'll get the coffee and fix the oven door," Krafchenko said. He cursed in some foreign tongue Marko didn't recognise and released his grasp slowly to let Marko down. His little old mother held more power over Krafchenko than the strongest man in the world ever could.

Marko sat on the ground and pressed his hand against the side of his head. Krafchenko leaned over and whispered into his ear in Ukrainian. "Keep your lips buttoned or I will most certainly make you pay. I know where you work. I know where you live. I know everything about you. I can convince the authorities you helped me with the operation. You don't want to help me in Plum Coulee, fine. You will when I get back. If you breathe a word of anything to anyone, you better pray hard, because only God will be able to save you."

"Do you understand?" Krafchenko said in English.

Red-faced, wide-eyed and wet from sweat, Marko nodded emphatically in agreement.

"Good," Krafchenko said in a calm voice. "Now get out of here before I change my mind."

"Johnny, Johnny! You coming? What taking so long?"

"I'm coming, I'm coming!"

Marko sprang to his feet, grabbed his suitcase and ran out the door, not bothering to say goodbye to any of the others. He stepped out and immediately felt the cold chill. But it didn't bother him. He wiped the blood away from his face and ear and stood silent for a moment with his eyes closed while the pain in his head subsided.

Mike's bike vanished. Marko swore to himself. That same thief took it. Mike will not be happy.

Kraf's Dark Past
November 30, 1913

Mildred opened the large oak door and allowed Marko in. Every time he entered the mansion he almost had to pause. Like a king's castle, the gleam from the polished white marble floor blinded him.

"Good to see you again," she said in a cheerful voice. She leaned against a small, ornately carved bureau that held a single, large lavender vase. On this occasion Mildred put her hair up. She wore a bright and pretty pink and light blue dress edged with red lace around the wrist and neckline. She held what looked like a small piano.

Sensing his gaze, she held it up. "Oh, this. It's actually a jewelry box." Mildred opened the piano-shaped box to reveal a green velvet interior. The material on one side had been torn. A small ballerina on a little pedestal was missing it's head and one arm. "It's an old box I received from my grandmother when I was a little girl. It's seen better days. The ballerina is supposed to spin in a circle, a pirouette. It's also supposed to play a little melody when you open the lid but this one's been silent for years. Even the lid is broken." She tossed it in a small garbage bin beside the bureau. "Were you able to complete your assignment?"

"Da."

Immediately Mildred held up her finger with a coy smile. "What did I tell you about using 'da'?"

Marko smiled. "Yes, yes, yes. No da."

"Correct. Try to use proper English."

Marko followed her into the living room for his English lesson. The thick area rug in the room felt like walking on a cloud. The mansion seemed quieter than usual. Perhaps Mildred's mother stepped out? She seemed to spend much of her time socializing. And why not, especially if you have your own staff to cook and do chores?

He seated himself next to her on the red velvet couch. Like he did each visit, he ran his hand slowly along the fabric, soft and luxurious. He never sat on something so comfortable. The intricately carved wooden table in front of the couch would cost a year's wages. Maybe more.

Mildred quickly reviewed the sentences and paragraphs Marko wrote since their last lesson. Once again, he still mixed his b's and d's. His difficulty telling the difference between 'there,' 'their' and 'they're' continued. Although still bad, his spelling showed signs of improvement. He caught Mildred's faint smile when she complimented him on completing his homework.

Several times during the lesson Marko stared at a large oil painting depicting a fox hunt in the English countryside. On each occasion the image of Krafchenko holding a knife to his eye hounded his thoughts. How could it not? The confrontation with Krafchenko unnerved him all week. He ate little and had trouble sleeping.

"Is everything alright? You don't seem yourself today."

"Uh, yes."

Mildred lowered her head and widened her big brown eyes. "Are you sure…?"

Marko dropped his shoulders and exhaled. Enough. "No … something is wrong. Very wrong. A few days ago I went to meet people I know. While I was there I find out they had my suitcase … the one that was stolen."

"I get the impression you should not see them again. They seem unsavory."

"They want to take money from a bank," Marko said. "They want me to help. The main man, he's a strong leader. He says his friends and I could make lots of money. But I know it's wrong. I went to tell him I don't want to rob a bank."

Mildred lowered her voice. "You were going to rob a bank? You know that's not right. That man you are talking about … the leader … he does not sound like an honest person."

"Everywhere … everyone knows him. Almost like they are afraid. They don't want to make him mad. He's strong, too. Not tall, but very powerful. Very smart."

Mildred grabbed Marko's hand. "You must not associate with him. It appears to me like he's nothing but trouble. Anyone that is able to convince others to rob a bank does not have a shred of good moral fiber."

Marko squeezed her hand. "I'm not robbing a bank."

She tightened her hold on his hand. "Who is he?"

"His name is John Krafchenko."

Immediately Mildred let go her grasp and cupped her hand to her mouth. Her back arched and eyes widened. "John Krafchenko? Are you certain…?"

Marko nodded.

"Oh, Marko." She touched his shoulder. "John Krafchenko is an animal. From what I've read, that man has been in trouble with the law numerous times. I heard he passed around bad cheques…"

Marko looked down, feeling shame. "He said bad cheques all accidents. That he mean to—"

"Nonsense. He knew what he was doing. Writing a bad cheque is just like stealing money and don't let anyone convince you otherwise."

"He said he escaped a train going to prison. Officer was bad to him."

"Somehow I doubt that. I'm sure he was never treated like royalty, but I doubt his life was in any immediate danger. All I know is he escaped from a prison in Saskatchewan. He immediately stole a large amount of money and went to the United States where he robbed some banks and eventually slipped back to Europe. If he stayed in Europe that would have been fine. Good riddance, I say. But his crime spree continued. Eventually he came back to Manitoba to continue his life of crime."

"How you know so much?"

"Krafchenko is quite notorious, I can assure you. While he may have many evil allies, there are many, many more honest, law-abiding people terrified of him. His exploits have been in the newspapers. Why, just a few years ago he robbed another bank in Southern Manitoba. Somewhere near Winkler, if I recall. Listen … if you know that man is about to commit a crime, you need to notify the authorities. He must be stopped before someone gets hurt."

The ticking from the gold and silver clock on the mantle above the fireplace provided the only sound in the room. Finally, Marko looked up to Mildred. "I'm in trouble. Krafchenko is mad at me. I can't go to police. He's a powerful man. He knows where I live."

"So what will you do?"

"Nothing," Marko said. "What happens, happens. Krafchenko will rob bank. Police will find him. He will go to jail. Problem solved."

Dr. Fairchild
December 5, 1913

"Ya might want to get in," Benny Rolph said from inside his taxi. "Kraf wants to see you."

Marko stood dumbfounded on the street corner. On his way to the store to pick up a few things, he didn't expect this. He had kept his mouth shut like he promised when Krafchenko pressed a knife against his throat. He did tell Mildred, but she could be trusted.

"What he want?"

"Can't say. All's I know is Kraf wants to see a few of his fellers…" Benny spit out on the sidewalk. "…and you're one of them."

Marko pressed his lips together. Kraf did say that he'd expect help when he got back. What if he didn't go with Ben? Krafchenko knew where he lived. He had nowhere to hide. It would be a bad idea to anger the man.

"Look," Benny said. "I don't want to go either. But have ya got a choice? I'm in the same boat. I didn't go to Plum Coulee either."

Marko exhaled, opened the door and slipped inside the Overland.

Benny tipped his driver's hat up to the top of his forehead and tightly gripped the steering wheel with his gloved hands. Within a few minutes car #350 rumbled on the Arlington Bridge, overtop the wide CPR shops. Whatever Krafchenko wanted from him or Benny or any of the others would not be good and certainly not legal. The last thing he needed was to be mixed up with the hardened criminal.

"You read any of the papers?" Benny said over the noise of the engine.

Tight lipped, Marko nodded. How could he not know? Everyone talked about the sensational news from Plum Coulee. A few days ago a man, dressed all in black, walked into the Bank of Montreal, robbed it, and in the process killed the bank manager. It had to be Krafchenko. Who else could it be? Krafchenko said he'd rob the bank. Who knew the truth or who to believe? He obviously didn't get caught by the police.

The vehicle pulled up to Krafchenko's hide-out, a rooming house on

William Avenue. Benny leaned toward Marko. "Before we go in, be sure to refer to Kraf as Dr. Fairchild. That's what Kraf's calling himself. Don't call him 'John' or 'Kraf' or anything else. Just Dr. Fairchild."

Around the rear of the rooming house they noticed evidence of wood cutting from the sawdust in the back yard sprinkled on top the unusually little snow cover. Benny led the way through the backdoor.

"Are you here to see Dr. Fairchild?" a woman in the hallway asked with an air of authority.

"We are."

"You can go right up the stairs," she said with a smile. "What a lovely man he is."

Benny and Marko walked past the woman and up the creaky staircase. Benny knocked on the door to a suite.

"Who is it?" came Krafchenko's voice from within. Marko's heart sank.

"Uh, I'm from New York. Uh … are you the man from Gibraltar?" Benny answered.

Within moments, the door to the suite sprung open. Krafchenko stood at the doorway bearing an effortless smile.

"Good to see you Benny. You too, Marko. Come, come … come inside." Krafchenko stepped aside and waved his arm, urging the two men to enter the suite.

Benny entered. Marko paused for a moment, but followed. Krafchenko placed a reassuring hand on Marko's shoulder. "I'm glad you could make it to my humble flat. I very much appreciate it."

Like a snowflake in the hot July sun, Marko's worry and concern melted away with Krafchenko's soothing words. How could he do that? In one instance he could bring about cold fear, but a moment later, unyielding trust, like that from a sibling or life-long friend.

Not much bigger than a bedroom, the small room looked neat. Although older, the furniture and fixtures appeared to be in good shape with very little dust. The lady at the bottom of the stairs took good care of her rooming house. Bert Bell and John Buxton had already arrived. Bell sat on a wooden chair while Buxton relaxed on the couch. Another two chairs remained available. A brown leather bag sat on the ground beside a comfortable-looking blue high-back chair. With his hair greased back and parted neatly down the middle, Buxton dressed in a full brown suit including a sharp vest. Bert looked a little rougher on the edges with thick black trousers held up with brown suspenders. His messy hair made it look like he just got up while his white shirt featured an old coffee stain.

"Have a seat," Krafchenko said. "Johnny, pour them a shot. Johnny was kind enough to bring a bottle of whiskey."

"Hey, time to celebrate," Buxton said. He rose from his seat to get more glasses.

Once all the whiskey shots had been poured, Krafchenko lifted his glass to propose a toast. "To all my friends and comrades," he said. The four other men raised their glasses and downed their shots. Immediately Buxton refilled the glasses.

"I'm sitting in that chair," Krafchenko said to Benny, who was about to sit in the high-back. Benny immediately moved to a place on the couch beside Buxton. Marko grabbed a chair and moved it closer to the coffee table.

"Well, my friends, the deed has been done. I will need a bit of help over the next little—" Krafchenko stopped when a knock came to the door.

He walked to the door but didn't open it. "Yes?"

"Is there anything I can get for you and your guests, Dr. Fairchild?" asked the landlady from the other side of the door.

"No, Mrs. Thomas. I believe we are fine."

"Dr. Fairchild," Mrs. Thomas said after a short pause, "one of the guests was wondering if you could help him? It's Mr. Lunn. He has the most horrible tooth ache."

"I can see him later, but not at the moment."

"Very good. Thank you, doctor. I will leave you be and send Mr. Lunn later."

Krafchenko lit a cigarette and took a sip of whiskey. He chuckled slowly and nodded his head. "That landlady, she's as easy as apple pie. She thinks I'm a doctor. Yesterday I saw a sign in the window that there was a room to let. Two chaps were in the backyard cutting wood with a gas-powered saw, but the motor was not running properly. It sputtered because the gas mixture was too rich. It required the simplest of adjustments. Marko would also know what to do in an instant. Immediately I was able to improve the efficiency of their operation.

"As I did, I learned about Mrs. Thomas's husband, who happens to be working at Oak Point. I learned that her husband – whom I never met before – was short and has a moustache. Well … armed with that information, I was able to convince the lady I knew her husband and that I had four farms in the

Oak Point area. I didn't have a problem securing this room. Ha! I even made up the story about being a doctor," he said with a wink. "I had her believing I amputated the legs off a man yesterday morning. So remember … while here, I'm Dr. Fairchild." He took another drag of his cigarette and played with the snake ring on his little finger.

"But enough fantasy," Krafchenko continued. "On to the matter at hand. The withdrawal from the bank in Plum Coulee generally went without a hitch."

"What about the bank manager?" Bert Bell said quietly.

"Oh, that. It's a problem, I suppose, but I didn't shoot the manager. Curly did it. He was with me on the heist."

Marko frowned slightly. Curly? He never met a Curly. Krafchenko nor anyone else ever mentioned anyone named 'Curly.'

"The job was going off without a hitch. I cased the bank for a few days before. I stayed at Willy Reigie's place and even got to do a little rabbit hunting. It's been such a mild winter that not many are hibernating. I had some drinks with a bank employee and he unwittingly provided information pertaining to deposits and the safe. The bank has a Gary safe. Those are tough to crack. I could do it, but it would take time. Because of that, it was easier to strong arm the job. I obtained a long, black coat and put a disguise on. A local liveryman by the name of William Dyck has a stable a block away from the bank. He drove us out of town. We drove all over the country side, but Dyck eventually dropped us off at different points. Myself, I asked to be let off near Osborne Station."

"Is he in on it?" Bert asked.

"Sure he is. I gave him some silver and bundles of currency. He fancied my watch so I threw that in. Besides, I can now get any watch I want. Although … I'm worried he might squeal. Once the bank manager was shot, I reckoned Dyck might get cold feet, so I discharged my revolver in his car and put a hole in the side. I hope that keeps him mum, but you never know."

"What about this Curly?" Buxton asked. "Where is he?"

Krafchenko butted out his cigarette. "He skipped the province. He thinks – and I obviously concur – that he will be a wanted man for pulling the trigger on the bank manager. He left all the money with me then hitched a ride on a train bound for the United States. He'll hide out there. I don't think we'll ever see him again."

"Me, I stayed the night at a place on Cathedral Avenue here in Winnipeg.

Then I stumbled upon this spot, although I will not be staying long. I need to move around. Stay a step ahead of the authorities."

Krafchenko finished his glass and motioned to Buxton to refill it. Buxton topped up everyone else's glass in the process. Krafchenko lit a fresh cigarette and blew a puff in the air.

"Now, Benny …" Krafchenko said. Rolf sat erect at the mention of his name. "I really did not want to involve Dyck in this operation. I expected you to come down to Plum Coulee. I even sent Willy to Winnipeg to get you."

"I … uh … I," Benny's face reddened with each passing second.

"So I had to involve someone outside our little circle. That could come back to haunt us. I'm sure the authorities already have Dyck in custody. Hopefully he will stay loyal and stick to his story, but if he doesn't … it will pose a problem."

"The roads. I was worried about the roads. The weather was not the best," Benny said, now sweaty.

"Oh, really?" Krafchenko said. He crossed his legs and cocked his head to the side. "If that's the case, then why was Dyck able to drive me to Osborne Station and then go all the way back to Plum Coulee without a hitch?"

"And Curly, too," Buxton said.

"Huh?" Krafchenko said. "Oh, yes, of course. He also drove Curly around. Dyck had no problems driving Curly and myself all around southern Manitoba."

"Well, I … ya know …. I … uh … wasn't too sure. Ya know? I mean it's real tough for me to take my taxi outa town. The weather … it was kinda rough…"

Krafchenko downed his whiskey in one shot and slammed the glass on the table. In the same motion he rose and picked up the bag that was on the ground beside him. He slowly walked to Benny, unfastening the bag along the way.

Poor Benny looked like a sweaty, nervous wreck. What could be in the bag? Evil instruments of torture?

Marko held his breath waiting to see what Krafchenko would do. Frowning, Krafchenko stood in front of Benny and reached into the bag. His hand grasped something inside the bag and pulled out … a small, tightly wrapped package.

Wide-eyed, Benny Rolf's bottom lip quivered.

Krafchenko smirked and laughed. "Fooled you, didn't I? Here, take this loot. I need you to hide it. Like I said before, I don't want it all in one place. It's not safe."

Benny took the tightly bound package and carefully unwrapped a corner of it. Sure enough, a thick stack of Bank of Montreal currency poked out.

"That's about a grand-and-a-half." Now standing behind Benny, Krafchenko placed his hand on Benny's shoulder and squeezed. "You will be able to keep part of that bundle. Maybe a hundred or two. But you better not let me down like you did by not driving out to Plum Coulee. Do you understand?" Krafchenko's broad smile could not conceal the sinister aspect of his veiled threat to Benny.

"Y-yes K-Kraf … er … I mean Dr. Fairchild…" Benny stuttered. He moved the heavy bundle from hand to hand like a hot potato.

"Johnny B," Krafchenko walked over to Buxton while reaching into his bag. "Here's a bundle for yourself. Maybe a thousand. Same thing, hide it somewhere safe, maybe in the southern part of the city. There will be a cut for you."

Buxton smiled and nodded his approval.

Krafchenko gave a bundle to Bert Bell. "There's about $2,000 in that package. Plant it for now, but I want you to eventually send $500 to my wife in Graham, Ontario. From the remaining $1,500 you will need to get disguises and pay for a lawyer, if I need one. You understand?"

Bell nodded, but almost too enthusiastically.

Krafchenko laughed. "Don't get too excited, Bert. Maybe you should have another shot."

Bell treated Krafchenko's idle comment like an order and immediately downed his glass.

"Oh," Krafchenko added, reaching into his bag. "Here's a letter to my wife that goes along with the money. You are going to be able to take care of this, correct?"

"Yes, Dr. Fairchild. Not a problem. I'll take care of it."

"Good, good. I would not have it any other way," Krafchenko said. "You were supposed to go to Plum Coulee in place of Marko, but like him, you chickened out. Curly went instead. I'll give you one more chance to prove your worth," A slight smirk formed on his upper lip.

Krafchenko finally walked over to Marko, again, reaching into the bag. About to accept a heavy burden, Marko shoulders drooped. He didn't want to be involved in the robbery, but now had no choice.

"And here's your little package." Krafchenko held out a thick bundle right in front of Marko's eyes.

But Marko did not take the bundle immediately. Krafchenko flicked his wrist twice, urging Marko to accept the stolen money. Finally, after a long moment, Marko took it. The money felt substantial in his hands. He never held so much money before in his life. But instead of excitement, he felt dirty and ashamed. He took a sip of whiskey and felt it burn down his throat.

"Come now, my dear Marko. Everyone has to help a little bit. You need to do your part. We are all in it together now. Don't you see?" For some reason Marko believed the man, despite not wanting to.

"Be sure to hide it in a very safe place close to home. There is about a thousand there. You, too, will get a cut when all is said and done. But not till then. Got it?"

Marko nodded slowly.

"Good. That settles that," Krafchenko said, slapping his hands on his thighs. "I have a little bit still with me, but all of you have the lion's share. We will meet again to discuss—"

But before Krafchenko could complete his thought, a series of loud knocks came to the door.

"Dr. Fairchild," Mrs. Thomas said from the other side of the door," I'm sorry to bother you. It's me again."

Krafchenko silently motioned for everyone to hide their bundles, which they did between cushions, behind pillows and inside jackets. He then opened the door a crack.

"Yes, Mrs. Thomas. How can I be of service?"

"It's Mr. Lunn here. The toothache?"

"Yes, yes, please come in Mr. Lunn," Krafchenko said in a professional manner. He opened the door and a dark-haired man with a medium build entered. Mr. Lunn held the side of his red and swollen mouth gingerly and appeared to be in some distress.

Mrs. Thomas followed in, smiling. "I think it's simply wonderful there is a physician in the house."

Krafchenko stopped Mrs. Thomas from entering any further. "That will be all, Mrs. Thomas. I will examine the tooth and may need to perform an extraction. It would not be proper for a woman to be present."

"Yes, of course. I understand. Thank you, once again." Mrs. Thomas left the room and closed the door behind her.

"Now, have a seat on the couch, will you Mr. Lunn. I need you to be able to bend your head back." Both Benny and Buxton vacated the couch for the ailing man.

Krafchenko walked behind to the back of the couch. "Now, open up. Let's have a look."

Lunn opened his mouth and Krafchenko stuck his fingers in the man's mouth to help him better examine Lunn's teeth.

"Ah, yes. I see the problem. You have a badly infected molar. The infection is spreading to your gums. I will need to perform an extraction. Are you up for that Mr. Lunn?"

"Ah, ahhh," Mr. Lunn said, his mouth still open.

Marko could not believe his eyes. Krafchenko planned to perform a tooth extraction right in front of them.

"Mr. Gregory, I will require a small pan," he said to Bert Bell. "I believe there is one in the lavatory. Wash it out with soap, if you please. Also, kindly ask Mrs. Thomas for some cotton balls."

Bert hesitated and appeared initially confused as to why Krafchenko called him 'Mr. Gregory,' but he caught on quickly. "Yes, Dr. Fairchild," he said and scuttled out the door to fulfill the request.

"Mr. Barnes, I need you to get me a pair of pliers." Krafchenko motioned to Benny. "Perhaps from the trunk of your vehicle." Benny nodded and exited to fetch the tool.

"Mr. Cole," Krafchenko said to Buxton. "Pour this poor man a very stiff shot. He will need it."

"Yes sir, Dr. Fairchild." Buxton filled a glass to the top with whiskey.

Krafchenko tipped Mr. Lunn's head forward so he could drink the alcohol. But Mr. Lunn raised his hand in protest. "Ah gonk grink algoal."

"Nonsense," Krafchenko said. He forced the hard liquor into Mr. Lunn's mouth. "Swish it around and gulp it down. It will help ease the pain. Consider it like medicine. I am a physician, after all."

Mr. Lunn exhaled heavily through his nose, but downed the entire contents of the glass, gasping and sputtering after he finished.

"There, that was not so bad now, was it?" Krafchenko said with a broad smile.

Bert and Benny arrived from their errands. Sensing Mr. Lunn's concern over Benny's dirty pliers, Krafchenko ordered Marko to clean them in the lavatory.

Marko stopped for a moment on the way to the bathroom down the hall. He could make a run for it, fleeing from the strange scene taking place in Krafchenko's new flat. No, it was better to go along with the show, despite the uneasiness.

When he arrived back in the room, everyone had gathered around Mr. Lunn. Krafchenko rolled his shirt sleeves past his elbows. "Ah, the pliers." He took them from Marko.

"Alright, Mr. Lunn. Open wide," Krafchenko said.

Mr. Lunn complied, although in obvious distress. His eyes could not possibly open any wider, lest they popped from his head.

Slowly Krafchenko sank the pliers into Mr. Lunn's open mouth. He paused for a moment. "Gentlemen, please. You must stop crowding around me. You are blocking the light. Please give me some room." The men took a step back.

Mr. Lunn's contorted face changed several shades of red and purple. Nervous sweat dripped down from his forehead. Krafchenko placed the pliers around the sore tooth and with a single, swift motion, pulled the tooth away from its foundation.

Krafchenko raised the bloodied tooth in the air triumphantly while Mr. Lunn howled in pain. Krafchenko placed the tooth in the pan and gave the pliers back to Benny. Blood filled the man's mouth and dripped down the side of his mouth.

Sensing this, Krafchenko grabbed a small handful of cotton balls and inserted them, one by one, into Mr. Lunn's mouth. "Now, now, Mr. Lunn. You must not squirm. The cotton will soak up the blood until the wound heals." Krafchenko continued to fill the side of Mr. Lunn's mouth until his cheek resembled that of a squirrel in the late autumn.

Although in pain, Mr. Lunn appeared grateful. After a few minutes he rose from the couch and wiped his face with a towel Bert Bell provided him.

"Hank yu," he said to 'Dr. Fairchild,' shaking his hand.

"Oh," Krafchenko said. "It was nothing. A simple tooth is child's play."

Mr. Lunn grabbed his wallet and motioned to ask how much money Krafchenko would like for the procedure.

"No, no. I will accept no payment," Krafchenko said. "Consider it a public service. It is the least I can do."

Mr. Lunn bowed his head slightly and left the room. Krafchenko could not only pose as a doctor, but also get away with pulling out a man's tooth —

such charisma and confidence.

"Well, that takes care of that," Krafchenko said, rolling down his sleeves. "Gentlemen, you know your tasks. I will likely have to move to a different location. We will stay in touch. Eventually I will need to leave Winnipeg."

The men all left Krafchenko's apartment at the same time with their illicit bundles. No one said a word. They looked at each other with wide-eyed expressions. Someone who could, at a whim, pull out a tooth, could also likely inflect considerable damage if agitated or annoyed. Clearly, it was in everyone's best interest to do as Krafchenko said, or else.

As Benny drove him back, Marko wondered what he would do with the proceeds of Krafchenko's robbery. A dull throbbing pain appeared at his right temple.

Second Thoughts
December 7, 1913

Marko is holding scissors in his hand. Beside him at the kitchen table Anastasiya flips through a magazine. The gentle warm breeze through the window makes a wind chime tinkle.

"This one, Tata."

"All right, a horse." Marko carefully clips the picture out.

"And this one … a doggie."

"You try this time." Marko gives his daughter the scissors. She struggles with them, too large and cumbersome for her. Marko puts his hands around hers and helps clip out the photograph from the magazine.

Olena walks in from outside. She is carrying a bucket of water. "Clipping more pictures? I don't think I finished looking through that one."

"But Mama, the animal pictures are so pretty."

Olena smiles and rolls her eyes before placing the bucket on the counter. She is wearing her white summer dress, the one with the blue beads.

Anastasiya takes both pictures in one hand and Marko's in the other. "Can we put them up?"

Marko smiles and nods. How can he refuse? He allows Anastasiya to pull him to her room. She drops down to both knees in the corner. Monkeys, cats, snakes, rabbits, pigs, chickens …there are already fifteen to twenty pictures of animals pinned to the wall. Like the two in her hand, some pictures are from magazines. Yellowed and curled ones had been clipped from old newspapers. Anastasiya drew some by hand. Above them all is a crude sign written in red crayon: ANASTASIYA'S ZOO.

Anastasiya takes two pins from her dresser and carefully attaches the new additions beside a drawing of an elephant.

She snaps her fingers.

Marko stares at the photos.

She snaps her fingers again.

*****

Buxton snapped his fingers in Marko's face. "Hey, Marko. Snap out of it."

Marko shook his head. "Huh, what is it?"

"Bert and Benny finally showed up."

Marko looked up. Sure enough, the other two men sat at the other chairs at the grimy, uneven table in a speakeasy located at the end of a dead-end street near Annabella.

"We gotta do something," Benny said. "The cops are hassling me."

Grim-faced, all the men nodded.

The smoke-filled speakeasy featured four or five tables stretched across two rooms. Back in the day, decades ago, a well-to-do family likely resided in the home. The two rooms of the after-hours club could have been a dining room and a sitting room. Now it housed drunken men, some passed-out at their tables. If they had the gumption and stamina, only a few staggered steps away separated them from the sins of the flesh.

The clientele of the speakeasy looked rough. One wore an eye-patch, another an ugly scar on his forehead. One man smelled outright awful – likely due to an infected wound covered by a poor, soiled dressing. At one table a grimy-looking labourer with shabby, torn clothes picked his nose while his friend continually scratched his head.

The waiter, a man with extremely hairy forearms, placed four shots on their table.

"This place won't be confused with the fancy new Fort Garry Hotel," Bert said after the waiter left their table. "We should have met at the Moose Club."

"Forget it," Buxton said. "Kraf likes going there." He glanced around. "Alright, let's start at the beginning. Bert, how did your visit with Kraf go today?" The men spoke in hushed tones. No sense taking any chances, despite the sorry, drunken condition of the other patrons.

"Fine, I suppose," Bert said. "I got the woman clothes and things he asked for, but he agreed that dressing like a woman may not be the best approach. He actually thought we could take the train out of Winnipeg as a couple. What if someone saw me on the train with him?"

Benny poked Bert in the ribs. "New girlfriend? What would you say to your wife?"

Bert rolled his eyes. "I don't want to think about it. Thankfully we're not doing that. Buying all those clothes and cold cream and talcum powder was a waste of money."

Benny took a sip of his whiskey. "He sure moved to that house on College Avenue pretty quick."

"Yup," Bert said. "He likes moving around but I reckon all it's gonna do is raise suspicion. Who leaves an apartment after only a day or two? He even changed his alias again. Now he's Professor Andrews from St. John's College. While I was there he was helping the landlady with a real estate deal."

"The man's armed to the teeth," Bert continued. "I don't like how this is going. You been reading the papers? I bet he killed that bank manager. What he said about that Curly … maybe it's a load of malarkey?"

Benny slammed his fist. "Damn, I wish I never got mixed up in this, no thanks to you." Benny shot a quick glare to Bert.

"How did you meet him?" Marko asked Bert.

Bert shook his head slowly. "It was sometime in the middle of November. Not even a month ago. I met a friend around Portage and Main one day. He asked about work. I told him it was slow. If they ain't buildin' houses, then I can't decorate the ceilings. He took me over to the St. Regis Hotel a few blocks away. We go up to a room and there he was. But he went by the name of Mr. Ryan. Kraf asks me if I want to make money. I says I wouldn't mind and ask him what kind of job it is. He says, 'No, something a little easier than a job.' Then he goes on about robbing banks in Winnipeg and the one in Plum Coulee. I suppose he picked the Plum Coulee one."

"Dummy here told Kraf I'm a driver," Benny said, pointing his thumb to Bert. "Kraf needed to go down to Plum Coulee. Said he was going on a huntin' trip. He arranged for me to pick him up. We drove down, but he didn't do no huntin'. He was checking out the bank and had a gun with him." Benny shivered. "Hopefully he leaves town and never comes back. That means he'll want his money back soon."

"He ain't said nothing to me yet," Bert said. "I hid the loot he gave me in a sock and buried it in St. James, across town. No one will ever find it. Where'd you guys hide yer packages?"

"Just in the shed behind my place," Benny said. "I put it under a bunch of dead rabbits. No one will look there."

"I hid my stash in the southern part of the city," Buxton said.

Marko remained silent. He took a sip of whiskey and looked away at another table.

Buxton motioned to Marko. "What about you?"

Marko winced and forced out a stream of air. "I bury money," he said, looking down at his lap.

"So did I," Bert said. "We all planted our bundles somewhere. Big deal."

"I bury it last night at Krafchenko's new hideout on College Street."

Benny put his hand to his head and momentarily looked up in disbelieve. "What are you, crazy?"

"Keep it down," Bert said, grabbing Benny by the collar.

Benny looked around quickly and lowered his voice. "Why'd you go and do that?"

"I don't want that money around where I live," Marko said. "What if the kids find it? What will I say to my landlord? Anyway, it's Krafchenko's money, so he can deal with it." Damn. What a pile of money. Marko could have used it. He should have taken a few bills.

Benny shook his head while Bert crossed his arms.

"Wonderful," Buxton said. He nodded toward Benny. "What happened with you?"

Benny took a sip of rum and struck a match to light his cigarette. "After I dropped Bert off this afternoon the cops hauled me in."

"What did you tell them?" Buxton said. He straightened himself in his chair.

Benny furrowed his brow. "Nothing so far. But they know I know something. And they're giving me heat. I've been threatened that if I don't talk, they're gonna haul me in."

"They got nothing on you," Buxton said.

"How do you know? Maybe they do? My mom's sick. My dad's no better. I can't go in the hoosegow again...."

"I know the police have been on my tail," Bert said. "Everywhere I go, someone's been following me. It could be to a corner store, a tavern, it don't matter."

"The problem is none of you know how to lay low. That's what I've been doing," Buxton said. "Listen, Kraf and I go way, way back. The last thing he'll do is turn anyone in. Especially one of his own."

"There's another issue," Bert said. "Remember Mr. Lunn? Kraf ripped out his tooth. The word is that Lunn thinks Kraf's a fake. He's mulling over going to the police that Dr. Fairchild is actually Kraf."

Buxton crossed his arms and shook his head. "This is no good. Between the cops hounding Benny and Bert to this development with Lunn, we may have to come forward. That's the only way."

Marko remained still while Benny and Bert both nodded their heads. The men sat in silence for a moment while refills arrived from the hairy-armed waiter.

"If Lunn goes and tells them where Kraf is, we'll be mixed up in it," Buxton said.

"Why?" Marko asked.

Buxton frowned and slapped Marko in the back of the head. "Because Lunn and that landlady have seen us. What are you, stupid? They'll have descriptions of us and that'll be it. Then the lady from the College Avenue hideout will corroborate everything. We'll be considered confederates and they'll lock us all up. The way the justice system is around here, maybe all of us will hang."

Benny downed his shot. His face turned red.

"But if we come forward," Buxton said, "then we can make it sound like we were not really involved. We can say we were scared of Kraf or something."

"We wouldn't be lying," Bert said. "I'm scared. What about you Marko?"

Feeling his guts tightening with each passing moment, Marko nodded.

Buxton slowly rubbed his chin and glanced away from the table for a moment. He started to laugh then slammed back his half-filled shot. "This is what we'll do."

The three other men moved their heads closer to the table.

"Marko hiding that bundle ... that'll work out perfectly for us. So far only Benny and Bert have been approached or followed by the cops. One of you has to fess up. That will put you in the clear."

"I'll do it," Bert said. "I'll even bring my money to the station. It's a few bills short, but no one will notice."

"No, it has to be Benny first."

Benny frowned. "Why me?"

"Because they hauled you in already. They haven't touched any of us," Buxton said. "You go with your money and tell them you're scared and everything. Tell them you know he's in the North End but you don't know the address. Be vague. Tell them Bert does. Tell them that you and Bert go way back and you've been friends for a long time. Tell them Bert's also scared and wants to help with the investigation. Both of you have an out because you just met Kraf a little while ago. That makes you look innocent and makes Kraf look like he took advantage of you."

"Then, shortly after, maybe the next day, Bert, you go to the police station with your bundle. Tell them you're the man they want to talk to. Tell them you're scared of a reprisal from Kraf and that he planted money outside."

"The cops will show up, arrest Kraf, find the money and it's all done. You can direct them to where I hid my bundle. That way they get Kraf and all the money."

"What about you?" Bert asked Buxton. "How come you don't come to the police, too?"

"Because I'm too close to Kraf. It would be too obvious. Besides, I don't think they've been following me. No sense in complicating things. Both of you will be witnesses and get off scot-free because you did nothing. You weren't in Plum Coulee that day."

"And me?" Marko said.

"You're done. You have no money. It's been planted already. Mixing you up will complicate things. You're a foreigner, so no one might believe you."

"Oh yeah?" Benny said, pointed his finger at Buxton. "What if we mention you to the police?"

Buxton put his cigarette out on the table. "I'll deny it and you'll have nothing on me. If you go pointing fingers, it will make you look suspicious. Remember, the cops were following you, not me or even Marko."

After a long silence, Buxton folded his arms. "So it's a plan?"

Sweet Justine
December 11, 1913

Mildred sat with her mother at the elegant grand piano in the conservatory. It felt good to be with her to plunk away and sing a few songs. Only recently did she have the gumption to sit at the piano with Mother. To think they used to do it regularly, perhaps several times a week. But since the incident their personal time together practically ceased.

Mother practiced the piano almost every day, sometimes for hours at a time. An accomplished pianist, it took up her time like knitting or other handwork occupied other ladies her age.

Located at the rear of the mansion and far enough away from the hustle and bustle of the kitchen area, the conservatory provided peace and tranquility. A true refuge in the home. North facing, it displayed a spectacular view of the spacious back yard through several high windows. Sometimes just sitting in the conservatory and staring at the birds and trees calmed the nerves. The walls of the large room held oil paintings of famous composers and a smattering of photos from recitals and performances. A few featured Mother when she was a younger woman living in Ontario. Luxurious couches and chairs accompanied with carved wooden side tables offered plenty of seating. On many occasions Mother hosted meetings for the Women's Musical Club of Winnipeg.

"Do you remember this one?" Gertrude said. She played a few bars.

"Of course," Mildred said. "You used to sing this to me when I was a little girl." She smiled.

"Join me. I'll play the left hand, you play the right."

Mildred arched her back and began to play alongside her mother. They both sang together:

"O'Malley came back after six months at sea
Pinin' for the touch of his new bride, Justine
She weren't at the pier, nor waiting at home
Dear Lord, he couldn't wait to give her the …

Shirts and socks he'd worn earning a living
Catching fish, swabbing decks for wee little pay
He went to her mother's, hoping for luck
Had Justine found a new man to …
Oh, no! Oh, no! Where did O'Malley's sweet Justine go?
He kissed her goodbye on Southampton Dock
It was the last time he laid eyes on her
Before another bloke's key fit in her lock"

They both stopped playing at the same time, laughing and giggling.

"Mother! Shame on you," Mildred said in a faux scolding tone. "Introducing something so lurid to an impressionable young girl. Your daughter, no less."

"What's the problem?" Gertrude said with a playful wink. "You turned out just fine, did you not?"

After a pause Mildred felt her cheek and looked down.

Gertrude squeezed her daughter's hand. "I'm sorry, dear … I didn't mean anything in a bad way."

Mildred nodded and they embraced.

When they broke, Gertrude rose. "Well, that was lovely. We should do it more often."

"I would like that."

"Very good. Well … I should prepare for an engagement I have with your father tonight. Seems we are going to a show. Have a good day."

Mildred watched her leave the room. She continued to play on the piano for a few more minutes before she also left the conservatory. While walking past the kitchen she saw several of the house staff all gathered around in the hallway.

The staff stepped aside when Mildred approached revealing Gladys holding that day's *Manitoba Free Press*. The headline at the bottom read: *KRAFCHENKO, DESPERADO, CAPTURED BY POLICE IN WINNIPEG HOUSE.*

"They finally caught him," Gladys said. She gave the newspaper to Mildred. "The police burned the midnight oil to find him."

"Thank goodness," Mildred said. "No one could ever be safe while that criminal was at large. It's all everyone has been talking about."

"Yes, but did he do it?" a younger staff member said. "Do they have enough against him? I heard they don't have much evidence."

Mildred frowned slightly. "I think he's guilty. He has a checkered past.

He had previously been incarcerated. I imagine the authorities have enough evidence against him. Why else would they make such an effort to apprehend him?"

"Oh, I hope he's not guilty," another maid said, a cute young one with curly blonde hair and dimples. "He's quite handsome..." Several maids squirmed and giggled. The cute maid crunched her apron and brought it to her face, now red as a tomato.

Mildred paged through the paper and spotted Krafchenko's photo. "He certainly is rugged-looking...," she said. A wry smile broke over her face. The women staff went into another round of giggles and laughs.

Just then the chime for the front door signaled a guest. Immediately the house staff broke off and went about their tasks. One answered the front door for William.

Mildred smiled and held William's hand. "How was your visit with Thomas Kelly? How is the parliament building construction progressing?"

"Uh, just fine," William said in a dour tone. "Are you ready to go?"

"Not quite yet. I was just with Mother. I shan't take long. Please, come in." William stared off in the distance, emotionless. "Are you well? Is something bothering you?"

"Oh, nothing. Just a drab day, I suppose. Going out with you will certainly boost my spirits." He could only provide a weak smile.

Just before Mildred left, she held up the newspaper. "Oh, did you hear. Krafchenko has been captured."

"Yes, the news is everywhere."

Mildred sat in a chair in the sitting room and scanned the newspaper article. "Says here he went without a fuss. A house on College Avenue in the North End. All he said was 'It's all up. I guess I'll come quietly. I didn't intend to shoot anyway.' Oh my, the rogue had two loaded guns in his room! Thankfully none of the officers were hurt. They certainly had enough of them. Twenty police officers were present for the arrest. They even found bundles of stolen cash buried in the yard. Quite sloppy on his part, I would say. Why would he bury money he stole so close to his hideout? Seems a little too obvious, does it not? Oh well, I suppose hardened criminals don't think straight."

William took Mildred's hand. "From what I heard he was not that bad of a chap. I suspect he was set up. Like you said, who would hide money in such a sloppy fashion? There is still over a thousand dollars not accounted for."

"The women-folk are certainly attracted to him. There's something about the man, I will grant you that. Funny, though. The police captured him at 9:50 yesterday morning. He was scheduled to meet a friend at 10:00. Looks like they just got him."

"So it seems," William said.

Wound

December 21, 1913

With Christmas around the corner, massive red bows adorned the entrance and exit to the Spencer estate. Smaller red bows decorated the base of each window and along the staircase leading up to the front door. With about two feet of snow on the ground, some of the windows had been difficult to reach. Marko shivered remembering when he mounted the decorations on some of the more difficult spots.

Mildred opened the front door and smiled. "Come in. Come in. It is frightfully cold out."

"Good to see you again." Marko stamped his feet in the front entrance of the mansion. Wreathes and boughs from pine trees gave the home a smell of the outdoors. Red and gold garland draped the staircase.

Mildred wore a lovely green dress accented by a red bow across the middle. Her patent leather red shoes gleamed. Although usually brought up, Mildred's hair hung past her shoulders. When she turned her head, tiny diamond earrings gleamed and twinkled like distant stars.

"I'm all dressed up because William and I will be attending an engagement at his father's home in a few hours. But come, let's do your lesson. Here, let me take your coat."

Although Marko had seen the Christmas tree for a few weeks now, it still awed him. Positioned near the window and decorated with a variety of ribbons and silks, the tree stood a full ten feet. The waxy remains of candles lit in the evenings decked the ends of various branches. Frail, yet intricately designed glass ornaments hung from the branches. Coloured red and green, they almost seemed to be arranged in a particular order depending on the decorator's specific plan. A large red and green star at the very top appeared to be porcelain or some type of ceramic.

Still clutching his books, Marko stood in the center of the lavish living room.

Mildred's long locks from her fancy hairdo swayed to and fro whenever she turned her head. "You can have a seat. You don't have to wait for me to tell you."

Marko sat on the soft couch. She sat next to him. He could smell her sweet perfume.

"Christmas is such a busy time. Do you have any family back home in Austria?"

"I'm not Austrian. I'm a Ukrainian from Galicia. Austria controls Galicia."

Mildred tilted her head slightly. She didn't seem to follow.

Marko continued. "I lived on a farm and had a good life. Hard work, but good. I have two sisters. My father was good man. He teach me many things. I learn how to fix everything. But mother and father, they dead now. Sisters are older and helped run the farm but soon I ran it on own."

"Did you start your own family?"

Marko nodded but looked away. "Yes. Wife and daughter. But they are gone."

"I'm sorry to hear that." Mildred touched his hand. "Perhaps we should start?"

Over the next hour the two worked on understanding what Mildred called irregular words. He was baffled by the senseless arrangement of some words such as 'laugh' and 'build.'

"Why letter 'u' in laugh? Why 'ph' make *fff* sound? Why 'u' in build?" Marko asked, scratching his head.

She smiled and nodded. "I know. You are correct. It really does not make any sense. It's certainly not phonetic. The only thing I can say is that's the way it is. The English language evolved over the years and there are certain rules, but sometimes it doesn't follow the rules. Some words stand out on their own. The only thing you can do is try to memorize the difficult words. The more you see those words and write those words, the more you will remember them. Like everything else, it only comes with practice. Here, let me write a list of words on separate pieces of paper. I want you to try to read them aloud, use them in a sentence, then write them down." She held up one word at a time. They included 'knew,' 'know,' 'their,' 'eight,' and other rule-breaking words. He had difficulty with each.

The last piece of paper had 'wound.'

Marko knew the 'ou' combination made the sound like in the word 'ouch.' "Wound," he said. "I wound my pocket watch. That is easy one, no?"

Mildred looked at the word on the paper and giggled into her hand. "Oh my, you are correct. When I first wrote this word down, I intended it to be pronounced 'wound' like the wound someone would get on their body."

Marko squinted his eyes. He didn't understand.

"I'm sorry. Some words in the English language have two meanings and can be pronounced two different ways. This word can indeed mean 'wound' like the way you wound your pocket watch this morning. But it can also mean 'wound' like someone sustaining a wound in an accident. Perhaps we should set this one aside for now."

He tried to repeat the different pronunciations of 'wound' several times to himself, shaking his head at the new language's absurdity.

"I think we are finished our lesson for today," Mildred said. She straightened the various books and papers they had worked with.

"Two meanings," he said. "I wound my watch." He held out his thumb from his otherwise closed right hand to count. Then he stuck out his index finger. "She has a wound."

Mildred stopped and reached for her own wound on her right cheek. She dropped her head down and turned away.

"Oh! I sorry. I no mean to talk about your…"

Mildred exhaled and closed her eyes. After a short moment she regained her composer. She reached over and grabbed his hand and gave it a reassuring squeeze. "That's fine. I know you did not mean anything by it. There are times recently I actually forget about it."

She didn't move her hand. He slowly brought his other hand on top of her hand and looked into her pretty brown eyes. She looked away, but after a brief moment accepted his deep stare.

"I no ask…" Marko paused to correct himself. "I *never* asked you because I think it's wrong. Not my business. My mother said it important to talk … to talk about things that bother. It eases the mind." Mildred pressed her lips together and looked down. "How you get your mark? You don't have to tell me. That's okay. But if it helps you to clear your mind, you can."

Mildred withdrew her hand from Marko's clutch and ran her fingertips along the right side of her face, down the entire length of the large, deep scar. She straightened herself on the couch and swept her wayward hair to behind her ears. She placed her hands in her lap.

"It happened one year ago. Longer actually, this spring it will be two." Mildred paused and fidgeted with her hair. "A few years ago my family went on a holiday to England. We have several relatives in London and various other cities. We spent most of the time with Uncle Felix and Aunt Mabel. It was the summer of 1911. We had a wonderful time. I had not been to England since I was a child and much enjoyed spending time in the lush English gardens. We went to numerous shows and musical engagements.

"Originally we were only going to stay for a few months and come back in late August, but somehow Muriel caught the eye of a theatrical producer. The man offered her a small role in a musical in the West End. The Queen's Theatre, I believe it was. She was mainly part of the chorus line and only had two speaking lines – hardly anything, really – but she wanted to stay. She said it would better her career. Another notch on her resume, if you will. You see, my sister was an accomplished performer. She could do it all: sing, dance, act. And to Mother and especially Father, it was like she could do no wrong."

She paused for a moment and stared at the clock on the mantle, but continued on. "I'm being too hard on dear Muriel. After all, she was naturally gifted. No one could doubt that. Not even I. Maybe I was jealous, I don't know. Muriel was always better at everything. She was younger and prettier and had a way about her. The moment she entered a room, she was the center of attention. Like a bouquet of freshly cut flowers. She always knew what to say and what to do. I'm convinced my parents thought she was perfect. Of course that made me the afterthought, but….

"The play was scheduled to run until the spring. Father and Mother went back to Winnipeg at their scheduled time. Father could not stay away from his businesses for too long. It was expected Mother would accompany him on the voyage home. The opportunity was too much for Muriel to pass up. It was decided the children would stay behind to be with Uncle Felix and Aunt Mabel. They wanted me to remain to watch over Muriel and Andrew. Andrew was about fifteen at the time. It was decided he would enroll in a school in September. I was teaching here in the North End. Father made arrangements for the school to hold my job as I would be missing a large portion of the school year. Ha! Originally it was even suggested that I home-school Andrew while waiting for Muriel to finish her commitment, but of course I refused. Why should I be his handmaiden? Instead, I wiled away the fall and winter months at tea parties and other get-togethers."

Mildred smiled. "I even had a gentleman caller who was quite courteous and doting. We went for dinners and long walks in parks and gardens. Then I found out he was married and, well, that was the end of that. I was not going to be made out to be a harlot.

"The days changed to weeks, the weeks to months. Come March, Muriel's play finally came to an end. She earned the notch on her resume, although I suspect it was the oily theatrical producer who carved a notch on his bed post. Quid pro quo, I suppose."

Marko cocked his head to the side. "Kid po co?"

Mildred smiled. "I'm sorry. Quid pro quo means tit for tat. Anyway, Andrew continued to do well in school, although he did find himself getting in the odd bit of mischief. He discovered a taste for scotch. Although he turned sixteen while we were away, he was still far too young in my opinion. But he was the little brother of Muriel, so he was fawned and pampered. He would sit with the men after dinner each night to enjoy a smoke. He was acting like a man but was still immature."

Mildred turned her head and looked off in the distance. "Finally, it was time to go home. In thanks for keeping us in their manor for such a long visit, Father arranged for Uncle Felix and Aunt Mabel to accompany us for the voyage. It was Father who suggested we come home in grand fashion. After all, Muriel was a star in the West End. No simple steam liner for us. No, we were coming back in style: aboard the *Titanic* for its maiden voyage across the Atlantic."

"Oh…" Marko could not hide his shock.

"I must admit, I was also excited by the possibility. Although I made the best of the time I had in England, I wanted to go home. But to go home on the biggest, finest boat in the world was like a special treat that would make up for my forced exile.

"But the crowds … there were thousands and thousands of people in Southampton in early April. I heard someone say there was a hundred thousand people at the launch. That is as if you took the entire population of Winnipeg and plopped them all on the dock. It was such a festive scene.

"And the liner itself was something to behold. Naturally Father had us travel First Class. He always insisted, and I have to agree, that it really is the only way to travel.

"Our stateroom, which the three of us shared, featured a private bath and an adjoining parlour room. It was absolutely beautiful. There were two separate bedrooms. I shared one with Muriel. Beautiful furniture and tastefully decorated, lace quilts and pretty curtains, it was everything I would have wanted for my own bedroom here at home. I'm sure it cost Father thousands. Uncle and Auntie were in the next stateroom over.

"It was not just the staterooms. Everything about the ship was fantastic.

The dinners were exquisite. For the meals everyone dressed in their finery. There was enough jewelry present at each dinner to purchase Prince Edward Island, I'm certain. Of course Muriel was the center of attention wherever she sashayed. Unattached men hung off her like the clouds in the sky. It made me feel a little like a frump, but what was I to do? Thankfully I had enough money prior to the voyage to purchase appropriate evening gowns and daywear.

"The facilities, at least in First Class, were the best of the best. I was even told that Second Class would have rivaled First Class on other liners, for that matter. The reading room was in a lovely Georgian-style theme with rose coloured carpeting and pink draperies. Absolutely lovely for tea and coffee with Aunt Mabel and some of the other ladies on the voyage.

"Muriel and I generally got along. We whiled away many hours talking and enjoying each other's company. She was so excited about the future and I felt good for her. Of course she also spent many evenings dancing the night away with various potential suitors.

"Andrew continued to be caught between being a boy and being a man. He was considered too young by most standards, but clearly did not belong with the other children. He ended up spending considerable time in the men's smoking lounge with a few others who were also bound for Winnipeg. One of my father's business associates, Thomas McCaffray, managed to sneak him around and provide him with the occasional Scotch and cognac. Uncle Felix did not watch Andrew closely.

"For the next ten days we had a lovely voyage. We met some truly extraordinary and successful people. Muriel was having the time of her life. For Andrew it was almost a coming of age. Each night it seemed he was tipsy.

"That fateful night after dinner Muriel and I sat in the reading room. We did this each night. Usually after a few cups of tea Aunt Mabel would call it a night after which Muriel would change into something glamorous and continue on." Mildred smiled and shrugged her shoulders. "That evening she convinced me to go dancing. She leant me a beautiful pink sequin gown adorned with white ribbons and exotic feathers. Quite daring, I must say. It featured a swooping back that came down to the small of my back." Marko raised his eyebrows trying to visualized the dress in his mind.

"I danced and danced that night. I had a smashing time, the most fun I had in several months. Oh, my trip to England was wonderful, but I never really had an opportunity to let my hair down like I did on that evening in the middle of the Atlantic Ocean. The band was marvelous.

"Around ten in the evening we had enough and decided to retire to our stateroom. I'm not sure where Andrew went earlier that evening, but I suspect he was smoking and drinking with some of the Winnipeg contingent. In any case, McCaffray and two of his associates, Thomas Beattie and John Ross, pounded on our entrance. After Muriel opened the door Andrew fell from their arms to the floor. Drunk. Mother and Father would not have approved.

"The men threw Andrew in his bed but then produced a bottle of sherry. I wanted them to leave. It really was not appropriate for them to be in our stateroom. Although they were gentlemen, they were inebriated and somewhat older than us. But of course Muriel let them stay until the bottle was dry.

"By that time it was eleven. Unfortunately Muriel became quite tipsy. She would get flirty when she was drunk and I could see it was having an effect on the men. Thankfully, through my strong urging, the men went on their way. Of course I had to threaten to summon Uncle Felix and a battery of stewards if they did not leave our stateroom. I remember when I went to close our door, the top of Muriel's dress *accidentally* slipped off revealing her naked bosom.

"So Muriel and I had a row. Very disappointing." Mildred raised her hand to wipe a tear. Marko moved closer to hold Mildred's other hand. "A perfect evening, spoiled. I told Muriel how inappropriate and embarrassing her actions were. She called me a prude. We went back and forth. Now that I think back, it was such a waste of time. She was so drunk, it was obvious she would not listen to reason.

"But she kept going on and on. 'You are just going to be an old maid.' 'Why don't you ever want to have any fun?' 'I knew we should not have went dancing.' All the while her dress was barely on her body. I slapped her and she fell to the floor."

Mildred turned away while she continued. "She rose up slowly from the floor of the cabin and began to laugh. It started a slow chuckle, but then ended up in a full howl. 'Do I offend you, big sister?' she said. 'What's the matter? Are you jealous of this?' she said and grabbed her bosom. Then with a flick of her wrist she dropped the rest of her dress down to the ground. To my amazement, she was completely naked. The entire evening she never wore any under garments. Like a cheap call girl.

"Infuriated, I demanded she go to sleep. I had enough. Still in her heels, naked as a jay bird, she sat down and continued her tirade. I could not be bothered and ignored her. I changed into my sleeping attire and prepared for bed while she rattled on.

"Right at that moment we heard an awful scrapping sound and the ship lurched. That was the exact moment the ship struck the iceberg. We did not know, of course, and assumed it was something to do with the engines and what not. Ignorant of the ship's impending doom, we retired. The alcohol fully took hold of Muriel and I was able to ease her into her bed. I didn't bother dressing her. I shut off the light and retired to my own bed.

"A few minutes later I heard Muriel frantically stumble and bumble while she tried to locate the water closet in the pitch darkness. She vomited all the alcohol from her stomach. Probably for the better, I thought, as I drifted off to sleep. I was extremely exhausted and had quite enough of my sister at that point and dreaded the thought if Aunt Mabel had heard our row.

"I don't know how long I was sleeping – it could not have been very long – when I was awoken to wild banging and thrashing on the entrance to our stateroom. It scared me at first. It sounded like someone was trying to gain access. Suddenly, thinking of Muriel's deplorable condition, I sprung up and turned on the light to the cabin. The banging and shouting was incessant. Muriel wasn't in her bed. I put on my robe but was still reluctant to open the cabin door. The man on the other side insisted we get up and prepare to leave. The ship was sinking.

"I opened the door to a scene of complete mayhem. Porters and stewards attempted to raise everyone from their slumber. Some passengers were already dressed and wore life preservers. The steward at my door was as white as a sheet, like he had seen a ghost. From his expression I could not doubt the urgency and severity of the situation.

"Panic set in. What was I to do?" Mildred spoke at a quicker pace. "The door to the water closet remained shut. That's where she had to be. It was locked. I pounded on the door, but there was no response. She was likely sleeping off her drunk on the floor. I ran to Andrew's room and tried to shake him out of his stupor. He was still fully dressed. After several long minutes Andrew's eyes opened, glassy and red. He was still drunk. It then dawned on me that not much time had passed from when I fell asleep. Judging from Andrew's condition he was perhaps also infested with some sort of opiate.

"Fortunately, Andrew began to stir. I ran to the lavatory and pounded on the door screaming for Muriel to open it, but there was still no response. By then all my banging and yelling caught the attention of Andrew. He also tried to rouse Muriel but there was no sign of life on the other side.

"Andrew encouraged me to go on ahead and that he would take care of Muriel. I steadfastly refused. My sixteen-year-old brother was not in a correct frame of mind to care for himself, much less Muriel.

"A steward stepped into the cabin to give us a last warning. Most of the lifeboats had already launched. If we didn't reach the deck immediately, we would be left behind. We explained the situation, but the steward did not have a key and seemed to be in a frantic state.

"Despite my protests, Andrew convinced the steward to take me away while he would remain to try to get Muriel out of the washroom. The steward threw a life vest over me and grabbed my arm in a rough manner, manhandling me all the way to the deck. I fought against him the entire way. I didn't want to leave Muriel to die, but he was not going to relax his firm grasp."

Mildred stopped and her voice began to crack. Tears filled her eyes. Marko tightened his hold on her hand. She continued, but in a quieter tone between sobs.

"When we reached the deck, the steward directed me to a lifeboat. The moment he released me I turned around to run back to the cabin. But in my haste and because I was wearing a bulky life vest, I was clumsy and fell awkwardly. Unable to catch my fall, the side of my face smashed into a jagged metal railing.

"I got up, my life vest stained with my own blood. I must have looked like someone from an industrial accident. The other nearby passengers and crew were shocked to see me. I was led on to a life boat. I screamed for Andrew and Muriel and pleaded for the crew to wait, but they lowered the life boat. Someone gave me some linen, maybe a table cloth or a dress, I don't know. I pressed it against my face. I lost a considerable amount of blood and the conditions were not the best."

Mildred regained her composure. "We rowed away from the doomed ship. A few life boats had yet to be launched. But there were so many people. There was no chance everyone aboard the liner could fit on the remaining life boats. My cheek ached. It was cold. It would take several hours before we were rescued by that other ship.

"A doctor on board the rescue ship sutured my cheek, but it was beyond repair. The damage was indeed permanent. I rested on a smelly bunk with a straw mattress. My mind reeled at the stunning change of events. One moment I was enjoying myself with my sister, dancing the night away. The next I was bleeding, disfigured and separated from my siblings.

"Of course Andrew survived the ordeal. He visited me at my bunk many hours later. His face was bruised and beaten. He somehow managed to jump on one of the last life boats. There was a bit of a frenzy and the scene became violent. It appears some passengers did not take kindly to a young man attempting to find passage when there were women and children more worthy. How ironic. Andrew spent the entire time on *Titanic* in the company of adults and indeed tried to emulate adulthood, yet when it came to life and death, that same membership into adulthood worked against him. Andrew was never the same since the tragedy. Now he seems so distant and removed. Perhaps he's guilty that he was never able to get Muriel to open the washroom door. I don't doubt he would have traded places with her in an instant. Later we learned Aunt Mabel made it to a lifeboat. Uncle Felix did not.

"Father and Mother were naturally beside themselves. In some ways, I think Father blamed me for what happened. Naked and cold, poor Muriel likely drowned in the darkness of the water closet.

"And that is how I received the wound on my face."

Letting go of Mildred's hand, Marko exhaled audibly at the conclusion of her fantastic story. No wonder she didn't like talking about what happened. "I'm so sorry to hear your story."

Mildred glanced at Marko, her eyes still red with emotion. "Thank you. Your mother was correct, it does help to ease the mind."

He stood up and gathered his books and papers. "I go now." She followed him to the door and helped him with his jacket. Before he opened the door to leave, he reached into his pocket and pulled out a beautifully wrapped box with a purple bow. He handed it to Mildred. "For you. How you say? Merry Christmas and Happy New Year. Thank you for help. I read better now. Talk better, too."

Mildred took a step back in amazement, her face flush. "Oh my ... you should not have gotten me anything."

"No, no, you take," Marko insisted.

Mildred accepted it with a curt smile. Carefully and slowly, she undid the bow, unwrapped the gift and opened the box. Her eyes twinkled like glitter on a Christmas tree. With a broad smile she pulled out a piano-shaped jewelry box. She put her hand to her mouth. "Oh, my. A new box to replace the old one I discarded. You shouldn't have, the cost...."

"It cost very little. It's the same one. I took it out of the garbage and fixed it."

Mildred turned it around in her hand. The shiny new hinges reflected the light. He had repainted the outside of the box. She opened the box and it instantly played a tinny-sounding tune. The ballerina, a different figurine from before, spun in one spot, like she said it did years ago. Instead of the original green, brilliant red velvet lined the interior.

"I find parts from other boxes. Music, dancer, everything. I found fabric in garbage behind a furniture store. It's not the same and not new, but…"

Mildred hugged Marko, her eyes red from delight. "Thank you very much. This is a wonderful gift."

Dear Fanica
January 11, 1914

Mildred opened the service door beside the kitchen. Marko gave her a weak smile. He looked dirty and filthy after working in the garage for several hours. "Have you completed your tasks for today?"

"Da … er … yes. I'm finished. I go now." His nose wet from mucus, Marko cupped his reddened hands up to his mouth to blow on them. The red and white tips of his ears also needed immediate warmth.

"Oh, dear. Please step inside for a moment before you leave. Warm up. You look chilled to the bone."

She saw him staring at a tray of uneaten meats and bread. "You did not stop for a lunch break, did you?"

"No, too cold to sit. Can't eat lunch if frozen." Sniffing, he rubbed his hands to get the circulation going.

"Oh." Mildred held her hand to her chest. "Well, I suppose. Silly me, I should have known that. Here, clean up and have a bite before you go, will you?"

Marko washed his hands and arms, although he still left some oil and grease on the towel provided for him.

Gladys prepared a plate for Marko and set it on the table in the kitchen.

Mildred watched Marko devour the sandwich, complete with noisy grunts and swallows. "Thank you for being able to come today. I know Father prefers no work to be done on a Sunday, but the repairs needed to be completed before winter took hold and the vehicle was stored away."

He wiped his runny nose on his sleeve. "Repairs were not hard. Replace headlight. Stop the backfiring. Change oil."

Mildred nodded. Such a hard worker. He never seemed to complain and just went about his tasks. Definitely not like other immigrants.

"How is your English assignment coming along?" Mildred asked.

"Difficult," Marko said, one cheek stuffed with food. "Hard putting words together."

"Yes, but that is the next step. It's one thing to be able to spell individual words correctly, but you need to learn how to string those words together into meaningful, coherent sentences. That's why I wanted you to write a letter."

"But who I write to?" Marko finished his sandwich. A crumb clung to the corner of his mouth.

"Do you not have a relative you can write to? An aunt, an uncle? Anyone?" Marko looked down at his plate.

"Well," Mildred said, "just pretend. In fact, there was one such letter in the newspaper yesterday." Mildred picked up Saturday's *Manitoba Free Press* on the counter. She turned to the page and began to read it aloud:

"'My dear and beloved Fanica. Accept my love and be healthy. My dear, do not believe all that which you read in the papers. I am not guilty of the trouble which the papers write about. And now, my dear Gipsy, I send this money to you. No one should know where it comes from. Hide this money and stay at Graham until I would send someone to bring you where I am. Do you understand, my dear? May God be with you. I cannot write to you sooner, because the police are after me like the devil. This man is a friend, and he does not know what he is giving.'"

Mildred stopped reading. "See," she said, "something like that."

Marko furrowed his brow. "Who wrote that letter?"

"John Krafchenko. You know … the fugitive. They published the lovely letter he wrote to his wife. The police must have found it when they apprehended him."

Marko nodded. "I try to write a letter for next week."

"Very good. Although, you must be concerned…"

"Why?" he said with a bemused smile.

"Have you not heard? John Krafchenko escaped from jail early yesterday morning. Every police officer in Winnipeg is looking for him. See." Mildred showed him the headline at the bottom of the first page of the newspaper: *KRAFCHENKO MAKES SENSATIONAL ESCAPE.*

All the colour left Marko's face. His breathing became erratic and he fidgeted in his seat.

"Is everything alright?" Mildred asked.

"No, everything fine. I go now. Thank you for sandwich. It very good."

Obviously troubled by the news regarding Krafchenko, Marko quickly made his way for the door.

Audience With the Snake
January 15, 1914

Bundled-up, Marko stood on the corner of Wellington and Agnes. He felt his fingers beginning to numb. The cold temperature kept the streets quiet. He took out at his pocket watch. 7:00 pm. Where was Buxton? If Krafchenko escaped from jail then he must have murdered the banker in Plum Coulee. Why escape if you are innocent? And the jails here … they were like fortresses, no?

A few minutes later John Buxton arrived. He looked in every direction, perhaps to make sure no one followed or watched. The cloak of darkness helped.

"Come with me," Buxton urged. They walked a short distance to Toronto Street where Buxton turned. He led Marko to a three-storey apartment building called the Burris Block not far from Wellington Avenue.

"Here we are," Buxton said. He continued to scan the vicinity for any prying eyes. "Remember now, you don't know about this location. You've never been here. You know nothing."

"Da," Marko said, nodding his head. Earlier that day Buxton had waited outside the factory for Marko. He said Krafchenko wanted to see him. Buxton wouldn't say why. Marko didn't want to help the man, but same as before, did he really have a choice?

Marko stopped before entering the apartment block.

"Wait," he said, "Kraf knows someone turned him in the last time, doesn't he?"

"Of course he does," Buxton said."

"Bert and Benny…?"

"Kraf has a long memory, so I'd be worried if I was them. As for you, I don't know."

Marko swallowed and took a deep breath. He could feel a headache coming on. His right temple began to throb.

"You're not worried? Doesn't he suspect…?"

"He doesn't suspect me. I wasn't directly involved in his capture. I didn't

go to the police nor was I a witness at the preliminary hearing. Besides …
I helped him escape by setting up the lawyer and the cop that Kraf turned.
How do ya think he got out of jail? It was an inside job I helped put together.
For that, Kraf will be eternally grateful."

One day Buxton turns his friend into the police. The next he arranges for
his escape. He couldn't be trusted.

The two men walked up the steps of the apartment building and down
to the end of a hallway to Suite #4. Buxton knocked on the door three times
quickly, paused, then knocked two times.

A tall, balding man opened the door slowly just a few inches to peer out.

"It's me Johnny. I have a guest with me," Buxton said.

The man opened the door the rest of the way and Buxton and Marko
quickly slipped inside the dark apartment. Marko felt damp with nervous
sweat. The balding man immediately closed and latched the door shut. Why
no lights?

"Marko, this is John Westlake. This is his apartment. John, this is Marko
Gobinski. He's the man Kraf wants to see."

The two men shook hands. Westlake did not look particularly imposing.
In fact, he seemed like a regular fellow. The man had not shaved in a few days
and had bags under his eyes. Why was everyone in Winnipeg named John?

From the tiny apartment entrance, two closed doors lead to other areas
of the apartment.

"He's in here." Westgate opened one of the doors. A few candles in the
room provided some light, but not enough for reading or much else for that
matter.

"Ya gotta pay your electricity bill," Buxton said, half-teasing, to Westgate.
"You know there's very little light in the winter."

"I know, I know. Once I get paid. I'm a little busy at the moment, you
know…"

The three men entered the room. Marko took a deep breath. Krafchenko
lay on a couch bed in the corner of the room, his leg up on a small table. The
flickering candles gave him a devilish look.

"Marko, my good friend. Good to see you again. Have a seat. John, pour
the man a drink."

Marko's heart thumped like a knocking engine. Expecting fire and
brimstone and bracing for physical pain, Krafchenko's bubbly greeting
unnerved him. But then again, perhaps that was just Krafchenko's style.

Expect the unexpected.

Marko sat at a chair not far from the couch, but far enough to be away from Krafchenko's reach. John Westgate filled several glasses with whiskey and passed them around.

Krafchenko raised his glass. "A toast to a successful escape," he said before downing the booze in one shot. Westgate immediately refilled everyone's glass.

Krafchenko definitely looked worse for wear. Not wearing socks, his ankle had ballooned to twice the size. White cloth tied together with black cotton bandaged both hands. Wearing an undershirt, Krafchenko's chest and muscles still looked intimidating.

"Nice, eh?" Krafchenko said, pointing to his ankle. "I also burst my knee and my back is bruised up. I cut my hands going down that infernal rope. They got me some medical supplies, so I fixed myself up as best as I could. Mr. Westgate here has been putting ointment on my back. He fidgets too much in bed, so I had to kick him out."

Marko glanced at Westgate. Pale and expressionless, the man stared at the ground. Being forced to sleep on the ground or on a chair would account for his rough appearance.

Krafchenko downed his shot and beckoned Westgate to pour another. Krafchenko played with the snake ring on his little finger. He lit a cigarette and blew the smoke into the air emphatically. No doubt he was a survivor. On the wrong side of the law, but a survivor, no less. Like a snake, slithering in the bush, hypnotizing his prey before pouncing. And just when you thought you had him, he'd be gone.

"You were the one who hid the money on Collage Avenue, were you not?" Krafchenko said.

"I ... I ... no." Marko stumbled for his words, fidgeting with his hat at the same time.

"Do you play poker?" Krafchenko asked.

"N-no."

"Well, you better not." Krafchenko blew out another stream of smoke. "You see, in poker you must evaluate your hand against that of your opponents. The thing is, you do not know what they are holding. But if you look at their mannerisms and gestures, you can make a calculated guess. You can tell when they are sitting on a good hand, or simply bluffing. I can tell what an opponent will do and the strength of their hand by just looking at their actions. And judging by your actions, I can read you like a book. You hid the money, my friend." Krafchenko forced a crooked smile.

"I no do anything. I no rob bank. I no want money."

"That money was not yours. It was mine. You were supposed to take care of it for me. When the police found it in the same yard where I was staying, well, that does not look good, does it?"

"You're a smart man," Marko said. "No one would think you hid the money there."

Krafchenko downed his shot and in one motion hurled the glass at Marko. Not expecting the move, the glass smashed against the right side of Marko's head. Blood dripped from the new wound. Instead of a dull pain, the side of his head now pounded like a sledgehammer. Despite being seriously injured, Krafchenko could still exact punishment with the fury of a cobra. Immediately, Westgate ran to get Marko a towel to stem the flow.

"Do not make me for a fool," Krafchenko said through clenched teeth. "I know what you did … what the others did."

Then, instantly, Krafchenko completely changed his expression to one of smiling calm serenity. "Another glass, please," he said. Westgate complied and filled it with whiskey.

"Y-you might want to take it easy, Kraf. I-I don't want the neighbours hearing. These walls are kinda thin, you know…"

"Of course, of course." Krafchenko waved his bandaged hand.

Krafchenko brought his attention back to Marko, still sitting on the ground with a bloodied towel pressed against his head. "You see, my dear Marko, I know how it works. We are all jackals. Everyone in this city, in this new province, looks out only for themselves. I know there was a conspiracy and took the chance. I was caught. Benny and Bert … perhaps they will have to answer to me one day. As will you … unless you redeem yourself."

"Why not ask Benny or Bert?"

"Why?" Krafchenko took a sip of whiskey, "because they are too public now. The cops have an eye on them. It's best to leave them be. But you … interestingly, you were not mentioned in any story. Not one single article. It's as if you do not exist." Krafchenko paused to take a drag of his smoke and pointed to Buxton. "It's the same with Johnny B. over here."

Marko opened his mouth to speak, but then shut it. He could have blown everything open by telling Krafchenko that Buxton actually organized his capture … but Buxton would only deny it. Who would Krafchenko believe?

The man who hid his stolen money at his hideout or the man who helped spring him from jail? No, it was not the time for that, especially when dealing with desperate men, the lot of them. Even injured, Krafchenko wielded significant power and control over others. Buxton played both sides. He probably took some of the money Krafchenko trusted with him before the police claimed it. And Westgate? An unfortunate pawn hiding a fugitive.

"How did you escape?" Marko asked.

"It was easy. The police station jail cell on Rupert Street is not really a proper jail. Just two months before it was a kitchen. The *Old Kitchen*, as everyone calls it, was reconverted into a jail cell, but was really no better than a detention room. Two unarmed cops were with me in the cell at all times except if I was getting council from a lawyer. It turns out Johnny B. happened to bump into a lawyer at the Clarendon Hotel. A man by the name of Percy Hagel. Buxton told Percy that I needed a lawyer. Hagel jumped at the opportunity, given the high-profile nature of the case. He's a defence lawyer and correctly figured that this case would put him over the top because it is being reported all across Canada. Everyone would know his name. The opportunities would come streaming in.

"Hagel and I became friends. Before long he also believed, without a doubt, that I was innocent. But if we went to trial, I would likely end up dangling at the end of a rope. The two police guarding me? They were nothing more than lazy pea-brained thugs. They took turns taking naps. When one nodded off, it gave me the opportunity to talk to the other. Constable Flower would not fall for anything, but Reid was a push over. I had him eating out of my hands. Reid practically drooled when I talked about the Australian Gold Bonds I have hidden away. All $252,000 worth. It was the same for the $8,000 in diamonds I stashed. Soon Reid was convinced of my complete innocence and that a travesty to justice was about to occur.

"As luck would have it, Reid also frequented the Clarendon. Once Buxton knew Reid was the night-duty guard, it was a simple matter to slip him a fiver and see if the man in blue would help. Reid, Hagel and Johnny B. did everything. Of course it helped that Hagel was able to meet with me in private under the guise of lawyer-client privilege. The guards left the cell whenever Hagel needed to consult with me.

"Buxton arranged for the gun, a Colt, to be stolen from Ashdown's Hardware. The serial numbers were filed off. Reid purchased a skeleton key from Eaton's. Same with some rope. Reid hid everything under his tunic and when Flower went for a nap, gave the items to me. I hid the gun in my pocket and everything else under a mattress. Reid acted like he was surprised when I pulled out the gun and urged Flower not to blow his whistle until I was free and clear. Too bad the damn rope broke while I was climbing out."

"So what you want me to do?" Marko asked. He took a sip of whiskey.

"It's obvious I need to leave Winnipeg. For a few days I was holed up at a storage warehouse on Ellice Avenue, but the conditions were deplorable. Thankfully Mr. Westgate over here was able to offer this wonderful abode." Krafchenko tipped his glass to Westgate, who gave him a slight, almost reluctant nod.

"But it's time to move on," Krafchenko said. "I need you to contact someone from your place of employment."

"Who?"

"William B. Dalton. I need to see him. Arrange for him to come here this weekend."

William Dalton? The name hit him like a ton of bricks. That filthy-rich weasel? Why would he be hanging around with the likes of John Krafchenko? What would Mildred think of that? Should he even tell her? Maybe not. Dalton would deny everything and Marko's meddling would only get him fired.

"What do you want me to say?"

"Tell him that Pearl Smith needs to see him. I used to go by that name. He will know what you mean. William will be able to get me out of town to somewhere safe. I don't know where, but I'm certain he has some ideas. It's hard for me to move around, so I will need all the support I can get."

Marko nodded, but how could he approach William Dalton? He already fell in too deep to squeal or walk away.

Krafchenko smiled and played with the snake ring on his finger.

Playing Pool
January 17, 1914

Marko winced when he bumped his head getting out from under the sink. The kitchen sink at the Spencer mansion had acted up again, but he fixed it for good this time. He ran the water from the tap and peeked underneath with a flashlight. No drips.

He wiped his dirty hands on a damp cloth then washed them properly in the sink. With the last task in the Spencer manor complete, it was time to go home. His pocket watch said quarter to four. He could have easily finished all the required repairs before noon, but dragged it out by pretending to have problems with the repairs, not that anyone could tell the difference anyway.

Where was that damn Dalton? He visited just about every Saturday, doting over Mildred or taking her out to some restaurant or play. Marko could only connect to Dalton through Mildred. But he couldn't tell Mildred to pass Krafchenko's message on to William. Even with William present, how would Marko approach him without it being awkward or raising suspicion? The man never said a word to him in all the months he'd seen him at the Spencer household.

And why should he be the one to inform Dalton? Would it not be easier for Krafchenko to simply call Dalton on the telephone? Perhaps Krafchenko didn't have access to a telephone? Marko didn't notice one in the apartment. Or maybe because a call could be spied by a telephone operator? The Krafchenko escape captivated the entire city and everyone remained on high alert for any knowledge of his whereabouts. No, Krafchenko was smart by keeping things quiet and only involving a few, select people in his plans. That way he maintained better control of the situation.

Krafchenko might end up dragging him down. He never should have agreed to meet him about the 'opportunity' in November. But the man seemed so trustworthy.

Marko gathered the tools he used and went downstairs to put them away. The preservatives and other foods were stored in the dank and dusty room with a low ceiling. Although he went into the Spencer basement frequently, he never could get used to the amount of alcohol stored below. Rows and rows of wine bottles. Cases of scotch, whiskey, gin, rum … just about every type of alcohol imaginable. He enjoyed the bottle of vodka Mr. Spencer gave him for Christmas a few weeks ago.

Back upstairs, he heard voices coming from the front of the mansion. He stopped to strain his ears. It sounded like Mildred but he couldn't make out any words. He walked to the front hallway. Both Mildred and William stopped their conversation.

"Have you completed all your tasks today?" Mildred asked. She held William's hand. William still had on his overcoat and must have just entered.

Marko bit his bottom lip. "Ah, da … I mean yes. No! I'm not finished."

Mildred narrowed her eyes and cocked her head. "Which one is it?"

"I'm not finished," Marko said quickly and turned around back to the kitchen. He opened the cabinet door below the sink, dropped to his knees and stuck his head in. He grabbed the already repaired pipe with his hand to make it look like he was doing something.

After about five minutes he pulled his head back out and glanced around. Silence. They must have left to another part of the mansion. He shook his head. He could feel his heart racing. How long before William left? What should he do? His right temple felt tight and uncomfortable. He brought his fingers up to his temple and pressed hard. Not now. He closed his eyes and tried to slow his breathing down. Concentrate. Concentrate. Calm thoughts.

"…an odd fellow, isn't he?" Marko heard William from the kitchen floor.

"He can be at times." Mildred replied. "But come, let me show you the dress I'll wear tonight. It's hanging up in Gladys's room. She still has to do a quick alteration."

Footsteps went upstairs. He had to act now.

Marko sprang up and walked quickly to the front landing. William had draped his overcoat on a chair in the hallway. Marko reached in his pocket, grabbed the envelope, folded it in half and with nervous, shaking hands, rammed it in one of William's pockets.

Just as Marko turned to leave, William spotted him from the top of the stairs.

"What are you doing? Leave my overcoat alone."

"I done now," Marko said. He gave William a wink.

William looked puzzled.

Marko put on his outerwear and left the Spencer mansion. A block away he determined that winking at William was probably not a good idea.

*****

Sitting in the front room at home after dinner, Marko tried to read the newspaper. While he couldn't understand every word he got the general idea of each article. If anything, looking at the paper every day improved his reading. He could not believe the amount written about Krafchenko. Lines and lines of story every day.

Mike's children ran about the house and occasionally received a stern warning from Maria. Ann crawled on the ground licking and sucking an old, used shotgun shell.

He took a sip of coffee. The articles discussed all the rumours regarding how Krafchenko escaped and where he could be hiding. Someone offered a large reward in the neighbourhood of $13,000 for his recapture. Marko looked up for a moment. That would pay for a garage and then some.

He sat back in the chair and stared at the wall. Caught again in Krafchenko's web. When would it end? Maybe never. There will always be something else Krafchenko would want.

Marko looked into his half-empty coffee cup. Why get dragged down by the man? Krafchenko can't run forever. Eventually he will be recaptured. And when he is, the authorities will surely be vigilant that he'd have absolutely no chance of escaping again. Getting involved with the authorities would plunge Marko into the thick of it. Instead of being cleared he'd end up in jail. They'd wonder why it took him so long to come forward. And being from Galicia, would the police trust him?

"Hey, Marko … let's go out tonight. How about the Woodbine?" Mike asked in Ukrainian.

Marko paused for a moment. "Sure, but let's make it the Clarendon."

*****

Marko and Mike played several games of pool, taking turns breaking and racking. On his breaks Marko liked to get really low to where his eyeball almost touched against the cue. Then, like a single-stroke piston, he would bring his right arm back and drive the cue ball into the group of balls on the other side of the table. On most occasions at least one ball would find its way into a pocket.

But not this time. Marko glanced at the stand-up bar while waiting for Mike to finish his shot. Johnny Buxton stood at the bar ordering drinks.

Buxton did a quick double-take when he saw Marko, his cheeks red and

148

eyes glassy. "Hey ya, Marko. Can I buy you a shot?"

Marko frowned. "No, I buy my own." Something didn't seem right about Buxton. Something smelly. Everything about Kraf's capture and escape seemed like a set-up. And the only man getting away with everything? John Buxton.

Marko positioned himself to get a better view of Buxton's transaction at the bar. The bills practically popped out of Buxton's bulging wallet. The man was loaded. Buxton handed the barkeep a Bank of Montreal note – the same bank that Krafchenko robbed. Buxton put his thick wallet back in his jacket.

Marko tapped him on the shoulder. "C'mon. We need to talk."

Buxton frowned but then smiled. "What's got into you? Nothing wrong with having a few drinks with my friends."

Marko wasn't smiling. He motioned with his hand for Buxton to follow. They both walked into the washroom to the overpowering smell of urine. Both men checked to make sure no one else was in the dimly lit room.

"Yeah, what do you want?" Buxton said. "Did you give William Dalton the message?"

"Yes. I put it in his pocket. I hope he reads it."

"What do ya mean 'you hope?' Kraf was very specific. You wouldn't want to get on his bad side, would you?"

"Bad side? What about you?"

Buxton jerked his head, the alcohol exaggerated his confused expression. "Me? Kraf is indebted to me. I'm one of his trusted friends."

Marko shook his head. "Trusted friend. You're no friend. You're just like him. A criminal."

Catching Buxton by surprize, he reached in and grabbed Buxton's wallet from his inside jacket pocket. He grabbed a handful of bills and held them up. "What's this? The money Krafchenko stole. He killed the bank manager and stole money. Krafchenko gave you this money but you only gave police little bit. Not all of it."

"I wasn't around when the cops picked it up…"

"You got him captured," Marko continued, "then you arranged everything to get him out again. All behind scenes. Of course Krafchenko trusts you. But you don't care for him or anyone. I read paper. I know lots of money is missing. You have it."

Buxton crossed his arms and looked away for a moment. "Yeah, well what are ya gonna do about it? You think the cops'll believe you? I'll just hide the money and no one will know any different. Then you'll get mixed up in the investigation. You'll end up doing time. We already talked about that."

"Yes, but Krafchenko will figure out you still have money."

"I'll tell Kraf it was for the lawyer."

"But the lawyer Hagel was not paid. It said so in the newspaper. And if he wasn't paid, then where is the money?"

Buxton didn't have an answer. He stood silently looking down, swaying slowly back and forth.

"Krafchenko will figure it out," Marko said.

"How's that gonna happen?"

Marko pointed to himself with his thumb. "I'll tell him." Marko tightened his hold on the wad of cash and held it in Buxton's face. "I'll bring the money to him and tell him. Then you're in big trouble."

"Alright, hold yer horses," Buxton said, placing his hand on Marko's shoulder. "You crazy? Don't go to Kraf…."

"Why not? Now I'm in Kraf's favour, no? Listen … you know what to do. You tell police where he's hiding. Hurry before William gets to him."

"The truth is, I can probably plea my way with the authorities. Squeal on everyone else and come out scot-free. You were not involved in the escape, so I can't mention you." Buxton burped into his hand. "Gotta stick to my story and it'll all work out. Hagel, Westlake, Constable Reid – they were all lackeys in Kraf's escape."

"And you keep money," Marko said. He threw the money back at him. "I don't care for it. Once Krafchenko's in jail, the problem will go away. Who knows? Maybe the police are on to you already."

Marko left Buxton to pick up the assorted Bank of Montreal notes from the washroom floor. He put his hand in his pocket to make sure he could feel the twenty he had slid in.

686 Toronto Street
January 18, 1914

Marko stood near the back of the throng of people outside Krafchenko's hideout. He pulled up the collar of his overcoat to block the cold wind. Although it was quarter to eleven at night, there still had to be over a hundred gawkers. Word got out fast. At least a half dozen police cars blocked the road in different directions.

Just twenty feet away, a fast-moving vehicle stopped so quickly it slid two feet on the ice on the road. William popped out of the back seat, breathing hard. He took two quick steps toward the apartment block, but stopped.

"Look, there he is! There's Krafchenko!" a bystander shouted. Everyone looked at where the man pointed and, sure enough, officers assisted Krafchenko into a police vehicle.

"He looks pretty banged up," another said. "I wonder if he put up a fight?"

A newspaper reporter standing beside William threw his finished cigarette down and pressed on it with his foot. "No, no struggle at all." The reporter closed his notebook and put his pencil away. Marko cocked his ear.

"Were you there? Did you see?" William asked.

"Yup, saw it all. I'm just waiting for a ride to go back to the office to write it all up. It seems the police were giving Reid, Krafchenko's guard, the heat. They figured he must have been in on it. But it all came down when they picked up Buxton earlier in the morning. He ended up spilling the beans. The lawyer, Hagel, got arrested a few hours ago. And now they finally got Krafchenko at the apartment building. They also nabbed Westgate … they'll have him in for harbouring a fugitive."

William nodded and the reporter walked away. He motioned his driver for them to leave. Just as he turned to go he caught a glimpse of Marko. He waved him over to get in the back seat of the car.

"Did you slip me this note?" He took it out of his pocket and read it: "Pearl Smith needs to see you. 686 Toronto Street."

"Da."

"Why didn't you tell me about it yesterday? I was going to hole him up in an old abandoned cabin along the Red River just north of the city. After a few months or so, we could have smuggled him out of the province in a piano box or in the trunk of a car."

"In front of Mildred? You want her to know you're friends with Krafchenko?"

"Well, now it's too late. They'll watch Kraf like a hawk. You should have got word to me earlier so I could do something. That Buxton double-crossed poor old Kraf. And you didn't help much."

Marko fiddled with the door handle. What would happen when William found out he forced Buxton's hand? "I—"

William clenched his jaw then raised his hand to cut off Marko. "Enough. The fact is I didn't read this note until just an hour ago. Far too late. How do I know you didn't delay giving it to me on purpose?"

Marko stared into William's cold brown eyes.

"Get out. Not a word of this to Mildred. You got that?"

It Looks Like a Lamp Shade
April 4, 1914

Mildred examined herself in the mirror in the hallway at the bottom of the stairs. She wore a full-length beaded white dress augmented with little red bows along her neckline. She tipped her white sun hat up and down and moved her head in various angles to try to find the best look. It didn't matter, really. Her scar would never go away nor could it be hidden.

She breathed out forcefully, flapping her lips like a horse. Not much she could do about it. One time, maybe a year ago, she would have tipped her hat far down and to the right. She would also keep her head down. That first reaction after initial eye contact always bothered her.

But she was beyond that now. Not as fragile. She'd never be the same, but had more perspective. Was this what they called acceptance?

Smelling cigar smoke, Mildred sensed Father nearby. She turned away from the mirror to see him walking with a newspaper under his arm.

"Have you seen Mother?" Mildred asked.

Thomas muttered something Mildred couldn't make out. He stopped in his tracks and frowned at a lamp that was missing its lampshade.

"Your mother must be making adjustments to the decor again."

Mildred shrugged her shoulders.

"Is this the new lampshade?" Thomas said. With his cigar firmly wedged in the right side of his mouth, he put his newspaper down and picked up an item from another table nearby. "It looks terrible. It's too narrow and not very deep. All the feathers would make it a fire hazard." He turned it over. "And look, there are no metal hoops to attach to the bulb. Certainly a hot bulb is not supposed to rest on felt."

Mildred smiled and looked away, pretending to be still doting over her hat.

"I suppose we will be going soon," Gertrude said, just entering the hallway. "The ladies are having an afternoon tea at Ashdown's residence down the street." She put on a new, floor-length dress made of a very fine material, perhaps even silk. Light purple, the material billowed down in several layers right to her feet, which were in matching high-heeled shoes. Several strands of pearls adorned her neck.

"When will you be back?" Thomas asked. "I fancied we were going out for dinner this evening?"

"I shall not be long. It's just a tea."

"More like a hen gathering."

Gertrude frowned. "Now, now. You get to go out with your male companions. I like to get out once in a while." Her elbow-length white gloves looked a touch too extravagant for the circumstances.

"Well, don't be long. I can't stand it when we're late for anything."

Gertrude cocked her head to the side. "But it's quite alright if you're out late or otherwise away?"

Mildred went up the nearby stairs and stopped when she reached the next floor. Best to leave the developing situation. Father may have had too many afternoon scotches.

"Now you listen," Thomas said. "I have very important business meetings and other matters. They take time. Don't forgot where the money comes to put this roof up and food in the pantry and the memberships to all your clubs. I'm not sitting around sipping tea."

"That's right," Gertrude said. "What you drink is far more potent."

Mildred strained her ears. It sounded like scuffling. Poor mother.

The front door opened. "The vehicle is all set," said James.

"Thank you, I will be out momentarily," Gertrude said. Her voice sounded shaky and uncertain. "Mildred," she called. "It's time…"

Mildred walked slowly down the stairs. Father crossed his arms, his face red with anger. Mother's face also had turned crimson but it didn't appear that he hit her. James's timely arrival saved her. Perhaps he just grabbed her. Sometimes she had bruises on her arms and elbows. That's why she fancied long gloves.

Gertrude looked around. "Now where is my hat? Did you hide it so I would not go out?"

"I don't know what you are talking about," Thomas said.

"My new hat. I just got it from—" Gertrude stopped when she saw the lampshade, only it wasn't a lampshade. "What is that doing there?" She pointed to her hat.

"Huh? Oh, I saw you purchased a new lampshade, so I placed it on the lamp. All those feathers and fluff are not very safe you know."

Gertrude grabbed her hat. "It's not a lampshade! It's my new hat."

"Sorry," Thomas said in a somber tone. "I thought it was a lampshade."

"You are impossible." Gertrude shook her head. She gently placed the hat on her head and examined herself in the hallway mirror.

Marko entered the front door with the original lampshade. With a meek smile he walked past and placed it carefully on the lamp. "All fixed now," he said and continued on to the back of the house toward the kitchen area.

Gertrude raised her eyebrows and walked out the front door.

"Goodbye, Father," Mildred said before she followed.

She could hear Father scream from inside. "It still looks like a lampshade!"

The Weight of the World
May 31, 1914

"I do not believe there will be a lesson today," Gladys said at the Spencer mansion front door. Her eyes seemed unusually red.

"She told me to come today," Marko said.

"Perhaps, but plans have changed, I can assure you."

He shrugged his shoulders with a glum smile. "Okay, I go. You tell Mildred I was here?"

But the door had already slammed. With nothing he could do, he turned to leave.

About halfway up the driveway he heard Mildred call his name from the house. Dressed all in black, she waved a handkerchief in the air.

"Marko, come here please." She dabbed her eye with the handkerchief.

Marko quickly walked back to the front step. "Are … are you okay?"

Mildred hid her rosy cheeks and wet eyes in her handkerchief.

"What's the matter? What's wrong?" He put his arm around her shoulder.

"I'm sorry. I-I will not be able to provide a lesson for you today. I received word from England that my Aunt Mabel has passed away." Tears trailed down her face. "So sad, just two years after Uncle Felix."

Marko stood silently. He did not know what to say.

"I have to go back inside. I'm sorry."

"No. Don't be sorry," he said. He gave her a warm, comforting hug.

Mildred gently waved at Marko and stepped back in.

He took a deep breath and exhaled slowly then adjusted his hat and left the estate to go back home.

*****

Mother sat in an upright chair in the sitting room, sobbing into her handkerchief and dressed head to toe in black. A few other ladies in equally bleak colours stood around. One held Gertrude's hand while another gently stroked her hair. A few other relatives and close friends mingled quietly in the room. Everyone spoke in whispers and subdued tones.

Andrew sat on the couch between Thomas and Mildred. She reached over to hold Andrew's hand. He moved slightly and offered only a faint smile.

"How are you holding up? Aunt Mabel was such a sweetheart." Mildred said.

Andrew took a sip of the whiskey and stared off in the distance. Was Mabel's death bringing up his memories of the *Titanic*? With Father already on his third scotch, it was going to be one of those nights.

*****

Marko sat on a streetcar on his way home back to the North End. Still downtown, he noticed an old baba, wearing black. Despite the warm day, she had tied a black handkerchief around her head. Why do old ladies from the old country always do so? Why couldn't the babas look like the other old ladies?

A kind old lady, his baba would always sneak him a sugar cube when he was a boy. She could also be stern and never thought twice about hitting him with her wooden spoon if he was naughty. One time a small portion of the spoon broke off when she hit him on the bum. Despite that, she continued to use the same spoon. She would not replace it with a newer one because it still worked. Not that well, but good enough. Even as a teenager – long past the age he would ever need to feel the end of the spoon – whenever he saw Baba using it, it reminded him to be good and listen. After she died, Marko's parents cleaned her house and wanted to throw it away. But he picked it out of the garbage, cleaned it, and kept it. Occasionally, when looking for something else, he would stumble upon it. Just the sight of it would bring back powerful memories. Some, like the beatings, were not so good, but many happy memories lingered. Marko cracked a faint smile thinking of her cooking. Easily the best cook in the world, she made the tastiest treats and pastries anywhere including her flavourful apple pie and the sugary halushki filled with poppy seed. And, of course, the kutia at Christmas. But best of all was her torte. She only made it on special occasions, like birthdays. No one could make a torte like Baba. Not even Ma.

He tried not to think about Baba and even adjusted himself to look straight ahead in the streetcar. But the old memories could not leave. Like that fateful day years ago when he walked back from his friend's farm.

They had both been fishing in the creek. Marko caught two fish and was taking them home for Ma to clean. Seventeen at the time, he had been gone most of the day while his parents went into town with the wagon to fetch some supplies. Earlier that day Pa told him to finish the chores before going fishing. Marko did, but didn't do a particularly good job. He raced home to try to finish what he left behind.

As he approached the farm, he noticed his sister's wagon. She must have been visiting. Older than Marko by about fifteen years, she had been married for a dozen already. Then he noticed his other sister's horse. She was even older and married off when Marko was an infant. Why would they be visiting?

But oddly, no sign of Pa's wagon. They should have been back by then. But at least it gave him a chance to finish his chores without having to worry about Pa being cross. If one thing infuriated Pa, it was a half-completed job.

Marko stepped into the house with his fishing rod and basket of fish. Both his sisters sat in the kitchen. "Hello. I didn't know both of you would be here. Are you staying for dinner?"

The two sisters remained silent while Marko placed the fish on the counter.

"I caught some fish in the creek by Luca's place. They might not be enough for all of us, though."

The oldest, Kateryna, slowly rose from her chair, wringing her hands. Only in her early 30s, she looked older. She had her hair tied up in the back, but a few wiry strands dangled around her ears. Vira was about five years younger than Kateryna, but still much older than Marko. She did not marry until she was twenty-one, just a few years ago. For a long time Marko's parents worried she would end up an old maid. Shy and withdrawn growing up, Vira learned to become more outspoken and independent in her ways. She eventually found a man who would marry her, although occasionally he raised his hand against her.

"I have to finish up a few chores before Ma and Pa get back from town…." Marko walked toward the door.

"Marko," Vira said, still seated at the table.

"Hmm?" Marko turned.

Vira's face turned pale and appeared troubled. "I … we … need to tell you something."

"Yes, what?"

"Ma and Pa are dead," Kateryna said.

"What?" Marko smiled form the corner of his mouth. "Is this some sort of joke?" If so, he did not find it particularly funny.

"No," Vira said. "They're gone." Almost on cue, both sisters began to weep.

Marko stood at the back door. "How?"

Vira dabbed her eyes and blew her nose in her handkerchief. "The wagon lost its wheel while they were going around the bend at the big hill near town. The horse panicked and ran. They were thrown from the wagon and tumbled over the edge. Ma hit her head on a rock. Pa fell down the slope. It was a long fall. The horse somehow still made it to town dragging the broken wagon. They found Ma and Pa shortly after."

Marko could tell this was no joke. No one makes a joke like that. He stood silent for a moment while his mind raced. Instinctively, he stepped out to tend to his chores.

He walked toward the barn, but with each step the enormity of his sisters' news broke through. Tears welled up in his eyes. The weight of the world suddenly burdened him. He leaned against the outside of the barn, rested his head against his arm and cried uncontrollably. His sisters ran up to him and gently comforted the new orphan.

The Gallows
July 9, 1914

At three minutes to seven in the morning, Deputy Sheriff Pynicker led the way through the provincial jail at the end of Vaughan Street. Reverend Heeney followed, then Krafchenko assisted by one warden and finally another warden bringing up the rear. A black sack had already been placed over Krafchenko head. While a condemned man would normally have the bag put on his head at the scaffold, Krafchenko requested darkness for the entire walk.

They descended the narrow, dark stairs from Krafchenko's second storey cell, then on toward the courtyard. Krafchenko's head drooped low, swaying rhythmically from side to side, as if in a hypnotic state.

The scaffold greeted the entourage when they entered the open air, already illuminated by the brilliant morning sun. Forty-nine men stood to watch the execution within the gated confines of the prison's courtyard including elected officials, dignitaries and several newspaper reporters.

*****

Krafchenko's trial took place in Morden, a little over fifteen miles straight west from the scene of the crime in Plum Coulee. It started in March and captivated the entire province. They remodeled the courtroom to accommodate a large audience. Nearly every day of the trial it filled to capacity. The newspapers had arranged for a nearby house to be strung with telegraph wires where operators could tap the latest about the trial to get the news to streets as it occurred.

The trial had lasted three weeks, lengthy by any standards. Seventy-two witnesses testified including young school girls and people with little or no English. Their testimony affirmed that a man who looked like an old Jew dressed in black with a false beard robbed the Bank of Montreal and murdered manager Henry Arnold with a single shot behind the building.

The jury brought in a guilty verdict. Krafchenko stood proud in the prisoner's box and delivered an eloquent statement. He thanked everyone for a fair trial and even noted that the decision was fair given the evidence presented. Still, he maintained his innocence. While he admitted to committing crimes in the past and even being in Plum Coulee the day of the robbery and murder, he swore he did not end Arnold's life. He claimed the involvement of three others and that some testimony was less than genuine. Shaken and moved by Krafchenko's speech, the judge's voice quavered through the sentencing. He seemed reluctant to sentence Krafchenko to hang, but the facts indicated that he had no choice. Women in the audience wept openly.

After the April 9 sentencing dozens of petitions had been organized calling for Krafchenko's sentence to be changed to life imprisonment. Despite some 16,000 people having signed those petitions by July, the government refused to be swayed. While many of those 16,000 sympathized with John Krafchenko, a considerable portion simply expressed moral opposition to capital punishment.

*****

William Dalton, being from a prominent family, received permission to stand with the other witnesses in front of the gallows within the jail walls. He threw down the stub of his cigarette. He had done everything he could for Krafchenko. For Kraf's last request William arranged for a physician to examine Krafchenko's body. His mind drifted to tomorrow's provincial election. All his work with Thomas Kelly had come to fruition.

About three hundred had milled around outside the high stone walls of the prison the evening before. Mostly women, they hoped to catch a glimpse of the handsome, condemned man through the second storey window. After a few hours police dispersed the crowd. When dawn broke, people slowly converged again. This time the police didn't bother keeping the thousands of people away. Although still early in the morning, people came to be near the site where Krafchenko would finally meet his fate.

Some threw shouts of encouragement over the wall.

"Keep up your courage, Kraf!"

"We know you're innocent!"

"May God bless you on your way to heaven!"

Marko stood outside the wall of the prison with his hands in his pockets. He could feel the tension mount. At long last, the evil snake would be gone from his life, back down to the gates of Hell. He couldn't wait.

A short distance away down the street, Benny Rolph and Bert Bell leaned against Benny's taxi. They took a little bit of money from the packets that Krafchenko had given to them, but could have lifted more. In any case, cleared of all wrong-doing, both appeared as witnesses at Krafchenko's trial. They played their parts perfectly by twisting the facts to serve their needs.

Also not far away and dressed in a blue three-piece suit stood John Buxton. Sporting a new felt hat, Buxton looked down at his pocket watch. Exactly seven. The cops had picked him up the same night he met Marko at the Clarendon. They had to wait for him to sober before grilling him. But he played it cool and gave them just enough information to get them on their way. He didn't say a thing until they guaranteed immunity, then testified at both the preliminary hearing and the trial itself. The Crown tried Hagel and Westgate together. Hagel got three years at Stony Mountain Penitentiary. Westgate got two years. Reid paid the stiffest price, sentenced to seven years in Stony.

Forty feet away Krafchenko's mother wept into a handkerchief. Her neighbour, Bernice, comforted her. Such a good boy. Sure he had some troubles, but did it warrant this? It seemed too much. What everyone said about him, all lies.

Even Krafchenko's wife and infant son, both of whom travelled all the way from Graham, Ontario, joined the crowd on the other side of the wall, waiting for the fateful moment. The guards never permitted them to even hold hands that one time she visited him in jail. He promised her the stars and the moon but now what would she do? Her face had become a mess of snot and tears.

A warden led Krafchenko up the steps, one by one, to the top of the scaffold. The entire time Reverend Heeney whispered prayers from a ragged Bible. During the past few months Krafchenko had poured out his heart and soul to Heeney. He told him his darkest secrets including all manners of crimes and other vile deeds nobody knew about. But through it all, Krafchenko staunchly affirmed his complete innocence related to the murder of the banker in Plum Coulee. Sure, he was involved in the robbery, but remained adamant he did not kill the banker. Heeney saw Krafchenko shed tears of anguish and disappointment that he would never, ever see his wife again. He would never see his son grow to become a man. Through Heeney's guidance Krafchenko faced his wrong-doings and sought forgiveness from the Creator. Heeney could tell Krafchenko had never been happier in his life when he accepted his fate like a man. By the end of their time together, Heeney wondered how Krafchenko could commit any crimes, so transformed was he.

But the last night seemed strange and unusual. Reverend Heeney had decided to spend the night alone with Krafchenko. At about four in the morning, Krafchenko suddenly stood up in his cell and tensed. This caught Heeney by surprise. "Listen!" Krafchenko said. For about two minutes he didn't move while every muscle strained in his neck. Without warning, Krafchenko said, "Ready!" and immediately fainted and fell to the ground. Heeney called for the guards. One rushed in while another ushered Heeney out. Krafchenko remained prone in the same position until just before seven o'clock.

Once at the top of the scaffold, something within Krafchenko snapped … as if he suddenly became aware that the end was imminent. "No, no. Not me. It's a mistake! No!" The condemned man shook his head violently, like he had just woken from a bad dream.

Deputy Sheriff Pynicker shook his head and motioned for Arthur Ellis to do his job.

"Take your hats off," Ellis said. Everyone in attendance in the courtyard complied. Arthur Ellis stood only about five-and-a-half feet tall, but still appeared strong in his compact, wiry frame. He had killed more men than anyone in Canada, being the official executioner. All told, he had performed 314 executions in Canada and Great Britain over the past twelve years. John Krafchenko was number 315.

Ellis could tell a condemned man's guilt or innocence just by looking at him, and this one appeared innocent. He did not know why, but it did not seem proper. He frowned slightly but went about his task.

Ellis strapped Krafchenko's legs together then immediately placed the noose around the condemned man's squirming head.

"No! No! Not me. Please, listen to me!"

Ellis stepped back and activated the lever. The trap doors opened with a hard crash.

Motionless almost immediately, the guilty man hung for seven minutes.

"You can put your hats on now, gentlemen," Ellis said. "It's all over."

The Dance
July 19, 1914

It had to be one of the hottest days of the year. Even the inside of Mildred's elbows felt moist from perspiration. Far too unbearable for wool, especially on a Sunday, she wore a long white skirt made of cotton. Still, with the petticoat, she found it rather uncomfortable. Her predominantly white blouse had splashes of colour in the form of roses, carnations and other flowers embroidered in the material. With white stockings and shoes, the only exposed skin on Mildred was her hands and head.

Through the front window she noticed Marko walking up the drive carrying his books. She closed the curtains and quickly checked her appearance before opening the front door.

"Just about everyone is away today," she said. "Mr. Spencer is off golfing with business partners. Mother is at the park with some ladies. My brother is away at the lake. The cook is downtown to stock the pantry and get a few other supplies. The other staff also have the day off. Gladys is the only one here and she's upstairs mending some of her clothes. No one should interrupt us. Have a seat and let me see the sentences you wrote in your work book."

Marko handed his notebook to Mildred and eased into the red velvet chair on the right. She sat on the couch, nearest to Marko. She opened the notebook and examined Marko's most recent entries. "'The derds fly south in the fall.' Very good try. First off, you have mixed up your b's and d's again. Next, the 'er' sound … many "er" sounds are spelled with an 'e' and an 'r,' but not all. For 'birds,' it's actually 'i-r.'"

"So confusing."

Although the enormous curtains prevented the sun from entering the sitting room, it remained oppressively hot. Several times Marko excused himself to dab his brow with his handkerchief. Occasionally Mildred fanned herself with his notebook.

After reviewing and correcting several of Marko's sentences, Mildred demonstrated the differences of several homophones including 'to, too, two' and 'their, there.' She opened the textbook to a series of spelling lists and helped him read and recite each word on the list. Their warm hands occasionally touched.

After about an hour, she assigned some homework to be completed for the next lesson. Mildred sighed and slumped back into the couch. "That's enough for today. Do you think?"

Marko nodded. They stared at each other briefly. The awkward moment lasted for several seconds.

They stood up at the same time. "Thank you for lesson. I should be going…"

"Oh, you are very welcome. All the work you do around the home is much appreciated. I know Mr. Spencer likes it."

Marko grabbed his hat and motioned to pick up his books.

"Wait." Mildred stopped him. "How rude of me. It's so hot and I never offered you any refreshment the entire time you were here. Please, let me get you a lemonade."

"No. I no need…"

"I insist. Besides, I'm having a glass myself." She motioned for Marko to sit back down and left for the kitchen.

She returned in five minutes with a silver tray holding two tall glasses of lemonade. Marko had moved to the corner of the room, running his hand over the gramophone.

She set the tray down on the table. "My mother is with the Women's Musical Club and when she hosts the occasional tea they listen to classical music."

"Very good cabinetry. A nice model."

She picked up both glasses and gave one to Marko. Each with a wedge of lemon affixed to the rim. Marko guzzled his drink like a thirsty camel. Mildred winced slightly. She took small little sips.

"Do you listen to any music?" She gestured to the gramophone.

"No gramophone here. I had in old country."

"Oh, that's unfortunate. What type of music did you listen to?"

"We have much folk music. For dancing at weddings, birthdays, celebrations. Some classical."

Mildred's eyebrows rose. "Oh, what type of classical…?"

Marko closed one eye, training himself to recall. He counted off the composers with his right hand. "Hmmm … Bach, Tchaikovsky, Mendelssohn,

Strauss…"

"That's a very good group. I didn't realize you were familiar with classical music seeing as how you only work…" Mildred stopped, catching herself. How could she belittle him, assuming that just because he was a labourer he could not have any appreciation for fine music? She shook her head and grabbed his arm. "I'm so sorry Marko, I didn't mean to disrespect you."

"No worry."

Mildred took another small sip from her glass, still not even one quarter empty. Marko seemed so honest and dependable. A pure and clean soul. Even his awkward foreign nature could not hide that. While his clothes were not the best fitting nor in the latest fashion, his chiselled jaw and soft brown eyes coupled with his natural good nature, at times, made her pause.

"Come, let's see what there is." Mildred strolled to the gramophone and opened the bottom compartment revealing the modest collection of records. She bit her bottom lip and bent down to take out a few records and read the labels.

"Ah, here's my favourite," Mildred said. "'Blue Danube Waltz' by Strauss. Strauss was from Austria, was he not? Let's have a listen." Mildred placed the record on the turntable and turned the unit on. A loud click followed by a humming sound came through a hidden speaker. The record spun. Mildred dropped the stylus.

The first few bars of the intro to 'Blue Danube Waltz' filled the sitting room. They looked at each other with little grins. Mildred took another small sip of lemonade and turned the volume up. The strains of the Viennese waltz dominated the room. "I absolutely love dancing to this piece."

"My mother showed me how to dance to this one."

"Really? Come, let us dance." Mildred held up her right hand offering Marko the lead. William would take her places, but he never danced.

"No, no." Marko shook his hands. "I'm no good."

"Please. I insist."

He did not have time to debate the merits one way or the other. Once the telltale signature movement began, she grabbed his hand and put her arm around his left shoulder. From the angle of his arm and the appropriate distance he stood away from her, she could tell he had been trained. Marko squeezed her hand gently, placed his other hand on the middle of her damp, warm back and began to dance.

"You are dancing a Viennese style. Very impressive," Mildred said. The two twirled around the spacious sitting room, an ample size for the two of them to not bump into anything. "Many men only know a simple box step. They do not realize this type of waltz requires more technique."

"My mother said, 'You must know how to dance. One day you will be asked. Women will appreciate.'"

"Your mother was correct."

The pair twirled to the romantic melody pouring from the gramophone. When appropriate, Marko switched and they rotated the other direction. They switched directions several times. In each instance, Mildred followed his lead. No ordinary peasant labourer from some poor, obscure, Eastern European nation, this man could dance.

The two sped up during the faster moments of the piece and slowed during the tender passages. The heat of the room, the intense, prolonged activity and the uncertain emotions worked together to make the dancers perspire profusely. Rivulets of sweat poured down Marko's face. Drops of perspiration glistened on Mildred's brow and above her lip. Beads slowly rolled down from the top of her neck straight down to the small of her back. She could feel sweat around her bosom.

As the waltz neared its intense finale, they spun and circled at such a speed that the surroundings became a blur. The red velvet couch and chairs, the ornaments, all the furnishings, even the walls themselves, all became invisible to the dancers. No longer smiling, the two stared in each other's eyes.

At last, the song ended. Mildred and Marko held their pose, their faces only inches away from each other. They could feel each other's breath. Both glistened. Their hands clenched tight. For ten long seconds they stared at each other, stuck in a romantic no-man's land. Each waiting for the other to make the first move.

Coming to their senses, both released. Marko stared at the ground. Mildred backed off and cupped her mouth with her hand. Did something just about happen?

"I go now," Marko said quietly. He picked up his hat and books.

"Yes," Mildred said, still trying to catch her breath. Mildred shook her head. What was she thinking? What about William?

Marko walked to the door and opened it. Halfway out the door he stopped and looked back but then continued on.

She watched him walk quickly down the drive and vanish from view behind the trees near the street. She turned around to see Gladys standing with her arms crossed.

Everyone Loves Parades
September 5, 1914

"What's that sound?" Marko said. Having just stepped out of the beverage room at the Clarendon Hotel, the bright afternoon sun forced him to squint. Winnipeg Iron Works closed earlier on Saturdays and Mike convinced him to go for a few drinks.

"It's coming from there," Mike said, pointing east down Portage Avenue to a loud din, like that from a marching band. The barrage of vehicles, horse buggies, bicyclists and pedestrians blocked their view, but no mistake, the sound approached.

Others noticed the racket and craned their heads for a view. "Mummy, is a parade coming? I love parades!" a small boy standing nearby said. About six years old and holding his mother's hand, he wore a blue naval-themed serge.

A block away all traffic moved to the side or escaped down cross streets to get out of the way. People quickly lined Portage Avenue two or three deep to catch a glimpse of the parade.

The band played militaristic music, heavy on the snare drums. A lone drum major led the parade. Fat with an extremely large black moustache, he wore an oversized brown bearskin-style hat and swung a staff in time to the beat. The band followed behind him. Every musician wore a military uniform and walked in perfect formation to the beat of the music.

Behind the band, also in perfect step, walked perhaps a hundred military men, all in uniform. The men smiled and waved to the crowd. The crowd, in turn, clapped and cheered when the men passed by. Occasional shouts of "Go get 'em! or "We're proud of you!" shot randomly from the crowd. Every so often, the military men, especially those at the edges of the parade, would encourage people from the crowd to join in.

Other, regularly dressed men followed in the parade behind the men in uniform. From time to time a young lad would bolt from the crowd and eagerly join the back of the parade. He would be greeted by hugs and pats on the back from those already marching. The non-uniformed men did not walk in strict precision like their uniformed comrades. The back of the parade looked more festive and congratulatory.

"Come. Join us. Let's kick the kaiser," one soldier yelled to the crowd. Other soldiers made similar comments. Some broke formation and grabbed young men from the crowd lining the street.

Marko and Mike turned away from parade. An older lady in a bright red dress with a large blue and red wide-brimmed hat grabbed Mike's arm. "Shame on you! How can you turn your back on your king and country?"

Mike looked at her with a blank stare. Red-faced, he swayed gently from side to side. "Yes, I am talking to you," the stern-faced woman said. Her pencil sharp nose pointed at Mike while her eyes bored a hole through his head.

"I … I … we…"

"And you as well." She pointed at Marko. "Both of you should be marching along and supporting our compatriots. What's the matter with you?"

Mike graciously took off his floppy felt hat, held it to his heart, and with a sorrowful expression said, "I'm sorry, madam, but you will have to lick me where I urinate before we join that parade. Besides, my comrade and I have better things to do than waste our time with pathetic Anglo trash such as yourself." Only he didn't say it in English; he said it in Ukrainian.

Wide-eyed, Marko could not believe what Mike had said to the oblivious woman. The man could say just about anything with a few drinks in his belly.

"Well, I understand you might have a personal situation that makes it difficult for you, but that's the same for all of us, is it not?" the woman said.

"My lady," Mike said, still in Ukrainian, now looking at the ground and appearing even sadder than he was before, "the only situation I would find difficult is how far up your ass I should ram that stupid hat of yours. The good news is when one of your bastard children pulled the hat out, it would smell like roses because obviously your shit doesn't stink."

Marko took his hat off and feigned coughing into it. Really he was trying to control his laughter at the fun Mike had at the expense of the respectable woman.

"You do not understand a word of English, do you?" the woman asked.

"Oh, I understand it all, you silly old bitch. Now please go away before I vomit all over your ugly dress," Mike said, again, still in Ukrainian. Marko did not know how he did it, but it looked like Mike somehow managed to force a tear from his eye.

The woman rolled her eyes and walked away.

Mike slowly raised his sad-looking face and looked at Marko. Instantly he winked and smiled. Both men laughed, slapping their thighs. It caught the attention of a few men marching in the nearby parade. Quick as a flash, about five or six men accosted them and dragged them into the parade.

Caught by surprise, the two found themselves part of the militaristic parade. Both Marko and Mike laughed and shook their heads, but continued walking along and waving to the crowds at the edges of the wide street. Mike stumbled occasionally as he walked.

Along the way a few more men actively joined the back of the parade or were strongly encouraged by others already marching. Some squirmed away or otherwise did whatever they could to not join the parade. In fact, it appeared the accosted men, those made to join the parade against their will, quickly ran off. Why would they? The parade seemed like a fun diversion. The men that joined the parade appeared young, some no older than sixteen years old. One man even appeared injured, his face partially bandaged.

At Osborne, the parade took a sharp left turn towards the construction site of the new parliament buildings, idle now due to the war. It continued for perhaps a block, then stopped abruptly. When the band disbursed, the soldiers at the front greeted the civilians. Most shook hands or appeared otherwise appreciative. The civilian marchers, all men, slowly began to approach a nearby building.

"Come this way, everyone," a soldier said. Eagerly, everyone followed and formed a queue.

"What's this for?" Mike asked the person in front of him in line.

The young man looked to be perhaps 19 years old, maybe younger. "Why … it's to sign up, of course," he said in a matter-of-fact tone.

"Sign up? What you mean?"

"The armed forces. You know, to help our mates fight the Germans and Austrians and Hungarians in the war. What do you think this is? A kissing booth?"

Marko and Mike exchanged surprised glances: not the type of line they wanted. They stepped out of line, to the derision and teasing of others.

"What's the matter? Got cold feet?"

"Hey, where're you two going?"

After only a few steps from the line, a group of uniformed men surrounded them. A skinny man with a pencil-thin moustache and a cigarette hanging from his mouth said, "Alright, what's the problem here, lads?"

"We're not signing up," Mike said. "Sorry for the misunderstanding."

Mike and Marko continued to walk, but the skinny soldier grabbed Mike's arm. "That's not how it works. You went in the line. That means you're signing up." He paused for a moment. "You don't want to defend your country? You live here now, you know."

"We didn't join parade. We were pulled into it…"

"That's not my concern. You're here now. That means you made a commitment to join."

"No," Mike said. He pulled away his arm. "Run for it!" he yelled and took off at full speed. Several soldiers ran after him. Taking his cue, Marko ran the other way.

A tall, strong-looking soldier grabbed Marko by his shirt near his shoulder. Filled with a combination of fear and nerves, Marko kept moving to try to break the soldier's strong grasp. His shirt ripped, loosening the leverage the soldier once had. With a quick tug, Marko freed himself.

He continued running, but out of the corner of his eye could see other men closing in on him.

Another soldier dove and managed to trip Marko to the ground. Fortunately, Marko sprang up and continued running before that soldier could get up and pounce on him.

He ran across Osborne Street, narrowly avoiding traffic and bicycles. Several automobiles honked. "Hey, watch where ya going, buster!" yelled one fellow commanding a horse-drawn delivery carriage.

Now on Broadway, Marko continued running west past apartment buildings and shops. Not far behind, a few soldiers still tried to catch him. He built about a half-block lead, but couldn't keep up the pace for much longer.

He ducked down a back lane. Before the soldiers could see, Marko veered off into a yard and hid behind a shed. A few trees and shrubs obscured his hiding spot from his pursuers.

Marko crouched down and waited. He could hear his heartbeat throb in his head. The pain in his right temple appeared again. Calm down. He closed his eyes and tried to slow down his breathing. If the soldiers caught him now, he would not have any strength to offer resistance. Sweat poured down his face and stung his eyes. Mosquitos buzzed around his ears, but he dared not move for fear of giving his position away. He didn't come to Canada just to fight in a war.

Finally, two soldiers jogged past on the back lane. He exhaled. Safe for now.

A few houses up they stopped. "Ah, he's gone. Let's go back."

Marko held his breath when he heard the soldiers walking back, just on the other side of the shed. But then he heard a screen door open.

"Hey. What are you doing in my yard?" came a gruff voice of a man. Petrified with fear, Marko maintained his silent pose squatting against the shed between shrubs.

"I'm talking to you, mister," said the voice again, this time sounding more agitated. By now the two soldiers walked into the back yard, level with the edge of the shed. Marko remained concealed by foliage, so the soldiers could not see him.

"Excuse me, sir," one of the soldiers said. "Did you say someone is in your yard?"

Wearing a dirty undershirt and barefoot, the gruff-sounding man had one foot outside his home. Grease lined the edges of his mouth. He appeared to be in the middle of eating something messy. "Darn tootin'. He's right there." The man pointed to Marko with his stubby fingers.

Immediately the solders spotted Marko. He tried to run past, but a soldier caught him. They dragged him to the ground and began to give him a beating. Marko curled up into a protective ball, completely submitting to the punishment. One kicked him in the side of the head, knocking him over. He tried to block the blows with his arms.

"Go get 'em, Rex," the greasy man said. A loud bark came from the direction of the screen door. Marko caught a glimpse of a large black and brown dog, possibly a German Shepard. He closed his eyes, expecting the worst.

The snarling from the dog intensified. He braced himself … but instead the dog pounced right over Marko and firmly chomped on the arm of one of the soldiers. The soldier screamed and tried to shake off the vicious beast. The other soldier looked to be at a loss, his hands on his head. The dog owner ran towards the scene. "No, no, you dumb mutt. Not him. The goon on the ground."

By this time the dog knocked over the soldier and worked him over while the other picked up a stray piece of lumber and attempted to prod the angry dog off his mate.

Missing his right sleeve, the soldier on the ground bled from a deep bite on his arm as his comrade tried to hold off the dog with the chunk of firewood. He threw the wood at the dog, hitting it on the head. This further angered the German Shepard. Eyes wide open with fear, the scared soldier ran back up the back lane with the dog in full pursuit, the dog occasionally nipping at his heels and bum.

Sensing his opportunity, Marko jumped up and ran across the yard to the front of the house and down the front street. He ran for several blocks straight north without stopping until he came to Portage Avenue where he leaned against a building to catch his breath. Pedestrians stared at him or otherwise provided a wide berth. A few women looked and frowned upon him. Those with children clutched them tighter.

After a few minutes Marko caught his breath. He walked past a store window on Portage Avenue and glanced at his reflection. He sported a nasty gash on the right side of his face – likely from the boot of a serviceman. Blood trickled down his neck and soaked into the collar of his ripped shirt. His head throbbed in pain and a dark bruise decorated his forehead just above his left eye. He also lost his hat. A complete mess. No wonder mothers were making their children avert their eyes.

He heard a tinkling sound on the ground. Then another. He looked down. Someone actually thought he was a pauper and threw a few pennies near his feet. Marko turned around, "Now listen. I no…"

Marko stopped mid-sentence. Mike laughed at him after he threw another penny at his feet. "So you survived, did you?" he said in Ukrainian.

Marko's scowl changed to a wry smile. He could see Mike fared no better. With a bloodied nose and also missing his hat, Mike's tussled and dishevelled hair looked like he just got out of bed. A ripped shirt pocket and an ugly red stain on the left side of his trousers provided evidence of the struggle Mike faced.

"Someone threw those pennies at me while I was sitting on a sidewalk a few blocks over," Mike said.

"How did we get into that mess? It happened all so suddenly."

"I should have known better. That was a recruitment parade. Any man who joins the line is expected to sign up for the army and go to war." Mike put his arm around Marko. "C'mon. These two vagrants need to drink a few shots to ease the pain."

Manitoba Club
September 17, 1914

"Milly!"

Sitting on a bench in the back yard, Mildred lifted her head up from *A Modern Chronicle*, a novel she picked up recently. William ran to her. She put the book down and stood up just in time for his strong arms to grab her by the waist and spin her around. Laughing, her lavender hat flew off to the ground.

"What is it?" Mildred put a stray strand of hair behind her ear. Rarely was William so excited.

Smiling, William put his hand on his chest to catch his breath. "Your father … I just met him at the Manitoba Club. He's offered me a position at the factory!"

"That's wonderful! When do you start?"

"It's effective immediately. He's already talked to my father about it. With Andrew off in the war he wants me to be the manager of production. I make sure outputs are completed on time and on budget and that there is a good work flow on the factory floor."

"Can you do it?"

William's look changed to one of bewilderment. "Of course I can. I'll require a little bit of training to learn the industry but I should have no problem. Your father said business has slowed down on account of men volunteering for the war effort."

Mildred squeezed William's hand. Father must have thought highly of William if he offered him a position, a high one at that. Maybe Father figured William will be part of the family in the future?

"I'd never been to the Manitoba Club before," William said. "I'm surprised my father never took me." He picked up Mildred's fallen hat and placed it on her head.

"At least you can go. It's men-only unless you're one of the serving staff."

"Everyone who's important in the city is a member of the club. I even bumped into Thomas Kelly in the billiard room. Now that I work with Winnipeg Iron Works and with the parliament buildings needing more steel, let's just say business will be very good."

She tried hard to not roll her eyes. Most of those dandies at the club were born into money and had no business sense anyway. Why couldn't women be members of the Manitoba Club?

"I'm so proud of you. You're obviously very good at business." Mildred smiled and gave William a warm hug. She felt something hard between them. "What's this?" She reached into his jacket and pulled out a thick envelope with 'Dr. Simpson' written on the front.

William snatched it from her hand and smiled. "Don't worry your pretty head. It's just business."

A Few Shots
October 15, 1914

Lily slammed back the shot of whiskey and pounded the glass back down on the table.

The young serviceman across the table belched. With glassy eyes and a flushed face, he teetered from side to side in his chair. Around the table his comrades, about five of them, urged him to take another shot. A few slapped him in the back. One massaged his neck and shoulders. Another raised the whiskey-filled shot glass up to the serviceman's mouth. All the guests in the brothel stood on their feet, shouted and raised a ruckus.

With a shaking right hand, the young lad accepted the shot. A drop or two spilled down the side of the glass.

"You drink it all up," Lily said. "Don't spill nothing." She leaned over the table from her seat. Her crooked smile and ample cleavage had to be a distraction for the new soldier. He looked so young and straight-laced, this may have been his first time near a woman like Lily. Or any woman, for that matter.

Marko leaned against the entrance to the waiting area with his arms crossed, the only person not around the table. His visit with Lily ended fifteen minutes ago, but he couldn't resist the spectacle.

His hand shaking with sweat running down his cheeks, the serviceman put the shot glass to his lips and downed the poison to a chorus of cheers and shouts. But before he could put the glass back on the table, his eyes rolled to the back of his head and he fell to the side, dropping the glass to the floor. Done.

"Davey! C'mon Davey. Get up! You can't let this woman beat you," one of his friends said. Another tried to stir him up with gentle slaps to the face.

Lily grabbed another shot from Chang. She walked over to the fallen soldier and put her foot on him revealing a large portion of her bare leg. Again, she shot back the whiskey and slammed the glass on the table. "That's how it's done, boys. Now pay up!"

The servicemen shook their heads and put their fivers on the table. Onlookers yelled and shouted. Once again, Lily drank a man under the table. She collected the cash, gave the wad to Minnie and sauntered to Marko.

He shook his head. "You do it every time."

"Hey, easy money, no?" Lily smiled and flicked Marko's stubbly chin with her long red fingernail.

"How many shots did you really have?"

"Two. Just the first one and the last one."

Marko shook his head and rolled his eyes. "How do you do it?"

Lily sauntered over to Chang where he was wiping a table from a spilled drink. She whispered in his ear. Chang went into the back and came back and fetched a bottle and a shot glass for Lily.

"Have a shot," she said to Marko and poured a glassful.

Marko sniffed the glass and frowned. Something wasn't right. He gulped down the drink. It didn't have the burn he expected. "This is watered down," he whispered.

Lily winked.

Such an actress. She should be in the moving pictures. She goads a greenhorn into a drinking game. Of course, his friends egg him on. After all, there's no way he can lose to a woman. Chang pours them shot after shot. But most of her shots are nothing more than flavoured water while her opponent gets the real McCoy. Everyone bets against Lily. She wins and splits the cash with Minnie and Chang.

"I bet I could beat that farm boy straight up anyway," Lily said.

"No, I don't think so."

"I bet I can beat you."

Marko sniffed and shook his head slowly. "Never."

"One day," Lily said. "You watch, I'll drink you under the table. See you in a few days…." She bumped him with her hip, knocking him off balance before continuing up the stairs for her next trick.

Marko paid close attention to her shapely legs the entire way up, half-tempted to go for another round. But the late hour and work in the morning stifled the lure. He waved goodbye to Minnie on the other side of the room.

Outside on Annabella Street he blew out a stream of air that formed into a cloud. Winter loomed around the corner. He pulled down his hat, hunched over and dug his hands in his pockets. The long walk back home in the cool air would be good for him.

He turned the corner on Sutherland Avenue. Just before Euclid, Marko stopped. Up ahead a group of men approached from the opposite direction. There had to be about four or five.

What should he do? Cross the street? Too obvious. Take his chances and continue on? Marko's breath shortened. He felt a twinge in his right temple. He should have hired a car.

Now just a few houses away, the loud voices and rambunctious mannerisms of the men gave away their rowdiness. Drunk, they joked and poked at each other. They must have wondered from a Main Street tavern to go to Annabella.

Marko squinted in the darkness. Soldiers. He felt a sudden urge to flee but fear kept on him on the straight path. Walking fast, he tensed as he neared the soldiers.

"Look who's in a rush," one of them said when Marko was just 10 feet away.

Marko ignored the comment and continued on.

"We don't bite," another said. The men parted, allowing Marko to pass.

"Hey … I know him, that's Marko!"

Marko looked over his shoulder at the mention of his name by a familiar voice. Under his large, unmistakable moustache, Eugene pointed at Marko. But instead of dirty overalls, he donned a soldier's uniform. Marko quickened his pace away from the men.

"That bohunk is probably still working at the factory where I was let go," Eugene said. "He's a foreigner. An enemy alien."

Marko's ears perked up. He could feel his heart thump through his chest.

"Bastard," another said. "Walks around like he owns the place."

"Look at him. Just keeps on walking. Turn around like a man! We're talking to you."

Marko began to run. No sense trying to reason with a bunch of drunk soldiers.

"Get him!" Eugene yelled and the group ran after Marko like a pack of hounds.

Where could he go? Marko turned a corner down a dark back lane. The familiar throbbing in his right temple started. He glanced behind. The soldiers chased after him, maybe 25 yards away. His foot landed awkwardly, tripping on the washboard road. He fell in a heap. Pebbles from the road stuck into the bottom of his palms.

He scrambled to get back up, but it was too late. Two soldiers pounced on him. Defeated, with his face pressed into the dirty gravel back lane, his mind raced at what would happen next.

The two soldiers brought him up to his feet. In the gloom of the darkness he could make out the fast movement of a fist. It came down hard on his left eye.

Eugene rubbed his knuckles. "Good to see you again, Marko. You enjoy taking a job away from a Canadian?"

Marko winced from the pain of the blow and from the increasing pain at the side of his head. These soldiers had him dead to rights. He couldn't fight back, only absorb the blows.

A punch caught him on the cheek. Another broke his nose. Blood poured on to his jacket and dripped on the ground.

"Nice shot, Albert," Eugene said. Marko glanced at the larger man beside Eugene. Albert had the stocky build of a rugby player. Missing a few teeth and with a short nose bent slightly to one side, he looked to have been in a few tussles in the past. A scar ran from the edge of his left eye and down a few inches along the edge of his face. His uniform looked tight and almost too small for him. Albert's suspenders appeared to strain in pain while they held up his pants.

"Please. I do nothing wrong...."

"Shut up," Eugene said. He grabbed Marko by the hair. "You're just getting what's been coming for a long time."

Again, Albert socked Marko in the face. Defeated, Marko lowered his head.

"Hey, gimme a turn," the soldier holding his left arm said just before letting go.

"Me first," said the other holding his right arm. He also freed Marko's arm.

Taking advantage of his opportunity, Marko ran down the back lane in the opposite direction, back toward Sutherland Avenue.

"Why'd you guys let go?" Eugene said. "Go get him."

Just as Marko reached Sutherland, a soldier caught up and tackled Marko to the ground. The other soldiers pounced on him like savage hyenas. Kicking and punching, all the men attacked Marko at the same time. Curled up in a ball and already bloodied, he could not defend himself.

For a long minute the soldiers kicked and pounded Marko. Finally, Marko raised a bloodied hand. "Stop. Please stop. I did nothing wrong. I'm only walking home."

"Hold it lads," Eugene said. "It appears our friend's had enough." The men backed away.

Sensing the punishment had ended, Marko uncurled from his prone position. His entire body ached. All the kicks and punches certainly bruised his back.

Just as he tried to help himself up, Eugene kicked him hard in the mouth. Marko's head flew back. He spit out two teeth. He felt another sharp blow to the head and everything went dark.

Blood
October 16, 1914

Marko opened his eyes. He felt intense pain in his head like he had been run over by a train. He ran his tongue around the inside of his mouth and felt a gap where there should be teeth. It was not a bad dream. He moaned. Every breath hurt.

Slowly, he cracked open his eyes. His vision still blurry, he could sense figures hovering over him.

"He's coming to." The woman's voice sounded familiar. He lay on a bed, but where? He tried opening his eyes but the room started to spin. He shut his eyes.

"It's okay, you're safe." Another woman's voice. Lily. He could feel her holding his hand.

Aside from hurting, it felt like he wore a hat. With his eyes still closed, Marko reached up and felt a thick bandage wrapped around his noggin.

"He'll have to rest to recover from the beating. He's lucky he wasn't killed out there." The voice came from a man. Marko opened his eyes again. This time he could adjust to the light. The man draped a stethoscope around his neck. A doctor. He placed medical supplies and instruments into a black leather bag. Lily and Minnie stood beside him.

Her arms crossed, Minnie nodded. "I imagine so, but it'll have to be somewhere else. I can't have him taking up a bed. Thank you, Dr. Brooks."

The doctor put his hat on his head. "I've done all I can. His dressing should be changed daily until it heals over. Let me know if you need me for anything else." He left the room.

Minnie motioned to Lily and they whispered near the window. Lily nodded and Minnie also departed.

Alone with Lily, Marko said, "How long?" in a raspy voice.

"You have been out for about ten hours," she said in Ukrainian. "It's about 11 in the morning."

Marko looked away and exhaled through his mouth. Late for work. He tried to get up, wincing, but Lily ran over to him and eased him back down.

"You can't go to work. The doctor figures you have a few broken ribs along with your broken nose and the teeth you lost. You also have a big cut on your head from where someone bashed you with something."

"How did I end up here…?"

"Lucky. Your friend Benny drove by in his taxi. You were lying on the street all beat up. He recognized you and dropped you off." Lily held his hand. "The doctor noticed the notch on the side of your head. He thought your skull was crushed but I told him you've always had it. How did you get it?"

"I think it's a birth defect. I still get bad headaches. I don't think about it that much. It's always been like that."

Lily poured Marko a small shot of whiskey. "Here, take your medicine."

"Is this the real stuff or that watered down mix you use to win money?"

"Try it."

Sure enough, Marko felt the burn down his throat and into his gut from the real thing.

"Minnie's not going to want you here. You'll have to go home. You're lucky she likes you to let you stay even one night. I'll get you a car. It's not too safe in the streets if you're from Galicia."

"I left to get away from Galicia. Why am I considered an enemy?"

"You want to explain it to a group of drunk soldiers? They don't care. You're from there so you're the enemy. So am I. But enough." Lily ran her hand gently on the top of his head. "Rest up."

Marko nodded and settled back on the pillow. He could see his bloodstained jacket and shirt at the side of the bed.

After Lily left the room he slowly closed his eyes and drifted off.

*****

Anastasiya and Olena are sitting with him in the carriage. They are on their way back home from a wedding. Olena's white dress billows in the wind. It's the same brilliant summer day when Anastasiya ran through the field, but later in the evening. The sun has set, but the full moon in the cloudless night sky provides enough light to see where they are going.

Marko holds the reins of Zelony, the lone horse pulling the carriage. The sounds of the Zelony's clip-clopping and the wooden wheels of the carriage mingle with the belches from frogs and insect chirps.

They arrive home. Anastasiya is very tired. Olena prepares her for bed while Marko stays in the yard to unhook Zelony from the carriage and put the animal away in the barn. Approaching the barn door leading Zelony, he notices it open. He could have sworn he closed it before they had left for the wedding.

Marko puts Zelony away and fills her water trough. The cow will be calving soon. He heads back to the farm house. A single lantern illuminates through the window.

He enters the farmhouse, but realizes he's not wearing any shoes. He doesn't remember taking them off. He obviously had them on while he was outside. He turns and sees them near the floor. He concludes that he is just tired.

He takes two steps towards the bedroom when he notices he's holding a knife. A very sharp one. The one his father gave him years ago that he uses for butchering. Why is he holding it now? Did he pick it up? He must have.

Marko looks at the counter in the kitchen, then looks back at the knife. Now it is dripping with blood. Blood is smeared all over his arm and his body. He feels a sharp pain on the side of his head. He drops the knife. Did he cut himself?

Thinking he's injured he runs into the bedroom and calls for Olena to help him. But she is already asleep in the dark bedroom. The light from the lantern in the kitchen isn't quite able to penetrate the darkness within the bedroom.

Marko walks over to Olena's side. She's covered in blankets. How can she be asleep already? He tries to rouse her, but she still will not wake. He takes off the top blanket. Olena is covered in blood. She's been stabbed multiple times. Twenty, maybe thirty times. Marko jumps back in horror. His heart races. Someone murdered his wife. His dear, lovely wife. Who would do such a thing? What rogue would commit such a horrible crime?

Marko runs out of the bedroom. He slips and falls from a pool of blood near the entrance to the bedroom. He gets up. Anastasiya!

He runs to his daughter's room. It, too, is clouded in darkness, however the window is open. The curtain flaps in the light breeze. Magazines are littered on the floor. The moonlight shimmers and dances on little Anastasiya. He approaches her bed. Marko's hand shakes. He clutches the blanket and throws it back.

Marko's eyes widen from shock and disbelief. Like his wife, little Anastasiya, his little flower, is covered in blood after being stabbed multiple times in the upper body.

Marko screams in anguish. Who did this? How can this be? He was only in the barn a short while.

Marko runs out of the house. He's in the yard, panting. He spins around looking for the assailant. He has to be there somewhere. But there is no one. He looks down. He's wearing his shoes again. He's holding the knife again.

He feels a sharp pain on the side of his head. He reaches back. Blood. Did someone hit him in the head? But there is no one around. He falls to his knees, clutching his head. His head hurts so much, it feels like it will explode.

Where's Marko?
October 21, 1914

"How did it happen? When? Where? Did he call the police?" Mildred threw a flurry of questions at the foreigner standing at the front desk, cap in hand. Liz and Peter approached the counter.

The man opened his mouth to speak when Peter interrupted. "Hello. Me name's Peter. I'm the shop foreman here." He held out his hand and the man accepted the handshake.

"I'm Mike. Marko live in my house. He's very hurt. He was beat up last week."

"How bad is he?" Peter asked.

"Not good, but better now. He has a cut on the back of his head. A few broken ribs."

"Oh my," Mildred said. She turned to Peter. "What can we do?" Marko not only didn't come to the mansion on Saturday to fix a sticky window, he also didn't show up for his English lesson on Sunday. Something had to be up.

"Not much we can," Peter said, taking off his derby and scratching his head. "The poor sap's laid up. We'll have to wait until he gets better."

"He's been gone for an entire week and never once attempted to contact the company regarding his status," Liz said. "I say we terminate him."

Mildred turned and glared. "Oh, Liz, how can you be so cruel?"

"He's an enemy alien. I honestly don't know why we keep him around. There are plenty of real Canadians who need work. Don't you think?"

Mildred frowned at Liz and was about to appeal to Peter when a familiar voice came from the stairs. "I also say we terminate him." Wearing his smart blue suit, William stood at the bottom of the stairs, arms folded across his chest. "That's just my opinion, of course. If a man cannot show up for work, what good is he?"

"Poor Marko was beaten by some ruffians and is convalescing," Mildred said, "certainly you cannot hold that against him?" William never did seem to care much for Marko. At best he ignored him. And he didn't fancy Marko's personal English lessons. Was he jealous? Or was it because Marko was a foreign alien?

William took out a cigarette and lit it, blowing away a nonchalant first puff. "It's a tough world out there. What about the poor soldiers sitting in trenches in Belgium and France? Even your own brother. If some alien gets caught in a dust-up, that's his problem."

"Please," Mike pleaded. "Marko good man. Hard working. He fixes everything. He doesn't make problems. Let him get better, then he comes back to work."

"We'll give him some time," Peter said. "The man's more than showed his value to us."

"Are you certain?" William said with a stern voice before taking another puff of his cigarette.

"I assumed he'd flown the coop. Blimey, after he missed the first day of work, I thought he'd finally gotten drunk or something. But when I checked the employee records I found out he'd never missed a day of work from the moment he was hired last July. He'd never even been late. In fact, he's the only employee who had a perfect record. Aye, and he's kept machines running that'd be idle. He's a genius with the wrench, he is. If the machines are running, that means we be making money. What are me options? Fire him? Who's around to do what he was doing? Nobody, that's who."

"Suit yourself," William said and turned to go into his office.

"Thank you," Mike said. He reached and shook Peter's hand and exited the building.

Peter turned to Mildred. "Get me Marko's address. I'll pay him a visit after work."

*****

Marko opened the front door. "Hello, Peter. Come inside."

Peter paused for a moment, likely jarred by Marko's rough look. A bandage still around his head, Marko's black eyes made it obvious his nose was broken. The side of his face featured dark bruises.

Peter gave Mike a nod, which Mike returned. Marko motioned for Peter to have a seat on the couch.

"Um, I won't stay long," Peter said. "I just wanted to see how you were fairing. Your mate over here told me ya got in a wee bit o' trouble."

Mike brought in glasses and a bottle of whiskey. He poured three shots. "Here, have a shot," Mike said, almost making it sound like an order.

"Thank you, sir," Peter said, accepting a glass and taking a sip. Mike left the room and barked orders to the kids in Ukrainian.

"So, tell me what happened," Peter said.

"I was walking home. A bunch of soldiers beat me. Eugene."

Peter lips formed a grim, thin line. "That bastard's always been a hot head. It don't surprise me. And his mates are a little off the deep end. Did ya go to the authorities?"

"No, not worth it."

"Perhaps you're right. In any case, ya don't look so good. Still, you've missed a bit of time. I can cut ya some slack, but eventually it will be difficult, if ya know what I mean."

"Da. I try work on Monday?"

"It's Wednesday today," Peter said. "Alright, let's aim for Monday."

"Thank you," Marko said. He poured another shot for both of them. When Marko smiled Peter's eyes widened.

"Blimey. They knocked out a few teeth as well."

Marko looked down and nodded.

Peter leaned towards Marko. "Listen," he said quietly, "I stuck up for you because I know you're a fine worker. For a foreigner, you're pretty good in me books, ya hear?"

Marko nodded.

"But I can only stick up for ya for so long. There's people in the shop, they want you and any other foreigner out. Ya understand? Being a foreigner, getting a job would be tough. I bet they wouldn't even hire you to work at the new parliament building. So be sure to show up if ya can. Okay? There's plenty of work for you." Peter downed his second shot in one gulp. "Well, I best be going. The missus will think I'm in a tavern again." He winked before he rose.

"Wait," Marko said. "Ukrainian custom. You not leave until bottle finished."

Peter looked at the bottle on the table. His jaw dropped: it was three-quarters full. "I can't leave until we drain the whole bloody bottle…?"

Marko frowned … but then quickly smiled. "I joke. It's not a custom."

Peter laughed and hit Mark in the arm. "Ya kidder, you." But Marko winced at Peter's innocent shot. "Sorry, mate. I forgot your condition."

Again Marko smiled and pointed at Peter, he had fooled him again.

"Ah, there ya go again. Why anyone would want to smack you around? I can't understand."

Back to Work
October 26, 1914

Mildred looked up at the clock on the wall in the office. Five minutes after Noon. She took a deep breath and walked to the door leading to the factory floor. She paused for a moment before opening it.

Most of the workers had their lunch in various groups leaving the factory floor quiet. Now would be her best chance to speak to Marko. Best to get it out of the way early in the week rather than waiting until the weekend.

She saw Peter sitting down with a few other workers at a tool bench. Their hands and faces streaked with grime and grease. Eating sandwiches with disgusting black fingernails.

"Peter, do you know where Marko is? I have to speak with him for a moment."

He pointed. "Over beside a pile of metal railings on the other side. Seems he wants to eat alone today." Spittle and crumbs flew from Peter's mouth as he spoke.

Mildred forced a smile. "Thank you." She continued on into the bowels of the factory. What exactly did metal railing look like? She peeked around a few corners until she saw him sitting on the ground, his back up against a large drill press. He took a bite from a hard-boiled egg.

"There you are! Oh, my Lord, let me see you. I can't believe what happened."

Marko looked up and winced, favouring his side. He offered a faint smile, perhaps embarrassed of his appearance. His black eyes gave him the look of a raccoon. His broken nose pointed slightly to one side. She could see a clump of hair missing in the back of his head where he had received several stitches.

"I'll get better. But my jaw still hurts when I try to eat." He looked away. "I'll be fine."

"Look at those bruises," she said quietly, careful not to be overheard. "That was a horrible beating you sustained. I – we were all terribly worried about you."

Marko nodded his head in agreement. "Da … I mean, yes, it was difficult."

Mildred crossed her arms and shook her head. "I can't believe the authorities did not attempt to apprehend those … those heathens. Do you know who did this?"

He hesitated for a moment. "No. Some soldiers. It was dark."

"Well, it's good to see you back at work again."

Marko smiled. "Yes. I will see you on weekend."

Mildred fidgeted with the material from her skirt. "Ah, yes. About that." She crossed her arms. "Yes, this Saturday there are a few items at the house that require repair. I will make sure to pay you for your time."

Marko popped the remainder of the egg in his mouth and frowned. "Pay? I thought my payment was English lessons?"

Arms still crossed, Mildred turned away. She couldn't look him in the eye. "William and I had a conversation a few days ago. He felt … we felt … it was best if I did not provide you lessons any longer. The lessons have been for over a year now and you are improved … much improved. You can read and write and while your grammar isn't the best, you've caught on quickly. With just a little more practice I am sure you will be fluent. I've taken you as far as I can…."

Marko didn't say anything. Mildred turned around. He stared straight ahead, chewing his lunch slowly.

She looked each direction to make sure no one was looking then crouched down to whisper. "I would like to continue the lessons … but William feels they are inappropriate. Remember that day in the summer when we danced? Gladys saw. A few days ago I got after her about something and in spite she told William. He was apprehensive about it to begin with, but after he found out, he put his foot down. I'm sorry. Father would still like you to come on Saturdays. He's grown to appreciate your handyman skills. And, of course, you will be compensated."

She looked down to the ground. "I'm sorry."

He reached for her hand and gave it a squeeze. "I understand." With bits of egg between his teeth the poor beaten and battered man looked sad.

Mildred patted him on the shoulder and stood up. Again, she checked the general vicinity for eavesdroppers. She examined her hand for dirt or grime after Marko touched it. "Well then. I should be getting back to the office…."

She wrung her hands on the walk back to the entrance to the front office.

Perhaps it was for the best. How long did she expect to provide English lessons for him? Being a foreigner, how much more could he learn anyway? Heeding William's wishes should take precedence. Should it not?

She stopped just before the entrance to the office and looked back. But still....

Pictures in the Office
January 6, 1915

Mildred gently tapped Thomas's office door at the factory. "Father? James is here with the vehicle. We can go now."

No answer. The door ajar, she slowly pushed it open. Father stood facing a wall while holding a drink. He took a sip.

"Father?"

Thomas jerked his head. "Oh, hello Mildred. It's time to go? Alright. Let me just finish."

Mildred closed the door behind her and slowly walked over to see what preoccupied Father.

The pictures. Of course. The wall featured several family portraits. One large, earlier painting of Mother as a young woman dominated the wall. Likely painted soon after their marriage, with her narrow cheeks and thin neck she appeared younger than Mildred today. Smaller portraits of Muriel, Mildred and Andrew surrounded Mother's. Mildred's sitting took place a few years before the *Titanic*. It seemed like a lifetime ago.

Father stared at Andrew's portrait. He never admitted it, but he missed Andrew. He had big plans for the boy, but the war delayed it. Since Andrew went off to the war Father seemed more distant. Morose. Edgy. The littlest things annoyed him. He drank more.

Time to change the subject.

"The factory seems busier."

"It is," Thomas said. "We got through the 1913 recession relatively unscathed. But things are picking up in support of the war effort. The shop floor is busy again. Now it's a problem finding workers with so many overseas."

"Peter tells me some of the employees are complaining about pay. Are you concerned about moral?"

Thomas scoffed. "That's their problem. I built this factory, just like all my businesses, out of nothing. When I was a young man never once did I ever ask for a rise in pay. If I didn't like a situation, I moved on. It's the same at Winnipeg Iron Works. If they didn't like it, they could go ahead and quit. Good luck finding decent employment for more pay. Spoiled bastards. They don't know how good they have it. During a war, no less."

Thomas poured another drink and sat down on one of the comfortable chairs. He stared again at the pictures. "Poor Muriel. I still miss her."

Mildred swallowed. "As do I. We all do."

"Then there's Andrew. I'm so proud of him joining the army and defending this country's and England's honour. When he gets back I'm going to teach him everything I know. It's hard to imagine the perils he faces every day. Trenches filled with every disease known to man. Strange gases able to wipe out a regiment in an instant. Barbed wire and whizzing bullets. Mines. Bayonets. Poor Mother is beside herself with worry."

*****

Andrew looked dashing in his crisp uniform. Mildred and her parents saw him off at the train station on Higgins. The station teemed with other freshly minted volunteers also saying goodbyes to their families, some certainly for the last time. The families all came from different classes, although most were Canadian or British.

Andrew carried his military-issued sack over his shoulder at the base of the train. Weeping, Mildred gave him a strong hug. Gertrude hid her face in a handkerchief. Andrew turned to face Thomas and gave him a military salute. Father smiled. He shook Andrew's hand then embraced.

"You take care of yourself, you hear me, son?"

"I will, Father."

"Watch your back. Those Germans are tricky buggers."

"Yes, Father."

Thomas broke the embrace and glared straight into his son's eyes. "And for God sake, don't be the first one to go charging into things. I want you back here in Winnipeg, safe and sound. You have a future here."

Andrew smiled. "Don't worry. We'll mop up the Krauts in no time. I'll be home before winter."

Thomas nodded and blinked, working hard to hold back his tears.

Gertrude kissed Andrew on the cheek and hugged him, her tears smearing against the lapel of his uniform. "Be sure to write. If you need anything, we'll send it."

Andrew nodded, his eyes red. "I'll write."

Moments later the conductor called for everyone to board. Mildred gave

Andrew another tearful hug. Andrew stepped on the train, waved once more and then was gone.

193

A Stroll in Point Douglas
February 18, 1915

Marko held out his right arm which Lily accepted. They stepped outside the bordello into the mild evening air.

"It's been such a harsh winter but tonight it's so beautiful outside. There's still more than a month of winter left, but we should enjoy this day, no?" Lily said, a faint hint of alcohol on her breath. They continued their conversation in Ukrainian.

"Da," Marko said. "So much snow and very cold. Not like last year." He patted her hand. "Not working today? It looks busy."

"It's that time of the month. Customers don't like to get all bloodied after they get their candle waxed."

Marko laughed. He liked that she made him laugh. She made him forget his problems, another reason why he visited two or three times a week.

Holding hands, they ventured outside the red light district and strolled west, in the direction of Main Street but still on residential streets. The homes in this part of Winnipeg looked older than those in the North End around Selkirk Avenue and almost all had been build from wood. The newer homes featured brick construction. Not far away, the click-clacking of another train entering Winnipeg broke the sound of soft snow squishing beneath their feet.

Marko and Lily walked past a modest two-storey wooden home. The white fence surrounding the yard looked weather-beaten and could use a new coat of paint in the spring. Suddenly, a woman stormed onto the veranda of her home. She wore an apron featuring a floral theme. Her rolled-up sleeves revealed arms caked with flour.

"Get out of here!" the woman yelled.

Marko stopped in his tracks, however Lily continued on to the point where she tugged Marko along.

"That's it ... keep going," the woman said.

"I don't understand ... why is she cross?" Marko asked.

Lily stopped for a moment and smiled slightly. "I don't really have to explain, do I?"

"Get off my street, you whore. Go back to Annabella and McFarlane. You already ruined those streets. We don't need any fallen women on this one. Take your trick with you and be gone." The woman put her hands on her hips.

Lily reached down her top and pulled out a breast. "Suck on this, you old hag," she said in English.

Mortified, the women turned around and ran back into her home.

"That will teach her," Lily said in Ukrainian. She readjusted herself.

Marko raised his eyebrows.

"That happens from time to time," Lily said. "It's not so bad. Most men don't care where we are or what we do. The police usually leave us alone. In fact, some of them are our best customers. The clergy sometimes raise a fuss, but that's only when they have nothing else to complain about. Recently they've been concentrating more on booze and bars. It's the women ... they hate us. I think they're just jealous. They hate that we dress better than them and that their men find us desirable. But I always say, if they opened their legs a little more for their husbands, my sisters and I would be out of business."

"But don't you miss a normal life?"

"Normal? What's normal? Me with four of five kids running around. No money. No food. Living from day to day. Is that normal? Because if it is, I want nothing to do with it."

Marko squeezed Lily's hand. "I don't know, there are bad times, but there are always more good times. But it's like that with anything. Even in your business. What happens when Winnipeg is not booming and growing? It's slowed down since I arrived. And now with the war, anything can happen. Sure, you might get some frustrated married men, but most of your trade is with young, single men."

Marko stopped and put both his arms around Lily and held her close. They kissed. "You can live an honest life. With me. I can provide for you. You will never have to work another day in your life."

Lily smiled tentatively, but the smile dissolved and she looked down and slowly pushed herself away. "Look Marko ... I really like you. I don't have to put on a show for you like the other men. I enjoy your visits and look forward to them. But ... the life you talk about ... that's not for me. I am what I am. I don't think I can change." She paused when Marko lowered his eyes. "Maybe one day, but not now. Do you know how many men have proposed marriage to me over the years? It's happened more times than there are stars in the sky."

Lily gave Marko a warm hug. "Let's keep things the way they are. I know I can't do what I do forever. There will be a time when I've had enough, but right now this is what I want. Besides, how else can I get a drink? Speaking of which, maybe we should head back and get a few. No?"

Eaton's
March 20, 1915

Mildred frowned at the mirror. She tried to put her hair up, but the bangs kept flopping down.

"James has the auto ready for you," Gladys said from just outside her doorway.

"Thank you. Can you help me with my hair?"

Gladys walked over. "You're making a mess of it."

"I'm half tempted to get it cut, but William prefers longer hair."

"Ah," Gladys said, "women are forever bound to do as the men of their life wish. That's the way it is." She gathered Mildred's errant locks and tamed them using bobby pins.

"I suppose, but sometimes it would be nice to do as I wish, would it not?"

"True, but we don't really have much say in the matter. We cannot vote, although that may change soon. We cannot drink in taverns, not that I would ever want to. I hear those establishments are quite loathsome. It's just best to listen to what's good for us. Your father, for example, is a successful upstanding businessman. I'm sure William will be the same."

Mildred nodded, but slowly. Men controlled everything, but men also started wars. They set all the rules, but the rules only benefit those same men. That would have to change one day.

"There, that should do the trick. Now hurry along," Gladys said before she left the room.

Mildred grabbed a silver clutch and looked in the mirror one last time. She touched the scar on her right cheek. It used to consume her thoughts every waking moment. Now it seemed an afterthought. Besides, it didn't seem to concern William.

She stepped outside the mansion where James waited near the opened rear door of the black Abbott-Detroit automobile. She paused for a moment to breathe in the spring air. A beautiful Saturday afternoon, most of the winter's snow had melted away. Dirty, crusty patches remained in shaded areas. A perfect day to go shopping at Eaton's.

While driving on Wellington Crescent, Mildred scanned the other large mansions and homes. Although seasonally pleasant outside, the bare trees and messy yards proved that spring was still young. Mud and muck prevailed. Certainly the worst time of the year in terms of cleanliness.

And everything stunk. Horse droppings mingled with slush. The stronger sun had slowly exposed assorted refuse and rubbish, hidden in snow banks since November or December. The underbellies of smelly dogs dripped dirty black water. Streets not paved became rivers of mud. Although Winnipeg residents longed for spring's warmer temperatures during each winter, they had to endure the mess that went with it.

James drove the automobile over the Osborne Street Bridge and past the construction site for the future Manitoba parliament building. The allegations of impropriety had just became public. Details littered the papers. During a public accounts committee the government had to explain why they had overpaid for building materials. William's friend, Thomas Kelly, being the contractor for the constructing of the building, figured heavily in the allegations. William didn't like talking about it. He would always wave it off or say that she simply would not understand. William had dealings with Kelly, but to what extent? Would he ever tell her? Why shouldn't she be involved in matters of business? After all, soon she would be able to vote.

The auto continued north and then turned right on to Portage Avenue, still a few blocks away from Eaton's. The pedestrians on the sidewalks featured a mixture of classes and creeds. Labouring over shopping bags, older Eastern European women waddled like penguins in homemade, ill-fitting jackets. Scarves covered their heads. They also wore unfashionable trousers or skirts, along with ugly, dirty, well-worn shoes. None smiled. Their life seemed a continual struggle, bad enough they lived in dirt and filth.

Beside them, fine, smartly dressed, upstanding citizens mingled about. Of course, all the men wore hats. The women from middle class or upper class households, especially those with an English background, tried to look their best in full-length dresses, colourful hats, and matching shoes.

Children ran about. Most came from poor families. Like hungry dogs, they would resort to stealing if they had to. But could they help it? They were brought up that way.

Eaton's looked particularly busy on this Saturday afternoon. Dozens of shoppers went in and out of the eight storey building, the largest retail establishment in Western Canada. It took a few minutes for James to negotiate the automobile to a good spot in front of the store.

Eaton's placed most of the clearance items in the basement for those living on tight budgets. Food and other household grocery-type items also occupied the basement. Mildred never bothered with the basement. The staff purchased all the groceries for the house and she never had much use for cheap-looking clothes.

Instead, she shopped for finer items: make-up, dresses, shoes, perhaps a good book. It didn't really matter and usually depended on her mood. She used to shop more frequently. Back then she did her best to keep up her appearance and looks. After the incident, shopping had become the last thing in her mind. Why bother with Eaton's?

The developing relationship with William certainly helped. It gave her confidence to face the real world. But what did he see in her? Just about every woman in Winnipeg looked prettier. Whatever it was, she wasn't going to complain. Although a charmer, sometimes he drank too much, like Father. He almost always had booze on his breath when they went out and likely ventured into bars and taverns well into the evening after their visit had concluded.

After spending a full hour examining footwear and yearning for a good book, Mildred decided to purchase *Beasts and Super-Beasts*, an anthology by Saki she heard good things about.

A few minutes before 4:00 Mildred made her way for the front door. The hustle and bustle on the first floor seemed more pronounced than when she arrived. The next visit would have to be earlier in the day or perhaps sometime during the week. Liz frowned when Mildred left to go shopping in the middle of the work day, but Mildred didn't care and, like whenever she showed off new items of clothing, got a thrill getting under Liz's skin.

A little girl accidently bumped into Mildred just before the doors facing Portage Avenue.

"April, watch where you're going," the mother said.

The little girl looked up to Mildred. "I'm sorry…" she began to say, but of course when she saw Mildred's face the little girl froze, mesmerized at the sight.

The mother grabbed her daughter's hand. "Stop staring at the lady. It's not polite," she said to her daughter. "I'm sorry," she said to Mildred with a faint smile before moving on.

A year ago Mildred would have been a mess of tears.

With her head still turned away from where she walked, Mildred accidently bumped into someone else.

"Oh! I'm sorry. That was clumsy of me—." She stopped when she realized it was Marko, a woman clutching his arm.

The situation awkward, no one said anything for the first few moments.

"Hello, Mildred," Marko said. At first he smiled broadly, but quickly replaced it with one less obvious. "How are you?"

"I'm fine, Marko. Thank you," Mildred said. Sheepish, she looked down at the ground, a nasty habit she had to break.

The pretty, well-dressed woman with Marko appeared racy. Her skirt revealed half of her calf. She also seemed to have far too much make-up on her face. Very red lips. An over-powdered face. Muriel told her the trick to make-up was putting on just enough to tease a man. That way your natural features came to the front. Too much and you look like a tramp. This woman looked like a tramp.

"Are you going to introduce us?" the woman said to Marko with an Eastern European accent. Perhaps just as well Marko found someone from his own ethnic background.

Marko looked nervous. "Yes, yes. I'm sorry. Lilia, this is Mildred. Mildred … Lilia. I work with Mildred at factory. She works in the office. I also do repairs at her parents' home."

Lily gave Marko a funny look. "Please to meet you. You can call me Lily." She turned to Marko. "Why you not tell me you're seeing other woman?"

Marko appeared flustered. "I'm not seeing Mildred anymore. I mean … no … we only work together." Marko's quick smile seemed to conceal the discomfort with the situation.

Lily stood up on her toes and kissed Marko on the check. "Relax. I only teasing you."

Now red-faced, Marko looked away.

Mildred put two and two together. Eastern European women did not dress or act like that in public. Lily was a fallen woman. She likely lived in a home of ill repute. "Well, it was nice meeting you, Lily. I should be moving along. My driver is waiting."

Everyone stood still for a moment until Lily broke the silence. "Come, I want to see the new perfumes." They exchanged farewells then Lily pulled Marko by the arm and he followed, like a dog on a leash. Too busy looking ahead, Lily didn't notice that Marko turned his head to give Mildred one last look.

Mildred noticed Marko's little peek and acknowledged it with a tiny smile before she herself turned and continued to her meeting spot. A fine man, Marko would certainly make a good husband. Mildred bit her lower lip. She missed the English lessons.

*****

Back home Mildred took off her jacket with the help of Gladys. "Master William is here to see you. He's in the sitting room."

"Thank you, Gladys." The maid went to the back of the mansion. William stood up when Mildred walked into the sitting room.

"Mildred, my dear," William said with a joyful lilt. "I waited almost an hour for you. I trust your shopping trip was successful?" Mildred traipsed into William's open arms. He gave her a peck on her good cheek.

Mildred clutched William hand with a firm grasp. She could smell his cologne. She loved the scent. One time William left his scarf behind. She went to bed with it. Made of cashmere, she held it to her face and felt its softness while inhaling William's scent. She felt naughty, like she was in bed with him.

"Did you get a haircut today? You look handsome." Mildred ran her hands through William's hair.

"I did." William gently grabbed Mildred's hand. She forgot he hated when she touched his hair.

"But I came here to talk…"

"Oh," Mildred said, somewhat surprised. "Well, have a seat and let's talk." She sat down on one of the upright chairs. "Can I get you anything? A hot cocoa? Perhaps some scotch? I'll get Gladys to—"

"That's all right, I have to leave soon anyway."

"Oh, where are you going tonight?"

"Just meeting a few men. All business. Boring matters that need not interest you."

Just like Father. Mildred nodded, almost reluctantly.

"Listen, Milly." William moved over on the couch to come closer to Mildred. "We have been together for some time. Done a lot.…"

Mildred frowned. Where was this going? Was he breaking up with her? He didn't want to see her. That was it. Mildred looked down at her hands on her lap.

"Look Millie. I really care for you and was hoping you would marry me."

Mildred looked up. William held a thin ring with a large, twinkling diamond solitaire.

The Wedding
May 29, 1915

Thomas Spencer clinked his glass with a fork to get everyone's attention. The modest gathering of about thirty guests collectively hushed. Smiling and looking dapper in his finest black tuxedo, Father raised his hand to silence the remaining few still chattering.

"Thank you very much for coming to our little reception. I cannot tell you how proud and honoured I am to have William as a new son-in-law. He comes from a fine family. I have known his father, Edgar, for many years now." Mildred saw Edgar Dalton a short distance away. Short in stature, William's father smiled and nodded at the acknowledgment. Despite being just in his early fifties, Edgar sported a head of white hair.

The flower arrangements in the backyard of the mansion complemented the joyous occasion. A large canopy provided some shade to those guests wishing to get away from the sun, although most chose to mingle in the open air. Chairs allowed guests the opportunity to rest their legs, if they so wished. The house staff had set up tables containing refreshments and light snacks. They replenished items as needed. A table under the blue wooden shelter at the center of the back yard held only one item: the white three-layered wedding cake. Women wore the latest styles including large, wide-brimmed hats decorated with colourful feathers and ribbons. Full-length dresses hung to the ground, although some of the younger ladies revealed their ankles. Men wore crisp suits with appropriate headwear. Many elected to wear top hats.

"William," Thomas looked at him while he spoke, "I welcome you to our modest family and I look forward to beating you at a round of golf in St. Charles this summer. I hope your arithmetic skills are better than your father's. Seems he's always one or two short when it comes time to add up the score." Everyone laughed at Thomas's poke while William smiled at his new father-in-law.

"I would like to thank all those who made the long journey from Ontario.

We hope your stay here in Manitoba's capital will be enjoyable. I have always felt that May is the best time of the year here in Winnipeg. As everyone knows, our winters are long and bitterly cold. The summers, though short, can be quite warm and depending on the year, infested with mosquitoes. But the month of May stands apart from the rest of the year. Winter has receded and the trees and flowers are beginning to bring their glory to the world. The temperature is warm and pleasant, and best of all, the insects have not yet hatched. Now if only my creditors would leave me alone in May, the month would be downright perfect." Again, another assortment of chuckles and guffaws.

"But alas, it would be remiss of me not to mention some of those who are not here with us today. My son Andrew is presently off in Europe, fighting on the front lines. I am very proud of my son and look forward to the day when I can shake his hand when he comes back from the war."

Several applauded and someone shouted, "Hear! Hear!"

Seated beside Thomas, Gertrude brushed away a tear with her gloved hand and smiled.

"And of course, our daughter, Muriel…" Thomas's voice cracked slightly. He paused for a moment to take a sip of scotch while everyone looked on in rapt attention. "Well, I'm sure everyone recalls poor Muriel's fate. There was a time when I looked forward to the day when I would be able to stand up here and address a similar crowd at her wedding. But sadly, that will never be. Muriel was a special, gifted young woman with many talents. Without a doubt she would have been a star on stages across the globe. I deeply miss her and continue to do so."

Thomas paused. Except for the chirping birds in the trees, complete silence lasted for several long seconds.

"But that is the past," he said with a lighter tone to his voice. He raised his glass of scotch in the air. "Please everyone, let us toast the new married couple. Let us toast to Mr. and Mrs. William B. Dalton."

The backyard became an instant cacophony of clinking of glasses and numerous "To the bride and groom" toasts.

"That was a wonderful little speech, was it not? Very touching." William whispered to Mildred, standing beside him only a few feet away from her father. William's breath smelled of scotch. She acknowledged him with a nod and a small, forced smile.

She felt stunning in her wedding gown. White with a high waist line and made of high-quality linen, lace and beads trimmed the gown in intricate detail. The dressmaker interwove beads into the lace itself. Although the dress dragged slightly across the ground, it lacked a train. That would be a waste of material. To distract from her face, Mildred's dress showed off more cleavage than she typically did in her day-to-day attire. Mother remained skeptical about it. When Mildred pulled the heavy veil back behind her head every guest likely had the same thought: *A pretty young woman, a pretty dress. Such a shame what happened.*

Mildred spotted Becky, her matron of honour, standing by herself a short distance away near a tree adjusting her large hat.

Becky smiled when Mildred approached. "That was a lovely church service … your dress is absolutely beautiful."

"Thank you."

"Where are you going for your honeymoon?"

"Banff Springs Hotel. We leave in a few hours."

"I would love to go there. I hear the mountains are breathtaking. George took me to Niagara Falls."

Mildred turned to look toward the river. She lowered her voice. "I can't believe Father never once said anything about me. I'm just like a head of cattle to be sold off to the highest bidder."

With a consoling smile Becky patted Mildred's back. "Well, just think about the wonderful time you will spend with your new husband. Let me get you some wine." Becky walked away.

A short distance away William stood off to the side with an older man leaning on a cane, his Uncle Charles. Mildred could hear the conversation. William face had reddened. "What do you mean?" he said to his uncle.

"You should be overseas right now. Young and able, what could possibly be your excuse?" Charles looked tidy with his well-maintained grey beard.

"Uh … I … uh…"

"I figured as much. If I was your age, I would not hesitate for a second to enlist. Shameful."

"Now listen here," William said. He poked his finger at his uncle's chest. "I'm not chicken. I'm an executive with my father-in-law's firm and he needs me to run things efficiently."

Charles snorted. "The only thing you've ever been efficient with is finishing your scotch."

*****

They prepared to cut the cake. Both smiling for the photographer, William held Mildred's hand on top of the knife. Becky stood with other guests about twenty feet away.

"That Becky's a bit of a looker," William whispered from the corner of his mouth.

Mildred frowned slightly. "Yes, she is pretty."

The photograph taken, William walked off to rejoin his best man. He picked up a drink along the way, stealing a glance at Becky.

Mildred crossed her arms and glared at him. Becky came to her side at the cake table.

"I hope he watches the alcohol," Mildred said. "He sometimes has a bit of a temper."

"Some men are like that. I know my husband gets a little crazy when he dabbles in the co-co juice. We might be better off if we end up with prohibition. Those temperance groups are picking up steam. But then again, I like my wine, too."

Mildred stiffened her back and raised her nose, feigning a high society duchess. "It is all about moderation, my dear," she said in a pseudo-English accent. Both women laughed.

"How has he fitted in your father's factory?"

"Right now Father has him in charge of production. But I've overheard Father complain a few times to Mother that he's not the most punctual employee. He does get along with most people, though. I've told him that he should consider a sales position but he scoffs. I'm concerned that some of his friends appear to be of the unsavory variety.

"But it's not just the stresses of work that has driven him to drink more. He appears to be unusually concerned with the scandal that's brewing regarding the parliament building construction."

Becky raised her eyebrows. "The headlines in the paper a few months ago certainly caught everyone's attention."

"'Manitoba Defrauded of $800,000.' How can I forget? It's all William talked about. Especially after the provincial government resigned and the Royal Commission that followed. I think William's father's firm was involved with that Thomas Kelly character who's in the middle of it all."

Mildred took a sip of wine. "So tell me, Becky. What happens next? Babies? Tea parties? Knitting doilies? Am I going to end up being just like my mother?"

Becky gave Mildred a companionate smile. "It's hard to say. I know I try to keep myself occupied. But it doesn't have to be all tea parties and visits to shoe stores. You can always volunteer for something. Many ladies do. It seems like the Christian thing to do and we have a considerable amount of time anyway. A few years ago I got involved with a mission that helps the unfortunates. It's called the All People's Mission. It tries to get recent immigrants acclimatized to the ways of Canadian life."

Mildred turned her head. "You never told me before…?"

"No, I kept it to myself. For the longest time I honestly didn't want to bother you with it. You know, right after your … accident … and all. I didn't think it would be something you were in the mood for. But now that you've been married off it's something you may want to consider. If you're interested, just come to the Mission. It's in Point Douglas on Sutherland Avenue."

"Not the absolute best part of town."

"True," Becky nodded slightly. "But there's not exactly a need for a mission on Wellington Crescent."

Mildred laughed and took another sip of wine.

*****

Mildred sat on the cot in her private cabin. The rhythmic click-clacking of steel wheels on the rails broke the silence. They had to be deep in the heart of Saskatchewan by now. The meal went well enough, but William practically ignored her to go play cards with some men from Ontario.

Her head shot up when she heard a knock on the door.

"W-who is it?"

"Special delivery for Mrs. Dalton," the man said from the other side of the door, immediately followed by a few muffled laughs and chuckles.

Mildred composed herself and opened the door.

Two younger men, well-to-do passengers dressed in crisp pants and vests with rosy cheeks and pasty complexions, held William. One had William's legs while the other carried his arms like they were lugging a dead body. William eyes remained shut.

"He's ready for you," the one carrying his arms said. The other man smirked and guffawed. "And I think you might have to change his diaper."

Mildred looked down at William's crotch. Her new husband had wet himself. "Take him inside. Lay him on the ground … gently."

"Your husband is not a particularly good poker player," one man said.

"…and not good at holding his booze" said the other.

Mildred closed the door after the men left. William smelled like a distillery accented with urine.

She smirked, then giggled. Soon she laughed loudly like she hadn't laughed in years. Her head swayed back and forth while tears welled in her eyes from the mirth of the situation. "Oh, William," she whispered in his ear. "What a lovely start to our marriage." Off in la-la land, he did not move.

She slipped out of her evening gown and carefully put it away in her new pink suitcase. Not concerned William would see her, she took off everything including her undergarments. She found her new nightgown, something she picked out for this special evening.

As she was about to slip it on, she noticed her reflection in the dark window. Dropping her nightgown to the floor, she stared at herself for a full two minutes. Gingerly, she ran her hand across her white body. Across her torso. Along her side. Over top one breast. Along her neck. Across her face.

But when she came to her right cheek, she stopped and turned her head away. She put her head down and began to weep.

Nothing changed. Everything remained the same.

The clacking steel wheels concealed her sobs.

William Comes Home Late
August 3, 1915

Mildred concentrated on the ticking of the grandfather clock near the landing at the foot of the stairs, the only sound she could hear. Every fifteen minutes it made a small chime. When the big hand reached the twelve, the clock proudly announced the arrival of another hour followed by the appropriate number of bongs.

She sat staring at the furnishings of her still-new Harvard Avenue home. The fabulous couch and matching chairs, luxurious and detailed, still smelled new. The expensive matching crimson draperies perfectly framed the large front window. Nestled in the corner, a Steinway upright piano craved attention. Various oil paintings of pastoral scenes filled the walls. Shelves contained assorted dishes and other nick-nicks, most of which were wedding presents.

Lydia walked into the sitting room, her hands clasped in front of her. "William's plate is in the oven … do you know when we might expect him?"

After a short pause Mildred turned her head slightly. "No. It might not be until later." Of course Lydia's question was rhetorical, but she still asked to be polite.

It worked well when Lydia agreed to leave Mildred's parents' manor for her new home. Younger and more open-minded than Gladys, she kept the home clean and did all the laundry, cooking and yard work. She also dusted every day. But with only William and Mildred to look after, Lydia had it easy. In her spare time she enjoyed crocheting and knitting.

"If it pleases you, I'll retire to my room for the time being. If William comes home soon I can help with dinner. But if it's too late…"

"Never mind, I suspect he won't arrive until much later. Go on and enjoy the rest of the evening."

"Thank you," Lydia said. She tipped her head down slightly and went to her room on the main floor.

Mildred curled up on the couch with a book. The silence of the house took over, save for the ticking of the grandfather clock.

Much smaller than her parent's Wellington Crescent manor, but located nearby in good neighborhood, she expected they would move into something larger once William's career further developed and they started having children.

The neighborhood seemed pleasant enough. Children played in the front yards. In the early evenings young couples strolled on the sidewalk, some pushing a baby carriage.

Gregory Browne lived next door, although they had never met him. They learned from Lydia that he was a bachelor in his early 30s and that his father made a small fortune from land speculation. Gregory followed his father's footsteps in real estate. He enlisted in the army once the war broke and has been overseas ever since. Although Gregory's home was usually vacant, the gardener came a few times a week to tend to the yard. He'd made arrangements for someone to pay the bills and ensure his affairs remained in order.

Three months into her marriage, Mildred found it odd that they never went anywhere after their honeymoon, especially considering the time of year, short summers and all. But William always had a reason. "I'm busy with work right now. We'll go somewhere later."

Busy. Always busy.

Almost immediately he paid less attention to her. He always went out. Practically every day, it seemed. Usually he came home drunk, smelling of booze and tobacco smoke. Through those foul odors sometimes she could almost swear she detected a slight hint of perfume.

Other than formal engagements involving her parents or some other evening event requiring the two of them to be present, William never took her out. No more quiet, romantic dinners. No more shows. No more concerts.

On weekends he went to the Manitoba Club to socialize with business associates. Sometimes he would play golf or maybe a bit of tennis. Each time he would stumble in the front door. Usually William's driver, John, would have his arm around William, propping him up.

After they wed William forbid her from working, despite her protests. "A married woman belongs at home. Only the man of the house is to provide for the family," he said. As an act of appeasement, William let her do whatever she wanted. She could shop anywhere and buy just about anything. But if she went too far or if William happened to be in a foul mood, he would order whatever she purchased be taken back. But generally, she pretty well got her way and could hide purchases or casually pass them off as a wedding gift he forgot about.

Bad with money, he spent it foolishly. He did so while he courted her, but she attributed his free spending as something all men did when they tried to win the hand of a woman. Because of this, she tried to rein in her spending and squirrel away money. Five dollars here. Ten dollars there. It was something women had to do, because you never knew what could happen in the future. Mother still did it.

But William's worst quality had to be his fiery temper. Without warning he could get angry. Already three times he had fired Lydia. On each occasion Mildred would quietly console her and she would be back doing her regular chores the following day. Of course on each occasion Mildred had to give her a little rise in pay to make up for the torment she had to endure. Perhaps that was one reason why Lydia made sure the house remained absolutely spotless and perfect: it gave William no reason to be cross with her.

His temper worsened when he drank. One evening after he arrived home late he threw a pretty porcelain figurine against a wall for the simple reason that he forgot they were to go to her parents' for dinner. Apparently he had inadvertently made other plans.

Typically she retired each evening after about nine or ten. Usually she would be fast asleep if William came home late. Sometimes she would hear him stumble around in the dark. If she awoke while he bumped in the night getting ready for bed she would tell him he could turn on the light, but he never would. "Uh, that's alright dear. You go back to sleep."

Through all the days and nights, week after week, like a sentinel, the grandfather clock ticked away and proudly announced the passage of time.

*****

Mildred woke with a start, still on the couch. The clock signalled the top of an hour. She listened for the bongs. One … two … then nothing. Two in the morning. She straightened herself in the darkness. Did William come home? He had to work tomorrow.

She reached over and turned on a lamp, illuminating the room. Perhaps William noticed her on the couch and left her there? A quick check of the empty bedroom upstairs confirmed that he had not come home. What manner of man does such a thing? Only on the rarest occasions did Father ever stay out that late on a weeknight.

She prepared herself for bed. After washing her face and slipping on her floor-length white sleeveless night gown, she made her way downstairs to turn off the lamp. Let him stumble around in the dark.

Halfway down the stairs she heard the click of the front door.

In a riot of noise, arms locked around each other, William and John sang something incomprehensible. One stumbled and both fell on the ground, laughing like school children.

William noticed her. "Hey ya, Milly. How ya doing?"

Frowning, Mildred gave William an icy stare.

Struggling to rise to his feet, William turned to John and said, "Oh, oh, Johnny Boy … me thinks I'm in the dog house."

"Me thinks you thinks correctly," John said. Both men laughed.

William looked dishevelled. His shirt hung out from out of his trousers. In addition to missing his collar, several buttons down the front had disappeared. One suspender hung limp from his side. Mud caked William's left knee of his black trousers. "Well, Johnny Boy, another successful evening."

"…and safe and sound at home," John said, red-faced. "Well, I ought be going. No sense in picking up any shrapnel from what's gonna happen to ya." Again, both men laughed heartily. John closed the door behind him, instantly plunging the house into silence but for the grandfather clock.

"You had a good evening?" Mildred said, still with her arms crossed.

"The tops." William ignored her cold glare.

"Why do you have to come home so late? You have to work tomorrow, do you not?"

"Ah, I can go in a little late. No problem. The factory's running ship shape now that the Old Man's got me in charge of things."

"You mean my father."

"Yeah, that's what I said."

"You said 'Old Man.'"

"Yeah, yeah, you know what I mean."

Mildred exhaled and walked down the remaining steps. "Come to bed."

"Yes, Mommy."

She noticed something white poking out from his trouser pocket. She grabbed it, a white feather. "Why do you have this?"

"Some old hag gave it to me. A bunch of women were pinning them on lads to shame them into enlisting for the war."

Mildred grabbed William's arm to help him up the stairs. "What happened to you? Why is your shirt ripped?"

"Ah, it was nothing"

"This was a nice shirt and that stain on your trous—" Mildred stopped when she noticed the bloodied and bruised knuckles on his right hand. "Were you fighting?"

William snatched his arm away from her grasp. "Lemme alone. It was nothing. Just a bohunk who needed to be taught a lesson. That's all."

Mildred wagged her finger six inches from his face. "I am sick of your drinking and fighting. You hang around with the wrong people. You never spend any time at home. We never do anything together."

In a flash William grabbed Mildred's wrist. Mildred struggled for a moment, but was at his mercy. Slowly, he bent her arm back while an evil sneer formed on his face. "I will do whatever I want," he said through clenched teeth.

Ever slowly, Mildred inched down until one knee touched the ground. "William! Stop it, you're hurting me. It hurts!"

Unwavering, William continued to apply force to her thin wrist. "You can't tell me who I can or cannot associate with," he said, his voice strong and almost devoid of alcohol-induced slurring. "I will go where I please, whenever I want. Do you understand?"

"Stop it!" Mildred screamed, her face twisted in pain. She cowered while William towered over her like a master would over his hunting dog.

"Do you understand?!?"

"Yes! Yes! I understand!"

William released his grasp. Immediately Mildred recoiled and fell to the ground, grasping her tender wrist. Sitting at the base of his feet, her long hair partially covered her face. She shot an angry glance at William.

William hit Mildred on the cheek. "Wipe that look off your face, you bitch."

Mildred fell back from the force of the blow. She realized too late that she had poked the tiger.

With authority, William stepped over Mildred and grabbed her by the hair, pulling her head back. Then with the other, slapped her in the face. He slapped her again the other way with the back of his hand. He continued slapping her hard in this fashion five or six more times. Finally, he threw her to the ground.

"You better watch what you say or I'll put a matching mark on the other side of your face. Stop hounding and harassing me. You have no say whatsoever. You do what I say or I will give you another thrashing."

William marched upstairs.

Mildred, bleeding from the nose and mouth, sat on the ground in a ball, her hands covered her head in case he changed his mind.

For several long minutes, maybe ten, Mildred stayed in the same position. In a combination of fear and sorrow, she sobbed quietly in case William heard her.

A door clicked open. Mildred tightened up.

"Mildred?" Lydia said softly. "Ma'am … are you alright?"

Lydia, in her nightgown, inched toward to Mildred. "Mildred. Oh, I'm so sorry for you…"

Mildred began to weep more openly. Immediately Lydia ran over and comforted her. "Oh, Mildred. What a thing to happen. You should know better than to confront him when he's been drinking…."

Tomorrow she would have two black eyes. Lydia would have to cancel all her appointments by telling everyone she fell ill. She would stay inside until the bruising healed lest her neighbors gossip. She would lay low for a few days, maybe a week. William would not apologize, but would likely buy flowers tomorrow. Nice, fresh roses. A dozen. He might buy her other things because maybe he would feel a little guilty. Then he will go out again.

And all the while, the grandfather clock would tick away.

All People's Mission
September 7, 1915

"Your new driver, Robert, is here," Lydia said from downstairs.

"Please have him wait for a moment," Mildred said. She splashed warm water on her face from the basin in the bathroom on the second floor. "I'm not quite ready. I'll require about ten minutes."

It took several weeks to heal from the bruises. She began to venture outside only a week ago. Crossing the hall to the bedroom, she could hear Lydia offer the driver some tea while she took his jacket from him.

Where was the hair brush? Not seeing it at her table in the bedroom, she opened a few drawers. Did she place it in one of William's by accident?

Last night ended with William stumbling into the home late. Another typical evening. She didn't wait for him anymore. Instead, she would retire around ten o'clock. He never bothered to wake her. Usually he fell in bed, fully clothed. Other times, with the help of John, he would sleep on the couch. One evening he fell against a small table in the hall and a pretty vase fell over, smashing on the ground.

Not that it mattered, really, because William paid so little attention to her. When was the last time they had been intimate? July? She didn't care. One morning, while he lay in bed, she noticed unmistakable lipstick markings on his cheeks and ears.

And each morning, like routine, he would stroll down the stairs into the dining room ignoring the events of the night before, all cleaned up, prim and proper, ready for another day at the office. Annoying chicanery, but both Mildred and Lydia played along with it. She could see Lydia roll her eyes whenever William mentioned the long business meetings or whatever lies he conjured. He left the house, driven by John, by 10:00 am each weekday morning. Why did Father put up with William coming into work so late each day? That cannot last.

She looked in one of William's drawers that she'd never opened before. Stuffed, it overflowed with envelopes. She looked in one. Money. Fives, tens, twenties. There had to be a small fortune in the drawer. Why didn't he deposit the money in a bank? It couldn't be safe just sitting in a drawer. What if someone robbed them? It didn't seem prudent. She made sure to have her secret cache hidden away in a hat box where William would never look.

Mildred found the hairbrush under a newspaper on the bed.

The trouncing the Liberals gave the Conservatives in the Manitoba election last month agitated William. The Tories never really had a chance, especially after the scandal surrounding the new parliament building. Thomas Kelly's firm overcharged for materials then gave the excess to the Conservatives as a political contribution through Dr. Simpson, an officer with the Conservative Party of Manitoba. William acted as the middle man exchanging envelopes, like the one she witnessed her first dinner with him. Such a smart man, why did William have to associate with a crook like Kelly?

But what did political developments matter? What could she do about it? Even Mother would say the primary role of a woman was to be a good wife. Yet, all the while, Father kept her in line whenever his temper reached a tipping point. Did it have to be the same for herself? Was there another way? Why did life have to be such a struggle?

She stared at her face in the mirror. What a fool to think her marriage would provide stability and ensure everlasting happiness. She wished she never met William.

"Mildred!" Lydia yelled from below.

"I know. I know. I'm on my way. Just a moment." She quickly powdered her face to cover the remnants of her bruising. She put on her light blue jacket, the first time this season she planned to wear it. From her hat rack she picked off a wide-brimmed number, white with blue trim. When tipped down, the brim of the hat mostly covered her face. Walking past the mirror, she instinctively glanced at her reflection.

To hell with the scar. It was a part of her, not unlike her arms and legs and bosom. Perhaps other people needed to accept her for the way she was instead of for what she was not. She could never be a better dancer than Muriel. Nor would she ever be pretty again. Nor a happy wife.

She took off the wide-brimmed hat and instead reached for one with a smaller brim. It didn't exactly match her blue jacket, but it would do. Before she went downstairs she glimpsed at the piano-shaped jewelry box Marko repaired for her a few years ago. She bit her bottom lip. How was life treating him? She hadn't seen him in months, certainly not since she married and left the factory.

Robert leaned against the wall, smoking a cigarette as Lydia dusted a nearby shelf. Once Mildred came down he immediately righted himself.

"Ma'am…" he said, but immediately flinched once he saw Mildred.

"Yes, it's a scar," she said abruptly and walked right past him to the door. "I was wounded while the *Titanic* was sinking."

Lydia and Robert gave each other surprised looks.

Mildred opened the door and looked back. "Come, come. I haven't all day. Let's go." She urged Robert with a wave of her hand.

"When will you be home, Mrs. Dalton?" Lydia said, sticking her head out the door.

"I'm not sure. And please, call me Mildred. Or Ma'am. But never call me Mrs. Dalton again."

"Yes, Mildred," Lydia said slowly before retreating back into the house with a puzzled expression.

Robert hopped behind the steering wheel. A middle-aged man with greying temples and a salt and pepper moustache, Robert appeared ordinary except for the missing pinkie on his right hand. "Where ya wanna go, Ma'am? Eaton's? Robinson's?"

"Sure, Eaton's, why not?"

Robert negotiated the automobile downtown and eventually down Portage Avenue. Mildred stared at the pedestrians along one side of the wide avenue. A wide assortment of nationalities and types of people, everything from prim and proper high society women to down and out pathetic bums went about their tasks and errands.

With their ill-fitting clothes and awkward manner, she easily picked out the immigrants. But where once she would have been disgusted, she now felt pity. Were those wretches any better or worse than she? Although miserable and destitute, at least those people had the desire and will to live. They travelled far from squalid conditions to try to carve out a better life. All their lives they only knew of struggle and hardship. Each day the sun rose to greet them with maybe, just maybe, the promise of a better day.

But unlike those pathetic Eastern Europeans, Mildred greeted each day with disdain. She hated her life. It lacked purpose. After over only a few months William suffocated any joy she had. She could not see a future, whereas the immigrants did. Why else would they journey so far with no guarantee of success? She came from a cultured, successful family, yet, in a way, was worse off than the immigrants.

It dawned on her: they had to work for it. Those immigrants had to work hard for every penny, every scrap of clothing and every tiny crumb of food. She didn't. In fact, she didn't have to do a thing and could live a life of utter luxury until her dying day. Other than household chores and rearing children, women served no purpose. They had no involvement in business or politics. Men – husbands and fathers – made all the decisions for them. They may let the wife pick the colour of the couch or the design on the drapery, but nothing more.

When they arrived at Eaton's Robert stopped the vehicle at the side of the road, got out and opened the back door for Mildred.

Mildred paused for a moment before she started to step out. She put her hand in the pocket of her jacket where she felt a piece of paper. It was the address of the mission given to her by Becky one day last year. One foot already on the side walk, Mildred stopped and stared at the note.

"Ma'am? Everything alright? Yer coming out, aren't ya?"

Mildred looked at Robert's outstretched gloved hand.

"No, I think not. I changed my mind." She plopped back into the automobile.

"All right, suit yourself." Robert closed the door and walked back to the driver's side. A vehicle honked from behind. Robert shook his fist. "Hold yer horses! I'm going, I'm going."

Robert quickly jumped back into the vehicle. "Alright, where to?"

She handed him the note.

Robert squinted his eyes. "All People's Mission? That's no store. On Sutherland?" He put the automobile in gear and sped off to the approval of the impatient vehicle behind them. "That's in Point Douglas. There's nothing there but factories, old houses, and ..."

"That's fine. That's where I want to go."

The vehicle went to Portage and Main where Robert turned left up Main. There, Mildred got a good view of the social condition. Although still the early afternoon, many men appeared visibly inebriated. A police officer practically dragged one man by the collar. In another block a man slept against the side of a building while others paid no heed, like it were a common occurrence. The upcoming possibility of prohibition should take care of some of those miserable scenes.

Not long after, their vehicle rumbled on Sutherland Avenue. "119 – there it is," Robert said. He pointed to a two-storey brick building. The automobile came to a stop right in front of the building. Robert opened the door and helped her out.

"Should I wait for ya here or do ya want me to come at a certain time?"

"Just go."

"Now, I can't go leaving ya here. This ain't exactly the best part of town, ya know."

Mildred thought about it for a moment. She had never even taken a streetcar before in her life. Never had to. "Come back at 5 o'clock, please."

She stood alone at the steps of the building. A plain-looking structure with a high stone foundation, the flat roof featured an iron cornice and parapet. She climbed the steps to the double door entrance and looked up at three larger windows on the second floor. There on the second floor, Becky waved at her in an enthusiastic fashion. Mildred gave her a quick wave and entered.

Although the street seemed relatively quiet, the same could not be said for the interior of All People's Mission. A hive of activity, people buzzed about, the majority being immigrant women or children. Most of the children dressed normal, although their clothes looked older, an inappropriate size, worn or all of the above. The women wore clothes that looked like they had just arrived from Europe. Bland designs and mismatched colours. While the children seemed to be in good spirits, the women, likely mothers of the children, spoke amongst themselves in their own native languages.

Becky came down the stairs. With a broad smile and wearing a smart-looking, yet plain yellow dress, she ran up to Mildred and gave her a strong hug. "Milly! How have you been? How's the married life? You must be so happy to be with William."

"Everything is fine." Mildred tried to fake a reassuring smile.

"I'm glad you're here. See, I told you that you would get bored sitting at home all day or shopping."

"Yes, well, I saw your note and thought I would pay a visit."

"Let's sit and have a tea."

Mildred nodded and gave her coat and hat to Becky. "How long have you helped here?"

"Oh, about five years."

"And you don't get paid?"

"No, not a penny. I do this because I want to and strongly feel that what

I do will make Winnipeg a better place."

"What made you want to volunteer? It seems like such an effort…."

"That man there." Becky pointed to a photograph on the wall of the thin-faced man with a receding hairline. He featured a thick, light-coloured moustache and a beard shaped into a point at his chin.

"J.S. Woodsworth," Becky said. "He was involved with the Methodist Church and became the superintendent here. He moved on to other things a few years ago, but I don't doubt he'll be well-known and regarded as a great man very soon."

Becky opened a door into an office. "Helga, can you please get us some tea?" she asked a heavy-set foreign-looking woman with thick, bushy eyebrows.

"Have a seat," Becky said. The office appeared plain and free of adornment – perhaps befitting a religious-based mission – although the walls held an assortment of photographs of volunteers, workers, children and homely-looking women. A crucifix about six inches in length hung on the wall. Against a wall on the other side of the room stood a pale green couch, old and lumpy, easily the most inviting place to sit. Mildred walked over to it.

"Don't sit there," Becky said. "It may have lice or bed bugs. You would hate to bring those little buggers home. Not the kind of guests you want. Here, let's sit on these chairs. Certainly not from Hotel Fort Garry, but they will do."

Helga arrived with a tray holding two cups of tea, a small container of sugar and a very small cup of cream.

"Thank you, Helga," Becky said, taking the tray from her and setting it on the wooden desk. A large old stain, likely from coffee, dominated a sizeable portion of its well-worn working area. The varnish, perhaps applied sometime in the 1800s, had long ago begun to peel away and fade.

"A wonderful, thoughtful man, Mr. Woodsworth had great regard for the human condition. Very selfless. He told me once of a trip to England. Oxford to be precise. He could not believe the state of the slums in London. There he was, in one of the finest, most refined cities in the world, and the wretched conditions of some areas were completely deplorable. He became convinced that Canada, being the virgin territory it was, should not ever develop those conditions."

Mildred scooped some sugar into her tea and added a dash of cream. "Well, from what I've seen on the streets, especially on Main, the conditions are not the best here in Winnipeg. I recall when I was a teacher in the North End that it was also the case with many of the families."

"Very much so. Most of the central and eastern European immigrants were already poor and destitute before they arrived from their native country. Like paupers, many lived in medieval conditions. They lack any formal education and had little means for advancement."

"Why come here? Why trade one form of poverty for another? Especially in, what is to them, a foreign land with foreign customs and a foreign language."

"Hope." Becky took a sip of her tea. "Hope, faith and hard work. That's all they have. Those three things are what keep the immigrants alive. Part of the problem is that the children of immigrants are not encouraged to have a decent education. Many leave school because they have to. Their family is poor and they need to get income from anywhere they can. Some children leave school as young as eleven, twelve years old. Horrible. Half their childhood is taken away for want of survival. Many immigrants are illiterate. And, of course, those children grow up to become adults and have children of their own. They, too, will also see little use for education and thus the cycle repeats itself. Here at All People's we have two kindergartens. We try to give immigrant children a start on the right path."

"My father would say that you're wasting your time. That those immigrants are lazy, uncultured and unintelligent by their very nature."

"Yes, it's an uphill battle, it certainly is … but I don't necessarily agree with your father's opinion. I think what we are really trying to do is assimilate the immigrants to be regular, ordinary Canadians. Start with them young and teach them the way to a civilized life reflecting our values. Same with the mothers and young women. After all, it's the woman of the house who upholds the moral fibre of the family. If we get them and the children to understand the proper way to dress and how to function in society, the men will follow."

Mildred sipped her tea. "I noticed the children all seemed to be dressed rather normal, just like any regular Canadian child, at least."

"True," Becky said. "The children are always the easiest ones to mould, if you will. It's more difficult for adults who are already set on their ways."

"Still, it must be a difficult task. I know when I worked at the factory, some of those immigrant workers were the filthiest creatures around." Mildred laughed.

"That's the other problem," Becky said. "Many new immigrants live in absolute squalor. There are six, seven, eight people to a room. Disease like typhoid runs rampant in closed quarters. The immigrants can't afford the rents and are forced to shack up in large multiples."

"Again," Mildred said, "my father and others attribute infant death and even typhoid to their poor hygiene and health habits."

"That may be partially true, but many homes in the North End do not have running water. It's a luxury for most. In addition, many mothers are forced to work because the father cannot bring home enough money to feed all the mouths leaving their small children with inadequate care."

Mildred finished her cup. "That hit the spot. Thank you for the tea."

"You're welcome," Becky said. She stood up. "But come, let me give you a quick tour of the facility."

Upstairs Becky led Mildred to several rooms. A group of young immigrant women recently vacated one meeting room. Several chairs of different styles occupied wooden tables of varying styles and heights. All People's clearly accepted whatever furniture it could find. The walls featured assorted slogans including 'Cleanliness is Godliness' and 'A Clean Kitchen Leads to a Pure Soul.' The wall also included several lists: direction on how to change and clean a diaper, cooking tips and advice on laundering.

"What about religion?" Mildred said. "Do you attempt to convert them to a proper form of Christianity?"

"We used to," Becky said, "but Mr. Woodsworth learned early in the process that the immigrants held fast to their beliefs. So strong is the bond to their religion that any attempt to reform them is met with absolute resistance and scepticism. So Mr. Woodsworth realized it was futile. Instead, he tolerated the foreigners' backward beliefs thinking that over time, they would come around to proper worship."

Mildred nodded in approval.

Becky showed Mildred a few other rooms on the second floor including classrooms and club rooms. In one room women and girls received instruction on how to sew and knit. Back on the main level Becky took Mildred through the kitchen and dining area. Downstairs featured a small gymnasium and a swimming tank.

"So you see," Becky said, "we have a wide range of activities to help immigrants and other unfortunates become viable members of society. We also have another location on Stella Avenue in the North End. Aside from the activities and programs we host in our buildings, we also offer summer camps to children and what we like to call fresh air clubs where we take groups of children to Assiniboine Park or other parks. Our programs are well-rounded in their approach and I would like to think we've made considerable progress in helping immigrants assimilate into our culture and be productive citizens."

Becky grabbed Mildred's hand. "How would you like to volunteer your time? We could always use more help."

"I think I would rather like that. As you said, it is somewhat ... boring ... just staying at home waiting for William to come home. It would be nice if I had some sort of diversion. In what manner can I help?"

"Well, you are a trained teacher ... we have English night classes. One of our instructors was forced to leave to bear a child. Since the war, immigration from Europe discontinued, so we don't have the numbers from a few years ago, but there is still a need for instruction. Many are able to speak enough English to get by, but they have extreme difficulty with reading and writing. We also have a good selection of text books and reading materials that have been donated."

Mildred looked at Becky. She smiled and slowly nodded. "Yes, I think that would be rather smashing."

Mildred Helps Out
September 23, 1915

"Alright, class," Mildred said, "that concludes tonight's lesson. I would like you to review the spelling words I provided. We will have a test tomorrow night. Remember – pay attention to the silent 'e.'"

Desks and chairs scraped against the floor. All the women, about a dozen or so, collected their English textbooks, notebooks and pencils and got up to leave the classroom. For the first few lessons Mildred felt sorry for the women. The recent immigrants wore the same ill-fitting and worn blouses and long skirts to every lesson. Not because of their uncouth and slovenly nature; they were simply poor.

Mildred stayed around to answer a few questions from some of the more eager students. She made sure to have time for every student, regardless of how trivial the query might be. She appreciated engaged students willing to learn. Little by little, she felt she helped improve society.

The women appeared to respect her. They seemed to listen to what she said and a few of the more adventurous ones would ask questions in broken English. But she could not help but feel self-conscious at times. One would point to her shoes. Another would feel the material of her dress. What were they saying when they whispered to each other in their foreign tongues? It had to be something about her scar. They likely tossed around scenarios. Maybe a terrible farm injury or perhaps something involving a horse.

After the final woman left the classroom and closed the door behind her, Mildred stood for a moment and smiled. She clasped her hands in front of herself. Another successful class.

She carefully cleaned off the chalkboard and marked tests from earlier in the class. After quickly planning tomorrow's pluralization lesson, she prepared to leave for the night. Robert would soon arrive to drive her home.

Becky was not at the Mission on this particular evening. Typically she had a quick cup of tea with her friend before going home. But on this occasion, she elected to step outside to wait for her ride. The cool, but not yet cold, September evening felt refreshing. Winter would soon be on its way, so it was best to enjoy the last remnants of agreeable weather.

Only the occasional vehicle drove by on Sutherland Avenue. The few people on the sidewalks looked dishevelled. Definitely working class. Father told her that years ago the more well-to-do families moved to Armstrong's Point south of downtown, then, better yet, Crescentwood. And with the Canadian Pacific line just a stone's throw away, living with the noise and smell from the trains would be revolting.

After ten minutes Mildred looked at her watch. What was taking him so long?

She turned to go back up the steps when she heard the sound of someone vomiting. It came from the side of the Mission, just around the corner.

She crept around. Stooped over, a woman leaned against the building with one hand. A thin line of saliva hung from her lower lip above the small puddle of vomit on the sidewalk.

Three boys, aged about ten to twelve years old, hovered near the woman. They teased and laughed at her. One boy held a stick, a branch ripped from a small tree or hedge. He poked the woman in the buttocks with the stick while the two other boys guffawed.

"Be gone! Leave this poor woman alone. Can you not see she is ill?"

Startled, the boys ran off, leaving their stick on the ground.

Mildred approached the sick woman and put her hand on the woman's shoulder. "Miss, are you all right? You seem ill…"

The woman wobbled slightly, paying little attention to Mildred. She wiped the drool from her mouth with her free hand.

"Miss, do you require any assistance…?"

The woman vomited again, this time against the wall of the Mission. It oozed down the brick wall. Mildred took several steps back for fear of having anything splatter on her overcoat.

What should she do? Her ride would arrive at any moment, yet she could not leave this woman to her own defences. She clearly needed help.

The ill woman spat on the ground. She struggled to maintain her balance, teetering from one foot to the next.

Mildred cleared her throat. "Ah, Miss?" Still the woman did nothing. "Do you require any assistance?"

"S'matter," the woman said, slurring in an Eastern-European accent, "ya never saw woman puke her guts out before?" She again spit out a loose chunk of vomit.

Revolted, yet concerned, Mildred took a step closer to the woman. "I have," she said. "You appear to be ill…"

"Ya, I'm alright. I'm always sick when I drink a bottle of whiskey."

"Oh my," Mildred said, holding her gloved hand to her face. "You … you're drunk."

"You're really smart, you know that?"

"Well, I never…"

"Never had drink before?"

"No," Mildred said. "I enjoy a good glass of wine and have had some sherry before."

"Ah." The woman disregarded Mildred's comment with a wave of her hand.

Mildred shook her head in disgust. "Well, it appears you don't require any assistance, so I will be on—"

She stopped mid-sentence. The inebriated women turned to face her for the first time. They both stared at each other. Brilliant red lips. Too much make-up. The woman looked familiar to Mildred, but she could not quite place her.

"Have I … seen you before? Maybe here at the Mission?"

"Da. With Marko. I see you in Eaton's."

Mildred thought for moment. She slowly nodded, "Yes, I remember now. I'm sorry, what is your name again?"

"Lily."

"That's right, Lily. Er … nice to see you again. My name is Mildred."

Lily recoiled from another pang of nausea.

Mildred helped steady Lily. "You are not in any shape to be on the streets tonight. Come, let's go inside the Mission. It looks like you could use a warm cup of tea or coffee and maybe a little bite to eat."

Mildred's tummy swirled with emotions. Perhaps she felt uncomfortable helping a woman romantically involved with Marko, even if she was just a prostitute. But in her condition, the fallen woman could not be left to her own devises, especially with packs of mischievous children roaming the neighborhood.

Lily broke Mildred's grasp. "No, leave me alone. I go back to house."

"Nonsense. Come with me. You can hardly walk a straight line. You'll just end up at the bottom of a ditch or floating in the Red River." Mildred tugged at Lily's arm more earnestly. Lily relented and allowed herself to be lead.

As they rounded the corner back to the front of the building, an automobile with its headlights on idled at the steps.

"Hello, Ma'am … ah … are you ready?" Robert said with a quizzical expression from the vehicle's open window.

"Please wait a moment," Mildred said, "I have to attend to this … lady. She fell at the side of the building."

The driver tipped up his hat with a smirk on his face. "Hey Lily, is that you?"

Lily did not reply and continued up the steps, stumbling and swaying.

Just before they entered, Mildred turned to Robert. "I don't know how long we will be. Perhaps come back in a half hour."

The driver smiled. "Sure thing, ma'am. But trust me, that lady never needed a half hour for anything. More like five minutes." The vehicle sped away and turned off a side street.

Mildred opened the door for Lily into All People's Mission. Two ladies wearing long, white aprons and bonnets noticed and immediately came to help. "Let's get her cleaned up. She needs a little food and maybe some coffee," Mildred said.

The women each grabbed one of Lily's arms and led her to the bathroom. In the light of the Mission, Mildred could see Lily's white dress had become soiled and dirty. The dress hung down to just below her knee and she did not have stockings. Lily's pretty lavender button-up shoes that went up to her ankles impressed Mildred.

"Perhaps wash her dress," Mildred said just before the bathroom door closed. "Give her something to wear from the donations."

Mildred went to fetch some coffee from the kitchen. When she returned, one of the women helping Lily stood outside the bathroom door, shaking her head in disgust.

"What's the problem?"

"That woman you brought inside, the prostitute, she's not wearing anything underneath her dress. Very inappropriate."

"All we can do is help. We cannot judge. Whatever brought her to this depth is her own cross she must bear. Perhaps through our support she will change her ways." Mildred mildly surprised herself. She would not have said or even thought of such a thing only a few weeks ago.

Fifteen minutes later Lily emerged from the washroom wearing a white frock a few sizes too big for her. Occasionally, a strap fell exposing her bare right shoulder. Mildred thanked the women and led Lily into the main office.

"Here." Mildred pulled out a chair. "Sit down and have some coffee."

Lily accepted the cup, still tipsy although more alert and sure of her step.

"The mission will be closing soon. Will you be able to walk to your residence?"

"Da. I no live far," Lily said. She had a mischievous grin.

Mildred folded her arms. "You really must be more careful. The streets are not safe for a woman, especially one of your ... your..."

Lily stared at Mildred with an unsteady head. "You mean for prostitute. What's the matter? You can't say it?"

"No." Mildred cocked her head back in defiance. "What I mean to say is that women of your ... persuasion ... ought to be careful lest you be taken advantage by unruly men."

Lily quickly finished her coffee and rose from her chair. "I'll be fine. You no worry about me."

"Very well," Mildred said. "You know, if you ever want to come by the Mission, you are welcome. Your command of English does not appear bad, but I can help you improve it. There are others who teach common household tasks and pursuits such as washing and cooking. You can even learn how to knit or how to manage money...."

Lily stopped and turned to face Mildred. "Maybe I will, maybe I won't."

"They are arranging to clean your dress. It is of fine quality, I can tell. You can come and pick it up tomorrow. You can also keep the frock you are wearing, although it looks big on you."

"Thank you." Lily opened the office door to leave.

"Oh, and be sure to say hello to Marko for me," Mildred said.

Lily winked.

Different Priorities
September 29, 1915

Spread across the work bench like glittering jewels, Marko examined the parts from the punching machine. Sprockets, levers, switches and a variety of other parts needed to be assembled together.

Located near the entrance to the front office, Marko preferred this particular bench because a nearby window provided more light than the other work benches deeper in the bowels of the factory. It reminded him of his old work bench back home in the barn on the farm. But instead of smelling manure, he whiffed grease and machine oils.

Marko closed his eyes for a moment, imagining what the final, assembled component should look like. He took a deep breath and slowly opened his eyes. He grabbed one part, eyed another and attached them together. With the simplicity of a children's puzzle, be began to reconstruct the component.

Before he could finish, the office door opened. Peter and William entered the factory. William crossed his arms while Peter's face burned red with fury.

"Ya haven't explained to me why we aren't working on the bridge for Saskatchewan," Peter said. "Why have ya got the shop knocking their heads off for the bleedin' building in Brandon? I'm sure the Saskatchewan bridge is more of a priority."

William pointed his finger at Peter's face. "Listen …I set the priorities for production, not you. You don't have a concept for what's important and what's not. Yes, the Saskatchewan bridge is important, but so is the Brandon project. Let me worry about priorities. You just need to make sure the grease monkeys do what they're supposed to without wasting time."

"That makes no bleedin' sense. Don't we stand to make more from the bridge?"

"It's not that simple. The owner of the Brandon job is connected. Very connected. We can get more projects if we do that one right. I'm thinking about the long term. And it's not easy with so many workers going off in the war."

Peter scrunched his nose. "Fine. The Brandon job it is."

William turned to leave when he noticed Marko looking on at the disagreement. "What are you staring at? Don't have enough work?"

Marko put his head down and pretended to fiddle with parts on the bench. William stepped back in to the front office.

Peter walked over to Marko and put his arm around him. "Don't ya worry about that pansy."

Three workers came to the bench. Michael Jones wiped his hands on an oily rag. Joey lit up a smoke. Russell always wore the same blue shirt with a ripped shirt pocket. Peter turned around and held his arms up. "It's not changing. Stick to the bloody Brandon job. Little Willy is daft. All I know is it'll be me who'll pay the price because of this. Once Mr. Spencer finds out what's happening, Willy'll weasel it up and blame me. There's something funny going on. That's all I got to say."

"He comes in late damn near every day," Russell said.

"Well, he's the son-in-law of the big guy, so there's not much we can do about it. Although …" Peter looked around and whispered to the small group. "I wouldn't doubt there's something mighty fishy about Willy's decisions. It'll come back to bite him." He went back to his loud voice. "Now go on back to work. Not much we can do about it now."

The men mumbled among themselves and scattered back to their work stations. Marko held up the reassembled machine component and twisted it in the sparkling sunlight streaming through the window.

Health Department
October 15, 1915

"You'll find no rats. We have a clean house," Mike said.

"You better let me be the judge of that," the inspector said. "If you don't let me in to have a look-see, I'll condemn it, sight unseen." Dressed in a blue suit, the short man wore wire-rim glasses and carried a clipboard. For someone claiming to be a health Inspector, Marko didn't think he looked very healthy. Skinny, he must have missed many meals as a youngster. He looked unwell with his pale, hollow cheeks and sour expression. When he opened his mouth it revealed that the Anglo's crooked and rotten teeth had seen better days.

Mike glanced at Marko, also seated in the front porch, and then looked back to the inspector. "Ok, come inside," Mike said. "But you'll see, there's nothing."

Marko followed Mike and the city inspector in through the front door. So much for enjoying the crisp Friday early evening with a drink. Why would an inspector come so late on a Friday? It had to be almost 5 o'clock. Didn't he have anything better to do?

The inspector began to walk into the living room when Mike held out his hand. "Wait. Please take off your shoes. You walk around your house with shoes? This is a clean house."

The inspector took a deep breath, but complied. When he did, it revealed his big toe poking out from a hole in a sock. Sitting a few feet away on the floor and playing with a small toy wooden horse, John pointed. "Oh, oh, your sock has a boo boo. Will your mama fix it for you? My mama fixes all our clothes."

A faint, embarrassed smile creased the inspector's mouth. He covered up his toe with his other foot.

"John, shush. Don't embarrass our visitor," Mike said. "He's an important man." Then in Ukrainian he said, "Go get Mama. Tell her an inspector is here."

John nodded and ran off.

The inspector grabbed a pencil from his jacket pocket and held his clipboard up. "Perhaps if we can start in the cellar, that's where we see many of the problems…."

Mike put his hand up. "Not yet. We have to fix your sock."

"What?"

"It's a tradition in Galicia. Men must have feet covered when visiting another man's home. Maria will mend it for you while we sit."

"You can't be serious…?"

Mike turned to Marko, who nodded. Slowly at first, but then more vigorously, "Da, da. It's very important. You would bring shame and disrespect."

"This is preposterous," the annoyed inspector said, rolling his eyes.

Just then Maria appeared in the living room, the top two buttons of her blouse undone. Barefoot, she had pulled her skirt up to almost her knee. She also let her hair down.

"Fix his sock," Mike said in Ukrainian. "Take your time." Before leaving the room, he quickly turned to Marko. "I'll be right back. Take him to the couch."

Marko nodded, but before he could Maria crouched down to remove the inspector's offending sock.

"What—?" He pulled his foot away. Colour entered his cheeks and he adjusted his glasses.

"I need your sock," Maria said. She fluttered her eyes and smiled.

"I'll do no such thing."

Marko rolled his eyes. "Please. Sit. It not take long. She's very good at sock repair."

"I am here to inspect this home. Not to…" Before he could finish, Marko had already led the inspector by the hand to the couch. Maria pushed him gently to ease him down.

Shaking his head with unwillingness, he put his clipboard on the coffee table. Now on her knees, Maria reached up the man's leg.

The inspected jumped back in his seat. "What are you doing?"

"Taking off your sock."

Breathing heavy, the man looked down. Bent over, his eyes caught Maria's cleavage as she bent over, her hand running gently up the inside of the pant leg to unhook the sock from the garter.

Mike was back from the basement. "Might as well have a drink while we wait, no?" A crooked smile on his face, he held up a bottle of Beefeater gin.

The inspector ran his hand over top his greasy hair. "I-I'm working. I cannot drink...."

"C'mon," Mike said. "Just a shot while we wait. It's almost five anyway. Beefeater. This must be your last inspection of the day, no?"

"No, I really can't..."

Maria stood up and dangled the man's sock in the air. She smiled and winked before she turned away and left the living room.

The inspector looked down at his bare foot. Then looked up at Mike holding the bottle of Beefeater. He licked his lips. "Well, I suppose a wee little sip wouldn't hurt."

Mike smiled. "Get three glasses," he said to Marko. Within five minutes Mike was pouring their second shots.

"So, why you come here?" Mike asked.

"A tip from a neighbor," the inspector said. "There's a report this house has vermin."

"It must be the Hendricks that live next door. We not get along."

"Whatever the case, we need to ensure conditions are livable to prevent the spread of disease. This part of Winnipeg is particularly prone."

"Maria, get some baking," Mike yelled in Ukrainian. In minutes Maria reappeared with a tray of her baking. She made sure to set the tray in front of the inspector, bending down in front of him in the process. The inspector could not help to look down her top again.

"You like?" Mike said.

"Huh? I ... uh ..." He instantly looked away.

"You like some baking?"

Now sweaty on his brow, the inspector provided a faint smile. "Oh, yes. The treats. Yes, I very much would like some. I'm famished."

"Very good," Mike said. He poured another round.

The three men drank for an hour, trading stories and jokes. During the time, the inspector's attitude ripened from his initial sour mood. He even put his arms around Marko on one occasion trying to recall the words of an old song.

Maria came back with the newly darned sock. She again gently lifted his pant leg and put it on. The inspector's eyes widened. Maria smiled and left the room.

"You still need to inspect our house?" Mike said.

The inspector hiccupped into his hand. "No, I think everything is in order." He rose, but stumbled, forcing him to sit back down. As he did, something broke with a small snap. He shot up immediately. John's toy horse lay where he sat, but now with a broken leg. "How did that get there. I don't recall a toy being—"

The inspector looked up. A rat scuttled across the living room floor, stopped for a moment to look around, then continued on into the kitchen area.

For about five seconds the room fell into complete silence. No one moved. The inspector's jaw dropped, like he couldn't believe his eyes.

John screamed. "My horsey! You broke my horsey!" He ran to the dumbstruck inspector and tore the pieces of his toy from the inspector's hand. "Why did you break it? Why?"

The inspector shook his head. "Huh, what?"

"The toy," John said. "Why did you break my toy?"

"I didn't break your toy."

"Sure you did, you sat on it and now it's broken. See." John held the evidence up high for everyone to see.

Mike put his face in his hand. "My son received that toy from his grandfather on his dying bed." John ran to his father's open arms for a big consoling hug. Frowning, Maria leaned against the wall with her arms crossed.

The inspector looked confused. "But didn't anyone see the rat?"

"What rat?" Marko said.

"The one that was in the middle of the floor." He turned to Mike. "Didn't you see a rat run across the room?"

Mike consoled John, still crying on his belly. He lifted his head up. "What? That?"

The inspector turned around. One of Ann's toys, a stuffed bear, lay in the middle of the floor.

"Wait, that wasn't there. It was a rat."

"Maybe you had too many of Maria's treats," Marko said. "There was no rat."

"But I could have sworn…."

"My horsey!" John screamed. "It'll be busted forever!"

"Look, I better get going," the inspector said. He burped into his hand. "Nothing to see here. Thank you for your hospitality. Thanks for fixing my sock." He put on his shoes and hat and went out the door.

By the time the inspector left the yard, John stopped crying and casually reattached the horse's leg to its body. He never did have any tears in his eyes. Maria buttoned her blouse back up and adjusted her skirt. Mike finished his shot, his cheeks red.

"I have to get more rat poison," Mike said. "That was a close call."

Maria shook her head. "We've had problems for years. You do nothing. A few traps, that's it. If that inspector wasn't drunk and I didn't throw Ann's bear on the ground, this place would have been condemned."

Mike waved her off with his hand.

Marko picked up the toy horse off the coffee table. The loose leg came off again. He could easily fix it. He wiped his wet brow. The gin hit him hard. He hated the swill. How could the English drink it? He felt a sharp pain in his temple.

*****

Marko is holding Anastasiya's toy wooden pig. The repair he made to the tail is still holding. He puts it down on the table. She sits beside him at the kitchen table in her white dress with the pink trim, cutting pictures and drawings from magazines. Aside from farm animals, she cut pictures of vehicles, wagons and even buildings.

Olena walks into the kitchen holding a picture in a frame. She is wearing the same white dress with blue beads as in the picture. "Look, I put it in a frame." Her soft smile could melt a pound of butter in seconds. She rubs her hand on Marko's back. It feels good, soothing. She gives him a little peck on the forehead and heads out to pick some vegetables from the garden for dinner.

Marko picks up the framed photo of her and Anastasiya. A pretty one. Their hair is done up nice and both have fancy dresses.

"This is a nice picture." Marko shows his daughter.

Anastasiya frowns. "I don't remember it."

"How could you not? It was just taken a short time ago."

She shrugs and continues to cut photos from the tattered magazines. That's all she seems to ever do. Always cutting and cutting, torturing magazines.

He stares at the photo for several minutes, examining every detail. Such a beautiful photo. He could look at it all day. Why is he not in the picture?

His head hurts. He feels the indentation at the side of his head, a half inch deep. No one really notices it unless they look hard. Ma told him he was born that way. Nothing that anyone could do about it. Growing up he did fine at school. But sometimes it hurts when things get crazy.

He places the photo on the table. Maybe they should move to Canada? Start fresh. Others have moved. Marak from the next farm over told him that his brother Mike went over years ago and is doing fine. He said he'd write a letter of introduction if they needed a place to stay.

Why is this photo the only one of Olena and Anastasiya? And where is their wedding picture?

A Messy Evening
June 13, 1916

Lily knocked on the door of the house on Aberdeen Avenue. Marko could make out music. Not too loud, but unmistakable. He looked at his pocket watch. Almost midnight.

Immediately the music stopped. The door opened only a crack. "Who are you? What do you want?" said a woman wearing far too much make-up.

Lily stepped in front of Marko and smiled. "It's me, Trudy."

"Lily!"

Trudy opened the door the rest of the way and the two entered. About ten people, mostly men, occupied the smoke-filled sitting room. Some sat on an older-looking couch while the rest stood and mingled. Trudy nodded to a man in the corner of the room who dropped the needle back down on a gramophone playing lively music.

Everyone in the room held a glass or had one nearby on a table or shelf. A thin woman with a tray wearing an extremely short red plaid skirt and high heels delivered new drinks to guests or free poured from a half-filled bottle of cheap whiskey in her other hand. The server-woman had blonde hair in tight curls and wore blood-red lipstick. Her most noticeable feature being that she was topless.

"Minnie giving you a night off?" Trudy asked Lily. Middle-aged in appearance, Trudy's blotchy complexion gave the impression that the woman had been around the block a few times. Barefoot, she wore a pretty green dress that matched her green dangly earrings. A thin black belt around her waist stressed her attractive figure, although most of the attention would be brought up to her plunging neckline revealing a good portion of her unsupported breasts. Trudy likely turned a few tricks on the side while being hostess.

"Yes, sometimes I need something different. It's boring being in same room. And … I need a drink."

"Minnie won't spring you for a bottle?"

"She doesn't like it if I drink profits. She only likes it when I drink with johns." She introduced Marko.

Trudy held out her limp hand, which Marko accepted and squeezed slightly. "Pleased to meet you, sir." She looked at Lily, "Is this a new man for you?"

Lily smiled and winked at Marko. "He's a good man. Good customer. He gets extra special treatment. You know what I mean…."

"I certainly do," Trudy said. "Well anyway, have a few drinks, enjoy yourselves." Trudy moved on to talk to a group of men in the corner of the room.

Marko pressed his lips together. Lilia referred to him as a good customer. Was that as good as it would get? They should be more than that. Could she not tell that he had strong feelings for her? He would make a good husband. He'd been in the city now for three years and had the same job despite being a foreigner in difficult times. Sure, everything ended badly in the old country, but that's why he had moved, to start fresh. Couldn't Lily also start fresh? She went to All People's Mission to improve her English. Maybe it would just take more time and persuasion for her to see the light.

They found two unoccupied chairs near the fireplace. It felt warm in the sitting area due to the number of people in the room. The lit fire in the fireplace didn't help. Marko removed his jacket and placed it on the back of his chair, Lily did likewise with her pink sweater. It matched her pink frock that went down to below her knees. In a rush when they left her place on Annabella, Lily slipped on a pair of brown, low-cut shoes on her bare feet.

The topless waitress came by. "What'll ya have?"

Lily held up two fingers. "Two whiskeys."

"Coming right up,"

Marko stared at the waitress when she walked away.

"What's the matter? You never seen a woman's breasts before?" Lily said in Ukrainian. She shoved Marko, breaking him out of his vacant stare.

He smiled. "Not so open like that. Even at your place the women cover up when they go downstairs, no?"

"True, but this place is not well-known and can get away with a little more. Remember, it's a blind pig. A booze can. Prohibition shut everything down a few weeks ago. Not that I'd be allowed in bars or taverns anyway."

"I tried that piss they call temperance beer. Horrible."

The waitress returned with their order and placed it on a little table near them. "Forty cents."

Marko raised his eyebrows. He paid the woman and she went off. "That's a lot for booze. It was half that before prohibition."

"That's the way it is," Lily said. "Everything is illegal. If they get caught by the police, the risk is all theirs. There's no place you can legally get booze."

Lily held up her glass. "Na zdrovya!"

"Na zdrovya," Marko said. They clinked glasses and downed their shots in one gulp.

"Another shot, Rose," Lily said to the waitress, now across the room. "You know … maybe just bring whole bottle, no?"

Rose looked back, smiled and nodded.

The man in the corner of the room put a slower selection on the gramophone. A couple stood up and started dancing in the center of the room, arms embraced. Maybe just a younger couple looking for a good time. Marko could not tell if the woman did tricks.

A few minutes later Rose arrived with a full bottle of rye whiskey, a lot of booze for the two of them. Marko paid her, all the while trying to look at only her eyes.

He poured a shot in each glass. "I'll take home whatever we don't finish. You know … for next time."

Lily poked him in the ribs. "Why? We'll finish it tonight."

"Are you sure? You already had quite a few at your place. So have I. I'll have a tough enough time finishing half a bottle of this rot gut."

"What's the matter?" Lily said. She put her arm around his neck. "You not man enough? You can't keep up with a little girl like me?"

He laughed and took a swig of rye. "Please," he said raising his hand. "You're a woman. You can't keep up with me."

Lily downed her shot in one gulp and slammed it down on the little table. "Hit me."

Marko filled both glasses. Lily shot back her drink and slammed it. "Hit me again."

Their torrid drinking eventually slowed down, but after 40 minutes or so, sure enough, the bottle of rye was bone dry. The evening spilled into the wee hours of Wednesday morning. Whenever someone came knocking, the music would stop and Trudy would answer the front door carefully. She only allowed entry to people she knew.

While Marko's cheeks reddened and felt fuzzy, Lily got absolutely plastered. She could hardly walk a straight line and slurred her words worse than a Main Street beggar. Time to go.

"C'mon, Marko. Let's have one more drink. Just one … p-please…?" Lily teetered from side to side.

"No, you had about ten too much."

"See. See. I told you I can drink like a m-man." Lily pointed to herself with her thumb.

"Da, you can drink … but I don't know if you can hold it."

"One more dance." Lily hugged Marko.

"Okay, one more. Then we go?"

Lily raised her hand and formed it to an 'okay' sign.

They slowly circled the floor while the gramophone played a slow tune. No one in the room paid them much heed and several had already passed out on couches and chairs.

Lily licked his earlobe. "What say we ask Trudy for a room? Eh, big boy?" she whispered.

Marko's alcohol-drenched heart quickened. "Okay … but not here. Let's go to my place. It's not far…." In bad shape, maybe the walk would do her good. Her place on Annabella was too far away. Besides, street cars stopping running hours ago and getting a hired car would be difficult. He'd have to sneak her out in the morning before everyone got up.

Lily walked awkwardly towards the fireplace to collect her sweater. Approaching her chair, she stumbled and fell to the ground. Marko tried to help her up and managed to get her to sit at the base of the fireplace.

"I … I don't feel good…" Lily said. "It's so hot here…" She began to take off her dress. Marko made her stop, but not before a few nearby men got an eyeful.

"You can't take your dress off," Marko whispered. "You don't have anything underneath."

"I don't care … too hot…" Sitting on the ground, Lily leaned forward and vomited down the front of her pink dress.

Trudy ran into the room. "Oh, not again, Lily!"

"She gets rough like this … always?" Marko asked.

Trudy gave Marko a funny look. "She's here at least two times a week, maybe more. I'm sure there are other speakeasies she frequents."

The man who operated the gramophone came over with a mop and pail to clean up Lily's mess, generally self-contained to the front of her dress.

Marko helped Lily up to her feet and put her pink sweater around her back. Somehow Lily slipped it on despite swaying like a branch in a breeze. She mumbled something incoherent. Marko led her to the front door while drips and globs of vomit fell from her soiled dress. He apologized for Lily's state, but Trudy seemed unconcerned. Just another night at a speakeasy, apparently.

They walked on the plank sidewalk on Aberdeen Avenue. He struggled to keep Lily upright. The awful stench of vomit almost made him lurch. He found it easier to breathe through his mouth. Thankfully they only had to go about four blocks to get to Manitoba Avenue. Lily still felt sweaty and warm, so the cool air did not seem to affect her much, not that she could do anything about it anyway.

When they got to his place he helped Lily up the stairs to the porch.

"I don't know what we're going to do. Your dress is ruined. Maybe you can wear something of mine to get back to your place, but it'll be too big for you. You can sleep for a short time in my room, but you should leave before everyone gets up." Marko couldn't help feeling he was making a mistake. How would he sneak her out before everyone woke?

He found the key and slowly opened the door, careful not to make any noise. He left it open a few feet but when he turned, his eyes widened. Lily still stood on the porch, but other than her shoes, completely naked. Her sweater and dress lay in a small, crumpled pile at her feet.

"Oh, my God … why did you take everything off?" he whispered.

"Y-you said my clothes are a mess. So I took them off. I don't wanna make a mess."

Marko raised his hands up to his head. What would he do? A naked hooker on the porch. If Maria found out, that would be it.

Quickly Marko grabbed Lily's arm. "Okay, come in, but be quiet, not a sound." The two stepped inside the dark home. To save money, Mike never left any lights on after they retired for the evening. Marko felt around and found the light switch for the landing.

Marko turned around to close the door behind him when he saw Lily's pile of clothes outside on the porch. He couldn't just leave them so carefully picked up the smelly pile.

But when he stepped back into the home, Lily disappeared. Wonderful. A naked woman walking around his landlord's home. What if she wondered into their bedroom? He didn't want to think of the implications. He quickly threw down the clothes, took off his shoes, and walked quickly and quietly into the gloom of the house.

No sign of her in the living room at the front of the house, he entering the hallway. Marko's heart rate quickened. Where could she be?

Why did they have to finish that entire bottle of rye at the blind pig? Just a slight woman, of course Lily couldn't handle the booze, regardless of how much practice she'd had. Besides, she rigged all those drinking contests at the brothel.

He dared not turn on another light for fear that it would wake Mike or Maria. What if one of the children saw Lily?

Marko heard a sound. Then another. He turned and went into the kitchen. There, against the moonlit window he could see Lily's naked silhouette.

"There you are," he whispered. "Why did you wonder around?"

"I don't know. Marko … I'm tired," Lily said, but not in a particularly quiet voice.

"Shhh. Okay, let's go upstairs." But definitely no fooling around tonight.

He led her arm, but with a slight stumble Lily accidently stepped on Marko's foot. He tripped and the two tumbled on the dark kitchen floor.

"Your shoes are still on. We have to take your shoes off." Marko helped Lily to a kitchen chair. He knelt over her feet and struggled to work at her shoes. He got one off when the kitchen light came on.

Mike stood at the entrance dressed in his nightshirt. It took a moment for Mike's eyes to adjust to the sudden shock of light, but even still he had to rub his eyes at the sight.

Calm, but pale as a ghost, Lily looked at Mike. "Hello."

Mike's jaw dropped at the sight of the naked woman sitting in his kitchen. He shook the last remnants of sleep from his head.

"Who is this?" Mike also spoke in Ukrainian.

"Uh, a … friend. Remember I was telling you about Lily? Lily, this is Mike…" The introduction sounded awkward and Marko knew it. Pretending to keep things normal, he worked off Lily's other shoe.

"What's going on here?" Mike said. "Why is she wearing no clothes? It's three in the morning,"

"She got sick all over them."

Mike paused. "I can't believe you brought a prostitute here. I have children. Both of you are stinking drunk."

Mike should talk; most nights he was drunk. It grated on poor Maria. But he never did something like this.

"I'm sorry. It was so late and we were close to here…"

Swaying, Lily could hardly sit in the chair. She rolled her head and smiled at Mike. "I can pay my way tonight. What do ya want?"

Mike frowned, "Nothing from you, thanks." Then he spoke to Marko: "She can't stay here. If Maria finds out…"

"What can I do? There's a dirty pile in the front landing. Maybe if you can get something from Maria that she could wear …"

"Oh, no," Mike said. He took a step back. "There's no way she's wearing any of Maria's clothes. What are you, crazy?"

"Look, it's too chilly and she can't go out like this. Let her stay here tonight. In the morning she goes. Tell Maria she ate something bad. Some bad meat or cheese."

Mike raised his hands in the air, as if at a loss. "Alright. I'll get the dirty clothes. Get her upstairs. Make sure she stays in the room. I don't want her wondering around. You understand?"

Marko nodded. He helped Lily to her feet and whispered in her ear, "Alright, let's go upstairs."

He opened the door to his room, but, just then, so did the children's door. Nicholas walked out, still half asleep. On his way downstairs he took a second look when he saw Lily, mouthing a silent, "Wow," at the sight.

Marko quickly led Lily into his dark bedroom, threw her down in the bed then walked back out to where Nicholas still stood in shock and disbelief.

"You should go back sleep," Marko said in English.

"Didn't you just take a naked woman into your room?" Nicholas rubbed his eyes, still puffy from sleep.

"What woman?"

"A woman … she didn't have any clothes on…."

"I don't know what you talking about. Go back to sleep. You want I tell your mother what you dream about?"

"No." Nicholas shook his head quickly and shuddered.

The Letter From Max
July 14, 1916

Marko opened the door to his apartment after another day at work. While he appreciated having his own place, he kicked himself over how things ended at Mike's house. He couldn't blame Maria for not wanting him around. The event with Lily proved too much for her. Mike tried his best to advocate for Marko, but what could he do? They gave him a week.

He found he drank more than before. Nothing else to do. Of course prohibition made it difficult to get a decent bottle of whiskey, but he had ways. At the very least, he could pick up a cheap bottle of vodka that a Russian distilled from potatoes the next block over. Or he could go to Mike's. Although Maria wanted Marko out of the house, she had no problem selling him bootlegged alcohol.

Lily visited every so often, something she never used to do. On slow evenings sometimes she would stay for the night. It felt good to be in bed with a woman in his arms. But he made sure to hide the picture of Olena and Anastasiya in a drawer. They didn't need to see him with another woman. In bed Lily would gently run her hands through his hair and message his scalp. It felt relaxing. She would be careful around the small indentation on the right side of his head. While his hair covered the scar on the back of his head from the attack a year and a half ago, his nose remained a little crooked. Every meal reminded him of his missing teeth.

He also found he drank more when with Lily. Sometimes she was already half-corked by the time he saw her on Annabella with a distant, vacant look in her eyes. She gave every impression that she enjoyed her profession and lifestyle, but did she really? She never had a chance to lead a normal life.

He'd already socked away about a hundred dollars from any money that was left over at the end of each month. But since the war started, saving became difficult. Sometimes he had to dip into those savings to cover the rent. If he had a wife and children there would be no way he could make ends meet. But he tried not to think about that. Thinking about a family only gave him headaches. Best to look ahead and dream about the repair shop he'd open one day.

Mrs. Dogaru ran the small apartment building located right on Selkirk Avenue. A little slovenly and rough on the edges, the landlady came from good Romanian stock. She also appreciated that Marko could fix things around the apartment building. It saved her money from having to hire someone. Marko liked the apartment's location, near shops and restaurants and a little closer to work. The previous tenant, also Ukrainian, left suddenly months ago and didn't pay the rent. Mrs. Dogaru reckoned her tenant died somewhere, maybe in the bush. And with no next of kin, what could she do? The man had a woman but she ran off to Regina to be with someone else after a few months. She didn't work and couldn't pay the rent. The woman took anything of value, but left many items behind including all the furniture.

Marko stepped across the threshold of the apartment when he felt something at his feet. An envelope. Mail? He never got mail.

The address was correct, but for an Olga Kostenko. He flipped it over. From Max Yagochuk, the previous tenant. He was obviously not dead. Olga must be his woman.

He tapped the letter a few times against his hand. What should he do with it? Olga flew the coop. Should he give it to Mrs. Dogaru? He poured a shot and sat down on the couch. Max's couch.

How would anyone know? He opened the letter.

Written in Ukrainian, Max possessed crude penmanship but Marko could make it out.

Dear Olga,

I miss you so much. How are you? I am sorry for not being able to write to you earlier.

That day in October when I didn't come home I was accosted on Main Street by the police. I did not have an Alien Registration Card so they threw me in jail. You were right. I should have gotten one. But at the time I would not think that they would intern me. I had an honest job making a fair wage. They let me into the country only to put me behind bars because I am Ukrainian.

It is hard to express to you how difficult it is here. We are prisoners. I am in a place called Macpherson Station. They consider me an enemy alien. I tried to explain that I am Ukrainian, not Austrian and that, like you, I am from Galicia and left Europe to escape Hapsburg rule. Insanity!

I no longer have any possessions to my name other than the contents of our apartment. I hope you are able to take care of it until I return. I can't wait to hold you in my arms again.

Most of the prisoners here are also Ukrainian. There are a few Hungarians and Bulgarians too, but to the Anglos everyone is the same. You know what's funny? There are only a couple of actual Austrians in the camp.

They have us working as slave labour. This MacPherson Station is in the middle of nowhere. All bush and trees. I hear they may change the name to Kapuskasing, some Indian name. We cleared off a good chunk of land from trees and bush. A guard told me the cleared land will be used for a farm.

But we try not to work too hard. We only do what we must. Still, it is very dangerous work. Many men have been hurt by fallen trees or an errant axe. The past winter was bitterly cold. Several men suffered severe frostbite. They actually pay us although it is little, just 25 cents a day. I am sure they would pay us nothing if they could, but I heard from someone they have to treat us just like a private in the army because we are considered war criminals. We live in little houses with six bunks each. I do not know how many prisoners there are in this camp, but it has to be over one thousand.

If someone wants to leave the camp, they can. But no one does. We are so isolated from civilization and society, there is no sense in leaving. The area is surrounded by a thick, wet bog and the mosquitoes are horrible. And that's just in the summer. In the winter the brutally cold temperatures would make escape impossible. And even if I did escape, where would I go? It's not like I could stroll into any town in Ontario, smelly, hungry and weary with no money, and not attract attention. Within moments I would be hauled back to the camp and I'm sure my captures would punish me severely for trying to leave. No, I have no choice but to stay.

Occasionally the men squabble and fight. That is what happens when you are miserable and in close quarters. But a month ago there was a riot at the camp. Some prisoners were transferred to our camp from a place with another Indian name. I think it is called Petawawa. Those men refused to work at their camp because they wanted them to do it during Christmas and Easter. The Anglos considered them trouble-makers. Anyway, once they came to our camp, most of us agreed with the Petawawa men. We ended up fighting with the guards. This was stupid, of course, because the guards had the weapons. Several men got shot or stabbed with bayonets. One was killed. Things have calmed down, but there is still distrust.

I gave this letter to a priest who visits us occasionally. All our correspondence must be written in English and first read by the Anglos before it is permitted to be posted. I tried writing to you before, but I was not allowed to say anything about the camp or have anything negative in the letter. There was no sense in sending you something that was not true. The priest will hide this letter in his pants when he leaves the camp. I am not religious, but he is a very good man and does help boost spirits when he visits. He gives us hope.

'But even when they allow us to leave, what will I go back to in Winnipeg? I will have a difficult time trusting anyone. The British are the worst vermin on the planet and I hope a good many of them die in the trenches in Europe.

'Do not even try to write to me. It's not worth it. If the commandant found out I was communicating with someone from the outside, there would be serious problems both for you and I.

'One day the war will be over and I will be back. I know we talked about moving to that new town called Transcona just east of the city. One day.

'I love you and can't wait to see you again.

'Love,

'Max'

Marko put the letter down beside him on the couch and took a sip. Poor sap. Max didn't know Olga had long gone. Marko looked in his wallet. Good thing he got his Alien Registration Card some time ago, but that might not be enough to prevent him from being put away in an internment camp.

Chocolate Mousse
November 17, 1916

Mildred moaned in delight. She threw her head back and let her eyes roll to the back of their sockets. "This chocolate mousse is to kill for."

"I thought you would appreciate it," Gertrude said with a coy smile. "The new cook picked up the recipe when he was in Montreal."

Mildred took another scoop from the long-stemmed desert cup with her thin, silver spoon. She let the rich chocolate melt in her mouth before reluctantly swallowing it. When was the last time she had something this good? Years? They have to visit Mother and Father for dinner more often.

"I know what to get Milly for her birthday," William said. Sitting beside her at the dinner table, he patted her gently on the back.

Thomas winked. "Lad, that's the easiest way to a woman's heart, I kid you not."

"Mmm, I think diamonds are better," Gertrude said. Everyone at the dinner table laughed.

Thomas squeezed Gertrude's hand. "Ah, forgot about that. I suppose you're right. Chocolate is lighter on the pocket book, though."

After taking another sip of red wine, Thomas wiped his mouth with his serviette and looked to William. "Let's go over to my study for a cigar and some scotch."

William rose. As usual, he looked particularly handsome in his best black suit and a new red tie.

Gertrude grabbed a spare serviette and began to get out of her seat. "Dear, I think you need to—"

"Just William and I," Thomas said, cutting his wife short.

"But Thomas…"

"We will not be long." The two men left the room.

Gertrude sat back down and rested her hand on her chin. "Suit yourself," she whispered, just loud enough for Mildred to hear. "But you will look silly talking to your son-in-law with a drop of mousse on your nose."

Mildred laughed and in the process snorted and choked on the smooth chocolate forcing her to gag. She poked her head in the kitchen to ask for more mousse and took a seat beside her mother. "It's nice having a quiet dinner like this, the four of us."

Gertrude nodded. "Yes. We don't seem to get together that much anymore."

"We'll see what happens after they've had a chat. I know Father's been less than impressed over the past two years." Mildred swirled her spoon around in her treat before sticking a glob in her mouth.

"Your father doesn't tell me much about his business affairs, but he has talked about William, unfortunately."

"His behavior hasn't changed much. He still stays up until the wee hours. And I…" Mildred stopped herself. How could she tell Mother about William's suspected infidelity? Or the times he manhandled her? And all the drinking? They hadn't been intimate in over a year. But on some occasions he seemed attentive and generally hospitable. Not many, but some.

"What is it?" Gertrude raised her eyebrow.

Mildred smiled and took another spoonful of mousse. "Oh, nothing. Everything is just fine. Uh, how is everything here at home? You said there is a new cook. Does Marko still come to repair vehicles or other things around the manor?"

"From time to time. The automobile repairs are relentless, but he has everything else in the home in peak efficiency. In fact, there are some Saturdays where he's not needed at all. If he had any sense he would slow down to spread things out, but that's not in his nature."

"I wish I could say the same. William does not do any sort of repairs. He feels he's above all that. I can't really blame him, to be honest. But it's difficult finding reliable help in the city for general repairs. I find I have to call and call before someone finally comes and even then the work can be shoddy. Many good men are off fighting overseas, so we're left with unreliable labourers."

Gertrude stiffened her back at the mention of the war. Her lip quivered. "I'm sorry," she said. "I can't help it. I find that I always have Andrew on my mind. I pray if he'll make it back. Every day the papers report on more and more soldiers that have been killed or crippled. It's awful. Just last week the Kensingtons from a few doors over lost their son. Bernice from the musical club found out her son was shot in the spine and will never walk again." She put her head down and covered her face.

Mildred leaned over and gave her mother a hug. "Our neighbor, Mr. Browne, returned from the front in the summer. He injured his leg and had to convalesce in the Tuxedo Military Hospital for over a month before going home. He needs a cane to walk. When it was warmer he sat out on a bench in the back yard just staring at the trees. He looks so sad and distant. I came by a few times to say hello. Very pleasant neighbor but the war's obviously affected him."

Gertrude brought her head up and took a deep breath, her eyes moist. "It's affected everyone. But, we all must soldier on. There's a reason, a purpose behind it all. All we can do is pray."

Mildred nodded and gently rubbed Mother's arm.

Dabbing her eyes, Gertrude forced a smile. "I'm fine. I get misty every now and then. But about your repair issues, why don't you use Marko? We can certainly share his services. I'm sure he'd be happy with the extra money. And you know he's quite proficient."

Marko! Of course. Why hadn't she thought of that before? "Tomorrow's Saturday. If you can arrange for him to come to our home, that would be wonderful."

"Very well." Gertrude turned her head and yelled toward the kitchen. "Gladys, can you come here please?"

Mildred rose. "I need to go up to my old room for a moment. There's a book I need to find for the teaching I do at the mission."

William would soon be finished his meeting with Father. He would likely be in a surly mood. Best to just agree and nod her head.

She walked up the stairs of the mansion. She hadn't lived in her parents' home for well over a year yet the firmness of the bannister, even the smell in the staircase, a hint of the cleaner Gladys used to polish the oak mouldings, made it seem like she'd never left at all. A strange sensation. She stopped at the top of the stairs and looked behind her. Everything looked exactly the same as before yet she felt pangs of longing in her belly.

Her room looked untouched from the day she left. Not even a speck of dust. Gladys always did a good job keeping the house cleaner than a hospital. She ran her fingers across the spines of books in her bookcase until she came to a red text book on mathematics. On the next shelf she grabbed a well-worn grammar text. As she did, an exercise book fell to the ground.

Dog-eared, the bottom front cover had creased over. Kneeling down, she picked it up gingerly, like a long-lost piece of art. She opened the first few pages. A broad smile formed on her lips. It was Marko's old exercise book from years ago. Gladys must have put it away, bless her grouchy heart.

She placed the exercise book inside the front cover of the grammar text.

Bird Watching
August 11, 1917

"I can see a blue jay," Mildred said. Holding her wide-brimmed, white sun hat, she pointed up to a tree in Gregory's backyard, perhaps fifteen feet away. She could already feel perspiration collecting along her neckline. How could she forget her fan?

"Indeed it is." Gregory craned his neck. "A very common bird in these parts. Intelligent, aggressive buggers. They do not shy away from a fight and are territorial. They're known to steal other birds' nests and eggs."

Gregory, Mildred and William sat in Gregory's backyard on heavy, white wrought iron chairs in an area elevated with brown wood planks nailed about a half-inch apart. The matching circular table held a large glass pitcher of lemonade with three lemons' worth of slices mixed in with the liquid. Just a few feet away, a large elm tree partially obscured the hot afternoon sun. The trunk was so thick that Mildred would not be able to wrap her arms around it.

William took a sip from his tall glass. "You know your birds…." He swatted away a few flies attracted by the sweet drink. Staring off into the distance, William looked bored. It took all her persuasion to convince him that it would be good to visit their neighbor but William always had an excuse. He couldn't come up with one when his golf game got cancelled.

"I had to do something while I was in the hospital," Gregory said. "You can only read so much before the words start running off the page. Someone left this behind." With his cane he pointed to a thick book also on the table entitled *Bird Watching*. "One day a friendly nurse saw me flipping through the pages. I wasn't particularly interested in the subject matter but the colour pages caught my eye. The next day there was a pair of opera glasses on my nightstand. I used them when they wheeled me out for some fresh air. I was able to spot and identify a half-dozen birds. From then on it's become a bit of a hobby."

"It must be difficult running your real estate business if you're looking through opera glasses." William looked at his pocket watch. Mildred scrunched her nose. Why did he always have to talk down to some people?

"I rarely go into the office. In fact, I do most of my work from home. Sometimes I'll venture downtown, but usually I'm able to handle everything from here. I arranged to convert my dining room into a meeting room. And with the telephone, I'm able to keep tabs on business fairly well."

"How is business?" William asked.

"It has its ups and downs. These days, with the war and all, it seems like there's more downs. The glory days are definitely over. But like my father said, good property will always be in demand. It's just a matter of managing your portfolio and understanding the true value of a property. Let the speculators chase their tails. My father felt fortunate making the money he did speculating thirty years ago."

"That sounds very interesting," Mildred said with faint smile. "I wish Father involved me more in business matters. I worked in the front office at the factory for a short time, but that ended when we got married."

"As it should, my dear," William said. He patted her hand.

Mildred frowned slightly. And why did he have to be condescending? Like she was his property. What did William know about business? He threw his money around like he was feeding pigeons.

"How hard is it for you to get around?" Mildred asked, hoping to change to subject.

Gregory smiled and momentarily fanned himself with his hat. "It's a chore. The doctors told me I have to be more active if I want to regain any sort of mobility in my left leg. When I was lying in a medical tent in Belgium they said they might have to amputate or, at best, that I'd never walk again. But it's improved to the point where I'm able to walk a block or two. When I was discharged from the hospital last year I couldn't walk across the room, so this is all gravy. As long as I have my friend with me." He lifted up his cane.

Considering his stature as a businessman, the cane looked rather ordinary. Made of oak, it had a curved handle and a rubber grip on the end. Some of Father's associates carried canes with mother of pearl inlay, perhaps also with a gold or silver handle. Some had precious gems embedded or intricate carvings. Not Gregory's cane. It made him look practical. A tall, thin and handsome man, Gregory always maintained a clean-shaven face. In fact, he never sported a single whisker in all the times she'd seen him. His long, thin fingers looked like he'd be adept at playing the piano, certainly not any heavy work. Judging from his family background, he likely didn't have to do any hard labour growing up. His mouth drew her attention the most. His perfect teeth gleamed like diamonds whenever he smiled. He certainly took care of them. He always dressed well, even when sitting in his backyard, likely because of the need to run his business from his home. It gave him a professional quality. How was it that he never had time for a wife? He must have looked dashing in his formal military dress.

William looked at his pocket watch again.

"Do you have somewhere to be?" Mildred asked.

"I'm expecting an important call," William said in a cold, sardonic tone. "Like our neighbor, I have business matters that are pressing."

Mildred rolled her eyes. "Whatever you say, dear."

"Oh, don't be like that. In front of the neighbor, no less." William turned to Gregory with a half-smile, as if expecting some sort of approval from the veteran. "Women…"

Gregory chuckled softly. "Better be careful, William. I just might steal her from you one day."

Mid-sip, William snorted, choking in his lemonade. Droplets dribbled down the side of his mouth.

Mildred frowned and looked away.

"That's a good one," William said, wiping his chin with a white linen serviette.

"Never know," Gregory said. "Milly might prefer a man in uniform."

Mildred's heart lurched. Only William called her Milly.

William patted Mildred's knee and gave her thigh a little squeeze through her long skirt and petticoat. "Never know." He winked at her.

Gregory squared his jaw after taking another sip of lemonade. "So tell me, how is it you never ended up in the service? They need good men now more than ever. Besides, conscription is coming."

William paused for a moment before answering. "I'd love to go, but work is too busy. The place would fall apart if I left for any extended period of time."

"Really?"

"Mildred's father has me in charge of the factory. I make sure every aspect of the factory is operating at peak efficiency."

Mildred smoothed the material on her skirt. Every aspect of the factory? What a lie. How could he keep a straight face?

"Well," Gregory said, "if that's more important than serving your country, I suppose so."

William put his drink down on the table and folded his arms, the top of his lip moist with perspiration. "What do you mean by that?"

"Oh, nothing. Just that I didn't let business get in my way." Gregory shuffled in his seat. In the process his cane fell to the ground.

"And look where it's gotten you," William said.

Gregory winked at William and picked up his cane. As he brought his head up, he glanced up to a tree and squinted his eye. Without taking his eye away, he reached for his opera glasses. "Hmm, there's a common yellowthroat. A warbler. Here Mildred, have a look." He handed the opera glasses to Mildred.

"I see it! It has black markings around its eyes. Like a bandit."

"It's rare for the yellowthroat to be in these parts in the summer. It's even uncommon in the spring and fall. Or maybe not so, eh William?"

Mildred tried her best to suppress a giggle in her hand.

"Mr. Dalton, telephone call for you," Lydia said, leaning over the fence with a pleated white headpiece on the top of her forehead. She went back into the house.

William stood up and looked at his pocket watch again. "Well, I suppose I should be going." He looked down to Mildred. "You can stay and keep Mr. Browne company." He tipped his hat to Gregory. "Good day to you. Happy bird watching." William left Gregory and Mildred alone.

Gregory topped Mildred's lemonade without asking her. A few slices of lemon slid into her glass. The man didn't seem to let his physical incapacity affect him. He made concessions and certainly had to change how he conducted his business and personal matters, but he seemed to take everything in stride.

"It's nice that we're able to get together like this," Gregory said.

"Yes, we should do it more often. I'd like to learn more about your business."

"I'll try not to get under William's skin next time. He seems to be a bit of a live wire."

Mildred took a deep breath. "He can be at times. But I suppose we all have our moments when we're moody and impatient."

The two spent the next hour conversing about the war, prohibition, women's suffrage, and some recent novels she had read including *The Rainbow* and *Virginia*. Certainly not anything William cared about. Mr. Browne seemed to have a genuine interest in everything. His teeth gleamed whenever he laughed. Never once did his eyes stray to the scar. Instead, they remained locked on her eyes when they spoke. Occasionally he would spot a bird and pass his glasses to her for a peek. Usually the birds would fly away before she could spot them.

Two glasses of lemonade later, Mildred rose from her chair. "I really should be going." She shouldn't overstay her visit.

"So soon? There's still some lemonade in the pitcher."

She smiled. Of course she'd prefer to spend the rest of the day with her interesting neighbor. "No, I really should. But thank you for the lemonade and the conversation."

"Very good, I hope—" Gregory stopped when something caught his eye. "Could it be…?" He looked through his opera glasses. "Yes, indeed it is! A spotted towhee. It's a kind of sparrow. Also rare for these parts. I swear Mildred, you are a lucky charm."

"Can I see?"

Gregory held up the glasses and pointed up in a tree. She looked but couldn't spot the bird.

"Here, let me look again." Gregory took the glasses back. "It's on a different branch now." Still seated, he held the glasses up to his shoulder. "Bend down here, the angle is better."

Mildred did so and looked in the glasses again, this time from behind Gregory's shoulder. She rested her left arm on his left shoulder for stability so she could perch tight against his right shoulder. She made sure her warm breath caressed his exposed neck. "I see it! It has a black head and a black tail. A white belly. Its sides are brown."

"It's rufous, a reddish-brown. This bird is more common west of here and to the south."

Mildred gave Gregory a tiny squeeze on his shoulder with her left hand when she rose slowly to give the glasses back to him. "What a wonderful afternoon visit—" But before she could finish, her heel caught the edge of a wooden slat on the deck causing her to tumble. Instinctively, she held out her hands to break her fall.

She toppled right on poor Gregory. He put his arms around her to make sure she didn't fall to the ground but her momentum knocked him off the chair and both ended on the deck. Their hats flew to the ground.

"I'm sorry," she said with a short giggle while still on top of him. "So clumsy of me. Are you all right? How is your leg?"

Gregory nodded with a grimaced smile that he was fine.

Her right hand on Gregory, Mildred pressed down to help herself up and felt something hard. She glanced and realized it was Gregory's groin area.

"Oh!" She quickly shuffled to her feet. Her face felt warm. "I really must be going."

Gregory righted his overturned chair and leaned on his cane to get up. His cheeks redder than a cardinal's plumage, he held his hat around his waist. He must have enjoyed the little tumble. "Uh, thank you for visiting. It would be nice to see you again…."

Mildred gave Gregory a faint smile. "Yes, it would."

Russian Revolution
October 17, 1917

"Do you hear from him?" Edgar Dalton asked. He sat on the couch in Thomas's office at the factory while Mildred leaned against her father's desk.

"I get the occasional letter," Thomas said. He stretched back on his chair with his hands behind his head, looking up at the ceiling. "Andrew's in the thick of it. Now that the Yanks are in it, maybe we can finally win the thing. He's been in many battles. He wrote about one battle at Passchendaele. We lost so many lads."

Edgar swirled his snifter of brandy. "But aside from the war, what's happening in Russia may be more troubling. They've overthrown the czar and the entire country is in chaos. That provisional government will not last. Who knows how long they will be in the war."

Mildred straightened herself to adjust her long white gloves. "From what I've heard over at the mission, the czar wasn't particularly good. One Russian woman immigrated several years ago. She said conditions in the country were deplorable. Food shortages while the aristocracy wined and dined."

Thomas shook his head. "I hardly think the prattling of a poor peasant from Eastern Europe qualifies as informed insight."

"She was there." Mildred frowned and put her hands on her hips. "She lived it. She knows more about the situation in Russia than any journalist in the Dominion."

Thomas sighed and rolled his eyes. "What happens in Russia is their problem. We need to be concerned with the situation here. It's difficult times we're headed for. I think it's time to cut back. Costs will continue to go up while the war rages. I know my profits are down so I'll keep my wages flat. Any raises I hand out directly affect my profit margin. And it's not as if the employees will work any harder if they get a raise. Everyone has to tighten their belts. The rank and file should know that more than anyone." Thomas took another swig of his cognac.

"I just hope they don't have any crazy ideas ... you know ... like what's happening in Russia," Edgar said.

"I cannot imagine," Thomas said. "The lot over here are too stupid."

Looking away to pour herself a splash of club soda, Mildred frowned.

"It's not them you need to worry yourself about," Dalton said. "It's the Brits. There are many dyed-in-the-wool labour leaders from the British Isles here in our city. They're smart and they have strong union backgrounds from back home. They're the ones we need to watch. The foreigners, they're just cannon fodder and the ones that will get blamed for everything. You watch."

Edgar looked at his pocket watch. "Where's William? The reservation is at six."

"I'll get Liz to track him down…." Thomas said.

Edgar waved his hand and rose. "Never mind. I'll go get him. I detest being late." Edgar left the office.

Thomas walked to the side table and poured himself another drink from a glass decanter.

Mildred crossed her arms. "That's your third drink and we're not even at the restaurant yet…."

Thomas turned around and glared at her. He tilted his head down like he always did when he meant business. "Don't go being like your mother."

Mildred turned around to look away. Someone had to be a source of reason. Why did he have to drink so much?

"Besides, I suspect William is taking his sweet old time because we had another conversation a few hours ago."

"Oh?"

"Our profits are taking a beating despite all the military-related orders. I've given him more than enough time but he's just not able to schedule jobs on the factory floor in an efficient manner. It was brought to my attention that some orders receive an unusual amount of attention to the detriment of more profitable orders. Suspicious, really. If he wasn't part of the family or the son of a very good friend, I would have thrown him on the street. In addition, he comes to work late almost every day. I've moved him to sales. He will be responsible for getting orders. His new position will require him to travel across the country, drumming up business for the company. He will not have any employees reporting to him and will report to my senior sales manager. Harold Morgan is a good man and will keep him on the straight and narrow."

"Will he be taking a cut in pay as well?"

"No, it will remain the same. But if he can't perform decently in his new position…." Thomas shrugged his shoulders.

Mildred swallowed hard and took a deep breath before taking a sip of her club soda. She could have scheduled production better than William. Tonight's dinner would be tense. William will take it out on her later this evening. She'd best turn in to bed right when arriving home or risk another black eye.

After ten minutes they heard a light knock on the office door. Seated at his desk Thomas motioned for Mildred to open it. "Perhaps your mother finally made it here."

Liz stepped inside. "I'm very sorry to bother you Mr. Spencer but there is a man to see you."

"Who is it?"

Liz remained silent.

Annoyed, Thomas waved his hand, "He's not another salesman is he? I told you I do not want to meet any more salesmen."

"It's not a salesman," Liz said, her head down. "I'll just send him up now. I know you need to see him." She scurried off downstairs.

"Wait. Who is it? You can't just send someone up…" Thomas shook his head in disgust. "Bloody secretary. Mildred, can you step out for a moment while I address this?"

But before she could leave, someone knocked on the door with far more force than Liz. A man with authority.

Mildred opened the door. A military man stepped inside. Older with a carefully trimmed white moustache, he wore his full dress uniform complete with shiny boots and white gloves. He tucked his officer's hat neatly under his arm.

Thomas stood up and buttoned his jacket. The colour left his face.

The officer took off his gloves and extended his hand. "Thomas Spencer?"

"Yes," Thomas said, accepting the handshake. "This is my daughter, Mildred."

The officer bowed slightly. She turned to leave but the officer stopped her. "Perhaps you should stay."

The officer cleared his throat. "I am Lieutenant Maxwell O'Brian," he said with a slight Irish accent. He put his head down slightly and reached into his lapel for a letter. "I regret to inform you that your son, Private Andrew

James Spencer, was killed in action in France on 13th of October, 1917. He died defending his country."

The announcement hit Thomas like a bullet. Mildred brought her hand to her mouth. Andrew dead? No.

"There must be some mistake," Thomas said. "Are you sure he was not mixed up with someone else?"

"I'm sorry, Mr. Spencer, we are certain and without a doubt."

Thomas walked over to his bar and poured a stiff shot of whiskey. With shaky hands he downed it. He took a deep breath, his face contorted as he tried his hardest to maintain his composure.

"What were the circumstances?" Thomas asked in a broken voice.

"Private Spencer's company was attempting to capture a hill in eastern France. He was one of the initial group of men that charged. He was cut down half-way up the hill by a German sniper."

Thomas remained silent, his back turned to O'Brien. Mildred strode over to console him.

The officer continued. "I know it will be of no consolation to you now but his commanding officer had nothing but praise for Andrew. He was a fearless fighter and practically challenged the Krauts to shoot him. He was the first to volunteer for any situation and placed his own life in peril on many occasions."

Mildred wept into a handkerchief.

Thomas approached the officer with a glass. "Here, have a drink with me, will you?"

O'Brian accepted the glass.

"To Andrew," Thomas said, raising his glass.

"To Andrew." The two men simultaneously emptied the contents of their glasses.

"Another?"

"No, I'm sorry. I must be going. I have a few other … appointments this afternoon."

Thomas nodded. "Of course, of course."

"I'm very sorry for your loss." O'Brian shook Thomas's hand again. He tipped his hat at Mildred before he walked out of the office, closing the door behind him.

Mildred slumped down on the couch, doubled-over in grief. Father poured another drink.

He stood directly in front of the photograph of her brother. "Oh, Andrew…" His voice broke. Large tears welled in his eyes and flowed freely down his face. "Oh, my dear Andrew. Andrew, Andrew, Andrew…"

Faulty Radiators
October 27, 1917

Lydia opened the back door to let Marko in. "There's something wrong with a few of the radiators upstairs. We turned them on a few weeks ago but they aren't giving that much heat. One of them bangs incessantly."

Marko took off his shoes and put his toolbox on the ground. "Where's Mildred?"

"She's in her room not feeling well. She's still grieving over Andrew and asked not to be disturbed. I'm sorry. No lesson today."

Mildred cancelled his visit last weekend because of the death of her brother. So sad. He wished he could give her a hug.

It had been a year since their lessons resumed. They only meet about once a month. He would make some repairs then the two of them would sit in the kitchen table at the back of the house for maybe an hour. Mildred and Lydia carefully selected the specific days, usually Saturdays when William was out. It would be a disaster if William knew Mildred resumed teaching English to him.

Although Mildred and William had only been married for a few years, they had problems. Marko could tell. Two months ago he saw a smashed mirror. Although she wore long-sleeved dresses with high collars, Mildred could not hide the occasional bruise. Sometimes she didn't smile and never mentioned anything about William when he made repairs. But during the English lessons she would always perk up.

Lydia followed him up the stairs and directed him to the water closet. "This room has been frightfully cold."

The spacious washroom had its own full-sized bathtub. The radiator stood against the wall under a window on the far side of the room. Marko smiled, shook his head and pointed. "There's your problem."

"You can tell already?"

"Sure, it's the shelf right above it."

He walked over to the crooked shelf and grabbed hold of it. Fastened to the wall with large nails that chipped and damaged the plaster, it wobbled at the slightest touch. "I don't remember this. When was it put here?"

Lydia whispered, "Mr. Dalton nailed it there a few weeks ago. I think he was trying to prove that he could also make improvements and repairs."

"A radiator can't have a shelf above it. The air doesn't flow good. This shelf should be taken down."

"I'm not sure if Mr. Dalton would like that."

"Then this room will stay cold." Marko tapped the shelf three times with his finger, but on the third tap the entire shelf dislodged from the wall and crashed down on to the radiator. "Oh … problem solved."

Lydia laughed. "You're going to have to explain it to him."

Marko smiled and shrugged. "He'll not like it but maybe with warm room he'll change his mind, no?"

"I doubt it. The other problem is with the radiator in the guest room. It keeps banging."

Marko examined that radiator and over the next half hour and found a faulty thermostat, an easy enough repair but would require him to get a new one from Ashdown's. He wouldn't be able to fix it until another weekend.

After putting his tools away and cleaning his mess, he went to leave. Lydia paid Marko for his visit and opened the back door for him.

"Wait," Mildred said from the far end of the kitchen holding a text book.

Marko averted his eyes. "You're not feeling well, Lydia said…"

Mildred raised her head up and pressed her lips together like she was trying to choke back tears. "I would like to do your lesson." She had a black eye, worse than the one last summer. She wore an unflattering blue dress that hung to the ground. She had put hair was up, but dangling, limp, loose strands looked untidy. Lydia left the room.

"Are you sure?"

"Positive. I'm fine."

Marko stood motionless for a moment then nodded. He pulled his exercise book out from the hidden compartment he had built at the bottom of his tool box. They sat down at the kitchen table where Mildred examined the paragraphs he wrote. Expressionless, Mildred appeared withdrawn. Ashamed.

While Mildred explained the importance of a good leading sentence in a paragraph and how a theme should be kept the same within a paragraph, Marko reached over and grabbed her hand.

Mildred stopped mid-sentence. She put her head down and began to cry.

He got out of his chair and gave her a hug. "I'm sorry about Andrew."

She nodded, her face red and eyes scrunched tight.

They held their silent embrace for several minutes. Marko pressed against her and stroked her hair. She buried herself in his shoulder.

"He hit you, didn't he?"

Mildred remained motionless in his arms.

"He's here!" Lydia yelled from the front of the house.

Mildred closed the textbook and rose. She scratched away her tears with the back of her hand and wiped them off on her long blue dress. Before leaving she gently put her hand on Marko's cheek. "Thank you." She lifted her skirt and ran back upstairs before William opened the front door.

"Hello, Mr. Dalton," Lydia said. "How was the Manitoba Club today."

"Good. How's Mildred…?"

"She's resting upstairs. Marko is here to repair the radiators."

Marko put his exercise book back in the secret compartment and sealed it shut only a moment before William came into the kitchen.

"Ah, I rarely see you here. You're like one of Santa's elves." He extended his hand.

Marko clenched his jaw but accepted the firm handshake. The man should be getting a punch in the face instead.

"You need a new thermostat for one radiator. The one in washroom is fine, but the problem is the shelf. It doesn't let air move around room. It fell down."

William frowned. "Fell down? I put it up."

"I touched shelf and it fell down."

William smiled and chuckled. "Oh, well. It just goes to show I will never be a labourer. If the shelf doesn't belong there perhaps you can mount it in a better location?"

Marko nodded. Lydia expected William to have a problem with the shelf. Maybe only when it came from the mouth of a woman? He put on his hat and shoes then grabbed his tool box. "Have Lydia arrange a Saturday that is good and I come."

"Very well."

Marko put his hand on the door knob to leave. "I hope Mildred is feeling better."

William folded his arms and paused for a moment. "What do you mean?"

His tone sounded serious and direct.

Marko's heart thumped against his chest. The familiar, old pain in his right temple appeared. He lowered his voice. "She looks like she's not feeling well. Sad about her brother … she also has a mark on her face."

"Mildred is of no concern to you."

Marko smiled. "Excuse me." He bowed slightly. "I mean no problem. I only notice. Something must have happened to her to leave mark like that."

"She slipped and fell in the tub."

Marko nodded, but slowly. "I know. Some things happen every now and then. She seems to get hurt every so often. How you say? Accident prone."

A small smile crept over William's mouth. "Yes, accident prone."

Marko turned to leave.

"Wait a moment. What's that on your shoulder. Why is it wet?"

Marko strained his neck to look. Mildred's tears. "Water from radiator dripped on me."

Letter from the Grave
November 10, 1917

Marko tapped on the guest room radiator twice with a wrench. "New thermostat. That should fix your problem."

"Thank you, again," Mildred said. "You're such a help." Handy and resourceful, if he opened his own repair shop, be it for automobiles or anything, his business would flourish.

Marko put his tools back in his toolbox. "It was nothing. Easy repair."

Mildred smiled and put her hand on his shoulder. "Maybe for you, but not for most people." Earlier Marko mounted the shelf that had fallen down from his last visit onto a different wall in the washroom.

Back downstairs, Marko turned to go into the kitchen where they always held the English lesson. Mildred tugged his arm.

"Today we'll have our lesson in the dining room. There's better light and more space to spread everything out."

Marko frowned. "What about William?" he whispered.

"He's off on a business trip in British Columbia and will be away for four days. It's just Lydia and myself."

Marko's expression changed into a broad smile. He looked like a boy on Christmas morning. She led him by the arm to the dining room where they reviewed Marko's essay on Ancient Egypt he wrote from the library books he used for research.

Not having William in the house for an extended period of time felt like a summer breeze. While he wasn't always an ogre, she needed a little break from him. Just sit back and enjoy each day without stress and drama. Do whatever she fancied like handiwork in her bedroom or perhaps visiting someone for a tea. Her choice.

An hour and a half later, with the lesson complete, Marko put his exercise book away and rose to leave.

Lydia popped her head around the corner. "Excuse me," she said. "Can I play something on the gramophone or will it bother the lesson."

"Go ahead," Mildred said. "We're finished here."

Marko paused for a moment. He looked reluctant to leave.

"Is everything all right?" Mildred asked.

Marko put his hands in his pockets. "I'm fine. I was wondering if you are. It's not my business, but I know you sometimes have a difficult time … with William."

"I do. I suppose it's obvious."

"I saw the mark on your eye a few weeks ago. You didn't fall down in the tub."

"No."

He looked straight into her eyes. "You should leave him. Before he hurts you bad."

Mildred crossed her arms and turned away. "I cannot. The bond of marriage is strong. Even my mother gets a few slaps."

"You want to wait until it gets worse?"

"There's not much you can do. He's not always bad. Just most of the time."

The absurdity of her last statement made her pause. She turned back to face Marko, brought her hand up to her mouth and started to laugh. Even Marko chuckled.

After her laughter subsided, Mildred reached for his hand. "Don't worry about me. I'll manage. Although I would have preferred to work at the factory, I still volunteer at the mission several times a week. William does travel more frequently now that he's in sales. And even when he's at home, well, he isn't really. He goes out most nights to drink and who knows what else. I've been questioning his fidelity for some time now. It's been difficult recently with the news of Andrew's passing, but I manage."

Mildred let go of Marko's hand. He meant well, but his queries opened too many wounds. She changed the subject. "Are you still seeing Lily? She still comes to English classes once a week."

"Yes. Not as much as before."

"Have you thought about making her an honest woman?"

"What you mean?"

"You know, marrying her. Taking her away from … her profession."

Marko looked down. "No, we only friends. She will not settle."

Mildred organized the books on the table into a neat pile. Since she began seeing Lily at the mission, she'd grown to appreciate the woman. Although

Lily's profession repulsed her, Lily remained open and honest about every aspect of her life. She did not care what others thought of her. A wonderful student as well. Pity the immoral relationship Marko had with her. Definitely not proper. Interesting that both seemed such fine people, despite a sinful relationship.

But Mildred's own marriage, while proper and normal in the eyes of most, became a wasteland, a mistake from the start. No love or companionship, only deceit. William could not compare to Marko. Marko would make a great husband. Too bad he was a foreigner.

"That's unfortunate," Mildred said. "I'm sure you will meet someone special. You've never really told me about your family back home. I think you said you were married and had a daughter…?"

Marko's shoulders tensed. His hand fidgeted with his tool box. "No family anymore. They died."

"I'm sorry. It must have been difficult. Was it disease? Consumption or influenza?"

"No. They were killed."

"Oh." Mildred brought her hand to her chest.

"I should go now."

Mildred nodded. Before he could take a step, the first bars of the 'Blue Danube Waltz' filled the house. They looked in each other's eyes for several seconds before Marko broke the gaze.

"Let me know when you need something fixed," he said then walked out the back door into the cold November air.

Mildred folded her arms and stared at the back door. What were the chances of Lydia playing that selection? Mildred smiled at the corner of her mouth. What if she had succumbed to temptation years ago that hot summer day?

She sighed and felt the warm radiator. Good as new. She looked through the coils and spotted something on the ground. A screwdriver. Marko must have forgotten it. She grabbed it and slipped on shoes before running outside into the chilly twilight. Breathing hard at the back fence, she looked down the back lane. Gone. She turned to go back to the house.

"Hey there, Milly." Mr. Browne from next door leaned against the three-foot fence. His other hand held his cane. He wore a brown overcoat with a matching hat.

"Hello, Gregory." She felt her heart flutter.

"He just turned the corner. If you run you might catch him."

"That's alright." She held up the screwdriver. "He can get it next time."

"Nice shoes."

Mildred looked down and guffawed. In her haste she put on two different shoes, one black and the other blue. "Thank you, I go to the best shops in town, you know." She threw Gregory a wink.

Gregory winked back. "I'm sure you do. Coming over again tomorrow for some tea? I have to finish my month-end accounting, if you care to help."

"I will. This time I'll bring the scones. Yours were rather hard."

"See you then." He tipped his hat and limped back to his house.

Mildred put a strand of hair behind her ear and stood outside for a few moments. Her broad smile warmed her soul.

*****

A few hours after Marko's visit, Mildred noticed a small pile of mail on the bureau near the front entrance. She held her breath when she saw a letter from Andrew. Holding the sealed envelope, she felt a pinch of sorrow and had to dab a few tears with a handkerchief. Obviously the last words from him before his death.

For several minutes, she stared at the envelope. Why didn't he send anything to her before? Nothing. He only sent letters to Father. Perhaps the strains of war proved too much for him?

Mildred first prepared some tea then carefully opened the letter and unfolded the single piece of paper. It was dated October 12, 1917.

Dearest Mildred,

I am sorry for not writing to you earlier. I really should have, but circumstances always prevented me from doing so. I did not mean it as a slight. On the few occasions I felt like sending a post, I did not have any paper available. On other occasions I had paper and a pen, but no ink. After a few years I thought it was not meant to be. I hope you are not disappointed.

Words cannot describe the horror and atrocities I have witnessed first-hand. Numerous comrades have fallen. Many others are blinded by poison gas or otherwise crippled for life, missing one or more limbs.

Myself, I have been fortunate. An enemy bullet grazed my leg a few years ago, but it hardly broke the skin. I was up and at 'em in no time.

I feel the tide of the war is turning. After a near stalemate for years, I feel the Allies are making progress and we will defeat the Huns. We will prevail, but of course, at a cost.

Although I have been spared from major injury, I sense my luck may soon run out.

Maybe quite soon. But before it does, I feel it is important for me to get something off my chest. My conscience has been bothering me.'

Mildred stopped reading momentarily to fill her teacup. Not bothering to add any sugar or cream, she took a wee sip.

'As you know, that night aboard the Titanic *has haunted me and continues to do so. I pounded on the door to the water closet in our suite, but Muriel would not stir. I used various pieces of furniture, anything I could lay my hands on, and banged on the door screaming her name until I bloodied my hands.*

'But then I panicked. I thought only of myself and left our sister to die. Like a coward. I should have gone down with the boat. But no, like a selfish oaf I fought my way on to a life boat. I tried to act like a man all through the voyage, yet at the moment when I should have stepped up to be one, I displayed extreme cowardice. I recall even pushing down a woman holding a baby so that I would be in a better position to get on a lifeboat.

'Surviving the Titanic *has damned me. I should not have survived. I still carry the shame. I contemplated ending my life soon after the ordeal. I reasoned that a better path was to join the army. If I die on the line, Father would think better of me. I would leave a positive legacy.*

'It is a miracle I have survived thus far. This, despite volunteering for all the most difficult missions. We are scheduled to attempt the capture of a hill tomorrow here in France.

'Mildred, please know I love you. You were always a kind and fair sister.

'Do not bother sending a reply. I do not plan to return to Canada. There is only one way for me to go. Perhaps it will be tomorrow. Perhaps the next.

'Good bye.

'With love, your brother,

'Andrew.'

Mildred fell back on the couch and stared off into blank space. She'd heard of other male *Titanic* survivors suffering through the same guilt. Some killed themselves from the shame. Yes, a German bullet took Andrew's life, but Andrew's joining the army was nothing less than suicide.

William's Deal Falls Through
November 19, 1917

Marko stepped into the office with his tool box.

"Well, it certainly took you long enough. I told Peter about it this morning." Liz stood by her desk with her hands on her hips, the frown on her face permanently etched like a bad army tattoo.

"What you need fixed?"

"The drawer on this desk," Liz said. "See." She grabbed it by the handle, but it would not budge.

Marko tried the handle. Sure enough, stuck. "It locked?"

"No, there is no lock on this drawer."

Marko scratched his head. Something must have been keeping the drawer jammed shut.

After Liz went away to the front counter to sort the day's mail. Marko crawled under the desk and shook the drawers, hoping to dislodge something. He ran his fingers along the edges of the drawers when he heard William's voice.

"Once I get the confirmation, this place will be buzzing."

"Don't count your chickens," Harold Morgan said. The head of sales, William's boss stood well over six feet. With broad shoulders and a thick build he looked like the type of man who could take care of himself. Marko stuck his head up from beneath the desk. As usual, both men looked immaculate in their expensive dark-toned three-piece suits and fancy neckties. They probably never touched a wrench in their lives.

"The meeting in Prince George was a piece of cake," William said.

"That's why we meet clients in person," Harold said, "to wine and dine them and make them your best friend."

"How is the drawer coming along?" Liz said. She walked over to check Marko's progress.

Surprised, Marko bumped his head on the bottom of the desk top. "Oww. Still stuck." He continued fiddling with the drawer. It would not budge, regardless of the jostling. Something must have moved or shifted within the drawer preventing it from opening.

He thought for a moment and then grabbed a long, thin file from his tool box. He carefully inserted the file into the drawer and moved it around. Sure enough, something blocked the way. He jiggled the file, rearranging the object. Once the object moved, the drawer opened easily.

With the drawer open, he saw what had been the problem: a booklet that had been lying on top of everything inside the drawer shifted up so that it pressed against the top edge, preventing the drawer from opening. To make sure he solved the problem and to ensure he didn't have to go back into the office and deal with Liz, he took the entire drawer out to inspect the runner.

The telephone on Liz's desk rang. She picked up the earpiece. "It's for you, Mr. Dalton," She handed the earpiece and the rest of the telephone to William.

William covered up the mouth piece. "I should have my own telephone."

Liz shrugged and went about her task at the front counter. William cleared his throat and spoke into the receiver. "William Dalton."

He paused for a moment.

"Wait a minute. What was that? … That's what I thought you said."

Marko stopped and peeked over the desk.

William cracked a nervous smile. "You must be joking, Steven. You're such a joker."

After another short pause, William's expression changed from jovial to a look of concern.

"What do you mean? Steven, Steven … wait a moment … that's not what we discussed. You said that …Wait a minute. Wait a minute. We had a deal. Did we not? I mean, I demonstrated the accomplishments of Winnipeg Iron Works. We've constructed many bridges over the years, all of fine quality. You can talk to any city manager or provincial official. Our work is top notch. No … I … yes … of course, I understand. Yes, you need to make your own decisions. But I was certain we had a deal."

William adjusted his collar.

"I thought I … ah … I thought I was able to smooth negotiations with the package I provided."

William shook his head.

"No. No, no, no, no, no. I sent the package. Are you telling me you didn't receive it?!? How can that be possible?" William covered the mouthpiece with his hand and glared at Liz, still leaning against the front counter with her arms crossed.

"Liz," William said in a stern, forceful voice, "Steven at Grand Trunk says he never received any package. Did you not send it out?"

Liz looked up. "Of course I did. Why, it was about two or three weeks ago. It should have already arrived at its destination."

"They never received the package."

"It was just an envelope, was it not? A thick one?"

"Yes," William said. He rolled his eyes.

Liz's well-worn crease lines formed a frown. "What was in it?"

William paused momentarily. "Papers," he said. "Papers for them to sign, of course." By now everyone in the office listened in. Morgan stood in the doorway of his office.

"I see," Liz said. "Well, in that case, I can't understand why the envelope would be lost in the mail. You told me yourself to just address it and stick it in the post. In the past when we have to send anything … of value … we never send it by mail. It's all hand delivery. Sending anything important through the mail can be sketchy. You just never know. But if it was just some papers for your client to sign, surely we can just prepare another set and send them out. They are not valuable to anyone, so I can't imagine they would get lost in the mail again." The edges of Liz's lips formed into a slight smile of delight.

William grimaced. He removed his hand from the mouthpiece and continued his telephone call. "I can prepare another package for you. I just need a little time. What do you mean it's 'too late?' You gave the contract to someone else? But we had a deal! Wait … we need to discuss this further. Wait … wait!"

William hung up the telephone and stood silent at Liz's desk, his head down in a combination of anger and disgust. Marko ducked back under the desk.

"William. Office," Morgan said.

William swore under his breath and slowly walked into his supervisor's private office. Morgan closed the door.

Everyone in the office remained silent to try to listen to the conversation. Good. William deserved it.

"I went to give him the envelope," William said, his voice muffled but still legible. "But I forgot it at home."

"You forgot it at home. A thousand dollars and you forgot it at home?"

Morgan voice shot out like a cannon, loud enough to be heard from across the street. "How can you forget the most important deal closer?"

"I ... I ..."

"And then ... and then ... you arrange to have the cash sent in the mail? What are you? Stupid? You never send cash like that in that mail. You know how long it takes a mailman to make a thousand dollars?"

"Liz should have known. I just thought it would be fast..."

"What? A fast way to lose a potential client? And don't go blaming Liz. Look ... Mr. Spencer put you in this position because he said you were more of a people person. Well, no amount of cajoling is going to get that bridge built in Prince George. You know how competitive this market is? Winnipeg used to be the number one city in the west, but now there's industry in Vancouver, Calgary and Edmonton. We can't win contracts by resting on our laurels anymore. Those days are over. The only way to get anything done is to sweeten the pot ... and you left the honey pot at home."

After a short pause, Morgan continued. "And do you know what the biggest problem is? Do you? We've already ordered and paid for the steel for the bridge we will not be building!" He screamed out the last sentence forcing several of the office staff to look down, pretending to do their work despite the door to Morgan's office being closed.

"I can get that replaced. That's not a problem."

"It's not, eh? Well, you work on that. Now get out of my office. I have to visit Mr. Spencer and break the news to him. It will not go well. I suggest you visit some of our city contacts. Maybe someone is constructing a building or something, but with the war going on, I seriously doubt it."

William left the office, grabbed his hat and overcoat, and slowly shuffled out the building.

Still seated on the ground under Liz's desk, Marko couldn't help but wear a smile. How long would Mr. Spencer put up with him?

"What are you doing?" Liz said, holding a parcel.

Marko snapped his head back and again hit it on the desk. He winced and rubbed the back of it. "I fixed drawer, see..." He took the drawer from the floor and placed it on the runner and demonstrated that it moved freely by opening and closing it a few times.

Liz tested it herself a few times. "Good."

Marko put away the metal file he used for opening the drawer into his tool box and prepared to leave.

"Before you go," Liz said, "what was wrong with the drawer? Why could it not open?"

"Too much in drawer. This was blocking drawer from opening." He picked up the booklet he took out of the top drawer. Liz's eyes widened and her face turned red when she saw the cover: HOW TO IMPROVE YOUR BUST SIZE IN THREE WEEKS.

She snatched the booklet from Marko's hands. "That will be all, thank you."

*****

That night Marko walked in the darkness to Selkirk Avenue to catch the streetcar to visit Lily. The strong wind gnawed on his face and neck. He felt a throbbing on the side of his head and shut his eyes.

For fifteen minutes Marko waited at the stop for the streetcar. Bundled against the cold, he stared ahead, concentrating. Breathing slowly. A woman with a head scarf clutching a child, a small girl, also stood at the stop.

"Why do we haveta go? I don't wanta visit Uncle Anton."

"Shush!" the mother said. "The operation is tomorrow. We need to see him before the doctor's knife."

Knife.

*****

Marko is walking away from his farmhouse on the narrow, dirt road. He looks down. He is holding a bloody knife, his hands soaked in blood.

He throws the knife down and begins to run. He wants to run far away from the farmhouse.

A stone trips him and he lands on the ground, hard. It is dark outside, but on the ground in front of him, shining against the moonlight, is something metal.

The knife.

But he threw it away a hundred yards ago. How can it be there, on the ground right in front of his eye? He gets up and continues running.

At the turnoff to the road that leads to town, Marko pauses to catch his breath. What happened to his family? Who killed them? He has to make it to town to alert the authorities.

He looks at his hands. Not a drop of blood on them.

"Marko! Is that you? I was looking for you!" He turns at the familiar voice. It is Boris, a police officer, sitting on a white horse. "A crazed man escaped from a lunatic asylum. I was on my way to your place to warn you.

Apparently he's dangerous. He will not think twice to slit a throat. If I had my way, he would have been at the bottom of the gallows pole long ago."

Of course, that explains everything.

Boris frowns. "Marko, why are you holding a knife? My God, you're covered in blood!"

Marko looks down. Indeed, he is holding the dripping knife again and his hand and upper body is drenched in blood.

*****

"Are you getting on or what?"

Marko looked at his hand. No knife, only coins.

"Hey buddy, you okay?" the streetcar driver said.

Marko took a deep breath and stepped on the streetcar.

Home Renovations
May 18, 1918

"This wall goes," Marko said in Ukrainian. He slammed his hammer into the wall of the office in Gregory's house. Plaster fell to the floor from the impact while cracks ran out from the new hole like tiny lightning bolts.

"That will make a big mess," Mike said. He stood behind Marko with his arms folded across his chest. He wore grubby blue overalls and shoes that had seen better days.

"You have to destroy before you can create."

Mike smashed his hammer against the same wall creating a second hole. The desk, a short bookcase and an end table rested in the middle of the room covered by blankets. Earlier they rolled up the blue carpet from the office and temporarily put it in the hallway, beside the stairs.

"Why is he renovating?" Mike asked.

"I think he's going to sell this house. He finds this room is too cramped, so he wants to move the wall. That's a bit of work if you ask me. If you want to sell, then sell. Why waste time? But he's well off, so who am I to argue?"

The two continued to demolish the wall. Plaster crumbled. Dust hung in the air and stuck to the thin film of sweat on the men's exposed arms and necks. Most of the laths needed to be pried off with a crowbar. Within an hour they reduced the short interior wall to rubble. They gathered the larger pieces of wood and plaster and threw them into a bin just outside the back door. Using a broom and dust pan, Mike swept the smaller pieces into a garbage can.

"Hello! How are things progressing?" Gregory had arrived and hollered from the front door.

"Good," Marko said. "The office wall is down."

Gregory appeared in the doorway, his trusty cane at his side. His eyes widened when he saw the new opening. "There, that looks better already. If you aren't improving your residence, it's only deteriorating." Gregory limped to Mike with his hand extended. "You must be Mike. Pleased to meet you."

Mike accepted the handshake. "I'm just the hired help. Marko is the brains behind the renovation. But thank you for the work. Things have slowed down since the civic strike started a few weeks ago."

Gregory looked at his now-dusty hand. "It was one after the other. First the electrical workers, then the waterworks employees followed by the fire alarm workers. I think the city has threatened to fire the lot if they don't get back on the job."

"Why strike?" Marko asked.

"Higher wages. That's the main reason. I think they also hope to simply have the right to strike. They want to bargain for that ability."

"And they do it by striking?"

"They're playing chicken. Can the city fire everyone? If they did then who would run things? There's only so many workers to go around. But I reckon it will be over soon. The city rejected all the offers from the unions. Business leaders even resolved that striking should be illegal during the war and formed the Committee of One Hundred to work against the strike. I heard today the railway freight handlers are getting involved. If so, then that will be it. The government will step in to end everything. I'm sure the unions will win some concessions and all it will do is give them more resolve."

Mike wiped his sweaty brow with the back of his dusty hand. "It's all about money."

Gregory nodded. "It always is." He glanced at his pocket watch. "Well anyway, it looks like everything is progressing well. I'll be stepping out again but will be back in a short while. Carry on."

Marko gave a small wave before Gregory left the room. He and Mike cleaned up the reminder of the mess. Around 11:00 am both stopped for an early lunch. Mike used an overturned bucket as a chair while Marko sat cross-legged on the floor.

"In a few years I won't have to worry about strikes," Marko said. "I'll have saved enough to start my own repair shop. You make more money when you are your own boss."

Mike took a bite from his bologna sandwich and nodded. "Then maybe I work for you?"

"Maybe." A general labourer, Mike knew a little bit about everything but not enough to be good at anything.

"One day I would like something more steady. It's hard to feed everyone. We don't make enough from just my wages. Maria has to work. She cleans the houses of rich people one, maybe two times in a week. And Nicholas … he's older now and out of school. He works at a corner store."

"What about getting rent? Like you did from me?"

"It won't be enough. That's why we moved from Manitoba Avenue. The rent was too high. Our new place on Henry Avenue is small. Sure, we can go to a bigger place, but who wants to live with five, six, seven other people?" Mike smiled and put his thumbs under his armpits in a boastful pose. "But that's okay. I told Maria we'd be living south of the CRP tracks … and now we are."

Marko laughed. Crumbs from his sandwich flew out of his mouth. "Henry Avenue is just south of the train yards. It's not a very good part of town. Your place on Manitoba Avenue was better."

"Da. But what can you do?" Mike shrugged. "At least my brother, Harry, lives next door. But he's in the war right now."

"How could he join the army? He's from Galicia, no?"

"Da. He changed his name to Sidon. Harry Sidon. It sounds Canadian, so they accepted him in the army."

For the next few hours Marko and Mike framed a new wall extending a different direction from the one they demolished. Mike brought in new lath slats from the pile in the backyard and Marko hammered each in place. When he finished, Marko mixed plaster in a large bucket and gathered the tools for applying it to the newly created wall.

"I thought this other wall had to go down too," Mike said, pointing across the room.

Marko frowned and put down his mixing stick. "No, I don't think so." He looked up to the ceiling where a few cracks snaked across and around areas where the plaster had fallen. "We better get Bert in here. He's better at ceilings than I am."

Mike followed Marko's gaze and looked up. Without looking, he sat down on the overturned bucket. The moment he sat down, he shot up. He'd sat on the stick Marko used to stir the plaster. A line of brown plaster decorated Mike's bum.

Marko shook his head. "What are you going to do? Wipe your ass on the wall to apply the plaster?"

Mike provided a sheepish smile. Clumsy. No wonder he didn't have a steady job.

The front door opened again. Gregory and Mildred walked into the room being renovated.

"See, they're doing a smashing job," Gregory said to Mildred. Mike immediately turned his back to the wall so no one could see his rear.

"We're just about to apply the first coat of plaster. We'll be finished in a half hour."

"Take your time," Gregory said. "Mildred is over for a cup of tea."

Mildred smiled. "Hello."

Mike nodded. Marko acknowledged her with a small tip of his hat. Gregory and Mildred walked through the old office area into the back of the house.

Mike leaned his head toward Marko. "A married woman coming over for tea on her own to a bachelor's home? It doesn't seem right…"

Marko waved Mike off. "They're just neighbors. She's home all day and so is he. That's nothing unusual."

"If you say so." Mike winked.

Marko pressed a three-foot board against the bottom of the new wall. Mike put fresh brown plaster on the board while Marko dragged the board up along the wall to apply it. Once they completed the coat, Marko stepped back to admire his work. "I'll do another coat tomorrow and then the white coat the day after that."

"Are you sure that other wall doesn't have to go down?" Mike pointed across the room.

Marko shook his head. "No … I think."

"You better check with Gregory, because I could have sworn he said this other wall has to go."

"He would have said something each time he was here, no?"

"Maybe you should check to make sure?"

Marko looked at the wall. Wasn't it only one wall coming down? He felt almost certain. "Alright. Stay here."

He walked to the back of the house careful not to trip over the rolled-up rug and almost entered the kitchen when he stopped dead. Beside the kitchen table Gregory and Mildred had embraced. Mildred buried her head in Gregory's shoulder. Both clutched each other tight. Marko took a step back and looked away for a moment. It didn't feel right intruding during a tender moment. He always felt they were close, but not this close.

He took another peek. They progressed to kissing. Mildred pressed her body onto Gregory. He stumbled slightly, but remained upright. Mildred rubbed her hands all along Gregory's back while Gregory's hands went lower and lower. Marko's breathing quickened. Sure, Mildred was a married woman but her marriage suffered. Beaten and ignored. Treated horribly. To see her so enthralled with another man, a good man, made him smile.

But then his smile faded. He could have been embracing Mildred. Kissing her. Like that time years ago in her father's home after they danced. He could have stolen a kiss and she would have accepted. But that was then. He stepped back into the shadows.

What about Lily? A strange relationship. Obviously intimate, but she got paid to be intimate with everyone. Sure, she shared some of her secrets with him, but it would go no further. He couldn't pull her out despite his feelings for her, like a barrier she would not cross.

Maybe one day.

Marko took another peek. Mildred and Gregory picked up the pace. Their lips locked together like train car couplings, intertwined, strong and true. The bun on Mildred's head become unravelled. The collar on Gregory's shirt partially detached.

*****

Marko is kissing Olena in the hallway. Her hair feels like silk. She never looked like a farmer's wife. More like a sophisticate from the city. He draws his hands down to her buttocks and gives her cheeks a little squeeze. She likes it when he does that. Her tongue invades his mouth like a wet snake. Olena lifts her bare leg and rubs it gently in his groin.

He hears a giggle.

It stops, but then there's another giggle. Olena smiles and licks the tip of Marko's nose before walking the rest of the way down the hallway. Marko catches a glace of the back of her legs.

But more giggling. It's Anastasiya. He sees her head poking from around the corner, that rascal.

He runs after her, but when he gets to the corner, she is gone. "Where are you? I'm going to find you!"

He hears a sound from the kitchen. Of course, her favorite hiding spot in the cupboard under the kitchen counter.

Marko knocks on the cupboard door. "Hello, is anyone home?"

"I'm not in here." Anastasija says in a teasing tone from inside the cupboard. "You can't find me. Look somewhere else."

Marko smiles and swings open the door. Empty. Where did she go?

There are only piles of magazines. Most have been cut into little pieces. He feels a sharp pain on the side of his head and touches the indentation on his temple. He closes his eyes for a moment.

"See, I'm never there."

Marko turns. Anastasija is standing behind him.

"How did you…?"

"There's a hole in the back of the cupboard, Daddy. You need to fix the hole."

"A hole? I'll have to take it down to do that."

*****

"Ok, we'll take it down," Mike yelled from the office. Marko heard a dull thud from the office area, the sound of a hammer hitting plaster.

"No!" Marko ran back into the office.

Mike stood poised to give the wall another shot. "But you said to take it down."

Spanish Flu
October 21, 1918

Lily could not possibly take any more clothes off. First she took off her sweater. Then she took off her stockings. She even went barefoot.

"Are you sure you're okay?" Marko asked. They were at a table in the brothel's waiting room having a few shots before they went upstairs.

"Da," Lily said in a drab tone. She didn't sound very convincing.

"Maybe you should call it a night if you're not well."

"I'm fine. What am I supposed to do? It's busy here tonight."

The house on Annabella Street had every seat taken in the waiting area with several men forced to remain standing. Many military men. Alcohol flowed freely and one of the prostitutes sat at the piano playing an upbeat tune.

"Look at all the soldiers," Lily said. "With more and more coming back from the front lines, we'll be busy again like we were before the war. Most of these men went months, maybe years without the touch of a woman. The good thing about soldiers is they usually have money and are quick on the draw. I can have more clients in an hour. We better finish up before Minnie gets after me."

Marko took a sip of his rye and glanced around the room. "They look so young."

"Most of the soldiers are pleasant," Lily said. She coughed in her hand, a phlegmy, sick sounding cough. "Real momma's boys. Somehow they dodged the bullets and mines and mustard gas and made it back home. Some looked like they haven't shaved for the first time. Some are virgins. Poor farm boys, maybe nineteen or twenty. Never saw a naked woman in their life. Of course they act real brave. But once I bring them upstairs, they would be nervous and shy. They would fidget. They'd be more afraid of me than the Huns. At that point, I swear, they'd rather get in a fist fight than have anything to do with me. I would sit beside the soldier on my bed and just talk. Sometimes we do nothing. On those occasions, I tell the soldier what to tell his buddies. I'd feel bad taking their money, but have to. Minnie expects something from each trick. Sometimes, the soldier would be fine. Others would break down and cry, telling me about horrible experiences on the front in France or Belgium. Some soldiers are missing limbs, perhaps an arm or a leg. Their comrades would bring them along because they are one of the boys and deserve a night out like the rest of them. How attractive would a one-legged man be to any regular woman? I make sure the crippled boys have a good time."

Lily hacked again, this time into a handkerchief. Flushed and sweaty with glassy eyes, she grabbed a magazine from the next table and fanned herself. Noticing her from across the room, Minnie walked over and felt Lily's forehead with the back of her hand. Minnie frowned and leaned into Lily. "Yer done for the night sweetie. Go on to bed."

"I'm fine, just hot…"

"No, I think it might be worse than that. Yer burnin' up. Go on. No more for you tonight."

Lily finished her shot and rose from the table but stumbled and nearly fell down. Marko caught her just in time.

"All of a sudden I feel so tired…" Lily collapsed into Marko's arms. He bent his knees to pick her up and carry her. With Lily nestled in Marko's arms, Minnie led the way up the stairs.

Carefully, Marko laid Lily down on her bed. Bathed in sweat and burning like a match, Lily removed the rest of her clothing with the help of Minnie then slumped back down in the bed. Sweat glistened, beaded and poured off her body. She reached for her throat. "Hard to swallow," she whispered.

Minnie stood by Lily's dresser with her arms crossed, her eyebrows knotted with concern.

"Do you think…?" Marko said.

"Yes, I fear it's the Spanish Flu. The papers have been talking about it for a few weeks now. Most of the cases have been out in the eastern cities and the U.S. Not many in Winnipeg so far, but it's a-comin'."

Chang poked his head in the door.

"Run over and get Doctor Brooks. Then get me a pan and a sponge with cold, clean water." Chang nodded and closed the door.

Fifteen minutes later Chang came back with Doctor Brooks, the same doctor who worked on Marko after his beating four years ago. Wearing wire-rim spectacles, the doctor carried a black leather medical bag. He sported a neatly-trimmed moustache and beard sprinkled with grey hair. His well-tailored three-piece suit and neatly polished black shoes looked out of place in the whorehouse.

"What have we got here?" he asked. He placed his medical bag on the side table and took out his stethoscope. Marko took a few steps back to get out of the doctor's way. Mildred once told him that the doctor lived in the area and made many calls to the establishments in the red light district. All discrete, of course. Other than money for supplies, he didn't charge anything. Instead, he bartered for the skilled services provided by the girls. Minnie and the other madams didn't mind the arrangement and he certainly didn't either, so long as his wife never found out.

"I'm real worried about the Spanish Flu," Minnie said.

The doctor nodded. "That is a distinct possibility. When did Lily first present symptoms?"

Minnie shook her head. "I'm not sure. Maybe yesterday?" Minnie bent down to the still shivering Lily. "Dear … when did you start feeling bad?"

"I … I," Lily tried to speak but had difficulty because she was shaking so much. "I d-don't know. Not l-long. M-Maybe j-just in morning…."

Minnie gently wiped Lily's brow. Just then, Chang returned with a small pan and sponge. The doctor turned and pointed. "Good. Just set that down beside my bag." Chang did so and left the room.

Marko felt useless standing there, but what could he do? His guts churned with concern. He thought back to when he was a child, maybe six or seven. Uncle Oleg had consumption. Watching Oleg spit up blood scared him. Mother cried for days after he died.

Doctor Brooks placed his stethoscope on Lily's chest. The cold device made Lily shiver even more. "Now, now. This will only be a moment. Please breathe deeply and exhale." Lily complied. He moved his devise up an inch and asked her to do the same.

"Sit up, if you can," he ordered. Minnie helped Lily up to a sitting position. Doctor Brooks placed his stethoscope on Lily's back. "Breathe deeply again, please." After a few moments he asked Lily to cough.

"All right, you can lie back down." The moment she did, Lily grabbed the blankets for warmth and continued with her shivering. "How is your head? Do you have a headache?" Lily nodded in quick agreement.

Doctor Brooks took out his gold pocket watch and with his other hand took Lily's pulse. "One-twelve," he said under his breath. He took his stethoscope off, wrapped it around his shoulders and crossed his arms.

"What do you figure?" Minnie asked.

"There's no doubt about it. She has la grippe. Her lungs are relatively free at the moment, but the sudden fever is a sure sign. So is the headache. I have to concur … this is the Spanish Flu."

Minnie brought her hand to her mouth and gasped. "Oh, my dear girl. What … what do we do?"

"You need to immediately quarantine her. No one other than a caregiver is to see her. She is not to leave this room. Naturally she will have to take a break from her regular tasks, so to speak."

"Of course," Minnie said. "If customers got sick, there's a chance they wouldn't be customers for much longer."

"The fever will make her perspire profusely, so please ensure her bed sheets are changed regularly. Try to keep her dry. In addition, she needs to be kept clean. A daily sponge bath is a good idea. Make sure she's eating good food, if she can. And plenty of fluids. Also, ventilation is key. Leave the window open. Good, clean fresh air will drive away any foul air resulting from the disease. I have other patients with the Spanish Flu. Despite the ban the Board of Health instituted on public gatherings a little over a week ago, more cases are popping up. Places like Toronto and Montreal are seeing hundreds of people die. So far Winnipeg doesn't even have as many deaths, but that'll change."

The doctor looked down at Minnie overtop his spectacles. "I know you do not want to hear this, but you may have to consider closing your operation until the pandemic runs its course. If not for the safety of your clientele, then for the safety of your girls."

Arms still folded firmly across her chest, Minnie stared out the window. Then she looked at poor Lily, still shivering away.

"In the meantime, there are other treatments we can try for Lily. Next visit I'll administer an enema. We can also try a glucose-saline injection. In may not hurt to try some old-fashioned remedies. A poultice of hot bran mixed with sulphur may help if she develops more congestion in her lungs. Perhaps a sip of cinnamon oil." Doctor Brooks looked towards Lily's dresser and spotted a half-filled bottle. "Also, some of that whiskey might help. With prohibition you're fortunate to have a stock of alcohol. It will come in handy."

Minnie thanked the doctor before he left. She poured whiskey in a glass and propped Lily up. "Now, now. Down the hatch. Take your medicine." Minnie helped Lily tip the glass into Lily's mouth, but a good portion spilled down on to her bare bosom. Before going back downstairs, Minnie changed Lily's sheets and called for Chang to take the drenched, dirty linen. Lily's tremors subsided and she fell into a sleep.

A crashing sound invaded the still of Lily's bedroom. It came from downstairs where a fight had broken out. "Oh, fer Pete's sake," Minnie said. She went to leave the room. "You need to leave soon. No touching. You just leave her be. I mean it." She closed the door behind her.

Marko stared at Lily. Poor Lilia. Many had already gotten sick around the world. All those soldiers carrying their sickness from across the ocean. Was there any doubt Lily would catch something? Especially in her line of work being in contact with so many complete strangers.

He shook his head. They could have had a life together. Was this worth it? Would it not be better to mind a house and cook dinner? Marko slumped down in a chair beside the bed. Through the door he could still hear a commotion coming from downstairs. Gus must have been showing the door to some unrulies in an aggressive manner. The violence downstairs opposite to the quiet stillness of Lily's room.

Although asleep, Lily's face twitched. Marko frowned. She looked far too warm. Gently and carefully, he pulled back the covers revealing her naked body, soaked with perspiration.

The fever raged. He had to do something. He opened the window about a foot. Instantly the cool late-October evening air invaded the room. He noticed the water-filled pan and sponge on the dresser.

He carried the pan to the edge of the bed then wrung the sponge, releasing access water. Carefully, he wiped Lily's neck in a caressing and calming fashion, mindful not to wake her up. After all, she needed to rest to combat the deadly disease that had invaded her body. While wiping her face, he made sure not to let any water drip into her nose. He put the sponge to her brow where he gently caressed her forehead.

He brought the sponge to her torso, still sparkling with sweat. He tried hard not to admire her nakedness in a perverted way by remembering that her illness needed special attention. Marko bent over and washed one arm before dipping the sponge in the water, wringing it and wiping the other arm. He slowly caressed her chest moving the sponge over each breast carefully and slowly. The cool sponge bath and fresh breeze seemed to have an effect on lowering Lily's fever. Marko noticed Lily's breathing calmed and the colour in her face lightened.

Then he moved down to her legs, carefully wiping away sweat with the cool water from the sponge. With care, Marko cleaned Lily's feet.

He put the sponge back in the pan and wrung it. After gently wiping her hips, he cleaned her nether regions. This didn't seem right at first, but it was just another part of her body.

She slept better now. Satisfied, Marko put the pan back on the dresser. Spotting a towel, he slowly dabbed the water from Lily's body, being careful to not disturb his sleeping lover. Through the towel he touched and caressed her entire body, from the bottom of her feet to the top of her head.

Right when he finished, Minnie came back into the room. "What the hell are ya doing?"

"I-I—"

Minnie ran towards Marko, lifting the bottom of her dress to make sure she didn't trip over it. She ripped the wet towel from Marko's hands. "I thought I told you no monkey business. You weren't supposed to touch her."

"I wash…"

"Get out of here. All you men are the same. You only think of one thing."

Marko's stretched his arms out. "Lilia sick. I open window. I wash. She too hot."

"Yeah, well that's not yer job. Git!"

No sense in arguing, Marko placed his hat on his head and left the room.

Visiting Lily
October 23, 1918

Marko walked up the steps to Minnie's place on Annabella. The door was locked for the first time since he began visiting the brothel.

The curtain on the door moved. "We're closed! Go away! Can'tcha read the sign?" came a woman's voice from within. Marko looked, sure enough, a little sign attached to the door read: CLOSED UNTIL THE SPANISH FLU PASSES.

"I hope to see Lilia…" Marko said through the closed door.

"She's very ill and is not taking any customers. We're closed. You should leave."

"I don't want anything. I only want to visit. See if she's okay. Nothing more. I know she's sick."

Marko could make out two women talking to each other.

"Is that Marko?" another woman said.

"Yes."

Minnie opened the door. One of her prostitutes stood by her. He braced himself for a tirade or at least some sort of confrontation.

"Are you ill? You got any flu symptoms?" Minnie said with a frown and her arms crossed.

He shook his head.

Minnie raised her chin. "Alright. C'mon inside. You can see her. But it'll be to say goodbye."

Marko stepped inside and removed his hat. Where normally there would be anywhere from fifteen to twenty-five johns waiting for a turn, only Chang, wearing a face mask, ran upstairs with a pan of water. Instead of a roar of laughter, a piano or perhaps even a fist fight, dead silence filled the brothel.

Although the Spanish Flu had not spread as quickly compared to other cities in Canada and the U.S., its presence grew in Winnipeg. Just yesterday Marko read in the newspaper that there were almost 200 new cases in the city. Three people died that same day. Since the outbreak started about a month ago, over a hundred people perished from the deadly disease.

Public gatherings had been banned for about two weeks now, including theatres, schools, clubs, churches – anywhere people would normally meet. It made sense, but most regular businesses still remained open including factories and offices. With workers in close quarters, shoulder to shoulder, could they not also get the Spanish Flu just as easily as they could in church? It seemed odd.

The hospitals overflowed with patients, so much that the authorities set up a special emergency hospital in a building on the corner of Main Street and Logan Avenue with enough room for two hundred patients. Peter told him that they even converted a local hotel into a hospital for military flu victims.

In addition to the epidemic, the war drew to a close. Each day brought more news of victories over the Germans and their allies. After several dark, miserable years, Marko sensed that the city braced itself and prepared to erupt in celebration. But the flu tempered the joy.

"Go on with Mary," Minnie said. "She'll take you up to Lily's room."

Marko followed Mary up the stairs. A pretty young woman of maybe eighteen or nineteen, she did not dressed provocatively, but still wore make-up. Some fallen women could not resist the urge to make themselves up even when they were not working.

Mary opened Lily's door slowly. Also with a face mask, Doctor Brooks stood by the bed, his head bowed. Chang placed assorted cloths into the pot, perhaps to boil them clean downstairs, then left the room.

"My God, you need to protect yourself, man." The doctor handed Marko a face mask which he attached around his ears.

"How is she?"

Doctor Brooks sighed and shook his head. He didn't say a word and placed his items in his medical case. Before he left he patted Marko on the shoulder.

Marko slowly approached her bedside, almost afraid of what he would see.

When he viewed her up close, he took a small step back in surprise. The young woman, full of confidence and life, had been reduced to a shell. Lily's radiant eyes were bloodshot and puffy while her once beautiful hair had become tangled and matted. Pale with hollow cheeks, her raspy breathing struggled from the junk in her lungs. It almost seemed like her skin had a slight purple colour. Only her head stuck out from the bed sheets.

"Lilia," Marko said. His heart sank.

Lily did not acknowledge him. Bits of dried blood speckled around her nostrils.

"She went downhill from the get go," Minnie said, just entering the room.

"But doctor…"

"The doctor said there was nothing he could do." Minnie began to lose her composure and choked up. "Some cases are mild, but others … well … this is what happens." She brought a handkerchief up to her eye.

"I-I know," Minnie continued, "I know that you meant well last time you were here. You were just helping. You know, of all the johns, she liked you. She always talked about you."

Tears formed in Marko's eyes. One sick john slipped through. That's all it took. Probably a soldier fresh from Europe. It didn't have to be like this. They could have had a life together. Too late now.

Lily's head lolled from side to side. She babbled something incoherent. Marko leaned closer to try to understand. Like the last time he saw her, her head dripped in perspiration.

Slowly, her glistening eyes opened, wet from sweat and tears. "M-Marko," she rasped quietly, followed by a coughing fit.

"I'm here," he said in Ukrainian.

"Marko … you need to move on. Don't … worry about me," she said in the same raspy, sick voice.

"No. Don't say that."

"It was not meant to be. You know that. You need to move on."

"I'll miss you," Marko said, his rolling tears absorbed by the face mask.

"Listen …." Lily smiled faintly. "Those horrible things about your wife and girl in the old country … I don't believe them. You couldn't do that." Another coughing fit consumed Lily, worse than before. She gagged on her own phlegm.

"She needs water. Get water," he said to Minnie. Minnie bolted out the door and through a congregation of several other fallen women.

"Don't worry, Minnie will get you some…" Marko stopped short. Lily's eyes and mouth remained open. "Lilia? Lilia?" Marko leaned over and shook her. "Wake up!"

No response. Marko slumped back down in his chair and sobbed. Several of the ladies shrieked and openly wept. "Minnie! Minnie!" one shouted.

"Come here, quick, Lily … Lily's passed away."

Marko put his hands to his face and cried into his hands. His temple began to throb.

Minnie, also crying, gave Marko a clean handkerchief which he used to blow his nose and dab his eyes. He closed Lily's eyes with his hand. He took off his mask and for one last time gave her a kiss on the forehead. It felt like his heart would burst.

****

Marko is running through a thicket of bushes, his hands still covered in blood. He is still holding a knife. Boris, the police officer on the horse, shouts at him but cannot follow. The bush is too thick for the horse. Marko escapes.

But where will he go? What will he do? What happened? It is only a matter of time before he is caught.

Marko continues running, through swamp and bush. It seems like hours and hours. He doesn't eat or drink anything and feels weak.

He comes upon a farmhouse, but stays in the woods, away from anyone's view. Should he turn himself in? He looks down at his hands. He is still holding the bloody knife and blood is smeared all over his jacket and trousers.

But where can he run? Surely everyone is looking for him, especially since he ran away from Boris.

He slumps down behind a thick, tall tree and begins to weep. Nothing is making sense and everything is going too fast.

"Mister, are you alright?" a little farm boy says. He is holding a fishing pole carrying two fish. He looks strangely familiar, like someone he has seen before or knows quite well.

Startled, Marko gets up on his feet. "No, no … stay away from me. Please!" Marko doesn't want to hurt the little boy. He already butchered two loved ones. What will stop him from murdering an innocent boy?

"Why? Do you need help or something? Maybe you should talk to my father or mother?"

"N-no … stay away. See." Marko shows the boy his hands and the knife.

Only he is not holding the knife any longer. And his hands are not bloody. There is not a speck of blood on him anywhere.

"What am I supposed to be looking at, mister?" the confused boy asks.

"Aaarrrghhh!" howls Marko at the lunacy of it all. He goes back into the woods and keeps running. He needs a place to stop and rest so he could collect his thoughts.

But he soon gets exhausted. He arrives upon a creek but he is not in a mood to get wet. He collapses beside the brook and closes his eyes.

He opens them. It is morning. But now he's on the other side of the creek. And he's naked. Not a stitch of clothing. He looks around frantically. Where are his clothes? Gone. Did someone strip him naked and take his clothing? Why would they do that? Or did he do it?

He looks everywhere in the immediate vicinity. Nothing. He even looks up in the trees, at the leaves swaying in the light breeze under the morning sun.

He looks down. Again he is holding a bloody knife. He throws it on the ground. His entire body is covered in blood. Screaming, he jumps in the creek. It is not very deep, maybe a few feet. He lays down completely submerged in the water. He stays underwater and can feel his lungs burning, screaming in pain. Maybe this is the way to go? No one will know. His body will decompose. The little fish and other animals will pick away at his body until it comes apart and washes away to the sea.

No.

He bursts from the water, gulping at life-giving air like a pathetic drunk guzzling down booze. He stands up. Water dripping down his face and body. He is wearing his clothes again, but now he is all wet.

"There he is! There's the strange man I saw by the farm."

Marko squints his eyes and sees the boy standing at the edge of the creek, pointing at Marko. Beside him is a man that may be the boy's father. But the father looks reminiscent to Marko's father when he was young. Boris is also there along with two other officers.

"Yes, that's Marko alright," Boris says. "Go get him boys."

The two burly officers step gingerly in the water towards Marko.

"No! It wasn't me! No!" Marko backs away from the approaching officers. He turns to run, but trips and falls back into the water. By that time the two officers are on him and hold each arm firmly. He's not going anywhere.

*****

Marko lifted his lips from Lily. Eyes shut tight, he rubbed the sore spot on his head. Silently, he walked past Minnie, Chang and the other prostitutes. Gus cried like a baby into a handkerchief.

Nurse Mildred
November 9, 1918

Mildred heard the honk and opened the front door. "I'm going."

"No, you're not!" William shouted, pointing a finger at her. Complete with crimson cheeks, disheveled hair and unbuttoned collar, he had stirred only minutes ago from his drunken nap.

She paused for a moment. "Too late. I've already offered my services as a volunteer nurse. What should I say? 'My husband will not allow me because he forbids me to help others who are dying from the Spanish Flu?' Or perhaps you would like to tell them? I have already visited several homes and the situation is dire." Mildred tipped her head up. What could he say to trump her logic?

"Well …. " Grimacing and red with anger, William continued to shake his finger. "I've had it … you're disloyal and don't listen. When I told you I didn't want you to be a volunteer nurse, you should have obeyed. What if you get sick? This is the last night I want you out and about. Your place is here. It's bad enough you teach those putrid enemy aliens at that mission. But this is too much."

The taxi out front honked twice.

"Are you finished? I have to leave now." She opened the door and left without saying another word.

William ran to the front door. "I'm warning you! No more of this or you'll get it." William slammed the door so hard it didn't close properly. He slammed it again.

Mildred rolled her eyes and shook her head. What a sad state of affairs that she would rather risk her life tending to the sick than be with her husband. William found Prohibition bad enough, but now the epidemic had shut down all his usual haunts, leaving him with nothing to do but drink at home. In a fit of rage he had dismissed Lydia in August. But who could blame the woman for not coming back?

"Hey lady, ya coming or what?" the driver said.

"Thank you," Mildred said. She climbed into the back seat of car #350. She wore a black coat to protect against the November chill and straightened the white armband with a green cross on her right arm. She brought a few hand bags containing nursing supplies, including gloves, bandages and masks.

"So where are we going to, ma'am?"

"Here's the address." Mildred handed the driver a card. "Somewhere in the North End."

Ben looked at the card. "I know where this is. It shouldn't take that long." He gave her a funny look. Must have noticed the scar. The driver remained silent for several blocks, his eyes glued to the road.

Mildred checked her bag to make sure she wasn't missing anything. The shuffling caught the driver's attention. "I reckon you've seen it all."

Mildred paused for a moment before answering. "I have, unfortunately."

"What's it like?"

"For my first call I went to Magnus Avenue."

"North End."

"That's right. I was with a few other nursing volunteers. A tiny house. A small child answered the door, perhaps five years old. I think our face masks frightened her. But the masks could not protect us from the stench. We discovered the mother on the couch. She had been dead for days. A smaller child was on the ground near her. Alive, but hardly. The father was upstairs in bed, incoherent, feverish and resting in his own vomit and excrement. Another child, a baby, lay dead in a crib."

"That's horrible," the driver said. He turned his head to check for vehicles on his right before making a turn. But his eyes seemed to gravitate to the scar. "My name's Ben Rolph, by the way."

"Mildred Dal—" she stopped herself. "Just Mildred."

Ben's taxi rode alongside a streetcar with only two passengers. "I reckon the North End's been hit hard?"

She interlocked her finger on her lap and looked down. "A few days ago I went to a rooming house on McGregor – and not a word of a lie – there were eleven people living in a two-room apartment. Most were foreign men. All but two were sick with the Spanish Flu. None were dead, thankfully, but it took me all day to help the sick and scrub the flat clean. Every day I don't know what to expect."

"How did you end up becoming a nurse?" Ben turned the cab left.

"I was helping at All People's Mission teaching English to new immigrants. They closed it down when the flu broke out. Reverend Rose offered the facility to the health authorities to do with as they pleased to help fight the flu. The call went out for teachers to help with nursing. It was the least I could do. So four days ago I went for training at Manitoba Medical College. And here I am."

Ben gripped the steering wheel tight. "But … aren't ya afraid of catching the Spanish Flu yourself?"

Mildred shook her head. "Not really. We take precautions. I always wear a mask when making a visit. I even wear gloves, although some find it silly. I wash my hands frequently. Besides, I suspect I may have contracted the disease early last month. I had the sniffles for a few days and it went away. The Spanish Flu is very strange. It affects people differently. Some die within hours or days of contracting it. Others, they may exhibit hardly any symptoms at all. I figure if I had it already, I may be immune to it."

Ben stopped at a corner to allow a couple to cross the street and glanced back for a moment, tipping his cap. "Well, everyone's glad you gals are helping the way ya are. I reckon I could help the cause by doing a bit of driving. Not like there's a lot going on these days anyway."

"Well, there is the end of the war, of course."

"Hoo wee, you got that right. Everyone in the street's full of joy. Can't beat that."

"All except the war is not actually over yet. There was an erroneous report. Now that everyone had mingled in the public, cases of Spanish Flu are sure to rise."

"Huh … never thought of that…" Ben navigated his vehicle through the downtown area. It being the early evening, most stores had already closed for the night.

"Got anyone coming home from the front?"

"No," Mildred said, looking at the street outside. Although a year ago now, Andrew's letter still made her swallow hard. He had kept everything bottled up inside. Why did he have to blame himself for Muriel? Bad luck and alcohol killed her. Wrong place at the wrong time.

"I tell ya," Ben said, "when those brave fellers get back, this city will be humming. I know business has been down for me since the war and all. Not many people need rides. Poor people don't take cabs."

Fifteen minutes later Ben pointed to a small apartment block containing just a handful of suites. "Do ya want me to wait for you?" Ben handed the card back to Mildred.

"No, I don't believe that will be necessary. I don't know how long I'll be. Each case is different." Mildred put on her face mask and a long pair of white gloves. It wasn't like she attended any shows or restaurants anymore so the gloves could be put to good use. She thanked Ben and watched him leave, her supplies in hand.

She looked at the address again. Ben had dropped her off at the wrong apartment block. He seemed pleasant enough, but maybe he wasn't cut out to be a cab driver if he couldn't get his fares to the correct address. It should have been the weather-beaten building across the street and beside an empty space, the remnants of a victory garden. So many gardens popped up in vacant lots during the war after the price of food shot up.

Mildred crossed the street. A placard in the window of the door indicated the apartment contained the influenza virus. Her breathing quickened and nerves took hold. Like they told her in training, expect the worst but hope for the best. It was the only way to deal with it. She took a deep breath and entered the door.

A single bare light illuminated the landing. She looked at the information on the card. She had to find suite Number 4. Last name: Goldman. Family of five. Three with the Spanish Flu. Mother and father both sick. Thirteen-year-old daughter tending to everyone.

The wooden steps leading to Number 4 on the second floor creaked and groaned. Dusty with worn floorboards, the building must have been built years ago. Bone dry, it was a fire trap. Since accepting her volunteer nursing role she learned that building standards differed in the North End. Builders constructed many of the houses and apartments quickly with little regard to quality. Most did not contain a bath. Several still had outhouses in the back yard. No wonder cholera had caused such suffering north of the tracks.

She stopped at the door to #4 and listened. Nothing, just silence. Strange. Some commotion would be expected from a large family in a small apartment. Especially this early in the evening. Not a good sign. She looked at the card again. No, she had it right, #4.

Perhaps the daughter was exhausted and resting? She could have contracted the flu. It would not surprise Mildred. Some of the requests for nursing support took days to fill. There were not enough volunteers available to handle the large volume of calls.

She knocked on the door. Still nothing. "Nurse calling! Is anyone able to answer the door?"

A door opened the floor below: "You nurse?" came a female voice with an eastern European accent.

"Yes, I am," Mildred said. "I'm here to see the Goldmans. I understand they have the Spanish Flu. The Board of Health sent me here to help them."

"Goldman? No Goldman here," the woman said, trudging up the creaky stairs. The stairs moaned and buckled a little louder for the large foreign woman than they had for Mildred.

Mildred looked again at her card. "But the address is correct, is it not?" She handed the card to the old woman.

Wearing a dirty bathrobe and worn slippers, the woman examined the card. She strained her eyes and held the card at arm's length. A cigarette dangled from the side of her mouth. Her greasy, grey-streaked hair stuck to her forehead and temples. "Da. This address here. But no Goldman." She shook her head.

Mildred pressed her lips together beneath her mask. Now what? Her driver had left. There must have been another mix-up at the office. Someone assigned the wrong address to the wrong case. It had happened several times before. With all the calls for help coming in from across the city, the telephone operators sometimes had difficulty keeping facts straight.

"But I call yesterday."

"You placed a call?"

"Da. Man here very sick. You here now, so maybe you see him, no? I let you in." The woman shuffled to the door and fumbled with the lock from a key she produced from the pocket of her housecoat. "I wait and wait but no nurse came. What I to do? I'm old woman. Maybe you help, no?"

When the woman opened the door a stale odour of disease escaped into the hallway.

"You go in, you help," the woman said before she left. "Please. He good man. Very good man."

Mildred nodded. The stairs squeaked again when the old woman descended back downstairs.

"Hello? Hello!? Is there anybody in there? Is there anybody home?"

Silence.

Mildred stepped gingerly inside the dark apartment. She knew from her training to step very carefully. Sometimes patients would lie on the floor, delirious from fever.

She felt the wall and flicked on a light switch illuminating a small kitchen. Near the entrance a hallway led to the living room.

Not seeing anyone, but definitely smelling something, Mildred walked slowly through the small hallway into the dim living room. From the lone light she could make out a figure on the couch. She spotted a nearby lamp and turned it on.

Marko.

A Domestic Squabble
November 10, 1918

Mildred opened the door slowly and peeked in.

Unshaven and disheveled with blood-stained eyes, William stood in the landing waiting for her. "About time you got back. It's ten in the morning. You were away all night."

Her heart sank. She hoped he would still be sleeping or nursing a hangover. Or perhaps he could have been away all night with his mistress. He could even still be drunk.

William grabbed her by the arm. "Did you hear me?"

Mildred broke his grasp by twisting her arm. "I heard you." She stormed past William and up the stairs. Why bother responding to him? It didn't matter what she said.

"How can you stay away all night? Lydia's not here anymore. Who was going to prepare my breakfast? I'm hungry."

She turned around at the top of the stairs. "Make it yourself. I was up all night tending to a man who is struggling with the flu. A foreign labourer. Likely someone you feel would be better off dead. He still needs help and I intend to go back to care for him." Not waiting for William's response, she headed straight for the bedroom and locked the door behind her.

Within a minute she heard him bound up the stairs. He tried the doorknob then pounded on the door. "Open up. What did I tell you about locking the door? You remember what I did the last time you did that?"

"Go away," Mildred said. It would not go well this morning. A price she had to pay. Almost sick with fear, she pulled random clothes from her dresser. Could the situation be any worse? No turning back now.

She grabbed her suitcase, the large, pretty pink one only used once for their honeymoon, and stuffed it with clothes. All the while, William pounded on the door. "You better open this door or I'm going to beat you into next Sunday!"

"You will anyway. What difference does it make?" She grabbed a handful of cosmetics and threw them into the suitcase. She found two hats, practical ones that could be squashed but then retain their shape.

William used his weight against the door trying to break it down.

Frantic, Mildred noticed her hands shaking. She should have planned better. Of course it had to be Sunday. During the week he would have been at work. How would she get past him? She looked out the window. A far drop. She would certainly break her neck or a leg from that distance. Besides, how would she get her suitcase down? It would break when it hit the ground. The more she looked at it, it became obvious she would have to endure another beating. And this one would be the worst. But maybe the driver….

The driver! Mildred slapped herself on the side of the head. She forgot to tell him to stay. Now she had to go downstairs to call another one. Or she could run next door to Gregory, twice the man compared to William despite his bad leg.

The pounding on the door stopped. Did he leave? Was he waiting for her to exit so he could pounce on her? She paced the room nervously looking for something to defend herself with, but what?

A loud knock came from the door. It swung open with ease. The damaged doorknob lay on the ground at William's feet. Looking like a crazed lunatic, he held a sledgehammer in his right hand.

He threw it aside and pounced on Mildred. Anticipating his move, Mildred moved to the side, but not without falling to the ground. William grabbed her arm and twisted it back. Once again, at his complete mercy.

He slapped her in the face with such force that he drew blood. Mildred shrieked.

"Shut up, you ugly bitch. I'll show you who's the head of this household." He hit her again, this time a punch that grazed the side of her head.

She managed to break his grasp and tried to escape, but he easily caught her and threw her down.

Near her nightstand, she grabbed a pair of scissors and swung them at her advancing husband. She caught his forehead only slightly, just enough to produce a small amount of blood. She swung again, but this time William caught her arm.

He broke her grasp and while she lay on the ground, held the sharp end of the scissors just inches from her eye. "I should carve out one of your eyes. It would make you look like a pirate. With that scar and an eye patch, you could sail the seven seas."

"Leave me alone," Mildred said, now sobbing. "I just want to go. Live my own life."

William threw the scissors against the wall, damaging the wall paper. He grabbed her hair and pulled it back.

"Leave? You can never leave. You are my wife, my meal ticket. The daughter of Thomas Spencer, wealthy industrialist. After Gertrude, you are the lone heir. His other children are dead. No, you are not leaving anywhere. Your father pounds the bottle worse than a sailor on shore leave. The way I figure, a man his age could only last so long before his liver gives way. One day you will be an extremely rich woman and me, as your husband, a very rich man. You can try to get a divorce, but I'll never allow it. Why do you think I don't want you attending to the sick? What if you catch the Spanish Flu? You will not do me any good dead. The Old Man has been giving me the evil eye at work and there's no guarantee I'll get a penny from him. So sit tight and be happy for the life you have. You're so ungrateful. No wonder your father hates you."

William let go his grasp. Mildred slumped to the ground, a whimpering mess.

He rubbed his forehead and noticed blood on his hand.

"You bitch! You cut me. How am I supposed to go out in public like this?" He kicked Mildred in the head. She flew back to the floor. He continued kicking her midsection, arms and legs.

She tried to get up, but William interlocked his hands and brought them down on her back like a hammer. He kicked her again in the ribs. She had covered her head, but that left the rest of her body exposed.

Why did she let the driver go home after dropping her off? She should have had him wait. Overcome by fear and pain, Mildred assumed the fetal position to weather the storm.

"I'm going to make it so you never leave this house again for anything, you ugly, useless bitch."

William picked the suitcase up over his head. The moment before he motioned to hurl the heavy suitcase on top of her, both latches sprang open. Over-stuffed, the contents spilled down upon William.

From the corner of her beaten eye, Mildred could see William momentarily distracted. Ignoring the pain, she sprang up and made a run for the door.

But before she could find her freedom, William dove and tripped her with his hand right at the doorway. He pulled her back and clenched his fists to strike. Exposed, Mildred looked into his hateful eyes.

She reached back. Her right hand came upon the broken doorknob. Acting on impulse, she drove the broken end of the doorknob into William's forehead with enough force to inflict damage. The sharp and jagged doorknob opened a painful cut.

William screamed and recoiled. Blood burst down his face.

Again Mildred scrambled up to her feet. Hobbling, she limped toward the staircase. Had to get to Gregory's. On her way to the top of the staircase, she could hear William charging towards her.

"You goddamn bitch! I'm going to cut you up so bad, you'll wish you were never born."

She tried to quicken her pace, but her painful left leg hampered her.

Like a deranged demon from Hell, William ran up to Mildred. Blood soaked the side of his face and stained his clothing. It looked like he had been shot.

She felt William's fingertips reaching for the top of her dress in an attempt to pull her back. Mildred dropped to the ground. Caught unawares and not able to stop in time, William's forward momentum put him off balance. He tripped on Mildred and fell over her. Now at the top of the stairs, he almost fell backwards down the staircase, but managed to grab the banister with his bloodied hand.

Strained and leaning awkwardly, William tried to right himself. Only his handhold prevented him from falling down the long staircase. Noticing his predicament, Mildred took off her shoe, clenched her teeth and rammed the heel into the middle of William hand.

William screamed and let go. Not able to prevent his fall, he tumbled violently down the stairs. Smears of blood stained every third or fourth stair.

Cautiously, Mildred pulled herself up and looked down. William lay unconscious at the bottom the stairs. Breathing heavily and still anxious, Mildred put her shoe back on and limped carefully down the stairs to examine her husband.

Despite still bleeding from his forehead, the gash did not look threatening. He got what he deserved. His limbs did not appear to be in any unusual angles or positions. No broken bones, not that she particularly cared.

Acting fast, she found some rope and tied his arms and legs. She also made sure to tie him to the staircase. The more knots the better. If he suddenly came to his senses, he would just attack her again. No sense in that.

She limped to a washroom and looked in the mirror. Never fond of mirrors, the moment she glanced at her reflection, she cried. With both eyes puffed and an ugly bruise on her cheek where William first hit her, the scar on the right side of her face now looked to be her best feature. Her jaw felt sore and fresh blood stained the side of her mouth. Smatterings of blood doused her blouse, a combination of William's and her own. Funny, about the only time they ever exchanged fluids came during a horrific beating.

She thought of Marko, gravely ill on his bed. Her crying stopped. She squinted her eyes and looked at herself in a new light: she did what she had to. She had to endure this punishment to move on. Now over, she felt free, unhindered.

She limped past William's still unconscious body, careful not to touch him or in any way stir him. While the fall down the stairs put him in la-la land, the alcohol that flowed in his veins likely also contributed to his state.

The spots and smears of blood on the staircase and along the upstairs hallway gave the house a macabre feel, like a horrible dream. But she ignored it all. Back in the bedroom, she eyed the sledgehammer William used to break off the door knob. It felt heavy in her hands. She could smash William's head, ending it all. He certainly deserved it for all he had done, all the abuse, both physical and mental, over the years.

But who would take care of Marko? She would not be much good in jail. She dropped the sledgehammer at her feet.

Quickly, she refilled the suitcase with her scattered belongings, stopping occasionally to wince in pain. Then she filled another. There would be no return trip. Some make-up, clothing, a few extra pairs of shoes, not much more. She could not take everything. Knowing she would have to start from scratch felt liberating, but daunting. She checked her pink hat box for the money she'd saved over the years.

Limping past William's dresser, she paused. She opened a drawer and threw all the bulging envelopes into the hat box. She'd need the money more than him anyway. Besides, after what she had lived through, she deserved it.

She dragged her suitcases and the pink hat box downstairs and placed them beside the front door. She changed and cleaned herself leaving her dirty clothes in the middle of the bedroom. William could deal with them later. Picking up the telephone earpiece, she called Robert to arrange for a ride.

After covering her face with a scarf, she ran next door and pounded on the entrance. When Gregory answered she hugged him immediately. He nearly fell over when he saw what William had done to her. She had to hold him back to stop him from limping over to cane William. After he promised to not call the police Mildred kissed him on the cheek and walked back into her home.

Gregory would find her a place to live but that was something to worry about later. Marko needed immediate attention.

Still tied up at the bottom of the stairs, William looked pathetic. Bleeding from his forehead, he didn't stir. She had to do something about the man. The police would be involved if she left him bound.

She picked up the telephone earpiece again. "Hello, John. It's Mildred. I was wondering if you could give William a ride. Fifteen minutes? Make it thirty. Where? You'll know when you get here. Let's just say we had a bit of a disagreement."

Fireworks
November 11, 1918

"Come on. Hold on. You can do it," Mildred said through her mask. She wiped Marko's feverish brow with a wet cloth.

That morning, Mildred learned, they had signed armistice in Compiegne. The war was over. Canada sent over 600,000 troops to Europe to help in the cause leaving many buried in the fields. Others suffered catastrophic injuries.

Mildred didn't have the time to celebrate and had not slept since she left William yesterday. Marko's condition worsened. He took very little fluids and whatever water or broth he did drink came up within a half hour. His pronounced fever did not ease.

She already changed the linen three times since she returned. Thankfully Mrs. Dogaru more than obliged by washing dirty or soiled linen and providing clean sheets. The importance of cleanliness could not have been stressed more during nurse training.

The windows in Marko's apartment remained open to bring in the fresh air. It seemed counterintuitive since she had to also ensure her patient stayed warm. How could he be warm with a horrible draft? Depending on the strength of the breeze, she opened some windows while keeping others closed. Generally, the bedroom window stayed open most of the time.

Once or twice a day a boy scout knocked on the door to present a box of bedside food, usually soup, jelly and fruit. Sometimes it contained something hardier for her. Such a blessing. She didn't have time to prepare anything for herself, much less Marko. Being a bachelor, he didn't keep much in his apartment and ate at restaurants frequently.

Despite her weariness, she gave him her full attention. Following her training, she wore a mask almost the entire time and changed it every two hours. She boiled used masks for a half hour. She washed her hands almost continuously and while Marko slept she disinfected a good part of the apartment.

Generally incoherent, Marko slipped in and out of consciousness. Most of the time she found it difficult to understand his mutterings. He frequently mixed English with his foreign tongue. In those instances when he appeared more aware, she urged him to go to a hospital, perhaps the temporary one put together just for flu sufferers on Main and Logan, but he flatly refused.

"No hospital. I die if I in hospital. Hospital for rich. I have no money. Not for me."

She would gladly pay, but no amount of convincing or cajoling could change his mind. But she understood. Being an enemy alien, how good would his treatment be? Perhaps he received better support from her in his apartment than he would anywhere else?

She continued to wipe his face and neck. Emaciated, he hardly resembled the man she knew. A critical time, the fever needed to subside. She didn't want to think of the alternative if it worsened.

Mildred stiffened impulsively when she heard a knock at the door. Could William track her down? Her face a puffy mess, the bruises on her legs had already started to turn blue. Her side still hurt and she didn't bother to inspect the bruising around her ribs.

She cautiously approached the door. "Who is it?"

"It's me," came Mrs. Dogaru's distinctive voice from the hallway. "Sheets dry. Also I have food for you."

Mildred turned the latch and opened the door allowing Marko's landlady into the apartment. Mrs. Dogaru wore the same housecoat and slippers each time she saw her. Were they the only clothes she owned?

"How Marko?"

"Not well. The fever is still very high."

Mrs. Dogaru shook her head and paused for a moment. "Come, come. You eat." she said in an excited tone. "I bring borscht." She held up a mason jar full of red liquid.

"No thank you. I'm not hungry."

"No, you eat, come." More an order than a request.

Mrs. Dogaru placed the neatly folded sheets on the couch. She took a bowl from Marko's cupboard and using a spoon, carefully poured half the contents of the jar into the bowl. "Sit."

Too tired to argue, Mildred took off her mask and began to eat. Immediately the medley of flavours danced on her taste buds. Carrots, potatoes, peas, celery and a multitude of spices. "Mmmm, this is delicious. Are these beets?"

"Of course. No beets, no borscht."

Mildred devoured the bowl in minutes. The second she finished, Mrs. Dogaru poured the remainder of the mason jar into the bowl. "No, thank you. This was enough…"

"You eat. What's the matter? You no like?"

"No, no, it's delicious."

"Then you eat," Mrs. Dogaru said, pointing to the bowl.

Mildred once again complied, but before she did, she slipped off her shoes to give her tired and sore feet a break.

"Your husband … he no want you here?" Mrs. Dogaru asked, her arms crossed while she leaned against the kitchen counter.

Mildred looked away from the chubby Romanian landlady.

"He beat you. I know. I can see. Your face. Arms blue."

Mildred nodded.

Mrs. Dogaru gave her a reassuring hug, like the one someone would get from a grandmother. Although Mrs. Dogaru smelled like tobacco, it felt good to be comforted by the Eastern European woman.

"I know how you feel. My husband, he beat me. He did it twice but only when he was drunk. He died of heart attack fifteen years ago."

"I'm sorry to hear that."

Mrs. Dogaru scrunched her nose. "We no live forever." She pointed to Mildred's luggage. "Two suitcases – you leaving him. Man always leaves woman. But woman … if she leave man, well, that's a big problem. You have problems for years, no?"

"Yes."

"Listen," Mrs. Dogaru stepped back and held Mildred's hands. "You do what you feel right. No one should suffer. Look at your face in mirror. Is that how a man takes care of wife?"

Mildred looked downward and shook her head.

"I know." The landlady pointed up with her index finger, yellowed from years of smoking, "You going to stay here with Marko? He is good man."

"No. I was in a hurry. We're … just acquaintances. I'm not certain where I will go, but it's being arranged. Speaking of which, I may need to use your telephone." Once Father saw the bruises and swelling, he'd fire William on the spot. He may not have been the most supportive father over the years, but definitely territorial. But then what? A divorce will be difficult. Where would she work? The factory?

Mildred put her bowl on the kitchen counter. "Thank you for the food and helping with Marko's recovery, but he is still very ill. I'm not sure if he will make it."

Mrs. Dogaru rinsed out the mason jar and motioned to leave. "You stay with him. What you do is good. But listen, put mothballs around his neck. That will help so you not get sick. Also, some cinnamon oil, just a small sip. Mix warm milk with pepper and sugar. That's how we do it in old country. If chest full, rub bran on it."

"Bran?"

"Da, da. Warm bran. Mix with lard and turpentine."

"Turpentine? Is that not used to remove paint?"

"Da, but good lotion."

"Uh, I'll try the warm bran."

Mrs. Dogaru smiled and grabbed the door knob to leave. She stopped before she shuffled out. "One more thing…," she said with a raised finger.

"Yes?"

Mrs. Dogaru lowered her voice to almost a whisper. "I no tell anyone … but if you want Marko to get better, you need to make his blood flow."

Mildred cocked her head. She, too, lowered her voice. "Do you mean bloodletting? I know sometimes they recommend…"

"No, no," Mrs. Dogaru waved her off. "His blood need move. Be active. He needs to be excited. You need to pleasure him."

"Excuse me…?"

"You know." Mrs. Dogaru held up her fist and made a subtle, almost lewd, stroking movements with it. "You woman. You no married now. You leave husband. It's okay. I no tell anyone. You want Marko get better? You do what all men want."

"Do you mean…?"

"Da." With a crooked smile, Mrs. Dogaru walked out of the apartment.

Staring at the door, Mildred's jaw dropped. Did Mrs. Dogaru actually suggest she pleasure Marko? Above and beyond the call of duty, indeed. Those Eastern Europeans certainly have their ways. No wonder they bore so many children.

She attached a clean mask to her face. Noticing that Mrs. Dogaru had washed her extra smocks, she tied a new one around. Tip-toeing, she went to see Marko.

He remained asleep, but fitful. Marko tossed his head from side to side, mumbling strange words and phrases. She didn't have to touch him to know his fever had worsened. Still congested, he also had difficulty breathing.

Mildred propped up his pillow and added another. Gently, she encouraged him to lie with his head raised. This way the mucus would not wallow in his lungs. Marko began to cough, expelling green bits in the process. She did her best to make Marko cough into towels. The more mucus expelled from his body, the better.

Marko motioned for some water. She helped him take a few sips.

Through the bedroom's open window came occasional shouts from the street of excitement and joy celebrating the end of the Great War.

"You … you should go," Marko said, his voice raspy and faint, a weak imitation of his former self.

Mildred stiffened. "Of course not."

"But you can get sick…."

"Nonsense. That is not something you need to concern yourself with. I'm here for you and I will remain until you improve."

Marko reached over and gave Mildred's hand a weak squeeze. She squeezed harder. He needed to be reassured that she would not leave his side. She placed a cool cloth on his forehead.

"Thank you."

"You need to rest. Conserve your energy."

Mildred turned to go back to the kitchen when a picture on Marko's nightstand caught her eye, the one of his beautiful wife and child. Both deceased. How sad. Each with light-coloured hair, the woman sat in a chair while the girl stood beside her. The girl looked to be about eight to ten years old. The woman had her arm around the child. Perfect smiles and poses, they must have made a special arrangement to have this photo taken. The Eastern European woman's white dress appeared to be of a fine quality. The same for the girl. Did the woman come from money? Marko certainly wasn't wealthy and gave no indication that he had any sort of wealth when he lived in Galacia. Why was Marko not in the photo?

"Very lovely photo of your family."

"It is the only one I could find before I left."

"Was there ever any resolution to their deaths? You said they were killed…"

"It was my fault."

"What do you mean?"

"I did it," Marko said, his voice cracking. Tears rolled down the side of his face.

Mildred stood motionless. Outside on Selkirk Avenue revelers sang and shouted. Occasionally the rapid staccato of firecrackers punctuated the lively celebration that had built down on the street below. Was he delirious from the fever? He must be. It did not seem likely that Marko could be capable of such a thing.

"What did you do?"

Before Marko could answer, he went into another messy coughing fit. The worst one yet. Small bits of blood intermingled with mucus. The towel Marko coughed into had already gotten far too stained from previous use. Frantic and unprepared, she reached into her pocket and pulled out a handkerchief. Marko coughed into it.

After about a minute of continuous coughing, Marko laid back down, exhausted. He could not drink any more water and nodded off.

Desperate, Mildred went to work. First she washed her hands. She then drew some water to clean and boil the soiled towel, handkerchief and her facemask. She made sure to put on a clean mask immediately. She should have called Gregory. Not only could he have arranged for help, but he also must have been worried about her.

But Marko's fever did not subside. If anything, it worsened. Despite being frightfully hot, he shivered as if he had been lying in the slush on the street outside. She tried to ease his fever by sponging his brow and face, but it didn't seem to help.

Later in the evening Mrs. Dogaru came with more linens and towels. She also gave Mildred some cinnamon oil to give to Marko. It didn't appear to have any affect. Marko's conditioned deteriorated. Would he survive the evening?

The ruckus outside on the street grew. Some revelers brought musical instruments to add to the developing festive atmosphere.

Marko's glassy eyes became thin slits, his red face a sweaty mess. Mildred wiped his face and neck area in a bid to cool him down, but it felt fruitless. She stepped away from him but tipped over the metal bowl filled with water she had used to keep him cool. The water created a mess on the floor. Still in just her stockings, she could not avoid the puddle and ended up with wet feet.

"Drat." She sopped up the water with a clean towel and wrung it into the bowl. Aside from feeling uncomfortable with her wet feet, she did not want to drag water around the apartment with her wet footprints. With her other stockings buried somewhere in a suitcase and given Marko's sorry state, it seemed insignificant to fiddle with stockings.

Mildred put her leg on a chair. She lifted her skirt, but had some trouble taking the stocking off the garter belt. After slowly sliding one stocking off, she did the same with the other leg. She carefully laid the two stockings on a chair to dry. Feeling warm, she undid her hair. She shook her head a few times, allowing it to flutter past her shoulders.

She turned to glace at Marko and paused for a moment. Despite his awful state, he stared at her. He must have seen her take her stockings off and he would have caught an eyeful, right up to the top of her thigh.

After filling the bowl with water she continued to sponge Marko, trying to ease his fever. Marko's shaking stopped, but his brow still felt frightfully warm.

Outside in the darkness celebrants shouted and screamed. Although only a Monday, the end of the war made it feel like New Year's Eve or a weekend on Main Street in the days before prohibition. The burden of war lifted, life would go back to normal. The soldiers would all return, reuniting families.

"Come on. Come back to me," Mildred said. She tore off Marko's covers and over the next ten minutes painstakingly changed the sheets of his bed. She learned how to change sheets for an occupied bed in her nursing class. She moved Marko to one side and unravelled the bedding from the open side. Then she put new bedding on the same side. After she cajoled Marko to the other side of the bed, she took the old sheet off and finished placing the new sheet on the bed. Before putting a new set of covers on Marko, she noticed his pajamas completely drenched from perspiration. They had to be changed.

She took off all his clothing. Marko seemed in a semi-conscious state, eyes closed, but still able to help with the task by moving a leg or a shoulder when needed.

Before putting new pajamas on him, she gave him a sponge bath hoping cold water would ease his fever.

But Marko's condition did not improve. He neared death's edge. Congested, he stopped breathing for a moment. She shook him. "Marko! Marko! Breathe, damn you. Come on!"

Marko coughed, expelling even more yellowish-green mess from his lungs. Mildred wiped his mouth then gently rubbed Marko's clean body hoping that perhaps a friendly touch would relax him.

"Oh." She brought her hand to her mask. Looking down, she noticed that despite his poor state, he was aroused.

She looked away for a moment, biting her knuckle through her mask while remembering Mrs. Dogaru's words of advice. Nothing to lose.

She stood up, reached between her legs, and took off her undergarments, letting them fall silently to the floor. Carefully, she went on top of Marko, straddling him.

She caressed his chest, stroking him carefully. Perhaps surprised at the sudden weight on his body, Marko gradually opened his eyes. His erratic breathing eased and became rhythmic.

Mildred's head slowly bobbing up and down, she made love to him. Marko brought his hands to her hips to help to guide her.

She arched her back, letting her hair fall back and began to moan.

Sure enough, Marko's heart pumped faster and more efficiently. His breathing improved. While the war in Europe indeed ended, at that precise moment the battle within his own body changed. The deadly Spanish Flu virus, ravaging his body for days, faced a new-found resiliency. Marko was winning.

Mildred quickened the pace, enjoying every second. Outside the open window fireworks exploded, lighting up the evening sky.

Getting Better
November 14, 1918

"You should have seen old Willy's face!" Peter said. "Blood red. The man was about to blow his top. Blimey, he wasn't gonna leave the office. Lizzy had to call me in from the factory floor to throw the bugger out. And I would've if he didn't go on his own. Wanker."

"He's fortunate Father only fired him," Mildred said. She wore long white gloves and a headscarf and also sat at the kitchen table while holding hands with Gregory. Now that she left William she didn't need to hide it. But what if William found out?

Marko yawned. He still felt weak and slept ten to twelve hours a day. Just sitting up felt like a chore. Although the fever broke days ago, at times his thoughts seemed broken and jumbled. He found himself thinking of all sorts of crazy things, some of them racy. His strength and energy slowly improved after he began to eat more but he still had to hack to clear his lungs.

"Another shot?" Marko asked, holding a bottle of homemade vodka.

"Don't mind if I do," Peter said, tapping his glass.

"Sorry that I'm not working."

Peter straightened himself in his chair. "It's alright. I can tell ya got the grippe. Many men are laid up all across the city."

Marko nodded slowly and took a sip of vodka. It felt good to appreciate a hard shot scraping down his throat.

"Nice stuff," commented Peter after taking a sip himself. "Where did ya get it?"

"My landlady. She knows people who sell. When I was sick she got me bottle. She says moonshine is the best for the flu."

Peter winked. "Can't say I'd argue."

"Still edgy at the factory?" Marko asked.

"Aye, same as before ya got sick: horrible. There's been no rise in pay for ages. Conditions are bad. No offence Mildred, but if Mr. Spencer and the other big wigs in Winnipeg think they can take advantage of the workers, they got another thing coming. All the business owners still eat in fancy restaurants and attend shows and concerts and drive around in their new-fangled automobiles. They cry that times are tough, but I don't see them suffering. No, they sip their cognac and take holidays. But it's the regular man, that's who suffers. Prices going up and up. Quality going down. Everyone's on the make looking to take every loose penny from ya. I tell ya, things are ripe for a bloody strike. A big one. That'll send a message to them and I'll support it."

"You have my support," Marko said.

Peter winked and stood up. "Well, I should be going. You're a good bloke, Marko. If there's anything I can do, let me know. We'll see ya in a week or so."

"We should get going as well," Gregory said to Mildred. He leaned on his cane to get up from his chair. "My driver can give you a ride home," he told Peter.

"Much obliged." Peter put on his black derby, much cleaner than the one he always wore at the factory.

"Glad to see you're feeling better, Marko," Gregory said and shook Marko's hand. "When you're up and at 'em let me know. A few of my properties could use your attention."

Marko nodded.

"I'll meet you downstairs in the automobile," Gregory said to Mildred. Both he and Peter left the apartment, closing the door behind them.

Her suitcases already downstairs, Mildred's pink hat box sat on the kitchen counter, her last item in the apartment. The poor woman, she looked horrible. While not as swollen, her eyes remained black. The headscarf attempted to cover the other bruises on her face and neck. Of course the long white gloves hid the blue marks on her arms. William, that brute. He saved the worst beating for last.

Mildred smiled and squeezed Marko's hand. "You're doing much better."

"Thank you for saving me."

"I was glad to help. It was the least I could do." She smiled quickly but looked down.

"So, where you live now?"

"I'm in one of Gregory's apartments on William Avenue, ironically. Gregory owns the block and made all the arrangements. It's even furnished."

He didn't know what 'ironically' meant but couldn't bother asking. He coughed into his handkerchief. "It's hard to believe he's a returned soldier. He's is a good man."

Mildred fidgeted with her gloves. Her brilliant eyes twinkled. "Yes, he is. You know … he accepts me for who I am. We have similar interests. He's an astute businessman, far more driven than William ever was. William's already bothered Gregory about my whereabouts. Fortunately Gregory found a buyer for his home for much more than he paid. He's going to be living near me a few blocks over on Ross. I daresay … Mother would not approve of our relationship, but I don't care. I have a feeling when the time is right both Mother and Father will appreciate Gregory."

Marko coughed again in his handkerchief.

She walked over and gave him a warm hug. "You take care now. Don't go back to work until you are completely healed. Before I go, I want to give you something." Mildred opened the hat box filled with envelopes. She took out one, looked inside briefly, then gave it to Marko.

It bulged full of currency. There had to be a few hundred dollars all in fives, tens and twenties. "Why?"

"You need it more than I do. I know you don't earn much at the factory. You have always been supportive and a good friend."

Marko held his hand out to give back the envelope. "I no take. This too much. Why you have so much?"

"I saved some money over the years. Maybe $200. I stored it in this hat box. When I left the house I took all these other envelopes from a dresser drawer. William received them from business associates over the years. I would not doubt the money is illegitimate. He likely received them as kickbacks and what not. You would not believe how many deliveries there were to our home over the years. Most are unopened. I suppose with all the money he received from his regular salary he didn't know what to do with this. Putting it in the bank would raise suspicion. He never was very good with money and frequently squandered it. He probably grabbed a packet whenever he was short. It's not his money anyway, so it might as well be put to good use."

"William will look for you, no? All this money gone, it will be a problem."

"I'll lay low. Besides, I hear he's more open about his mistress, some young debutant named Trixie from a well-off family." Mildred smiled and put her hand on his shoulder. "But don't concern yourself with it. You never know, what you have could be a good start for the garage you would like to open one day."

Mildred grabbed the pink box and walked to the door.

"Wait ," Marko said, "I have to ask you…"

Mildred raised her eyebrows.

"When I was sick. Very, very sick. I have a memory. I don't know if it happened or not…"

"What was it?"

"I had a dream that we were … that you … that we…"

Mildred frowned slightly. A very faint smile crossed her lips and colour invaded her cheeks.

He looked away briefly. "I don't know how to say it without offending you."

"Why would I be offended?" Mildred said with a straight face.

Marko whispered, "Were you on top of me?"

"On top? What do you mean?"

"Did you make love to me?"

Eyes wide, Mildred raised her gloved hand to her mouth.

"Maybe I was imagining. I always imagine things. I must have been thinking of Lily. She sometimes enters my thoughts."

Mildred inhaled deeply and exhaled. She put her hand on the doorknob. "Yes, you have a very active imagination. I can assure there was nothing of the sort. Get well." Mildred left Marko alone holding an envelope full of money. It felt similar to the stolen bundle he received from Kraf years ago.

Two Sides
April 17, 1919

"What do you think? Will it happen?" Davey said, a clean-shaven man in his twenties, his face caked in grime.

"I definitely think so," Peter said. "That's how it's shaping up." Marko and a few other Winnipeg Iron Works factory workers gathered around their foreman. For several months there had been talk of a strike.

At first, not everyone in the shop was on side. Some factory floor employees opposed any type of labour action. Why rock the boat? But after the months wore on and the snow from another harsh winter melted away into spring, those unsure also began to feel something had to be done. Working conditions didn't change. Pay remained the same forcing families to stretch their earnings even more just to survive. To complicate matters, the returned soldiers came back in droves. Naturally each one wanted full employment and expected it, especially considering they put their lives on the line in far off lands.

"What do we do?" Marko asked.

"For now, sit tight," Peter said. "Do yer jobs. I don't like it any more than any of you. From what I hear," he paused to look around cautiously before continuing in a softer voice. "From what I hear … the construction workers have also had it and may go on strike with us and the other metal workers. Maybe in a few weeks. Other trades might join in. It could be a big one. Blimey, the whole bloody city'll be shut down. Get yer wives to stock up on provisions."

The men nodded in grim acceptance. If the boss men didn't want to listen, they certainly would when all the machines shut down.

"Now git," Peter said. "Management will suspect something's afoot if we're standing around like a pack of lazy dogs."

The men left to go about their work, but Liz already noticed. She stood nearby, her arms folded.

Peter frowned. "What do ya want? I got work to do. Go back to yer cushy office."

"I was wondering when you were going to come into the office to remove all those boxes. We talked about that this morning." Nose in the air, Liz turned around and stepped through the door into the office.

Peter took a deep breath. He pulled out his flask and took a swig. "Bloody spy," he said to Marko still standing beside him. "C'mon, let's go see what's got Lizzy's knickers in a knot."

Marko followed Peter into the front office. Liz pointed to five cardboard boxes near the front entrance on the other side of the counter.

"Why are ya bothering me about this?" Peter said to Liz. "Can't you throw them out?"

Liz ignored Peter and walked up the stairs.

Peter snorted. "Bloody woman. It looks like office rubbish and papers. Alright Marko, take these to the drum in the back and burn them. When yer done ya can work on that welder that's shorting out."

Marko nodded and grabbed the first box.

The front door opened and Mr. Spencer walked in, a thick cigar in his mouth and dressed in a three-piece brown suit. Harold Morgan, equally well-dressed in a blue suit and a red bow tie, followed him in. "I'll get Jones to work on the Regina lead." Morgan continued straight for his office.

Mr. Spencer lingered at the front. He stood in the narrow gap beside the front counter that led to the office area. "Well Peter, fancy yourself in the front office?"

"Uh, no sir," Peter said. "Just doing some housecleaning for Liz."

Mr. Spencer took a deep drag of his cigar. "So tell me, how are the former soldiers fitting in?"

"All right … I suppose." Peter's voice quavered slightly and almost sounded uncertain.

"Just all right?"

"The blokes still have a lot to learn. They got some sense about them, but it'll take a while. There's quite a bit o' training to be done."

"It will take time. Those soldiers are resilient. They have been through significant stress." Mr. Spencer took another puff of his big cigar. Mr. Spencer positioned himself at the end of the counter preventing Marko from going back behind the counter. And Marko wasn't about to tell the owner to move.

"You know, some of our soldiers even fought against the Reds in Russia. Bloody Bolsheviks. Can you believe they assassinated the Czar? That same

Bolshevik mentality is sweeping across Europe. Other countries might end up falling to the Communists. It might happen here in Canada unless we do something about it."

"Oh?" Peter said, "How so?" With a slight squint in his eye, he tipped his derby up to the back of his head and leaned against the counter.

"It's those enemy aliens. They're spreading their evil gospel. They are the reason for the problems we're having. Do you not agree?"

Marko looked away. He felt his heart pound. Did Mr. Spencer really believe that? Yet he still wanted Marko to help with home repairs. And he was the last Eastern European in the shop. All the others had been let go over the years.

Peter paused for a moment. His neck and cheeks reddened. "With all due respect, sir, I can't rightly say I agree with ya completely."

The other office workers, about a half-dozen of them, all stopped to watch the drama. It wasn't often that someone stood up to Mr. Spencer.

Mr. Spencer put on a strange smile, like he'd heard something crazy. "What do you mean you do not? You are of British ancestry, are you not?"

"Indeed I am, sir." Peter shifted his weight again. "But from what I gather, the foreigners over here – most of them – are average blokes. They may speak a different language, pray differently, eat smelly, foul foods, but if ya prick them, they still bleed like the rest of us."

"Quoting Shakespeare, are we? I am impressed, Peter."

"All I'm saying, is they ain't all bad. They got families and problems just like the rest of us. In fact, some of them are better workers than the Canadian blokes. They left their countries in Europe to get away from oppression. That's why they're here. They just want a better life. They don't want any revolution or anything."

"Oh? Then how do you explain all those seditious foreign language newspapers? The government got them translated. They are rife with Bolshevik propaganda."

Peter scratched his head. "I can't speak to that sir, but from the blokes I've met, they pay no attention to that stuff. I'm sure there's bad apples everywhere. Look at Marko, he's a fine employee."

Marko's eyes widened at the mention of his name. No need to be brought into the middle of this.

Mr. Spencer folded his arms across his chest and glanced at Liz. She immediately put her head down and acted like she was working. "Listen, I know what's afoot. I know you're a union organizer in this shop. There's also something going on at Vulcan Ironworks in Point Douglas. I keep in touch with the other metal shops. I've just about had enough of this union business."

"Mr. Spencer," Peter said, "I know yer a fair man. A man of yer word and all that. But ya must know the times, they ain't the best. The prices of everything shot up. Some even doubled. Food, clothes, everything. For some of the workers … the wives have to work, even the kids, to make ends meet. And their wages, ya know, they've hardly moved. Certainly not to match the increases in food and all."

"And why should all this concern me?"

Peter snorted. "Listen … we all don't mind roughing it. That's how life is. Ya work hard and hope fer the best. But it's reached the breaking point."

Marko put the box he held back down on the ground and took a deep breath. He had no choice but to wait until both men finished sparring.

Mr. Spencer took a long drag from his cigar and blew a stream of smoke that quickly dissipated into the air. "Who owns this factory?"

"You do, sir."

"If this factory did not exist, would everyone be out of work?"

"Well, sure they would until…"

"And how many other businesses do I own in this fair city?"

"I don't know…"

"The answer is nine. I own nine other businesses, all of varying sizes. I own them all. Most of them are managed by others, but I assume all the risk. In lean times profits are down and I make less money. The employees? They are free to leave if they want. I do not force anyone to work for me. You or anyone else from this factory can go across the street if you do not like it here."

"But that's the problem," Peter said, tapping his index finger on the front counter. "It ain't better across the street. It's no better across town either. It's all the same low wages that don't keep up with the cost of living. And the workers … all of them … they've had it. No one listens to us. All we want is a fair shake."

"It can't be any more fair than it is right now."

The two men, both frowning and red-faced, stared at each other for several tense seconds. Mr. Spencer broke his gaze and walked up the stairs leading to his office.

Peter turned to Marko. "No sir" he whispered, "this is not going to end well."

*****

Marko walked into his apartment and noticed a letter on the ground. Mrs. Dogaru must have slipped it under the door. Addressed to Olga, he flipped it over. No return address.

He took off his shoes and put his lunch box on the kitchen counter before tearing open the envelope. Olga didn't live here anymore anyway.

The letter was written in Ukrainian and dated October 12, 1918. He looked up at the calendar on the wall and counted on his hand. Six months ago. Why did it take so long?

Dear Olga,

My name is Father Krapinski from a local parish near Kapuskasing, Ontario. I have come to write this letter to inform you, with deepest regrets, that Maxim Yagochuk has passed away.

He was clearing bush last week outside the camp when a tree that was being cut down fell on him. It was a large tree and he had several broken bones. I happened to be in the camp at the time. He was taken to the bunk house where he died shortly after.

Before he died he told me to write you a letter. He wanted you to have everything in the apartment, all his possessions. Max expressed his love for you and was remorseful that the dreams the both of you had never came to be.

It is very unfortunate because the war seems to be ending soon and he was looking forward to coming home to be with you again. I can tell you he was a very hard working man. Very skilled. He had the respect of all his comrades. Max will be buried here with all the other prisoners who died at the camp.

May the Lord look over you and protect you.

Yours sincerely in Christ,

Father Krapinski'

Poor bugger. Marko poured a shot of homebrew and sat at the kitchen table. So all the possessions belonged to Olga. But Olga already moved on.

He took a book of matches from the cupboard. After striking a match and holding it to a corner of the letter he laid it down in the ashtray and watched the letter burn into fragile black ashes.

Chicken Sandwich
April 30, 1919

"Thanks for fixing John's toy train," Mike said. He pulled a flask from his back pocket and took a swig.

"Ah, it was nothing," Marko said. They both spoke in Ukrainian while walking west along Selkirk Avenue toward Marko's apartment. Marko held a fresh chicken wrapped in newspaper under his arm. Late in the afternoon, the shops would soon close for the evening.

"So I can use your planer? I sold mine and need to fix a door that keeps sticking."

"Sure. The house on Manitoba Avenue had that problem. How are things going at your place on Henry Avenue?" Marko accepted the flask and took a shot before handing it back. It always seemed like Mike had some booze around him. Was he getting worse? It's hard to hold a job if you're always drunk.

"Not good. It's a rooming house. Our place is small but more and more people are moving into the other apartments. Four men live in one small room across the hall from us. It was five, but one died when the flu came back in March."

"And the kids…?"

"Nicholas quit school and works at a corner store stocking shelves and making deliveries. John … all he wants to do is read, read, read. He's good at school, but who cares? In a few years he'll need to work. School won't matter then. Ann is growing like a weed. And Maria, she cries all the time. Good thing her bootlegging business keeps her busy."

"At least your brother Harry is back from the war. It's nice to have family close."

"Maybe too close. Sometimes he gives Maria winks in the hallway. It's bad when you have to watch your own brother."

"I can't complain but even as an unattached man I've had a hard time saving. At least I still have a job. Many places are only hiring Anglos. All the returned soldiers want jobs."

His chin up in the air, Mike raised his index finger for emphasis. "Many of those soldiers will not find good jobs. They're not happy and you know who they'll take it out on?" Mike pointed to Marko and then himself. "But now with talk of a big strike, who knows what will happen? Tomorrow the building construction people go on strike. That will be just the start."

Marko spit on the sidewalk. "And the metal workers go on strike the following day. That includes Winnipeg Iron Works, Vulcan Iron Works in Point Douglas, Dominion Bridge, all of them." He transferred the chicken to the other arm. "But one day I won't have to worry about any of that. Maybe next year I'll be able to open my own repair shop. Be my own boss. I've already looked at a few shops. The dirty, messy ones with disorganized work benches, those are the ones that aren't making money. I'll go in there with a suitcase full of cash and buy it. I'll start small, maybe just myself, but then I'll add employees and train them. One day, but not right now. All this strike business has to end."

Mike nodded. "Hmm, maybe I'll work for you, eh?"

Marko gave Mike a faint smile. "We'll see." But not if Mike kept losing himself in the bottle.

They stopped for a moment on a corner to let traffic pass including three cyclists, one with a squeaky peddle. A streetcar stopped to let some passengers board.

Mike took another sip from his flask. "But mark my words: this strike will be much worse than the little one last year. It will include everyone and turn into a general strike, a sympathetic one. Everyone else will go on strike to support the building trades people and metal workers. Just about everything will be closed."

Marko nodded his head in agreement. "I wish there was another way."

"I've talked to workers from different industries. They figure it's the only way we can get the man to listen. I don't want there to be a strike, but enough is enough. But from what I hear, the trades want to be able to negotiate with the industry leaders. They call it collective bargaining. Right now that doesn't exist."

Something crashed behind them. Both turned. The large glass window of a Russian butcher shop shattered. Large shards littered the sidewalk in front of the shop. Five or six men stood in front of the store. A few clutched bricks. Two or three held bats. All dressed in suits and wore dark coloured hats.

"Go back to your swamp, ya Bolshevik," one man yelled into the store. A few customers fled from the shop. A bat struck one man. A glancing blow, the man continued running.

Mike and Marko looked at each other. Returned soldiers. Both started to run.

"There's a couple bohunks!" yelled another. "Let's show 'em who's the boss."

Marko looked behind. Three men pursued them. Pedestrians scattered to avoid being caught in the middle.

Marko trailed Mike by a few steps. He passed the chicken on to the other arm. The bird slowed him down. Mike crossed a street, but Marko had to wait for a moment for a vehicle to pass before he could cross. By that time, the men were almost upon him. If they caught him he'd get beaten like that time a few years ago. What angered the Anglos? He did nothing wrong. Just working and trying to make a living.

Two of the returned soldiers stopped running. One stayed on Marko's tail. Mike increased the gap to thirty feet ahead.

Marko could hear the footsteps of the returned soldier. What if he had a weapon? No sense in glancing back, that would just slow him down. Memories of the night in Point Douglas when Eugene and his cronies attacked him made his guts swirl.

Almost breathless, Marko stopped, and in a swift motion, launched his chicken at the pursuer. The returned soldier didn't have time to react. The raw chicken hit him squarely in the face, knocking off the man's hat and forcing him to stop.

Marko didn't bother to socialize. He left the returned soldier to deal with the bloody chicken and continued running. The man didn't follow.

Red-faced and still panting, Mike waited for him at his apartment door. "Where's your chicken?"

"I let a returned soldier have a taste."

Metalworkers Go On Strike
May 2, 1919

"What brings you here?" Liz said. Lines of concern on her brow. Not her typical nasty self. Understandable considering the circumstances.

"Mother asked me to see how Father was faring this morning," Mildred said. She stood by her old desk at the factory, now occupied by a blonde-haired young woman she'd never met before.

Liz nodded and fidgeted with the papers in her hands. The other office workers looked troubled and preoccupied. One woman at a desk stared off in the distance, expressionless. A young lad, he couldn't be eighteen, leaned against a desk with his arms crossed looking down at his feet, lost in thought. It had been a few years since Mildred worked at the factory, but the office workers usually traded healthy banter. Just soft whispers today.

"They're going to walk," Harold Morgan said. "You watch." With a cigarette dangling from his mouth, he leaned against the entrance of his office chatting with a few other managers.

"Even the smaller metal fabricators will go on strike," the manager of production said, a heavy set man with wide suspenders. "They're all joining the construction workers."

"They aim to cripple the city," Morgan said. "They should all be fortunate they have employment."

"Got that right," another said. "And from what I hear, other trades will follow suit in support of them. It'll be city-wide."

"It's all those Bolsheviks and foreign aliens. They mean to start a revolution and ruin our country."

The others nodded in agreement.

*****

On the shop floor, Marko glanced over to Peter. His foreman stamped out his cigarette under his work shoe and looked at his grubby, blackened pocket watch. 10:00 am. It was time.

Every other labourer within sight of Peter turned to look at their leader.

He stood motionless in the very centre of the widest aisle in the factory. At that moment, he became the most powerful person in the building. More powerful than Thomas Spencer or any of the office staff and managers. Peter turned his head to the closest worker, Cal, at a grinder. A loyal employee with many children, Cal had so much to lose if the stoppage didn't work. With a simple nod of his head, Peter signalled for him to stop.

Without hesitation, Cal shut off the grinder. He stood with his arms folded across his chest. Peter turned to Smitty, a welder, and gave him a nod. Smitty followed suit. Joey, Davey, Michael Jones … within a minute every employee stopped working. The factory fell silent save for the hum of the overhead lamps. It didn't feel right. Marko joined the shop workers and silently gathered to Peter, still standing in the large center aisle.

Peter stood silent still in front of his men. No smiles, the workers carried only grim expressions. Some had to be worried, especially those with families to feed and mortgage payments. But at the moment, they stood united. Only by shutting down can there be progress.

Without saying a word, Peter turned around and walked to the employee entrance. Every worker followed, silent and solemn. In moments the factory floor became completely vacant.

*****

Thomas walked down the stairs from his second floor office.

The nervous chatter of the office stopped immediately at the sight of their leader. All eyes trained on Thomas. He stood on the stairs to face the remainder of his staff. True enough, several left to join the strike in support of the factory workers. All told, about a dozen or so workers remained. Mildred waved, but he did not acknowledge her.

"As is evident," Thomas said, "we are now in the midst of a strike. I can assure you, this is not legal. Notwithstanding, this factory cannot function in its present state until this unfortunate situation is resolved."

Thomas looked at Liz. "Elizabeth, I want you to take down the names of everyone who remained loyal to this firm. Everyone in this room."

He gazed at the remnants of this staff. "I can assure everyone here that you will all continue to be employees in good standing once the matter is resolved. In short, you will all have jobs. But until then, this factory is closed. Unfortunately, I will not be at a liberty to pay anyone while the factory is shut down. I do not know how long this will last. I am certain this very same thing is happening at other metal fabrication factories and shops across our fair city.

So go home and sit tight."

Father walked back up the stairs, his face a seething caldron of anger. Mildred began to follow him, but before she reached the third step Thomas turned and glared at her.

"Now is not the time for a visit."

"Mother is worried about you."

"I shall be fine. Mother need not concern herself. You can wait for me outside. James is in the vehicle. I should be about 20 minutes." Thomas continued up the stairs.

He likely needed a few glasses of scotch. That's how he always coped with bad news.

Mildred exchanged pleasantries with a few old co-workers before going out the front door. Sure enough, James sat waiting in the driver's seat of Father's new Packard. Why did he get a new model every other year? Were the older models so dilapidated?

The last few factory workers disbursed from the factory. Mildred had her hand on the door handle of the vehicle when she spotted Marko. She looked away at first, not wanting to make eye contact. Over the past several months, certainly since he overcame his illness, she'd only seen him occasionally, usually in passing at Gregory's home on Ross. But when she did, her heart leapt into her throat. They hadn't had an English lesson since before she left William. As much as she wanted everything to be as it was before, how could it be so after she'd been intimate with him? He was delirious at the time, but he knew. He must have. Why else would he have brought it up a few days later? She tried to convince herself that her last-ditch act to save Marko came only because of the quirky advice of an old Eastern European woman, but was it more than that? Could there be something else?

She pressed her lips together. She felt dirty. Cheap. She had cheated on Gregory. But did it matter if she also had cheated on William over the past year? She loved Gregory, but was her relationship with him just a lie? Especially now that she spent more time with him to the point where she also helped him with his business?

She gave Marko a small, subtle wave. He looked away for a moment but then provided a weak smile. His face red, he looked ashamed and continued on down the sidewalk.

The General Strike
May 17, 1919

"What are you going to do?" Cecil Cavindish said. "This is not acceptable."

Mayor Charles Gray wrung his hands and stared out the window of the conservatory into the back yard. "I know, I know," he said. "I don't like it any better than you do. I just want things to be normal again. And I don't want any violence. It's those returned soldiers. They're a cranky lot. Some support the strike, others oppose it. Everything is upside down."

"This sympathetic strike needs to be quashed immediately," Thomas said. "For some of you gentlemen, the strike is a new thing. Everyone else walked off their jobs two days ago. But for my factory on Logan, it's been for more than a fortnight."

Mildred picked up a few empty plates and glasses and placed them on a tray. How annoying. She had been enjoying a nice visit with Mother on a calm spring morning when visitor after visitor arrived. About two dozen of the city's most influential and important men congregated, all dressed in their finest suits. Some even wore top hats. They wanted their meeting away from the usual locations and Father volunteered the manor, it being close to downtown and away from the prying eyes and ears of the unions. "There are no union people on Wellington Crescent," he said. He didn't provide any advance notice because he felt it would draw too much undo attention.

With Gladys and most of the rest of the staff away, it fell upon Mother and Mildred to provide food and refreshments. Thankfully, they found enough cheese and crackers in the kitchen.

Mayor Gray pointed towards Manitoba Premier Norris. "Along with the premier here, I met with the strike leaders a few days before the fifteenth. But nothing came of it. Their demands were fantastic. They want the right to bargain collectively."

Cavindish spoke up. "That strike vote was quite convincing. Eleven thousand to just five hundred. They obviously have the fortitude."

"That's why the Committee of One Thousand was formed," Thomas said. "We need to break this strike and reclaim our city."

Several men in the room agreed earnestly: "Hear, hear!"

"At once."

"They need to be driven to the ground."

Premier Norris scanned a tray of cheese Gertrude held in front of him. "If there is one thing that is apparent, it's that the enemy aliens are a scourge to our society. Surely they are behind all this labour unrest. I heard from reliable sources at the federal government that legislation is being tabled to deport all undesirable aliens." The premier rubbed his strong, cleft chin. Although his hair had thinned at the top, the grey at the sides gave him a distinguished appearance.

"It's about time," Frank Patton said. "The internment camps, while a good idea, are not enough. Most of them are communists. They came here with their crazy Bolshevik ideas. You saw what happened in Russia. The Red Menace will continue to grow if left unchecked. It needs to be stamped out."

Mildred opened her mouth to speak, but shut it. No sense saying anything. These men already made up their minds. What did they know about Eastern European immigrants? They wouldn't know a garlic sausage if it hit them in the head.

Mayor Gray moved away from the window. "Gentlemen, there is something else you should know. I have been in contact with Brigadier-General Ketchen. I asked for his help to protect property. The strike has been peaceful, but that can change in an instant. In the meantime, we need to rally our resources to ensure the city is not thrown into a state of anarchy. All of you are leaders in this city. Rally your loyal supporters. We need people to help fight fires, to guard our fire alarm boxes, get milk to families, to provide water ... even to walk the streets at night. We have to ensure that essential services are maintained. There are even roles for women."

Mildred rolled her eyes and left the room with her serving tray. Enough of being a handmaiden for one day. Time to go before the meeting thinned out and the heavier drinking started.

*****

"Hello, dear," Gregory said from the landing. Wearing a white bonnet, Gregory's maid Josephine, closed the door behind him.

Mildred scuttled into Gregory's open arms and gave him a kiss. He put his grey homburg on a peg and leaned his cane against the corner of the wall. His walking had improved considerably since they'd first met. These days he only took his cane when going out, although he really didn't need it. He hardly used it in the house but by the end of the evening his limp became more pronounced.

Gregory gave Mildred a hug, but sighed while doing so.

"What's the matter?"

Gregory looked away.

"Oh, no. Not again."

Glum, he nodded.

"We need to call the police…" She motioned to leave, but he held her wrist.

"No. Don't bother," he said. "It's just a bucket of ashes now."

"But that's the third time in the past two weeks. It cannot continue. Why would anyone want to burn down your properties? And who?"

Gregory shrugged and slumped down on the plush chair near the front door. "Strikers, I suppose. Perhaps they see me as part of the establishment? I don't have a great number of employees. A few apartment caretakers. I hire other firms to do any building or construction. Or it's side jobs with people like Marko. Maybe it has nothing to do with me? Perhaps setting my properties on fire is the strikers' way of making a point?"

"What are you going to do?"

"What can I do? Thankfully I have insurance, but rebuilding takes time. It's still a step back. I may have to acquire riot insurance as well."

Still standing, she pressed Gregory's head against her body. The poor man needed all the comfort she could provide. He'd been nothing short of a saviour. He gave her purpose and dragged her from the depths of despair. The only other alternative – running back home to Father and Mother – would have been a step back. Despite the clandestine living arrangement, she never felt more alive and free. But what could she do to help him now? Not much. But if a hug helped ease his soul, then she would hug him. Hard.

He gently squeezed her hand. "Thank you."

Mildred smiled and fixed some of the loose strands of his brown hair. She helped him get up and led him to his office.

Gregory arranged to have his modest two-storey tastefully decorated. It functioned as his office and his home so he made sure to furnish each room with the latest styles of furniture and wall paper. Blue, plush velvet couches and chairs in the living room felt like sitting on air. The modern office had a telephone, comfortable dark-hued furniture and an impressive floor to ceiling bookcase. Gregory claimed to have read every book on the bookcase and Mildred had no reason to doubt it.

Mildred converted an old servant's quarters located in the back near the kitchen into her own office. She enjoyed helping him with administrative tasks such as correspondence, typing and the mail. He also involved her in the odd business meeting with buyers and sellers of property but only with business people who would not remotely know of Mildred or William. She entered simpler transactions in a journal later verified by Gregory's accountant. Her experience at Father's factory certainly helped. She never answered the telephone as William or one of his sympathizers could be on the other line. Gregory tried to pay her for her help, but she refused. Besides, he didn't charge her rent for the apartment.

Living in exile wore on her. She carefully scanned every direction before leaving Gregory's and never walked to her apartment despite it being a short distance away. He insisted she be driven, to be safe. Gregory even arranged for groceries to be delivered to her. She never answered the door to her apartment unless expecting someone.

Maybe she shouldn't have taken all that money from William? She would have been able to live comfortably for some time with the money she saved on her own. Certainly William would look for his envelopes and know she took them. Gregory could only conceal her for so long. Although William's fidelity appeared dubious, a divorce would be extremely difficult. How could she prove his relationship with Trixie in court? And wouldn't that make Mildred a hypocrite?

"The strike means you still have no mail," Mildred said. "There were a few hand delivered invoices."

"Funny how those always find a way to their destination," Gregory said.

"I typed the letter you wanted for the contractor. Aside from that, there's not much to do."

"It will be like that until the strike is resolved."

"How long do you think it will last?"

"Both sides have a strong resolve. I could see it lasting a month or longer. It's a novelty at the moment, but we'll see what happens once bellies begin to grumble."

Someone knocked on the front door.

"Josephine, can you get that?" Gregory yelled.

The louder second knock sounded impatient. More like a thud from a clenched fist.

"She must be in the lavatory," Gregory said. "You stay here, I'll answer it myself."

Mildred remained beside Gregory's desk while he limped to the front door. His jaw tightened the moment he opened it. "Yes, can I help you?" Gregory's frown looked troubling.

"May I come in?"

William. He'd found her! Instinctively she grabbed a paper weight in the shape of an elephant from the desk.

"Now would not be a good time," Gregory said.

"But I insist."

Before Gregory could close the door William opened it further forcing Gregory to stumble backward.

Only a moment to spare. Where could she hide? With no place to run she dropped down and crawled on her knees under the desk.

"You leave my house this instant or I'll summon the authorities," Gregory warned.

"Where is she? I know you're hiding her. Word's out that you've been keeping her cooped up." She could hear William walking around the main floor. Hopefully he wouldn't poke around inside her office and see her personal items.

"I don't know what you're talking about but are you surprised she left you? I saw what she looked like after you beat her to a pulp."

"Oh, yeah, look what she did to me." William must have had a scar. Good.

"Suits you fine. Now get out. Or maybe you'd rather tangle with a real soldier. I'm not afraid of you."

"Don't make me laugh, you're a cripple."

"Get out of here."

"What are you going to do, hit me with your cane."

"If I have to."

"Oh my God!" Josephine screamed. She must have heard the commotion and just entered the room. Mildred moved slightly to take the pressure off her knees, but her long dress bunched up at the bottom, making it difficult. For a brief moment a hem poked out from under the desk, but she pulled it back. Her heart pounded like a runaway train.

"Call the police," Gregory said.

"Alright, I'm leaving. But before I go … how's business?"

"That's none of your concern."

"It must be difficult during the strike. I mean, with all those fires and all."

"What do you know about…" Gregory's voice dripped with agitation and contempt.

"That's none of your concern," William said, imitating Gregory's tone from when he said the same phrase. "But it will be unfortunate if more fires were to spring up." He paused for a moment. "Especially this fine home. I have a feeling they would stop if I had the whereabouts of my wife."

"Even if I did you'd never get that from me."

"As you wish."

Mildred heard footsteps and the door slamming.

"Josephine, never mind. Put down the telephone," Gregory said.

Mildred crawled out from the safety of the desk. Her hair had become partially undone and dangled along the side.

Josephine left the room, flustered.

"There you are," Gregory said. "And looks like you were prepared."

Mildred looked down. She still clenched the elephant paper weight in her white knuckles. She put it back down on the desk. "I'm sorry. This is all my fault. I should just confront him. It's not fair for you to be dragged into the middle of this."

He limped quickly to her and they embraced. "Nonsense, the man is a brute." He gently tipped up her head with the end of his slender fingertips. His teeth gleamed. "You mean everything to me."

"But your properties … he's destroying them because of me."

Gregory stroked the loose strands of her hair. "I don't see why. What does he have against you? Is he that jealous?"

Mildred bit her bottom lip. She shouldn't have taken the money. But it was just sitting there.

Victoria Park
June 8, 1919

Marko felt a tap on his shoulder.

"Blimey, they allow your kind here?" Peter said, dressed in a three-piece brown suit and his good derby. Actually, everyone in the park wore their best as they typically did when they went out.

Marko smiled and shook his foreman's hand. "I thought maybe I come to hear what they have to say."

Peter spit on the ground. "Where else ya supposed to go? The mayor forbade all marches. The drivel in the newspapers is rubbish and opposed to the unions. The only place ya get to hear things fair and square from the labour leaders is here in Victoria Park."

Marko marvelled at the scene. Just a few blocks near City Hall by the river, hundreds of striking workers continued to stream into the area. Unsmiling with serious expressions, they came from all walks of life: carpenters, brick layers, fire fighters, plumbers, sheet metal workers, telephone operators, police officers. Everyone.

"So many people," Marko said.

"Aye. It's been peaceful so far, but that'll change. People are getting hungry and fed up. They arrested eleven a few days ago on Main Street not far from here. But now they got those thugs. What they called? Specials? They hired them to control the order. All they care about is beating the tar out of people. They're returned soldiers with a bloody chip on their shoulder. All of them are opposed to the strike. They walk around with sticks and clubs. What do they expect? Of course heads'll get cracked."

"Mike told me police chief was replaced."

"That's because the police are on our side. Every last one of 'em. They're not happy with their wages like the rest of us. I bet they're dismissed real soon."

Marko looked at his pocket watch. Ten to seven. The program should be starting soon. Peter nudged him with an opened flask. Marko took a shot and wiped his mouth with the back of his hand. "Nice, where you find?"

"Your friend's wife on Henry Avenue. That's a tidy little operation she has."

"They still have troubles."

"I believe it. Been over a month since we walked off. 'Bout three weeks since the whole bleeding city shut down. It's tough for everyone." Peter lit a cigarette and blew the first stream of smoke straight up into the air.

More people poured into the congested park, forcing everyone to squeeze together. Victoria Park became a sea of men's hats of various shapes and styles. There had to be ten thousand people gathered, a good portion of the population of Winnipeg. Many talked amongst themselves with furrowed brows. A man beside him smacked his hand in his fist while making a point with a colleague. Another man with crossed arms shook his head in disagreement over some other matter. Everyone in attendance seemed burdened by frustration.

"Woodsworth is going to be one of the speakers," Peter said. "I hear he travelled from Vancouver, way out on the west coast."

A short distance away, a man appeared higher than everyone else at the massive gathering. He stood on a raised platform. Almost at once, all discussion stopped to pay attention to the man. A preacher, he led the congregation in a hymn and a prayer.

After him, Frederick Dixon, a strike leader, spoke. Greeted by applause, he criticized the anti-strike Committee of One Thousand. The large crowd clapped in agreement. City Alderman Robinson followed Dixon. Also welcomed warmly by the huge gathering, the alderman thanked the workers for their strength to withstand pressure from business leaders. He reminded them that ideas are more powerful than bullets and ballots are greater than guns. "Quit ye like men and be strong," he said before leaving the stage.

Reverend Ivens stepped up on the platform. He turned around slowly, scanning the crowd. He raised his arms. "Are you going back to work in the morning?" he shouted.

"No!" answered all ten thousand.

"Are you going to win this strike?"

"Yes!" shouted the hoard in unison amid whoops and hollers.

Ivens didn't speak for long, but while on the stage he made an appeal for those in attendance to donate whatever money they could spare to help feed striking women and needy families.

A war veteran, Canon Scott next appeared on the stage. The striking war veterans cheered wildly. Good-natured in his approach, Scott spoke about the importance of brotherhood and that love shall conquer all. While he claimed not to pick sides in the strike, he wanted what was fair for all. The crowd also gave Scott a loud ovation when he stepped off the stage.

Marko looked at his watch again. A full hour passed since the speeches started. Without notice, the general murmur slowly grew into a loud roar.

Peter grabbed Marko's arm. "There he is! There's Woodsworth!"

Marko looked up. Sure enough, a man climbed onto the stage. The massive gathering in Victoria Park cheered and shouted for a full minute at the presence of Woodsworth. He wore a well-tailored brown suit with a white hat pushed far back, not quite revealing his thinning hair.

Woodsworth smiled and waved to the crowd. After a short time he motioned with his arms for everyone to quiet down. Slowly, the cheering and applause calmed. Everyone inched closer to hear what he had to say. The only sound came from the leaves rustling in the breeze.

"Thank you everyone for the warm Winnipeg greeting. It is always a pleasure to come back to my old stomping ground. I am proud to be Canadian and of fine United Empire stock. Although I left this city about two years ago, my heart will always be in Winnipeg. As many of you know, for a time I was involved with All People's Mission in Point Douglas, not far from this very spot. We helped a variety of people, many of them hard-working, but caught in unfortunate circumstances. If there is one thing I learned, it was that poverty and destitution were sure to follow if a worker did not receive a fair and honest wage."

The crowd voiced its approval. Woodsworth went on to speak about industrial development, from its infancy a hundred years ago to today's modern factories. The one constant through time was the worker, the most important component to any enterprise. Without labour, there would be nothing. No development. No progress. We would live no better than cave men.

"Years ago, before the industrial revolution, each man was his own factory. His mind, his hands were what created product, whether it be a shoe from a shoe maker or a dozen eggs from a farmer. But the days of individual production are over. Now vast enterprises worth millions of dollars involving hundreds of workers are common. And these enterprises are typically run by one single man. While there are still some self-made millionaires, most rich industrialists are born into their wealth. They did not have to work for it."

Marko turned his head for a moment to look at Peter. With a red face and clenched jaw, his foreman – like everyone else in the park – stood riveted by Woodsworth's words. The crowd ate up everything the man said.

"I need to congratulate all of you," Woodsworth continued with his speech. "All of you have maintained law and order and have resisted the temptation to use force to express your will. As Alderman Robinson mentioned before me, ideas are far more powerful than bullets. I cannot encourage you enough to refrain from violent means. No good will come from it. In the end, love ought to prevail, but the social system we have prevents this. The system we have in place is controlled by a small group of extremely rich and selfish men. Oh, those men know love … but it is the love of money. Simple greed.

"Their greed has led to this situation, to this general strike. Their greed to make as much money as possible is why all of your wages are so pathetically low and unacceptable. Their greed is why they do not want to recognize collective bargaining as a basic right for all workers."

The crowd indicated its approval with a large cheer.

"And why not? Really now … think about it for a moment. Manufacturers and bankers have their associations. So why cannot workers have their own association? Workers … all of you in attendance here … were compelled to organize in the exact same fashion. This sympathetic strike is simply a logical development. What other choice do workers have? None!"

As Marko clapped, he felt a nudge from a man holding an overturned hat, the collection mentioned by Ivens. Weighted down, there had to be hundreds of dollars in the hat, most of it silver, but also several ones and a few fives. Marko and Peter reached into their pockets and threw in a few coins.

"Your struggle is a hard one, but solidarity is the key if you want to earn your rights. But let me tell you … everyone is on your side. I travelled all through Western Canada. The mayor of Edmonton told me to tell you that if a strike comes to his city, they will not hire scabs for public utilities. Saskatoon is equally supportive. I spoke to farmers in the North Battleford area. They also realize they are under the heel of exploiters. They know that farmers and industrial workers need to unite to overthrow the privilege capitalists were born into.

"And the war, my God, the war. All those lives lost. All the destruction. Many of you here served … you put your lives on the line. That war was caused by commercialization. It is up to the people to say 'never again.'

The tremendous war debt in Manitoba and the rest of Canada will cripple everyone. I feel the only way out will be heavy income taxes and to have the state assume estates when owners die. This great country has too many rich resources controlled by exploitive capitalists. These resources must be recovered for the people."

The crowd rumbled. Again, Woodsworth had to raise his arms to ask for quiet before he could continue.

"What do we want?" someone nearby asked.

"Very simple," Woodsworth replied. "Workers want a decent living for everyone. They want to be more than just well-fed slaves. They want a voice for fixing their wages and working conditions. Mark my words. The day will come when everything produced collectively by workers will be owned collectively by those same workers, not some cigar-smoking fat cat."

The mass of humanity in Victoria Park voiced their approval. Woodsworth reached into his jacket and pulled out his pocket watch.

"I have spoken now for two hours. Darkness is upon us here in this park. Thank you very much, all of you, for giving me this opportunity. I shall never forget this night. But most of all, I will never forgot your courage and resolve. Stand fast. Stand true. Above all, be civil and law-abiding. You are all making history. Each and every one of you. Because right now … right now … I can assure you the state is trembling. Thank you all."

Woodsworth stepped down from the crate amid wild cheers and shouts. Although weary and tired from the length of the strike, the speech seemed to ignite the strikers' passion and confirm their path as being correct. Fists shook towards the heavens. Like a battle cry, others stood and yelled at the tops of their lungs, their eyes bulging and veins popping out of their necks. Hundreds stepped towards the raised platform to shake Woodsworth's hand.

Peter took a sip from his flask and shared it with Marko. Both men nodded. They were in it for the long haul and to hell with the penny-pinching owners.

The two men tried to navigate their way through the crowd, but the volume of attendees held them up at times. At the edge of the park, someone called out Peter's name.

They looked down. There, on the ground against a tree sat a one-legged man with soiled and ripped clothes. He had not shaved for several days and looked like a beggar.

"Don't ya remember me? It's Michael. You know, from the factory."

"Mikey!" Peter said. "How are ya? Blimey, I haven't seen ya in years. Last time I saw ya…"

"…was on the back of the meat wagon," Michael said. Marko recalled the first day he stepped in the factory. The man never worked another lick at the factory.

"So how you been?" Peter asked.

"Not good. I was laid up for a while. The wife had to work. So did the older kids. I was finally able to work at a confectionary, but that ain't no man's work. Definitively don't pay much."

Peter took off his hat and bent down. "That's too bad. I'm … I'm sorry what happened to ya. Looks like none of us are working now anyway. Is there anything I can do? Blimey, how are ya gonna get outta here?"

"Oh, I'm fine. I got these things." Michael pointed to his crutches beside him on the ground. "But there's one thing … do ya think ya can spare a quarter or something? I gotta get milk for the kids."

Peter reached into his wallet and gave Michael a whole dollar.

Short Tempers at Portage and Main
June 10, 1919

Gregory held out a crisp ten dollar bill. "Here you go, sir. For services rendered."

"That's too much." Marko took a step back.

"It's what was agreed," Mildred said. "It took you two full days to repair that washroom in that apartment block on Salter." Marko had been in his kitchen sorting through his tool bag when they dropped in. When was the last time she was in Marko's apartment? Months? It had already reverted back to his bachelor messiness. Hard to believe it was once squeaky clean back in November. How could he carefully arrange and store tools in Father's garage but could not clean and put away his own dishes?

Marko smiled and took the note. Always sheepish, he possessed a cute smile when reluctant.

Gregory leaned on his cane. "It's the least we can do. All my properties are in shipshape. I know you're not making any money on account of the strike, so any little bit helps."

"Not as bad as others. I have some money put away." Marko gave Mildred a quick glance. She had to look away. She still hadn't told Gregory about William's money. Could she ever? Gregory would think she was a petty thief.

"Mildred tells me you have an interest in one day opening a repair shop."

"I'm saving money. One day. Not today."

"You never know, I might be able to help. You certainly have the skills and seem like a solid investment."

Marko raised his eyebrows and nodded. "Maybe one day we talk…"

Gregory tapped Marko lightly on the side of the leg with his cane. "Maybe sooner than later, you never know." He turned to Mildred. "Well dear, we'd best be going."

"You need to have one shot. That's what we do in old country when someone visits."

Gregory smiled. "I really should not."

"No, no. Just one. I have some rye you will like, not homebrew."

Mildred gave Gregory a wry smile.

"Alright, just a little one," Gregory said.

Marko pulled two glasses and a bottle from the cupboard. "Oh, before you go," he said to Mildred, "there are some things you forgot when I was sick. In my bedroom, on dresser."

That was over six months ago. Why didn't he mention it earlier? Mildred nodded and left the kitchen. The men could have their alcohol.

Marko's bedroom looked like a tornado had swept through it. Typical man. Clothes all over the floor. Unmade bed. A few dresser drawers partially opened. Why couldn't he shut them after taking something out? Three empty glasses stood on the night stand beside the bed. The man definitely needed a wife.

"Organizing your tools?" Mildred heard Gregory ask. She could hear their conversation clearly from Marko's bedroom.

"My friend Ben is picking me up," Marko said. "His friend has problems with his vehicle. It's somewhere near Portage and Main. Everyone says the corner is special. Why?"

Mildred closed the dresser drawers. She picked up the framed photo of Marko's family from the dresser. Such a pretty wife. High cheekbones. Handsome. She could almost be a star of the moving pictures. Cute little girl, too. Mildred frowned. He had been delirious and babbling at the time. It appeared preposterous that he could kill his family. Who would admit to something like that? Perhaps he blamed himself after a horrific accident or fire?

"Decades ago," Gregory said, "a man by the name of Henry McKenney opened a general store in what was then a section of land up a ways from where the Red and Assiniboine Rivers meet. Other development followed. Out of nothing, Winnipeg grew quickly and that same area became the corner of Portage and Main. Portage Avenue continues out west all the way to Alberta. Main Street follows the Red River north. McKenney's old general store is long gone, but the intersection is still here."

The pair of stockings hung from the edge of the dresser. How could she forget them? It must have been the pair that got wet. Marko held on to them for half a year?

"But I'd be a little careful out on the streets," Gregory continued.

"Nerves are a little testy now that the strike's been on for a while."

"I'll be fine," Marko said.

Mildred picked up the stockings. Her eyes widened. Her knickers laid underneath.

"If I were you," Gregory said, "I'd rather be bored in this apartment than be caught in the middle of something."

Mildred held up her underwear. Stockings were one thing, but how did she miss this? Maybe she didn't see them because they had been hidden under the dresser? Perhaps under his bed? She had stayed at his place for a few nights until he improved from his illness, sleeping on the couch. She thought for a moment. Yes, she had put on new undergarments. She must have neglected to put the old ones into her suitcase. But she could have sworn she had cleaned his room spotless. Although mad with fever that November night, of course he must have remembered what she did. How could she pretend like nothing happened? What would Gregory think?

She crammed her unmentionables into her carry bag.

From the other side of the apartment Marko laughed. "I always end up in the middle of something."

*****

An hour later Marko popped his tool bag in the back seat of Benny's taxi and settled in the passenger seat. "If your friend's vehicle needs new part, it will be difficult to fix. Hard to find now."

"Ya got that right. With this strike still going, who knows how long it'll be before everything's back to normal. I know so many men who are itching to get back to work. Look at Bert. He's a plasterer. He's been on strike for over a month. It's hard to pay the bills when you've been out of work that long. At least I can get the occasional fare on the side with the taxi."

Marko nodded. "Same for me. Always something must be fixed so I find little jobs here and there."

The taxi turned south on Main. A few blocks from Portage and Main Marko noticed two men in dark suits with white armbands. "Those are the new Special police?"

"Yup. The entire police force got dismissed yesterday. Can ya believe it? They didn't sign a non-sympathetic strike pledge. They all refused, every single one, and each was fired on the spot. Those thugs in their place they call Special constables are just former soldiers. They particularly don't like you aliens."

"Ah, no one likes us from Europe. Even strikers, they don't like us."

Benny parked his vehicle about a block from Portage and Main.

The two men walked to the corner. Marko's pocket watch told him it was almost 2:30. Several Special constables at Portage and Main attempted to direct traffic.

Marko would have normally been at work on a Tuesday, so he couldn't reckon, but there seemed to be more people than he would have expected. Certainly more than one would see on a typical Saturday afternoon before the strike. Why go downtown today with everything closed? Some of the men looked to be loitering or standing around in small groups waiting for something.

Benny pointed to the stalled automobile needing repair. Scratches ran along the sides of the black vehicle. Also with bald tires and a cracked headlamp, the Model T had seen better days.

"Hey Benny," said a short man who emerged from the driver's seat. "Glad ya can make it." Clean-shaven, the man undid a button from his black jacket. He wore a brown felt hat with matching shoes.

"Anything to help. This here is the mechanic friend I was telling ya about. Buck, I'd like ya to meet Marko."

Marko shook Buck's hand, but instead of a smile, Buck produced a sour expression. He also walked with a slight limp.

Immediately Buck took back his hand and motioned Benny to the other side of his stricken vehicle. Marko didn't have to lean in to make out the conversation. Words like "enemy alien" and "should be kicked back to the Kaiser" made it clear Buck was a returned soldier.

Benny's voice rose: "Listen, he's a good feller. I've known him for a few years. He ain't no revolutionary or nothing. Ya gotta trust me on this. Besides, what choice have ya got? Like I said, Marko's a mechanical genius."

Buck shook his head and smacked his vehicle with his fist. "Damn it. Ya should have told me. This ain't right. I didn't take shrapnel in Belgium to come home to this."

"Fine, we'll just leave. Have fun getting yer vehicle fixed on the corner of Portage and Main." Benny turned to leave. "C'mon, let's go," he said to Marko.

Buck grabbed on to his suspenders and spat onto the ground. "All right, all right. Let's see what he can do."

Benny motioned for Marko to get to work. "She's all yours."

Marko walked around the Model T slowly with his tool bag, examining it up and down with a trained eye. "What's the problem?"

"It won't start," Buck said.

"What sound does it make when you try?"

"Nothing. Here, I'll show you." Buck went to crank the motor.

But before he could, Marko grabbed Buck's arm, preventing him. "Brake on?"

Buck glared at Marko, but his angry expression quickly melted away. "Oh my God. I forgot." Buck went inside the cab to apply the parking brake. Doing so prevented the automobile from lurching forward and also locked the transmission by putting it in neutral.

At the front of the vehicle, Buck pulled out the choke lever, pushed the crank in and proceeded to prime the engine by adding fuel into the cylinders. Then he went back in the cab, turned the key, and set the throttle and choke. With his left hand he applied pressure to the lever, but the engine remained silent.

"See, nothing."

Marko motioned Buck away. He opened the hood and looked inside. He instantly spotted the problem.

Buck stepped back to stand beside Benny, nodding approvingly. "Have to admit, that's some mechanic."

"Got that right," Benny said. "That's why I want to make sure I stay chums with him. A guy like that's worth his weight in gold. One day he's gonna have his own shop."

While Marko worked on the Model T, more men congregated at the four corners of Portage and Main. Some of the men started to spill over on the streets.

"Scabs!" one man yelled at the Specials.

"Ya took jobs away from the real police. Shame on all of you!" another shouted.

"The crowd is getting a little restless," Benny said. "Hey, Marko, how's it coming along?"

"I'm finished." Marko closed the hood. "Try to start." Marko motioned to Buck.

It started on the first try. Marko reached in the cab to adjust the fuel mixture, making the vehicle run even better.

"Well, thank you." Buck slowly shook Marko's hand. "How much do I owe you?"

"One dollar."

After paying Marko, Buck pulled his hat down tight and went back into his Model T. But Buck had a problem. His newly-repaired automobile could not move. The crowd, now beginning to take the shape of an angry mob, stood in the way.

"Alright everyone, move aside. Let's let the traffic through," ordered a Special wielding a thick, wooden bat.

"In yer ear, ya scab!" shouted someone from the crowd.

Four Specials managed to cajole a group of men to move out of the way so Buck's auto could pass. After he did, the unruly men moved right back onto the street.

A Special motioned with his hands for the crowd to back up. "Stay on the sidewalks. No need for any of you to block traffic."

"You gonna make us?" someone teased from the back of the crowd.

A man in a fine-tailored suit walking nearby had enough. "Hey, lay off those men. Some of those Specials are returned soldiers. They're here to protect us from the riff raff. They served our country and deserve your respect."

Two goons grabbed the well-dressed man and threw him to the ground. Another kicked the man in the face. Stunned, the man screaming in pain, blood from a facial wound stained his crisp white shirt.

Seeing this, several Specials raised their batons and went to the man's rescue, beating away the attackers. By this time, rocks, bricks and glass bombarded the Specials.

One Special took a glancing blow to the head. His comrades beat anyone who stood near. Simultaneous fights broke out between the Specials and the mob.

"Let's take your bag to the cab and then come back," Benny said. "I want to see what happens next."

On the way back Marko noticed more men heading toward Portage and Main in small groups of three or four. Sporting grim, serious expressions, some appeared unshaven with pale features and dark bags under their eyes.

The Specials continued to try to control the swelling crowd on the corner. Sensing danger, older men and women scurried to leave the area. A wide-eyed woman pushing a baby carriage looked over her shoulder every few steps. A group of teenaged boys with their backs against a building hid their whispers with cupped hands.

"How you doing?"

Marko turned to the familiar voice, Mike sitting on his bicycle. He gave Mike a strong handshake and introduced him to Benny. "Why you here?"

"Same as everyone. No work, so I want to see what happens. It's not far from where I live, so why not?"

Before Marko could continue his conversation with Mike, he felt a hand on his shoulder. Peter.

"Hey there, Marko. Fancy meeting ya here." Peter tipped his derby. What luck meeting Mike and Peter at the same time right on the corner of Portage and Main during a riot.

"Look," Benny said, pointing, "they're bringing the horses."

Near the intersection several Special constables mounted on horses galloped toward the increasingly chaotic scene. They all carried clubs. From another direction newly arrived Specials joined the fray on foot.

As the mounted riders entered the disturbance, the riot intensified. Specials beat several rioters with their clubs, but Specials also received some blows. The crowd of agitators, all men, still continued to hurl rocks and other debris.

A rock hit a mounted rider in the head. Dazed, he fell off his horse. Immediately a group of rioters attacked the fallen Special, kicking and beating him with fists and other objects. Blood poured out of his nose. Specials ran to his aid and warded off the attackers.

But the presence of the mounted Specials began to have an effect. The rioters backed off. Specials captured some rioters and placed them under arrest. While hand-to-hand fighting continued, the Specials slowly began to push the agitators back to the sides and win back the intersection.

"There are too many gawkers around here," one Special said to a comrade.

Over-hearing this, Marko pulled on Benny's sleeve. "We go?"

"Naw. That's just what those scabs want," Peter said.

Three Specials carried away their stricken comrade, making their way for a vehicle. "Take him to the hospital. He looks hurt real bad."

"I recognise that man," another said. "That's Coppins. He's a war hero. He won a Victoria Cross."

A Special hit his club into his palm. "Those bastards. I say we crack all their heads. Most of them are likely foreign aliens anyway. I bet it was an alien who pulled Coppins off his horse."

Enraged, a group of Specials attacked rioters, hitting them with their batons.

"You idiots!" yelled Mike, raising his fist. A Special took exception from twenty feet away and turned to face Mike, his club raised over his head.

"Oop! Time for me to go." Mike found an opening for his bike and darted away from the congested intersection.

"Yer mate's a bit of a hot head," Peter said to Marko. "That'll get him in trouble one day."

The altercations came in waves. Marko's eyes darted from side to side. New eruptions bubbled up before others could be crushed. If he wasn't careful he could end up with a club to the head. Gregory was right. Better to be bored in the apartment than caught in the middle of a riot.

He couldn't help but notice one Special about twenty-five feet away. A brute of a man, he wielded his baton with such force he stunned strikers with just one hard swipe to the head. Three opponents knelt on the ground near his feet nursing sore noggins. Smarter rioters noticed the Special's fighting ability and backed off, unless they wanted a new dent on the side of their skull. Marko squinted for a better view. The large Special turned and looked directly at him. The Special paused for a moment while he and Marko stared at each other. The bent nose, missing teeth and scar by his left eye gave him away. Albert. One of the soldiers who had beaten him in Point Douglas a few years back. Marko reached up and felt his own slightly crooked nose.

Another Special with an enormous moustache fought beside him. Eugene. Short and stocky with a wry smile, the man swung his club like a crazed lunatic.

Eugene stopped for a moment when he noticed Marko. He said something to Albert and pointed directly at Marko's group. Eugene, Albert and three other Specials headed to Marko and his friends with clubs raised.

Sensing danger, Benny, Marko and Peter ran north on Main Street with the pack of angry Specials in pursuit.

"We did nothing. Why they chase us?" Marko said.

"It don't matter. Just run!" Peter said, breathless. "Eugene won't think twice to knock us with his club."

A sympathetic striker stuck out a leg causing a Special to tumble over. In turn, Albert tripped over the fallen Special forcing the group to stop momentarily.

The mishap gave Marko, Benny and Peter the extra time they needed to turn the corner. Benny lead the way and quickly veered off down a back alley just past where he parked his taxi. "Let's hide behind this garbage."

Breathing hard, the three crouched behind a half dozen overloaded rubbish bins that hadn't been emptied in weeks. Other trash including large pieces of discarded wood also helped hide their location. The rancid fumes ebbed from the garbage forcing Marko to breathe through his mouth. "Why here?"

"Those Specials are too la-ti-da," Benny said. "They won't come anywhere near here. Stay down."

 Marko poked his head up to take a look, but Benny quickly pressed it down with his hand.

Sweaty, nervous and breathing heavily, the men remained still and listened. Flies buzzed around the putrid bins in front of them.

"I think they went this way," a Special said from the street near the entrance to the alley. "Goddamn foreigners."

"I'm not a foreigner," Peter whispered.

Benny raised his finger to his lips.

"They must have gone down to the river. We lost them. Come on, let's go back to Portage and Main," Eugene said.

After several tense minutes, Benny peeked out and signalled that the coast was clear.

"We dodged a bullet there," Marko said.

Peter wiped sweat from his forehead with is sleeve. "Might not be so lucky next time."

Gregory's House
June 21, 1919

Mildred quickened her pace a few blocks away from Gregory's house.

Why were all men bull-headed? Sometimes they lacked common sense. She warned him numerous times not to go downtown during the strike. 'I want to see what the fuss is all about,' he said last night. A man in his condition wouldn't stand a chance. Yes, his walking gait had improved, but in no way could he outrun a hooligan. He should have followed the advice he'd been telling Marko and others and stayed safe at home. But his curiosity always got the better of him.

But then he had the audacity to tell her that she had to remain indoors because of unsafe streets. The nerve. Well, if it was safe enough for him, it was safe enough for her.

But that was his nature. Just like how he had gotten into bird watching. Once he found an interest in something, he dove in, regardless of the implications. But bird watching, a leisurely pursuit, could not be compared to the serious matter of the strike. And him, not even a striker.

She paused to catch her breath. A felled tree blocked the sidewalk. Just last weekend the city suffered through a horrible storm. Winds in excess of eighty miles an hour downed many trees and damaged structures. The city still struggled to clean up after it.

Moist from perspiration, she wiped her brow with a handkerchief. Despite being just 9:00 am, the back of her dress felt damp. Occasionally she saw groups of men walking toward downtown, likely to Victoria Park. Thousands of strikers hoped to gather today for a rally.

Not far from Victoria Park, Father planned to be at City Hall with the rest of the Committee of One Thousand, plotting their next move. He said if today's mob got too unruly they'd call the military. Anything could happen. Who could blame him? The factory had been closed for over two months, agitating Father considerably.

With no answer at Gregory's door, Mildred let herself in. Josephine must have been away. "Hello, anyone here? Gregory?" Mildred wiped her brow again. He'd left for Marko's already. So much for that.

She went to the kitchen and helped herself to some lemonade from the fridge. Sitting at the kitchen table, she rested her head on her arms. How long could she continue living her life this way? Hiding away from William with no realistic chance for a divorce. But without it, how could she ever be with Gregory? Her own purgatory. Free from William's clutches but unable to get on with her own life.

A knock came to the door.

Mildred's head shot up. Leave it be. No sense risking it, especially with no one at home.

Another knock.

What if there was a problem? What if something happened to Gregory?

She carefully moved the curtain slightly to peek out the front window. A boy of perhaps eight or nine and wearing a red plaid newsboy hat knocked on the door again. Fidgeting, he stood for a moment then looked back at the street to a waiting automobile. The boy shrugged. It looked like he said, "No one's home."

Someone in the vehicle waved him over where the driver gave him a few coins. Mildred frowned. Very strange.

But her eyes widened when the men got out of the vehicle: William with two others. One was Eugene. Peter let him go from the factory a few years ago. She didn't recognise the other large brute.

It felt like her heart skipped a beat. She immediately closed the curtain and placed her hand on her heaving chest. No one could help. What now?

Chewing a loose bit of skin near her thumb fingernail, she moved to the hallway, away from any window.

After a minute she heard loud pounding on the back door. The wooden door made a cracking sound. A break in! She could flee while they were out back. She ran to the front door and opened it.

"Hello, Milly," William said, his head tilted slightly to the side. He stood on the doorstep, blocking the way. He held a club, a thick white one like those the Specials used.

Mildred tried to close the door, but William threw it open with such force that she fell back. He stepped over the threshold and closed the door behind him. She curled up against the wall.

"Looks like the house isn't so empty after all," William said.

The sound of the back door splintering signaled that William's thugs had gained entry as well.

Eugene and the other man ran to the front of the house and stopped when they came to William and Mildred. Eugene pushed up his bowler hat with his club. "Look what we got here."

William smiled like a boy given a sugary treat. "Indeed." He tapped her with his club. "Get up."

Shaking with fear, Mildred remained seated on the ground.

William grabbed her arm with the strength of a crazed gorilla and forced her to her feet. He bent her arm back, a favorite maneuver of his, and marched her into the office. He stopped for a moment before continuing to the office desk where he threw her into the chair.

The chair almost tipped over backward but Mildred managed to steady it. William sat in the guest chair and lay the club on the desk directly in front of her.

She hadn't seen her husband since that day last November. The circular scar on his forehead certainly looked awkward; it indeed suited him well.

William turned his head toward his cronies. "Go fetch the containers from my automobile."

Eugene looked at his pocket watch. "Do we have time for this?"

"He's not here, so now's the time," William said. Both thugs leaned their clubs against the hallway wall and stepped out the front door.

"I always knew you were here seeing that cripple," William said to Mildred.

"He's more of a man than you'll ever be," Mildred replied under her breath.

William sneered. "Where's my money."

"What money?" Mildred looked away for a split-second before making eye contact.

"You know what I mean. The money you took when you left."

"I don't know what money you are referring—"

William picked up the club and slammed it down hard on the desk breaking the trunk off Gregory's elephant paperweight. "Where's my money!"

"I … it's … I … it's not here…"

"You better give me back every penny you took or I'll beat it out of you. And after that I'll get your limping hero."

Mildred crossed her arms and rocked back and forth. "It's not here."

"After we're done here you'll take me to it."

The men came back into the house, both carrying a jerry can in each hand.

Mildred frowned. "What are you…? Is that gasoline?"

William smiled. "You're about to see the biggest bonfire ever."

"You'll never get away with it. I'll … I'll tell the authorities."

"Be a shame if something ever happened to Gregory's other leg. How would he get around? One of those little carts I see some returned soldiers wheel around on? They use their knuckles to propel themselves."

Mildred raised her hand to her mouth.

"Albert, you start upstairs. Spread it all over the beds and draperies," William said to the large man with a crooked nose. William pointed to the back of the house. "Go over to the kitchen and spread it there," he said to Eugene.

Albert tried to get a cap off one of the cans. "Hey, how do you take these off?"

Eugene tried but it wouldn't budge.

William shook his head. "Righty tighty, lefty loosey. Don't you know anything?"

"I just can't seem to get it," Albert said. "Maybe it's cross threaded or something."

William walked to the hallway. "Do I have to do everything?"

Mildred picked up the earpiece of telephone and raised it to her ear.

"Please get me the Police." She paused for a moment. "Hello, Police? I would like to report an arson in progress. Three men are here at 376 Ross Avenue and about the set the home on fire."

William ran back into the office.

"One man is William Dal—"

Before she could finish William yanked the phone from her hands and pushed her down.

"What do we do now?" Eugene said. He traded glances with Albert. "We can't get caught here. Besides, we gotta go. Me and Albert have to be downtown with the other Specials."

"You call yourself Specials?" Mildred said. "Is that some kind of joke? You're supposed to be protecting everyone, not setting fires."

"Don't listen to her," William said.

"Don't worry," Mildred said. "Stay where you are. The real Specials and volunteer fire brigade will be here in minutes. You can explain it all to them."

Eugene's moustache twitched. "C'mon. Let's get out of here. This ain't worth it."

Albert nodded and followed Eugene out the front door, not bothering to close it behind them.

"Hey, where you guys going?" William said. "We have to finish this."

William snorted like a thoroughbred. Red-faced with clenched teeth and an evil scowl, he snatched his club from the desk. In a quick motion he raised it above his head about to strike.

Mildred raised her hands to defend herself. "Didn't you hear me? I mentioned your name. Kill me now and they'll know who to come after once you set the place on fire. No more snuggling with Trixie and trying to latch onto her family's wealth. Better be quick because it sounds like your ride is leaving."

The sound of the car revving its engine tore through the open front door. William turned his head. "Wait! Don't go! I'm not going to pay you if you leave." William ran out the front door.

Mildred exploded for the back door, its frame splintered from the break-in. She didn't bother to shut the door after she ran outside. But where would she go? She had to hide somewhere, just in case. Maybe in some backyard a few blocks away.

Then she had to go to Marko's. No sense in waiting for the authorities because Gregory's telephone line was still dead from last weekend's storm.

Bloody Saturday
June 21, 1919

Peter threw the *Manitoba Free Press* down to the table and waved a defiant fist in the air. "We'll show them. We'll shake City Hall just like that storm last week."

"There will be hundreds," Gregory said. "Maybe thousands." He sat at Marko's kitchen table while Mike poured shots for everyone. Marko and Ben also sat at the table cluttered with various hand tools.

"Ya got that right." Red-faced, Peter sputtered, spewing droplets of saliva. "How can anyone read this bloody rag?" He held up the messy, crumpled newspaper. Several pages of the broadsheet fell to the floor. "The mayor proclaims there are to be no parades until the end of the bloody strike. All we've got is parades and meetings! I can't recall how many times I've been at Victoria Park. Countless. The mayor's in the pocket of the industrialists and that bloody Citizens' Committee of One Thousand."

"I just want the strike to end," Gregory said. "I'm not in the Committee and I'm certainly not an industrialist."

Mike downed his shot in one gulp. He looked rough with three or four days of stubble on his chin and bags under his eyes. A few streaks of grey speckled his hair. "I can't remember the last time I made money. The kids go to bed hungry every night."

Marko stood up. As he did, he accidently knocked down a thick three-quarter inch wrench. He picked it up and played with it in his hands while pacing the kitchen. "Will marching matter? The owners all have deeper pockets."

"What else have we got?" Peter replied. He picked up the paper again. "Listen to this. The mayor has the gall to say... 'women taking part in a parade do so at their own risk.' So what? He's gonna have his Specials pound the tar out of 'em?"

Ben looked at his pocket watch. "It's ten. We should go. Everyone's massing in Victoria Park before they parade on Main Street at 2:30. With all the people showing up, I have to park my taxi a ways from Main."

Peter nodded and grabbed his derby. "It's all coming to a head. Especially after they jailed those ten strike organizers. They went in the middle of the night, Tuesday morning, and rounded all of them up. Ivens. Armstrong. R.B. Russell … even two aldermen: John Queen and Abraham Heaps. What gives them the right? Charged them with sedition and conspiracy against the constitution. Bollocks! I tell ya, I don't care if most of them get out on bail, everybody's furious and won't take it anymore."

Mike and Ben put on their suit jackets. Peter and Gregory had already walked out the door. Marko grabbed his hat and slipped the wrench in his inside jacket pocket. He might need it.

*****

Still breathless, Mildred knocked on Marko's door. She blew away a strand of loose hair hanging over her eyes.

She didn't need a mirror to know she looked like a sweaty, dirty mess. Stained with mud, the bottom of her dress near the hem had torn from a tree branch. The seam came apart near her right shoulder. She had hid in a back yard for almost an hour before she made her way for Marko's apartment. That took at least a half hour, maybe more. The whole time she expected William and his cronies to come barreling around a corner. The nervous walk across the Arlington Bridge seemed to last forever. If they caught her on the bridge, there would have been be no place to escape.

No answer. Damn. They had already left for Victoria Park. It would take the rest of the morning to walk there. A few streetcars ran on the streets, but she couldn't go looking like an automobile service station attendant.

She dropped her head down. Even if she was able to contact the police or Specials, or whatever they were called, they were all tied up at the demonstration downtown. Gregory should have addressed the arson problem a month ago.

Back downstairs, on her way to leave the apartment block, she passed Mrs. Dogaru sweeping the hallway. The older woman wore in an ill-fitting white floral-themed dress.

"You the nurse?" Mrs. Dogaru said with raised bushy eyebrows. Ash from her cigarette fell to the floor.

Mildred nodded.

"Marko and the others left half hour ago. You missed them. But why you so dirty?"

Mildred looked down at her filthy, mud-stained hands. She swallowed. If a foreign woman noticed then it must be obvious.

Mrs. Dogaru frowned. "You need to wash. Woman like you should not be outside looking like that." She reached into her pocket and pulled out a mass of keys. She sorted through them until she held one aloft. "Here, go to Marko's apartment and wash. He knows you good, so he not mind. You saved his life, no?"

Mildred accepted the key with a small smile. "Thank you."

Various grimy tools cluttered the kitchen table along with a half-filled bottle of alcohol surrounded by several shot glasses. They must have needed a little liquid courage before heading out.

Inside Marko's tiny washroom she took off her dress and washed her hands and arms several times. What would she wear? She crumpled her ruined dress and flung it. The dress sailed across Marko's bedroom and landed on his nightstand with enough force that it knocked over the framed photo of Marko's family. The frame fell to the ground shattering the glass.

She raised both fists in the air and screamed. Throwing herself on the bed, she pounded her fists into Marko's messy, disorganized bed sheets. Could the day be any worse?

"It's me," Mrs. Dogaru said after knocking on the door.

Mildred raised her head up. "Just a moment." She pushed the remnants of the frame under the bed along with the larger shards of glass. In the process she poked her right index finger, drawing a drop of blood.

She opened the door with her finger in her mouth.

"You wrecking the place?" Mrs. Dogaru said, holding a dress.

"Sorry, something fell."

Mrs. Dogaru snorted. "Here, take this dress. I no need. It from woman who lived here before Marko. She's in Regina now and not coming back. Maybe it fit, no? You can't wear other dress."

"Thank you, I'll try it on." Finally, some good luck. After Mrs. Dogaru left she tried the dress. Plain blue, it went down to her ankles and felt snug, but Mildred managed to pull it up past her hips. It didn't match her red hat.

Now she had to go downtown to get Gregory away from the demonstration. Marko, too. He shouldn't be demonstrating, especially being a foreigner. That Mike seemed sketchy and drank too much. He'd only get the others in trouble.

She threw out her old dress. Just before leaving the apartment, she noticed glass on the floor beside Marko's bed and rolled her eyes. How could she forget to clean that up? She picked up the frame and put it on the bed, face up before sweeping the bits of glass into a dust bin. She'd have to purchase Marko a new frame. Maybe leave a note in case she couldn't find them downtown.

She sat on the bed and looked at the photo again, flicking off a few glass fragments from the corner of the frame that resembled tiny diamonds. Such a beautiful family. Curious, she reached inside and took the picture out of the damaged frame. She turned it over to examine the back of it and frowned. She took a closer look at both sides of the photo.

Nowhere to carry it, she reached down her top and tucked it in her brassiere.

*****

"I think the speakers are over now," Mike said.

Marko, Mike, Peter, Ben and Gregory stood in Victoria Park with thousands of strikers listening to the end of a passionate speech. Attendees shouted and raised their voices more than they had in past gatherings in the park. Men seemed less reserved and more willing to speak their mind. The events of the past few weeks – fights on the streets, the arrest of labour leaders – increased the tension. Growling bellies at home and frustrated wives only added to the aggravation. Who can sit and do nothing for a month? Frustration set in and it became only a matter of time before frayed nerves led to frowns and eventually, to conflicts. Marko saw it on the boat coming to Canada. If idle men sat beside each other long enough, someone eventually got pushed or punched. The stubborn Committee of One Thousand pushed the strikers. The crowd at Victoria Park looked ready to push back.

"Let's go," Peter said. "Everyone's heading for City Hall."

But with everyone heading out of the park all at once, it took time for the jammed park to thin out, especially with the crowded sea of strikers and on-lookers wedged elbow to elbow.

A man with a pencil-thin moustache accidently bumped into Mike. "Outa the way, hunky."

"You watch it!" Mike said. He pushed the man away.

The man, an Anglo of medium build, clenched his fist and shook it at Mike. "Why, I ought to…"

"You do nothing," Mike said. "We're on same side, no?" He pointed to the man. "You strike." He pointed to himself. "We strike."

The man shook his head and trudged off in the direction of City Hall.

"Mike," Marko said, "you need to calm down. You'll get in trouble."

"Ah," Mike waved him off. "If I don't stick for myself, no one will."

Marko shook his head. It could have been worse. If Mike had been drunk there would have been a fight. Despite the company of many men of Eastern European descent, several thousand returned soldiers surrounded them, so any skirmish would end badly.

Eventually the strikers and sympathizers made it to Main Street just a short distance away. They completely overran the street. For several blocks in each direction the street became a mass of suits and hats. Only a few women joined the almost exclusively male crowd.

"C'mon, it's almost two. The parade starts at 2:30," a striker with a navy blue suit and a white Panama hat said to his comrade within Marko's earshot.

"To hell with the mayor and that blasted Citizens' Committee of One Thousand. I bet none of them have ever worked a real job anyway," said another man missing several teeth and wearing a scuffed Homburg.

"I tell you, I feel on fire," the blue suited man said. "As much as I've hated being on strike and all the hardship to my family, what bothers me more are the damn lies by the leaders. The mayor, the premier, the business elite, the whole lot of them are a bunch of greedy bastards. They haven't given us one inch. Well, they're going to learn what it's like when you rankle thousands of honest people."

"That's right," the man in the Homburg said. "I didn't go to war to come back to this. Poor as a church mouse with no future."

*****

On City Hall's parapet facing Main Street Mildred tapped her father on the shoulder.

He turned. In a split-second his blank expression changed to one of disbelief. "What are you doing here? You should not be here."

"I'm looking for Gregory," Mildred said. "He's somewhere out there." She pointed to Main Street, which had become a mass of humanity as strikers filled the street from the gathering at Victoria Park or directly from their homes from across the city. The clamor from the restless men on the street made it difficult to be heard. Some shouted at the top of their lungs. She spotted a few with bricks or rocks.

Thomas grabbed her arm. "It's too dangerous for you to be here. This demonstration can get violent."

"I can take care of myself." She broke her father's grasp.

He grabbed her by the arm again, this time more forcefully. "You will not find him. Besides, what's he doing there anyway? He's not on strike." With a quick tug, he led her into City Hall. "Come in here and wait things out."

Mildred struggled but couldn't break his grasp a second time. Thomas led her to a red, plush high-back chair in the mayor's office near the door. Although she had the urge to continue her search, the chair certainly felt inviting. The Committee of One Thousand, which included Winnipeg's leaders, filled the room along with the Mayor of Winnipeg and the Premier of Manitoba. All wore expensive tailored suits. A nauseating haze of cigarette and cigar smoke hung in the air.

Across the room Father spoke privately with Cecil Cavindish. He pointed to Mildred with his thumb, probably telling Mr. Cavindish of her silliness for coming downtown. Behind Cavindish on a mantle stood a clock that indicated a few minutes to 2:30.

Mayor Gray entered the office and hung his hat on the rack beside the door. "Dammit," he said, wringing his hands.

"What happened? How did the meeting go at the Royal Alexandra?" Thomas said, now beside Frank Patton near the mayor's desk.

"The negotiations fell apart. We had Senator Robertson, Commissioner Perry and A. J. Andrews. A few returned soldiers represented the strikers. It didn't matter. They refused to back down from the planned demonstration. Around quarter to two I received a telephone call from the new chief of police to tell me of the gathering crowd."

Thomas frowned. "Certainly you can see that for yourself. Just look outside the window."

"I know, I know … but he said he cannot handle the situation."

"So what are you going to do?"

"I don't want to have to read the riot act…."

"It doesn't look like you will have much of a choice," Cecil Cavindish said.

"It's those returned soldiers," Mayor Gray said. "They're so unpredictable. Some are ardent strikers. Others are staunchly opposed to it. About the only thing they agree on is that something has to be done about the alien problem."

"There's no time for that now," Edgar Dalton said. "Address the situation before those louts smash windows and loot all the stores."

Mildred stood up and looked outside. Indeed, the mob's ranks swelled each passing minute.

The mayor continued to wring his hands. "I already went to the Royal Northwest Mounted Police headquarters. They, along with the military, will quell this riot. It's the right decision, it is not? After all, I did make a proclamation that there would be no more parades of this sort. I reiterated it yesterday. I've done all I can. It's clear they would not listen … so it's time to bring on the constabulary." Mayor Gray scanned the group of selected aldermen and business leaders, perhaps hoping to get some confirmation that he had indeed made the correct decision. Father always said the mayor could have done more. He waited too long and now a major conflict had developed.

Mildred crossed her arms. The men continued to raise their voices and debate the predicament. No one would care what she had to say. Only a few feet away, the door to the mayor's office remained wide open. She glanced at her father, his back turned away from her while debating with the premier. She looked again at the open door. Casually, she got up and left the room.

*****

"What the hell?" Peter said. He pointed south down Main Street. They stood near the front of City Hall with several thousand strikers. "What's that?"

"Looks like some are the Royal Northwest Mounted Police," Gregory said. "See, they got red coats. The ones in the grey khakis are the military."

Sure enough, a line in perfect formation trotted slowly north on Main Street. The mob separated and moved back to the sidewalks when the row of horses approached. The demonstrators showed their displeasure by booing and jeering the show of force. One man ran out onto the street and waved his hat around, unsuccessfully trying to spook the horses.

"Boooo! Go back to the stables!"

"It'll take more than a few ponies to scare us off!"

"Go away!"

But the riders continued on, unaffected by the mob's verbal jabs. While the riders sat straight on their saddles and gave the appearance of authority, there must have been butterflies in the bellies of some.

The mixture of red-coated and khaki riders continued on for a few more blocks up north before turning back. All along the way, the gathered strikers gave the mounted police a wide berth, but the moment the line of horses passed, they went right back on to Main Street.

"Be gone, ya bastards." Peter shook his fist in the air.

"I don't believe it," Ben said. He grabbed Peter by the shoulder. "Look." He pointed north on Main Street where a lone streetcar approached. Slowly it clattered through the mob until it arrived near City Hall, unable to move any further due to the huge crowd of strikers. It stopped about twenty yards away.

"Are they daft?" Peter said. "That car, blimey, none of the streetcars should be running. Scabs are driving them."

"Yeah!" shouted a burly man with a thick black beard standing beside Marko. "The employees of the Winnipeg Electric Railway Company are on strike. I should know ... I'm one of them. Some have already been on the streets the last few days, but them driving that streetcar down here ... that's just so they can stick it in our face. No way I'm putting up with that."

Angered by the appearance of the streetcar, the men closest to it grabbed whatever they could find and hurled it at the streetcar, smashing its windows. With some help, the burly man climbed on top of the streetcar and disconnected it from the wire, stranding it in the middle of the hostile mob. Scared, the operator managed to flee, but not before being roughed up by the angry strikers.

Other men entered the streetcar and began to rip up the upholstery from seats. Another started a fire. A few ripped off a bumper. In a frenzy the strikers made sure the authorities knew how they felt about the presence of the streetcar.

"Come on," Mike said. He had to shout to make himself heard. "Let's help those men." Already about a dozen strikers heaved against the stricken streetcar trying to push it over. More men crowded around to help push.

Along with the other embattled strikers, Mike, Marko, Peter and Ben contributed their muscle. Marko could feel his back strain. The streetcar rocked back and forth, but despite the intentions of the mob, it stayed upright. After a few more attempts, the strikers gave up.

Leaning against his cane, Gregory stood a distance away, a grave expression on his face. He remained in the same spot and didn't try to help with the streetcar. He should not have come downtown.

Breathing hard, Peter looked at his pocket watch and laughed. "Twenty-five after two. This little parade is off to a smashing start."

"A might bit too violent for me," Gregory said. "I witnessed enough violence on the front line to have to see it in my home town."

Ben elbowed Marko. "Look, there's the mayor." He pointed to City Hall. Mayor Gray stood on the high parapet with a piece of paper in his hand.

Immediately the crowd jeered and yelled at the sight of the mayor. He raised his arms, asking for calm, but did not receive any.

"The Riot Act has been read," Mayor Gray said, reading from the paper, "and remains in full force and effect in Winnipeg. Riotous assembly of crowds, riotous attack on persons or property, riotous damaging of property are indictable offences, and all persons guilty of same are liable to imprisonment. Assembling in crowds, congregating and standing on streets is dangerous, and you do so at your own risk."

The crowd continued jeering to drown out the mayor's statement, despite the fact he shouted.

"Go to Hell!" Mike yelled from the crowd.

Main Street had become a mass of confusion of disorder and looked beyond Mayor Gray's control. He stood for a moment on the parapet. Someone fired a shot. The mayor held his hat and ran back into City Hall.

"What was that?" Gregory looked around.

"Maybe an engine backfire," Marko said.

"Or maybe they're given us a warning shot," Peter said pointing to the mounted police ready for a second surge.

Positioned south of City Hall on Main Street, the riders trotted again, but this time at a faster clip. Agitated and angry, the mob threw not only insults at the riders, but also various objects including bricks and stones. Panicked strikers, fearful of being trampled, moved out of the way to allow the horses to pass.

The riders rode quickly past City Hall. Strikers near the crippled streetcar shook their fists in the air and heckled the riders. Several blocks north of City Hall the riders turned their steeds around and went back down the street.

The last horse to pass the streetcar became entangled in the discarded, broken streetcar bumper. A stone hit the mounted officer. He fell down but his foot remained attached to a stirrup, forcing him to be dragged a distance by his scared horse. Eventually the fallen rider detached from the stirrup, but lay on the ground, dazed. Someone from the mob approached him, but the quick thinking officer pulled himself to his feet. Blood streamed down his face blending with his red serge. He fired a few warning shots in the air and staggered to a nearby hotel to seek refuge. All told, two riders fell off their mounts during the charge.

Now brandishing their side arms, for the third time the mounted riders charged the crowd in front of City Hall. The horses thundered north on

Main Street. Again the crowd hurled bottles and rocks and whatever they could find on the ground. The crowd upended two more riders. Instead of heading straight on Main, the group turned left sharply just before City Hall at William Avenue. The police fired shots when they turned the corner, hitting a few strikers.

"They're using live bullets!" Mike yelled. Everyone panicked and scrambled for cover. Some huddled near the steps of City Hall. Others ducked into buildings and hotels. Wounded strikers, bleeding from bullet holes, managed to be dragged into safety, screaming in pain. New pock marks decorated nearby buildings.

Marko looked around. "Where's Gregory?"

"He's been hit!" Ben said. Gregory laid on the ground fifteen feet away, their view occasionally blocked by rushing, panicked strikers. He writhed in pain, holding his bum leg.

"Bloody hell," Peter said. "Let's drag him to that barber shop." The four men grabbed Gregory and took him to the Palace Barber Shop on Main Street a half block away from City Hall. Along the way the poor man screamed at the top of his lungs. Someone took his cane, likely now using it as a weapon.

The mounted police travelled quickly around City Hall by first turning north and then right on Market Avenue to end back at Main Street. Peter, Marko, Mike and Ben ran back out on the street.

Peter looked north and pointed. Two blocks away Special constables started marching south waving their trademark heavy clubs. Panicked and disorganized, the large mob of strikers became sitting ducks. Some of the Specials involved in the June 10 riot likely wanted payback. "We gotta get out of here!" he screamed.

"What for?" Mike said. "You were on strike for almost two months. Now you quit?"

"Yer crazy," Peter said. "I don't want to die over it. C'mon …"

A shot rang out from close range.

Marko looked at Mike's eyes, wide as saucers. Marko looked down. The bullet hit Mike squarely in the chest. He crumbled to the ground.

"Mike!" Marko screamed. He went on his knees, but it was too late. A red stain appeared on Mike's chest and a trickle of blood oozed out of his mouth.

"Your friend should have stayed home, no?" the soldier in the khaki uniform said from his horse. Marko looked up to view the shooter. The soldier held a .45 pistol, but from the soldier's positioning on his horse, the sun happened to be directly behind the soldier's head. He could not make out his face but he recognized the voice.

Krafchenko.

"Good to see you again, my friend," the soldier said in Ukrainian. He aimed his gun directly at Marko.

Marko stood up slowly amid the chaos around him. Krafchenko. But how?

"Do you believe in ghosts, my friend?" the soldier said in English. "Because you are about to become one."

The soldier squeezed the trigger. Marko felt the shock of impact on his chest and fell to the ground.

Chaos in the Streets
June 21, 1919

"I suggest you move along," the mounted solider said, his pistol pointed at Peter.

"Y-ya murdered them…" Peter said. He stood dumbfounded with his hands up. Wide-eyed, Ben also remained motionless.

"The riot act had been read. Everyone was ordered to leave. Those who elected to stay did so at their own peril." He sounded exactly like Krafchenko.

"Jones, get over here. Fall in back with the ranks," a commander said from his horse, maybe twenty feet away.

"Yes, sir," Jones said. The soldier directed his horse back and galloped away south down Main Street to be with a group of other soldiers dressed similarly in khaki uniforms.

Peter and Ben looked at each other and immediately dropped down to examine Mike and Marko. Mike was clearly dead, the crimson stain on his chest continued to spread. Marko, on the other hand, had his head up and grabbed at his chest.

"Don't worry," Peter said. "We'll get ya to the hospital. They'll fix ya right up. It wasn't supposed to be like this. There wasn't supposed to be any bloody violence."

Marko moaned and winced. Peter helped open his jacket. His white shirt remained stain free. In fact, Marko couldn't find the bullet hole. Peter frowned and traded a perplexed glance with Ben.

His hand shaky, Marko reached into his jacket and pulled out his thick wrench and inspected it. The bullet had embedded in the body of the wrench. Only a small fraction of the bullet pierced through to the other side.

Marko showed Peter and Ben. "A good worker always has his tools, no?" He put the wrench back in his jacket.

But Marko didn't have a moment to ponder his good fortune. The scene descended into anarchy. Strikers ran in random directions trying to escape. Deafening shouts and screams mixed with the sounds of hoofs. The occasional shot rang out.

"C'mon. We gotta go," Peter said. He and Ben helped Marko up to his feet.

"We can't leave Mike here," Marko said.

Ben looked across the street. "Let's take him to Thomson Funeral Home. There's no other place for him to go."

The three men struggled to carry Mike's limp body across the street. Marko swallowed hard. Poor Mike. He didn't deserve this.

Gently, they laid Mike on the ground at the front door. Marko looked at his hands, now covered in Mike's blood. He felt that same old sharp pain in his temple. Olena and Anastasiya. The knife. Their lifeless bodies. Blood everywhere. On his hands. On his clothes. His head felt on fire.

He shook his head and frantically wiped his bloody hands on his jacket.

Peter snapped his fingers in front of his face. "Snap outta it, will ya! We gotta get out of here!"

Marko felt his throbbing temple and looked out at Main Street. Everyone scattered to avoid the authorities. The mounted police formed four ranks with each horse several yards apart. Other mounted police and soldiers blocked off Main Street at Bannatyne Avenue, south of City Hall. The Specials were almost upon them.

*****

Several hundred Specials marched down Main Street. Dressed in suits and jackets, they all wore white arm bands. Each carried a large club.

Mildred ran out to the middle of Main Street waving her arms in the air in front of the approaching Specials. "Stop! Stop! Enough!"

Two strikers ran out from the side of the road. One grabbed her. "What are you thinking? Get outa here." His horrible teeth exuded a foul odor.

"Leave me alone," Mildred said, fighting back.

The other man, his suit jacket sleeve ripped along the seam, looked at the advancing column of Specials. "Leave her be. We'll end up getting bashed." The men ran away and sought refuge in the first available doorway.

Mildred continued waving her arms, yelling at the Specials to stop. But they maintained their advance.

She fell to her knees and continued flinging her arms about. The Specials almost on top of her, she bent her head down, defeated. How could she stop their advance? She was nothing.

They walked around her, paying no heed. She obviously did not pose any threat to them. As they did, she examined the faces of the Specials. Frowning, steadfast, with a determined resolve in their eyes. They had fought for their country overseas and here they fought for it again, but this time against brothers and neighbors. But were the strikers the real enemy? If not, then who? Father and his Committee of One Thousand? The foreigners? Was it anybody?

Near the end of the formation Mildred puffed out her cheeks and exhaled. Time to find Gregory and Marko. But as the last column of men passed by, she caught a glimpse of Eugene and Albert. They marched one behind the other, clubs in hand. Both glared at her. Red-faced, Albert's nostrils flared out like a horse. Most of Eugene's scowl stayed hidden behind his enormous moustache.

Mildred's heart quickened. She had to find the men and leave before the Specials broke formation. Those two thugs would certainly come after her. But how would she find Gregory and the others?

After the last of the Specials passed, Mildred rose to her feet. Her mouth twitched and eyes moistened. All seemed lost. With a bowed head and a handkerchief to her face, she walked back to the sidewalk.

*****

The Specials attacked the strikers with the fury and force of a pack of wolves, merciless and bloodthirsty. Marko, Peter and Ben continued running.

At Pantages Theatre on the corner of Main and Market near City Hall, a grey-haired man, a striker, waved a hand gun around. Before he could use it, several Specials rushed him with clubs and beat him to the ground. Another Special grabbed a nearby abandoned bicycle and threw it on the man. The Specials struck the man in the head repeatedly. After dazing him, the Specials took his fire arm and left him on the ground, bleeding.

"Let's duck into here," Ben said. He led the way into a service alley behind the buildings on Main Street just off Market Avenue.

The moment Ben entered the alley, a club smashed him on the head, knocking him senseless. He crumpled to the ground, blood rushing out of his forehead. The Special emerged from the shadows of the alley. Albert. The brute continued to bludgeon Ben on the head and body.

Peter jumped Albert, but Albert threw out his elbow, catching Peter square in the face. Peter fell back to the ground. Blood spewed from his newly broken nose.

Albert turned his attention back to Ben, ignoring both Peter and Marko. Marko walked behind Albert, pulled out his wrench, the one that just saved his life, and crashed it down on Albert's head.

The blow left Albert with a huge gash on the back of his head. Albert fell on top of Ben. Badly injured and in pain, Ben could not push off his hulking, semiconscious punisher.

Marko helped Peter up. Filled with rage, Peter grabbed Albert's club and raised it in the air over the Special's head. "See how this feels, ya bloody git."

But before he could slam down the club, Marko grabbed the club. "No. If you kill him you go to jail and hang."

"Just one shot," Peter said. He struggled against Marko.

"No. Let's go." Other Specials began to close in and Ben could not be helped.

The two co-workers ran into the back alley, Peter still holding Albert's club while Marko had his wrench. Loud screams and yells echoed off the stone walls. Vicious hand-to-hand combat between Specials and other constables against strikers and their sympathizers raged. It felt like they had strayed into Hell.

One Special, bleeding from his forehead, wrapped a fallen striker's leg around a pole, cracking it at the knee. Two other Specials beat a man against a service door. A larger striker, wielding a club, had the advantage against a Special and proceeded to smack him on the head. Another man lay unconscious in a pool of blood.

But Marko and Peter had to ignore the horrible sights and sounds of the gruesome violence. Had to get away from downtown. Forget about the strike. Nothing was worth this.

Dodging around each separate fracas, the two men continued and almost reached the end of the alley when another Special charged after them. Marko managed to dodge the man after the Special tripped on the leg of a fallen comrade.

Out of breath, they reached the end of the alley. Peter doubled over. Blood still dripped from his nose, staining his jacket and shirt. His derby fell off his head long ago.

"I can't … I can't go no further." Peter gasped for air. "You continue on. Run. I have to catch me breath."

"No, we stay together…"

"Then you will go to jail and get thrown into an internment camp. I'm already all bloodied up. I'll go down to Victoria Park and wander home from there. But you…" Peter paused. His chest heaved up and down. "Ya gotta move on."

Peter stuck out his hand. Marko shook it and the two men, both soaked in blood, went separate ways.

Marko turned to snake his way north but ran right into a Special. The man wrapped his bear-like arms around Marko and tackled him to the ground.

"Got you now, you foreign scum."

Eugene.

*****

Mildred stood just outside the front door of the Palace Barber Shop scanning the violent scene. Backed by the mounted military personnel, the Specials beat the remaining strikers mercilessly with their clubs. Escape would be difficult. A striker would have to be fleet of foot. Not Gregory's forte.

The door to the shop opened. "Ma'am? Come over here," a man leaning outside said. He wore wire-frame glasses with one cracked lens.

Mildred hesitated.

"Git over here!" the man with the cracked lens said. "A feller here wants ta see ya." He waved his arms for her to come.

Mildred looked out into the mayhem taking place on the street one more time then lifted her skirt and walked into the shop.

"Who wants to see—" Mildred stopped when she looked down. Almost unable to breathe, she immediately dropped down to her knees to be with Gregory. He laid on the ground beside a barber's chair, clutching his bloodied bad leg. She grabbed his hand. As white as his perfect teeth, he looked to be in shock. Two men applied a tourniquet to his leg. He'd been shot. With a riot taking place outside, how could he get to a hospital? The ground felt moist. She had knelt in a puddle of Gregory's blood.

Gregory winced. "I figured it was you out there. Y-you were right, Milly. Should have stayed home."

"Don't worry about that now." Mildred rubbed her hands in his hair then turned her head. "Someone get me a cold cloth for his forehead."

Another wave of pain shot through Gregory and he screamed. One of the men put a flask to his mouth. Mildred could smell the hard alcohol as Gregory gulped it down.

Gregory sputtered and coughed. "I'll be fine. No worse than Europe."

Tears formed in Mildred's eyes. "Oh, Gregory…"

"Listen, when you see the others, tell them I'm fine…." Gregory's voice trailed off before he passed out from the pain.

Mildred stood up. The front of her dress bloodied, she wiped her tears away with her sleeve. She had to go back to City Hall. Perhaps Father could help.

*****

Marko and Eugene rolled on the ground, both struggling to gain leverage.

Eugene socked Marko on the side of the head. Marko returned the favour and tried crawling away, but just before he got to his feet, Eugene tackled him again.

Marko kicked his legs and caught Eugene in the gut, but only a glancing blow. Eugene punched Marko near the eye. Eugene jumped on top of Marko and began choking him.

Marko couldn't breathe. He reached up and tried to apply his own choke hold, but didn't have enough leverage. He tried breaking Eugene's grasp, but the man's hands had wrapped around Marko's neck like forged steel.

Eugene strained his face, eager to put Marko away.

Marko gulped for air that could not enter his lungs. Desperate, Marko groped around Eugene's mouth and managed to secure the man's over-sized moustache. He pulled down hard.

Eugene growled, but maintained his grasp.

Marko continued to yank on Eugene's moustache. Finally, Eugene let go of Marko's neck in an attempt to pry Marko's fingers from his facial hair.

But now it was Marko's turn to maintain a firm grasp.

Eugene plowed Marko in the face with enough force for Marko to break his hold. Marko brought his knee up into Eugene's crotch.

Eugene rolled over in pain. Marko remained on his knees for a half-minute massaging his sore neck.

"Hey look," said another Special a short distance away, "Eugene's on the ground. That striker must have got him." He pointed at Marko.

Marko sprang up and felt his forehead with his fingers. Blood.

*****

Marko is lying on a bed, his head killing him. It feels funny, like it's wrapped in something. There are no windows in the room. He sniffs. It smells like a hospital. A prison hospital?

He tries to move, but cannot. His arms and legs are in heavy leather straps, thick ones several inches wide with heavy buckles. He strains against the straps, to no use.

What happened? Why is he here? Then it all comes back to him. The trip home. Going to the barn. Olena and Anastasiya are dead, brutally murdered. The knife. The blood. Fleeing. Getting caught. Now here.

Surely they would dispense with a trial. Why waste time? They should just take him out back behind a tree and shoot him in the head. Done. He deserves it. He should be dead.

Marko strains against his bonds again. He screams. But why bother straining against them? He has nowhere to run. He has no home.

He hears sounds. Voices. They are getting closer. Yes, voices from two people. Maybe it will be his executioner. Was there a trial? Maybe it is still to come? He is tired and does not care anymore. He hears footsteps getting closer.

The door opens.

*****

Marko snapped back to his senses. He fled back to the same alley he and Peter previously entered just off Market Avenue. A gunshot missed him, but hit a nearby Special in the arm. The man dropped to the ground.

He entered the alley in full flight. Despite his head start, the Specials trailed not far behind. Bloody hand-to-hand fights still took place. The Specials seemed to have the upper hand in most of the struggles.

Marko ran past poor Ben being cuffed by a special. Now sitting upright, blood painted the entire left side of his face.

A few feet away Albert came to his senses and sat on the ground with a blood-stained cloth pressed against his head. "Hey, there's the guy who clubbed me. Get him."

Running back toward City Hall with several Specials in hot pursuit including Albert and Eugene, Marko's mind raced. What now? He looked both ways on Main Street, but a string of mounted police blocked both sides.

Run toward City Hall and then out behind. It looked like his only chance. He'd end up at Market Square and, if lucky, a side-street away from the commotion on Main Street to freedom.

*****

Mildred looked out the window in the mayor's office in City Hall. Father just finished admonishing her for sneaking out but she didn't care. If she hadn't stumbled upon Gregory, who knows what would have happened to him? Thankfully Father managed to arrange a trip to the hospital.

Most of the men huddled around the mayor's desk. A few smoked cigars. Two clinked their scotches. For them, everything went as expected.

She tried to remain facing the front window so nobody could see her blood-stained borrowed dress. She must have looked like a cleaning woman. More like a butcher shop employee.

"Mildred," Thomas said from across the room, "get away from the window. What if there's a stray shot?"

She ignored him. Would Gregory be fine? She should have gone to the hospital. What about the others? Marko?

Order had almost been restored on Main Street. The military, mounted police and Specials accosted anyone looking suspicious. Most of the strikers either fought in the back alleys and side streets with the Specials or had already fled for the safety of home. Occasionally a striker making a bid for safety zipped across the street. Sometimes he'd be caught, sometimes he found freedom.

She stared at the Volunteer Monument out front in the courtyard when some activity caught her eye. She moved closer to the window for a better view.

She held her breath when she saw Marko running away from several Specials including Albert and Eugene. Eugene looked to be limping. Albert had been bloodied. Good for them.

Could she pull Marko into City Hall for safety? No, bad idea. A striker in the mayor's office right when the demonstration had been quelled would land him in jail or worse.

He ran at full speed and seemed to be aiming to the get behind City Hall just north of the building. He ran past a mounted Northwest officer. With a straight arm he knocked down a Special trying to tackle him.

She put her head right against the window. A few Specials gave up the chase. Eugene and Albert continued at a slower pace. Eugene soon stopped and dropped to one knee. Once he saw his comrade falter, Albert did as well.

Mildred's pulse quickened. Still right against the glass, she could no longer see Marko. Her heavy breathing fogged the window.

She pulled away from the glass and felt her chest again for the photo from Marko's apartment. What should she do?

Pressing her lips together, she lifted her skirt and, for the second time, ran out from the safety of the mayor's office. Father would not understand.

Back outside, she stood briefly at the parapet but dropped down to crouch behind the wall. After a few moments she poked her head up. Eugene and Albert had turned away and walked slowly back to Main Street, their clubs resting on their shoulders. Running down the parapet, she almost stumbled down the last two steps.

Behind the building she saw Marko running down King Street. He, too, had slowed, perhaps noticing his pursuers had abandoned him. Mildred ran for a short stretch, but slowed down to a fast walk.

Marko turned left down a side street. Away from her view, Mildred quickened her pace. Her heart beat hard against the side of her chest and sweat formed on her brow.

She reached the corner with Marko just ahead. He stopped to catch his breath. She yelled his name.

He turned around and shielded his eyes from the sun to get a better view. Motionless for a few seconds while she approached, he ran toward her.

They embraced. He pressed his body tight against hers.

"What happened? Why are you here?" Marko said.

It took Mildred a few moments to catch her breath from her heaving chest. "I did not want Gregory to go. I was hoping I'd catch up with him before anything happened." She looked down the front of her dress. "I was too late. I chanced upon him in a shop on Main Street."

Marko nodded. "Yes, we took him there after he was shot."

"He's on the way to a hospital. How are the others?"

Marko crossed his arms, and turned away from her. "Not good."

She put her hand on Marko's shoulder.

He told her of his tussle with Eugene. "Benny was knocked in the head and arrested. Peter got smacked. But Mike … he was killed by a mounted soldier. Right on Main Street."

Mildred raised her hand to her mouth.

Marko turned around. "You will not believe me, but the soldier sounded exactly like Krafchenko."

"He's been dead for five years."

Marko raised his hands in the air. "I know, I know. It not make sense. But I swear it was Krafchenko."

Very odd. What a strange duck. This confirmed it. She scratched her head and looked away. "I don't know."

Marko grabbed Mildred's hand and they continued walking west, away from downtown. With both their clothes stained with blood and his face scuffed, the two must have appeared macabre to passersby. But anyone coming from the hostility downtown certainly had at least a few bumps and bruises.

Mildred took a deep breath. "There's something I need to show you." She reached down the front of her dress. Marko raised an eyebrow. She pulled out the photo that was from his broken frame and handed it to him, the edges moist from her perspiration.

Marko's eyes widened. "Why you have this?"

"I went to your apartment and accidently knocked it over. The glass broke. Look at the other side of the photo."

A vehicle came to a screeching stop right beside Mildred and Marko. William, Eugene and Albert jumped out. Mildred screamed. Nowhere to run, Marko stood in front of Mildred to protect her, but Albert's club felled him with one swipe.

William grabbed Mildred. "You shouldn't have left the safety of City Hall. My friends here saw you on Main Street but couldn't do anything about you then. It was a good thing Eugene took a look back and saw you running away from City Hall just now. I was waiting in a vehicle on King Street the entire time. Let's go back to Gregory's place, shall we?"

He threw her in the car and they drove off leaving Marko dazed on the sidewalk.

Gasoline
June 21, 1919

Sitting on the ground beside the sidewalk, Marko gently rubbed the back of his noggin. That knock will grow a good-sized lump. He closed his eyes and put his head in his hands. Tired, exhausted and beaten. A bed would feel good.

He heard a few men pass. One held his arm gingerly. From the strain on his face he must have been in pain. The other favoured his right leg. More strikers beaten by Specials.

Marko got up. No sense sitting around. Glancing at the ground, he noticed the photo of his family. The photo! He grabbed it and turned it over. It looked like part of an article about gardening written in German. Something about planting springtime flowers. He could only make out bits and parts of the article. Strange. He looked at the front again at Olena and Anastasiya. Why would there be something printed on the back of the photo? Did the photographer run out of regular photographic paper? The photo felt flimsy, like it came from a newspaper or maybe a magazine.

His eyes widened and jaw dropped. If the photo came from a magazine, was it reporting on their deaths? His temple throbbed. Why could he not remember when and where the photo had been taken?

Mildred seemed to know about it. Mildred! His breath quickened. How could he forget about her? She was in trouble. What did that crazy William have planned? It had to be about the money she took. He had to find them.

A man in a blue suit riding a bicycle came up from behind. He looked prim and proper in his straw boater hat with a black ribbon around the base.

Marko put the picture in his pocket and walked toward the cyclist. "Excuse me? Do you have matches?" He put two fingers to his mouth, making it look like he wanted to have a smoke.

With a puzzled look the cyclist slowed down. Marko's beaten face and blood-stained clothes made him waver. "Uh, I'm sorry, I do not have any with me."

Undeterred, Marko ran after the bicycle. The man tried to quicken his pace, but Marko had the jump and ran alongside of the bike. He pushed the man, knocking him to the dusty street. The man's straw hat flew off his head. Marko picked up the bicycle and jumped on. He drove twenty feet before the man could get up and run after him.

"Get back here, you thief! Damn foreigner!"

Marko pedaled hard, not bothering to look back. He didn't like taking the bicycle, but had no choice. Had to find Mildred.

But even if he did, what would he do? He could not stand up to both of William's thugs.

*****

"I have to admit, you had me going for a while, you know that, dear?" William said, a cigarette dangling from his mouth. He stood triumphantly above Mildred holding her pink hat box. She sat in a wooden chair in Gregory's office while Albert tightened the rope around her hands. "That's a nice little apartment you have. But I've got my money, so all is good."

"You have what you want, so why don't you let me go? You don't need me anymore."

William smiled. "I'm sorry, Milly. But you know too much. But don't worry, the end will be soon. Painful, but soon. That was a good trick you pulled earlier today, but Gregory's phone was dead."

His club in his hand, Eugene kept watch outside through a small crack in the drawn curtains. Albert stood near the front door, smarting from an awful, congealing head wound.

Mildred fidgeted with the tight rope wrapped around her wrists. The nauseating fumes from the gasoline made her breathe through her mouth. They poured it overtop the furniture, draperies, carpeting, the kitchen, up and down the stairs and even the beds upstairs. Luckily they spilled everything out of the jerry cans before someone thought it would be a good idea to douse her.

"You never loved me nor even cared for me," she said. "You admitted it yourself."

"Being from a prominent family, at one time you served a purpose. But your father was on to me. My fault really. I stayed up too late and didn't give the opportunity the attention it deserved. I suppose it was my own undoing. But I have another woman in my life. A pretty, young one. And her father is also rich and powerful. But you see, I can't marry her because I am currently married to you. We need to end our marriage. A divorce is too messy and complicated, although I'm sure you would want that so you could spend the rest of your pathetic days with Gregory. But that would be too public. No, we need to end it now. And as they say … until death do you part…" William blew a stream of smoke from his cigarette into the air.

"So you're going to kill me then?"

"A tragedy really. I can see the headline: City Woman Missing After Riot. When they sift through the ashes of this house you will be a pile of bones. The fire might even be blamed on you. Of course the fire brigade will be too occupied here to help with the one at the factory. Your father felt he should fire me. I'll show him what fire is all about."

Mildred slumped in her chair, defeated. Why did she go downtown? Of course someone would spot her. She only wanted to get Gregory away from the madness. She wanted to show Marko the back of that photograph, but why the rush? She could have talked to him about it later. She also could have stayed on the sidewalk on Main Street, but when she saw all those awful Specials marching with clubs in their hands, ready to punish the strikers, she had to do something. That's when Albert and Eugene first spotted her.

"When are we meeting Charlie?" Eugene asked.

"Right after we're finished here," William said. He looked over to Albert and winced. "You need to get repaired."

Albert shrugged his shoulders. Blood stained his collar and down his jacket.

"Eugene, take him to the hospital after you drop me off at the factory. I'll meet Charlie on my own. The other jerry cans are in the trunk?"

Eugene nodded. "We should go now."

She stared into William gloating eyes. His beautiful eyes. So handsome and fair, but all a sham. He grabbed a tea towel and tied it hard around Mildred mouth. The stench of gasoline invaded her nostrils.

Albert and Eugene left the home, William trailed behind.

"Good bye, Milly." He flicked his cigarette on a damp patch of carpeting. A small flame erupted.

*****

Marko jumped off the stolen bicycle before it came to a stop. Flames flickered through Gregory's front window and wisps of black smoke escaped around the cracks of the front door.

He felt the doorknob. Hot. He took out his handkerchief and wrapped it around the doorknob. Would William and his brainless thugs actually kill her?

Earlier he checked Mildred's apartment, a mess. She must have stalled for time while they searched for the money. They had to do it quietly enough so as to not make a racket. They must have put a sock in her mouth. Somehow she was able to write 'Go to G's' on a little piece of paper and place it on the music box he fixed for her years ago. To think she still kept the thing after all the years. The note looked out of place. It had to be a clue.

Marko opened the door releasing a cloud of foul, black smoke. Flames curled and deformed the wallpaper. Flames consumed patches of carpet.

After taking a step back for a few gulps of fresh air, he tore off his jacket and threw his hat away. He put his handkerchief up to his mouth and nose, closed his eyes and stepped through the flames at the entrance to Gregory's home. Thankfully the smoke thinned only a few feet in. The fire must have started at the entrance.

A few steps down the hall, he looked to the right into Gregory's office. Mildred! Tied to a chair and on her side, she must have knocked it over in her struggle. Her face puffed out in a muffled scream from a cloth tied around her mouth.

Marko ran over and propped her upright. Fire engulfed the draperies at the front window. The comfortable couch beside the window exploded into flames as the fire spread. Thankfully most of the office had so far escaped the fire. Lucky for Mildred the flames weren't yet upon her. But he had to hurry to untie her. He could smell the gasoline. That damn William aimed to burn her alive.

He tore the cloth off Mildred's red, sweat-soaked face. "Thank God, you made it!" she shouted.

"We have to leave … now." Marko struggled against the tight ropes that bound her hands. The smoke made it difficult to see anything. He clenched his jaw and tried working the rope, but couldn't tell if he was loosening or tightening it. Even under perfect conditions it would take some time to unbind.

Mildred screamed. Flames licked the bottom of her dress.

Marko looked frantically around the office. He had to cut the rope. What could he use? He didn't see a knife handy. It was too far to run to the kitchen and go fishing through drawers. The sharp pain on the side of his head returned.

"Just go," Mildred screamed. "Leave me. Save yourself…"

"No." With a surge of energy, Marko picked Mildred up, chair and all, and walked through the smoke and flames to the front door. Holding his breath, he bumped into the wall in the hallway just outside the office forcing him to drop the chair.

Mildred yelped when she hit the ground.

Marko picked up Mildred and the chair again and ran for the front door. Smoke stung his eyes, forcing them shut, but he continued on. Although he travelled just 10 or 15 feet down the hallway, it felt like a mile.

Screaming, Marko continued running until he ran off the front steps and fell forward. The full weight of his body landed on Mildred as both of them crashed on the concrete sidewalk just beyond the front steps.

The chair splintered. Mildred's head hit the sidewalk.

Marko rolled off her on to the front lawn, taking in deep mouthfuls of air. His head felt like it had been stomped by an ox. Mildred moaned. A trickle of blood ran down the side of her sweaty, dirty forehead. Pieces of the broken chair lay scattered around Mildred, her hands still tied together

Both remained on the ground for a full minute before Marko went on his hands and knees and slowly crawled to Mildred. She shut her eyes and her mouth twitched in pain from the horrible ordeal and the hard landing to safety. He wiped the blood from her wound with his soot-covered handkerchief.

"Sorry for the fall."

Mildred opened her eyes and shook her head. Still dazed, she bit her bottom lip.

He cradled her head in his arms. The fire fully engulfed the entire home. Coils of flame waved at them from the second storey window. Horrid black smoke rose to the heavens. Neighbors and onlookers had already gathered on the front street.

He untied the binds around her hands. Mildred rubbed the circulation back into her wrists. Missing a shoe, she remained on the ground, hugging Marko.

"I saw the note in your apartment." He stroked Mildred's dirty hair with his filthy hand.

Mildred nodded again. "I should have let you be when I saw you," she said, wiping snot from her nose with the back of her hand. "William's cronies, they followed me. I should have stayed in City Hall. I don't know why, but I felt compelled to show you the picture."

He pulled out the picture and frowned. "The paper, it's so thin. Not like a real photograph. Almost like it's from a …"

"Magazine." Mildred took the photo from Marko. "Do you remember when this photo was taken? Was it for a magazine?"

Marko shrugged his shoulders. Gregory's house continued to burn behind them as more people gathered to watch the scene. Someone ran to call the fire department.

"You don't remember anything about this photo?"

"Nothing." Marko winced as another sharp pain stabbed his temple. He tried to slow his breathing down. Concentrate. Hard to do while a house burned to the ground just a few feet away.

"Is that even your family?"

"I don't … I …" He stood up and turned away from Mildred. Was that possible? No. He remembered everything. All the birthdays and Christmases and snow storms. All the fun they had as a family. They never fought. Never argued. A perfect life until that day. The knife. The blood. But wait … they never fought? Never? Marko squeezed his eyes shut. Every memory was positive. How could that be?

The roof of Gregory's home collapsed into a chaos of sparks. The crowd of gawkers awed at the violent drama.

Marko picked Mildred off the ground and moved her away. "I have to think a little more about it. It doesn't make sense." Again, he wiped the blood seeping out of the wound on Mildred's forehead. He smeared it, making it look worse. She will need stitches. "William took all your money?"

"Yes, but there's more. He was going to go to the factory. Something about meeting someone. They were also going to set it on fire. Eugene and a Special named Albert were with him, but I think Eugene was going to take Albert to get mended at the hospital."

Marko stood up and pointed to the burning house. "No one does this and gets away with it. He tried to kill you." He went to the stolen bicycle.

Mildred crawled on her knees and grabbed his pant leg. "Where are you going? Don't go. I can tell the authorities what happened. He will not get away with this."

Marko could feel the rage bubbling from within. Time to get even.

Final Confrontation
June 21, 1919

Marko peeked around the corner. He saw no movement up and down the back lane behind the factory. He tried the doorknob at the employee entrance. Locked. He stood for a moment. He used to eat lunch in the very same spot. It also happened to be the spot where some of his first conversations with Mildred took place. It seemed like such a long time ago.

A vehicle screeched down the side street. He pressed hard against the wall of the factory. The vehicle sped past. He could hear his heart pound in his ears.

Taking cautious steps, he walked around to the front of the factory. A brown horse tied to the iron handrails of the front step snorted when it noticed him. The owner had to be inside the factory. Aside from a handful of pedestrians a few blocks away Logan Avenue remained unusually quiet. All the strikers went home to lick their wounds after the bloody confrontation at City Hall. Downtown had to still be crammed with Specials and the military.

Taking a deep breath, Marko stopped for a moment at the bottom of the staircase leading to the front door. He still had a headache, it seemed like for hours. His jaw felt sore from his fight with Eugene. Already a long day, he wiped his brow with the back of his hand. Covered in Mike's blood and ash from the fire, he must have looked like a tramp.

He hesitated. Should he wait outside? Catch William and whoever by surprise? But then what? Wait for the authorities? If William set the factory on fire, where would he work? No one knew to come here other than Mildred. No way her pleadings could change Marko's mind about settling the score with William.

Marko took a step up. Poor Mike. Too outspoken and brash. Maybe a little too quick to speak what was on his mind. He could have been rounded up for an internment camp at any moment over the past few years. With her husband dead, what would Maria do with the kids? Would she be deported?

He took another step. Bloody Jack crossed his mind. Like a demon from

Hell, John Krafchenko still lived. Or did he? The soldier that killed Mike certainly sounded like Krafchenko, but Marko could not get a good look at his face. But his commanding officer referred to him as Jones. How could Kraf cheat a public hanging? Did the horse belong to the soldier?

A step later he thought of Gregory. A war veteran, but wounded again and now with his house destroyed. The man did not act like the other returned soldiers. Gregory gave him work. He appeared to be a good match for Mildred, although his relationship with her seemed awkward and with her being married, well, that would have to remain in the closet.

Images of Lily washed over his mind the next step. So sad. Just Minnie and a few other women from the brothel attended her simple funeral. A vibrant woman cut down in the prime of her life. She never had the chance to live a normal life, something he could have provided to her.

Mildred came to mind the next step. So unlucky, yet tough. Able to overcome hardship. Even the scar on her face now seemed like an afterthought. She taught him to read and write. Unselfish, she did not have to volunteer at All People's Mission, helping the down-trodden. Sure, she came from wealth and privilege but she had time for everyone. A special friend. That dance they had years ago ... maybe if things had been different ....

At the top of the front step he paused before trying the door. He felt his jacket for the wrench. His jaw tightened. William had to be stopped. He would deny everything. His rich family would hire the best lawyers. Mildred would be jailed for taking the money from their home. What would her defense be? Especially after she went in hiding and wasn't discovered for months after. He would even lie about the fire. It would be her word against his with no proof.

Marko slowly opened the front door. Not a sound. Over the years he made sure each hinge in the factory remained greased. He opened the door wider. Still nothing. He had to be quiet like a barn mouse.

Holding his wrench tight in his right hand, he stepped into the factory office. The only light seeped in from the windows. He felt his right temple and winced.

He sniffed. Gasoline. In the gloom he could see three jerry cans beside the front counter. Why bother setting the factory on fire? Revenge for being fired? It seemed harsh. Tiptoeing to the dusty front counter, he noticed a pink hat box. He frowned. It looked like Mildred's. He peeked inside. Envelopes filled with money.

His breath quickened. If he took it now and ran he'd have more than enough for a repair shop. But that would be too obvious. Everyone would know the money wasn't his.

He shook his head. What was he thinking? That wasn't right. Some of it belonged to Mildred. Besides, he just about had enough already and with Gregory's backing, he might be able to buy a shop after the strike. And William's loot, well, Mildred should keep it, especially after what she went through over the years. The man tried to kill her today.

Thinking he heard a sound, he stood still and held his breath. Yes, from upstairs. He put the box under a desk and covered it with other boxes and papers then walked gingerly to the bottom of the stairs. He could make out men talking.

"Arrgh. I can't get this damn thing open. Let me try the combination again." The voice came from William.

Now it made sense. Break into the factory safe, rob money from the factory then cover your tracks with a massive fire.

Loud banging echoed from above before William cursed then said, "What the heck…"

"Obviously the lock is different," the second man said. Krafchenko. Or his ghost. "Spencer must have arranged to have it changed."

"But how are we going to open it? Drill out the lock…?"

"Observe."

For several minutes Marko heard nothing. Complete silence. Marko imagined Krafchenko placing his ear against the safe, closing his eyes and carefully listening to every click of the tumbler.

"Give it a pull," Krafchenko said.

A click.

"How did you do that?"

"Oh, just a little skill I developed over the years. Nothing really."

"Let's see what's in here," William said. "Stacks of currency. Very good. And a heavy bag of coins."

"I have no use for the coin. It weighs you down. I had problems with coin during the Plum Coulee job and it ended up being used against me in the trial."

"Let's go downstairs and count it up and get out of here."

"You've never pulled a big job before, have you? You don't count money at the crime scene. You do that after. Let's get on my horse and get out of here. We can do this at your place."

Marko heard them coming down the stairs. Now or never. Marko stepped to the side and hid beside the stairs where he wouldn't be seen. He licked his lips and held his wrench high up in the air.

The stairs squeaked and creaked when the two men descended. Marko shook his head to throw off the pain in the side of his head. He widened his eyes and held his breath.

William reached the bottom first. Without hesitation, Marko crashed the wrench on the side of William's head. Still clutching the paper bag, William dropped and rolled on the ground in agony. Marko went to take a swing at the second man.

But an arm shot up and caught Marko's right hand with the grip of a boa constrictor. Before he could react, a fist connected with Marko's right cheek, knocking him backward to the floor.

Marko looked up. His heart sank. Yes indeed, John Krafchenko. He now had a moustache, but it was him. He had survived the gallows pole.

Krafchenko kicked Marko's wrench out of his hand. It went clattering across the office floor. Marko scrambled to get back to his feet but stopped in his tracks when he saw the business end of Krafchenko's gun.

"My, my, my … what have we got here?" Krafchenko said. "Marko? I thought you were dead?"

"I thought the same about you."

Krafchenko snorted. "You'll be joining your friend Mike Sokolowski."

"You murdered him."

Krafchenko smiled and lit up a cigarette. "Tsk, tsk, tsk. No, I did not. He was holding a brick and was preparing to throw it at one of the mounted police. I saw it myself. The riot act was read. What happened was absolutely legal."

"He had no brick…"

"The newspapers will say he did."

"Why you kill him? He did nothing wrong and you know it. He had wife. Three kids.…"

"Why? No reason, really."

A few feet away William squirmed on the ground in obvious pain. He remained on his knees holding the side of his bloodied head.

"You going to be okay?" Krafchenko asked William. But William looked to be in too much distress to reply.

"So you just shoot me? Like an animal? Eh, John?"

"Why not? You were probably involved in getting Buxton to squeal. I can tell you were never really an ally like William. Do you know how many Germans I killed in the front lines? I have the medals to prove it. After the Great War ended, for fun, I joined the Siberian Expeditionary Force to try to quell the Red Russians. I just got back. Oh, and by the way, it's Corporal Charles Jones, not John. The John you know hanged in 1914. A horrible criminal, he was."

"But how … ?"

"I was locked in the Provincial Jail for a few months after my re-capture. During that time I had a chance to find God, or so thought Reverend Heeney. I easily gained his trust, like I did with the others. I also befriended two guards, Charles Jones and another named Earnest Brown. Guards, they have such weak minds, all of them, just like Constable Reid in the Old Kitchen. It seems Charles and Earnest didn't get along. Never did. I convinced them to hate each other even more. So much … that one time a fist fight broke out between the two. They would have torn each other apart in my cell if I hadn't stepped in to break it up. I convinced Jones that he should take a holiday right after the hanging to get away from Earnest. He told his superiors that he had to help his ailing father at a farm and would need to take a month off. In truth, Jones had no family.

"The Reverend told everyone that I had an epiphany, a vision, and that I suddenly fainted at around four in the morning and did not awaken until just before seven, the time I was scheduled to hang. Earnest took Heeney out of the cell while Charles attended to me. I was able to subdue Charles with some chloroform Earnest smuggled in for me. Heeney never suspected a thing. Jones was about the same height and weight as I. Earnest helped me switch clothes.

"We prepared Jones for the hanging in my place. He was still groggy from the chloroform when he walked the last few steps. Wearing a hood, no one could tell it was him. Thankfully the executioner was efficient.

"But by then, I was gone. Long gone. A friend of yours helped me flee, William Dalton here. William arranged for Jones's body to be examined by a physician he knew. An undertaker was called immediately. No one ever saw the body that is now under six feet of earth in Brookside Cemetery.

"Heeney met with the press and told them how much I changed and even cast doubt about the Plum Coulee incident. I had him convinced I was innocent.

"After laying low for a few months, the Great War broke out. It gave me time to grow some facial hair and step into a recruiting line in August of '14 posing as Charles Jones. Thankfully the recruiting officer was near-sighted. He thought nothing of a Manitoba jailer signing up to fight the Huns. I wrote an eloquent letter to the jail informing them of my decision. Of course they had no problem with their guard going to war. Earnest signed up with me.

"I don't know what those pampered Anglos thought. They felt the war was going to be like a little holiday. But I knew better. I enjoyed it. Oh, the things I did to the Germans and their allies. It was fun. I even took out a few of our own soldiers if they were a detriment. Earnest never made it back, the poor bugger.

"After that it was the Siberian Expeditionary Force. But now I'm back. Enough with the fighting. Time to start a new life as Charles Jones. You don't realize how easy it is to make a profit after all of the police were fired only to be replaced by mindless cretins.

"But enough about me…"

By now William got up to lean against a desk, but still seemed disoriented. He closed and opened his eyes several times rapidly and swayed from side to side. The colour had left his face. Marko broke a small, brief smile. At least he got one good shot in.

Krafchenko stepped toward William while still keeping his sidearm trained on Marko. "We have to leave but first need to take care of him."

Breathing deep and wincing, William pointed to Marko with an unsteady hand. "Kill him and burn the body."

Krafchenko trained his firearm on Marko.

"Mildred knows I'm here," Marko said. The pain in his head intensified.

"How?" William said in an uncertain tone, still clutching his head with one hand. The lump must have been the size of a chicken's egg.

"I saved her from the fire. You tried to kill her. Every Special in Winnipeg will be here when she tells her father."

"You're lying."

"How do you think I know to come here? A guess? And if I'm gone and money from safe is missing, they will come after you."

His lips curled in a scowl, William turned to Krafchenko. "Shoot him and let's burn this place down."

"Better hope I burn fast. It's a big factory. Will three jerry cans be enough?"

"As long as the office burns, I don't care," William said. For emphasis he waved his arms, but as he did, the bag of stolen cash he held caught something against a desk and ripped open. Bundles of cash scattered on the floor. William and Krafchenko dropped to the ground to pick up the scattered currency.

Taking advantage of the distraction, Marko sprang to his feet and ran for the entrance to the factory floor, the nearest door. Along the way he picked up his trusty wrench.

Halfway to the door he heard William shout, "He's running away!"

A shot whizzed by Marko's head just as he opened the door. He ducked into the factory when another bullet hit the doorknob. He looked to the right. He could try the employee entrance but if he had to fiddle with the door before it opened, Krafchenko would have him dead to rights.

Like a runaway stallion, Marko ran deep into the factory. His loud footsteps echoed through the silent emptiness. He had to get out and lose himself in the streets. But where would he go? Not his own apartment. They'd find out where he lived. The Specials wouldn't believe him, a bloodied, grubby foreigner. He veered off to the side.

Marko ran for an exit but it had been barricaded shut. Likely to prevent looting during the strike. Were all the exits on the factory floor sealed?

"You stay here and keep your eyes peeled," Krafchenko said, his voice rattling from every corner of the factory. "I'll flush him out. There's nowhere he can go."

Crouched behind a grinder and gripping his wrench tight, cold sweat dripped down the back of his neck. The pain in his head felt worse. He closed his eyes and massaged his temple. Full of promise and hope, the day became a disaster. The strike crushed. His friends killed, beaten or jailed. The fire at Gregory's. The resurrection of Krafchenko. And now this.

But maybe it was only fitting. Time to pay for his sins. He deserved his fate after what he did to his family in the old country. He should just stand up and let Krafchenko shoot him in the chest and burn his body.

Marko poked his head out to take a peek. Gun drawn, Krafchenko walked slowly down the main aisle in the centre of the factory. His head turned from side to side, carefully scanning every row of machines. His only hope for escape was to wait until Krafchenko ventured to the far side of the factory and then make a run for the office. He would have to get past William and then go out the front door. He should have tried to run out the front door when he had a chance.

He shifted his weight, but in doing so knocked over a container of rivets. They clattered to the ground, the sound echoing clear to eternity. His eyes widened. Time to move.

After a quick glance he ran to a neighboring bank of machines. Within thirty seconds Krafchenko arrived at the grinder he had just vacated. "I know you're around here somewhere. Might as well come out and get it over with."

Nervous sweat dripped down the side of Marko's face. The big, empty factory amplified even the smallest sound. Kneeling beside a lathe he noticed the start button and had an idea. He pressed the button. Electricity surged through the machine. He quickly engaged it.

He ran to a drill press and did the same. He moved from machine to machine turning everything on. Krafchenko couldn't hear him now.

A bullet hit a bench just in front of him. He turned, Krafchenko stood about 50 feet away.

He ducked behind a stack of wooden pallets piled up over his head, maybe fifteen feet high.

"You can't get away," Krafchenko said, hot on his tail.

Marko looked for cover between two machines. Another bullet pinged off a grinder.

"Like I, you have cheated death far too many times. This will be your last resting place. But this is what I enjoy. The hunt. Stalking my prey. It was the best part about the war in Europe. I spent most of my time in foxholes and trenches. Alone with a gun, just me and my adversary. Just like when I was a boy hunting rabbits in Plum Coulee."

Krafchenko stopped for a moment and cocked his ears. Futile, given all the racket from the other machines. "Come now Marko. Playing a little hide and seek, are we? It's only a matter of time…."

His gun stretched out, Krafchenko walked right beside the stack of pallets. Now. Marko pushed the pile over, tumbling them on top of Krafchenko. The man's scream boomed overtop the hum and growl of the machines.

Half-buried in pallets, Krafchenko shouted in anger. Marko leaped toward Krafchenko and swung his wrench.

But Krafchenko dodged the blow. He grabbed Marko's arms and threw him to the ground then disentangled himself from the mess. Kraf didn't have the gun. He must have dropped it when the pellets fell on him.

They both saw it on the ground at the same time near a fallen pallet. Both dove for it but Marko arrived first and kicked it away.

Krafchenko rose slowly, a small cut on his cheek. Smiling, he wiped it with his hand to inspect the blood. "Very good, Marko."

Marko remained silent, his wrench cocked.

Krafchenko and Marko sized each other up. "You don't have a chance, you know. Not against me," Krafchenko said with a smirk.

True enough. Krafchenko took on those two goons at once and easily beat them both in that vicious fight on Main Street years ago. Marko was no fighter, but to survive, he had to be.

"But listen, it does not have to be like this. We can stick together. Just you and I. You are a survivor. We can leave Winnipeg. Start our own career. We will accumulate wealth beyond imagination. Any woman can be yours. What do you say?"

Marko didn't answer. Enough with the lies. A master criminal and escape artist. Loyal only to himself.

"Eventually I'll get that gun and put a bullet in you."

Marko noticed a workbench near a drill press. While still maintaining his gaze on Krafchenko, Marko reached over with his left hand and grabbed a drill bit and threw it at Krafchenko.

Krafchenko easily dodged the tool. It fell to the floor behind him.

But Marko used the distraction to lunge at Krafchenko, pushing him to the ground. He struck Krafchenko on the head with his wrench.

Krafchenko reeled from the blow.

Marko swung again, but Krafchenko moved aside in a deft fashion again grabbing Marko's right arm, this time at the wrist. He applied immense pressure, forcing Marko to drop the wrench. Although Krafchenko's grip appeared effortless, it had enough force and leverage to make Marko cringe in pain.

Then, slowly, still maintaining his hold, Krafchenko brought Marko around so that they ended up face to face. The muscles in Marko's neck tightened. He tried to block the intense pain. Blood poured from the fresh wound on Krafchenko's forehead, but he didn't seem to notice. Instead, he smiled.

Their faces only inches apart, Marko could feel Krafchenko's sour breath. "Lucky shot," Krafchenko said. "You're getting your money's worth with that tool."

Marko head-butted Krafchenko on the nose.

Krafchenko recoiled. Blood erupted from both his nostrils and he let go his grasp.

Marko ran for the front of the factory, straight to the door leading to the office, the only way out. He didn't have much time before Krafchenko regained his senses and grabbed the gun. Marko heard his own heavy breathing over top the hum and rattle of the factory machines.

A shot hit the door just when Marko reached it. He opened it as another bullet hit the wall inches from his head.

Near the front counter William turned around the moment Marko entered. The side of his head glittered with blood from Marko's earlier blow. "Where's the damn box?"

Not bothering to answer, Marko ran for the front counter. He had to make it past William for any chance of freedom.

William looked chipper than before. He confronted Marko at the end of the counter in the little space that separated the front area from the back of the office. Marko tried barging through, but William held his own and pushed Marko back.

Marko swung his fist but missed and put himself out of position. William landed a solid right that knocked Marko to the ground. "Where's the box?" William said. "Where did you put it?"

Marko felt his jaw and jumped up. He didn't have much time. Krafchenko would be in the office any second.

Instead of trying to go through William, Marko dove over the counter, landing on the other side. He opened the door, but William dove and pushed Marko to the side. The two rolled on the ground.

Marko got up and grabbed the door knob. Again William pulled him away.

A shot fired. It hit William, exploding his skull. Drops of blood splattered on Marko. William fell dead like a sack of onions.

Krafchenko stood just on the other side of the counter, his gun trained on Marko. "Sorry William, friendly fire."

Kraf had him dead to rights. The next squeeze of the trigger would end it.

"Where's the hat box?" Krafchenko said. "There's more in there than what was in the safe."

Hands up, Marko slowly shook his head.

Blood dripping down the side of his face, Krafchenko expression transformed into a hellish scowl. "That's it. I've had enough of you." He slipped around the counter and grabbed Marko by the ear then dragged him back to the office area. He held his revolver hard against Marko's temple, the same sore and throbbing area. "Where's the money or I'll shoot you right now."

Almost ready to black out, Marko gnashed his teeth together. "You'll kill me anyway, so why should I tell you?"

Just then, the front door swung open. Soldiers stormed in, rifles drawn. "Drop the gun!" one of the soldiers shouted. A few attended to William's dead body.

"It's true," another soldier said. "Look at the gasoline cans. They were planning to start a fire."

With Kraf distracted, Marko reached for the gun. Both men struggled for control of the revolver. Once again both came face to face as the gun wavered in the air from the force of the struggle. Blood continued to drip from both of Krafchenko's nostrils.

"Drop the gun!" the same soldier yelled again. Marko and Krafchenko fought for control of the weapon.

Mildred ran in the front door.

"Shoot him," Krafchenko said. "He's a subversive enemy alien."

"Don't listen to him," Mildred said. "That's Krafchenko."

"Miss, you shouldn't be in here…" said another soldier who ran in after her and grabbed her by the arm.

Marko and Krafchenko continued their struggle with the firearm. They forced the gun down between the two of them. Krafchenko's eyes only inches away from him, Marko could see hate and fury smoldering behind the serpent's blue eyes.

The gun discharged. Instantly, both men stopped their struggle and stared at each other. Krafchenko pointed his gun to the group of soldiers, perhaps instinctively. One of the soldiers fired his rifle hitting Krafchenko in the chest. The snake crumpled to the ground.

Mildred ran to Marko, completely ignoring William. "It's all over. Father arranged for the soldiers. William's cronies were apprehended. He's even offered to help Gregory with…."

The pain in his temple increased. Marko could barely stand. His right hand shaking, he looked down. Blood dripped off his fingertips. He moved his hand to reveal a growing red stain on his gut.

Marko fell down.

*****

The leather straps are too strong. Marko slumps back in bed.

The door opens. The executioner, wearing white, walks over to Marko's side. He feels Marko's forehead and then his wrist.

A woman comes in wearing a funny hat. She also wears white. Why is a woman here? Women have no business witnessing an execution.

But maybe he's dead already. And the man and the woman are angels. He drowned in the river. They pulled out his dead body and put him in a hospital morgue. But then why is he restrained? Nothing makes sense.

"Is he awake?" the woman asks in Ukrainian.

"Yes, he appears conscious," the man says.

Marko forms his lips to say something, to ask where he is and what will happen next. But nothing comes out. He is too afraid to find out. Either way he is about to die or is dead already.

"It's alright, Mr. Gobinski. You're safe now," the man says.

"Huh?"

The man speaks to the woman. "He still appears feverish. Can you get a cloth for his brow?"

"Yes, doctor." The woman leaves the room.

"Doctor?" Marko says in a broken, raspy voice.

"Yes?" the man says.

"You are a doctor?"

"I am."

"Where am I."

"In a hospital."

"When will he take me?"

"Who?"

"My executioner."

The doctor has a puzzled look. "There is no executioner."

"No?"

"No. Why would you think that?"

"My wife. My daughter…" Tears form in Marko's eyes and he turns his head away.

The doctor frowns. "I don't know what you mean…?"

Marko turns to look back at the doctor, his face wet from tears. "They don't want to execute me after I butchered my own family?"

The doctor puts his hand to his side. "Well, that would explain everything."

"I don't understand? Why am I here? What happened? Oh, please kill me now."

"You experienced severe trauma. It affected your facultics." The doctor leans down closer to Marko's face. "As far as I know you are not married."

"But, the blood. The knife."

"You were kicked in the head by one of your cows soon after delivering a calf. Your skull was partially caved in. That cannot be repaired, unfortunately. That's why you have a bandage around your head. When they found you in the river you were muttering nonsense. Blood pouring from the side of your skull. When they went into your house they found a bloody knife on the floor of the kitchen. Torn and cut magazines on the floor. The real world and fantasy have mingled together in your brain."

"But Anastasiya … Olena …"

"Figments of your imagination."

"No."

"One of your sisters found you."

"No."

"She said you've been living on your own in the family home after your parents perished. Never found a wife."

"No." Marko moves his head again to face the ceiling, trying to make sense of it all.

"The restraints are more for your protection. We feared you would try to kill yourself again. It was either that or the straight jacket. I wanted to keep you here for observation to see if you would come around. If you did not, I would have you committed. Your sisters are very worried about you."

"My sisters."

"Yes. They visit you every day. They cleaned your house. They took care of your animals."

He feels a sharp pain on the right side of his head. In his temple.

The doctor folds his arms. "I'm afraid your headaches will come and go, especially considering the damage to your skull. I doubt you will be able to run the farm anymore. You need to start a new life. You should leave. Go away. Go to Canada. I hear they need young men."

The nurse comes back into the room.

"Rest up now. We'll observe you. Once you start acting rational, the restraints come off. Does that sound fair?"

Marko nods his head slowly in agreement. The doctor is lying. Olena and Anastasiya are real. They have to be.

The doctor speaks to the nurse. "Maybe give him something to eat. See if he takes it. It will be a slow process."

"Yes, doctor," she says. The doctor leaves the room.

The nurse smiles and looks down. She is pretty, but has a scar on her cheek, not a large one, maybe three-quarters of an inch, but still noticeable.

"What happened?" Marko asks.

"I thought the doctor explained…?"

"No, to you. Your scar."

The nurse reaches up and touches it, smiling. "Oh, that. A farming accident years ago when I was a child. Here, let me put this cold cloth on your forehead. It will help calm you while I get you something to eat."

*****

"Marko! Marko!" Mildred screamed. She had both hands on his belly, pressing hard.

Marko pried his eyes open. He felt weak, like the moment before falling asleep after a hard day of work.

Mildred looked up to the soldiers. "We have to get him to a hospital or he'll bleed out."

"I didn't do it," he said.

Mildred ran her hand through his hair. "Try not to talk. You have to conserve your strength."

Marko smiled slightly. "Olena and Anastasiya are not real. I thought they were real, but they're not. I didn't kill them. No one did. Just a picture from a magazine."

"I know," Mildred said, tears welling in her eyes.

"I was kicked in the head by a cow. Headaches. I … I must have made things up. Pretended to have a life I didn't."

"Shhh. Try not to talk," Mildred whispered. "Did anyone hear me?" she yelled to the soldiers.

Several soldiers on each side of Marko prepared to take him away. One shook his head in grim silence.

"It's too late," Marko said, his lips quivering. With his bloodied hand, he slowly reached for Mildred's hands that were still pressed hard on the entry wound. "I hid your hat box under a desk. Take care of Gregory. He's a good man. Thank you for the English lessons. I would have liked to be more than just your student. But I'm glad I was your dance partner that one day. And that time when I was sick."

"Don't die. Please don't die." She wiped away a few tears, smearing blood on her face. She shook her head. "We'll take you to the hospital. You'll get better. They'll fix you up. I love you too much for you to—"

Marko closed his eyes. That was all he needed to hear.

Blue Danube
June 21, 1936

Mildred opened the gate and walked through. She didn't need a sweater this morning. They called for it to be a warm one today. Maybe in the 80s again. She held her black hat so a gust of wind wouldn't blow it off. It had a blue ribbon that ran around its base and trailed off a few inches over the brim. She clutched a small bunch of flowers, red carnations with some baby's breath.

Michael caught up to her and held her hand.

"We can't be too long," Mildred said. "You have to go to school."

Michael squinted when he looked up. "I know, but I like comin' with ya. Besides, school's almost over anyway. Maybe I should just stay home…?"

Mildred tussled his hair and smiled. "You're sweet, but no, Maxwell will drop you off." The boy will be charming the school girls soon enough with his radiant blue eyes and blonde hair.

The two walked for about five minutes along the path. The lump in her throat grew larger as they neared. She swallowed hard.

"Why do you come every year?" Michael asked.

She took a deep breath. "It's important to pay respects. If you think about it, you wouldn't be around if it wasn't for him."

His modest tombstone read: MARKO GOBINSKI 1887-1919. She bent down and pulled a few weeds that had grown along the side of the marker. The groundskeeper never was very thorough at this cemetery.

"Are we going to the cottage this weekend?" Michael said.

"We'll see. It's only Tuesday."

Michael broke the grasp and wandered to a few other graves. "Some of the people here have hard names. Lots of letters."

Mildred nodded and reached for her handkerchief.

Michael rubbed his hand along the top of a grave stone. "Sally says she's gonna move to Toronto when she's old enough."

"She may. Your sister is only fifteen years old. She's still young." Mildred glanced over to Michael, then frowned. "Don't stand on the graves. It's not appropriate."

He jumped out of the way. "Why, Mom? Aren't they dead anyway?"

"It's about respect. Would you want someone walking all over you? Would you walk on Grandfather's grave?"

Michael looked down.

"Run off to the car. I'll just be here a moment." She watched her ten year old saunter toward the waiting vehicle on the other side of the gate. He didn't mean anything bad but has to learn how to conduct himself in a cemetery. So rambunctious. Always surprising her. Then again, the boy surprised them when he was born after they thought they'd only have one child.

A gust of wind came and her hat flew off and landed right on Marko's grave. Reaching down to pick it up, she leaned on his grave stone. Hard granite, the inscription may have been simple, but Gregory spared no expense with the stone. She carefully traced the inscription in the headstone to brush away the dust and dirt that had collected in the grooves over the past year.

She blew her nose in her handkerchief. Gregory became a fine husband. Despite losing his leg after he got shot during the Strike and with her help, they rebuilt his real estate business. It's been much more difficult the last few years, but thankfully he never dabbled in the stock market before it crashed. He always said stocks weren't worth the paper they were printed on.

Mildred smiled, recalling a few years after the strike when Gregory bought a vehicle repair shop in the West End. He hired the best car mechanics he could find and renamed it MARKO'S AUTOMOBILE REPAIRS. He said it was the least he could do to honour the man who saved his future wife's life. She couldn't help but cry when she first saw the sign. Even now she feels a fluttery feeling in her tummy when they drive past the shop even though he'd been dead for seventeen years.

The same day as his friend Mike. Shot dead right in the street. Someone said Maria ended up marrying Mike's brother only a month after Mike's death to avoid being deported. Mildred never did see Benny or Bert again.

Mildred put the flowers on Marko's grave and stood still for a few moments before returning to the car. Although each visit awoke sad emotions, by the end she felt better, like she'd just visited an old friend.

*****

"Sally, did you finish practicing your piano?" Mildred said. "Go on and finish up."

"Dinner will soon be ready," Bernice said. "Chicken soup." Originally they hired Bernice to help when they first had Sally, but she became such a good housekeeper they decided to keep her on. A heavy-set women in her late 50s, she possessed a jovial personality and, over time, felt like part of the family.

Tall and beautiful with long, straight brown hair, Sally stood almost eye-level to Mildred. She left the kitchen and in a few minutes the sounds of her plunking on the upright in the living room permeated through the house.

As Bernice set the table for dinner, Mildred heard the familiar sound of the Buick pull up the driveway in the backyard and enter the garage. The heavy door of the Series 40 slammed shut twice, once for Maxwell and the other for Gregory.

"Hello dear," Gregory said. He slipped off his one shoe and came over to her on his crutches to plant a kiss on her cheek. Mildred helped him remove his hat and jacket.

Gregory slumped down in a kitchen chair and leaned his crutches against the wall. "Whew, it's a hot one out there." His perfect teeth still gleamed. He'd put on a bit of weight over the years but having only one leg limited his physical activity.

"Here, let me get you some lemonade from the refrigerator," Mildred said. "Bernice just made some. Did you lay off Bradley like I told you to?" She poured two glasses and joined him at the table.

Gregory nodded. "It was difficult. I missed you at the office. You're much better at that than I. He was a good employee, but if there's no work .… I hope it turns around soon." Gregory gulped down half the glass then scratched the stump of his left leg.

They had to amputate just above the knee a week after he was shot. Either that or he would have died from infection. Those were the most difficult times. Gregory's house had burned down and he had to convalesce for months. The money from the pink hat box came in handy. She still found it hard to believe Gregory wanted to maintain the office out of the new home after construction. Thankfully they moved the office away from home and into a proper building downtown on Notre Dame. After the birth of Sally she didn't want a steady stream of business associates and customers coming through the front door every day. The old arrangement provided no privacy.

"I hope it turns around soon," Mildred said, "but I don't see it. It may take years. The economy is in tatters. Men can't find work. Crops are suffering. We are very, very fortunate. I'm so glad we diversified."

"Maxwell will be safe, though. I'll always need a driver."

"Until he finds something that pays more. We've went through many drivers. They all find something better."

"I'll worry about it when it happens. How was the cemetery?"

"Oh, fine." Mildred stood up and crossed her arms. She examined her features in the reflection of the little mirror just inside the hallway. Her hair was streaked with grey and no amount of creams would smooth those lines.

"You know, you're probably the only person on the planet that visits his grave. It's very commendable."

Mildred went to Gregory and stroked his hair. "Father used to always tell me that the factory was never the same after the strike. He missed Marko's skill as a repairman."

"True, but I think part of it was that he sacked Peter because of his involvement in the union. The poor bugger, he couldn't find a decent job in town and ended up moving back to England."

Bernice took the soup off the stove. She filled bowls and placed them on the table to cool before leaving the kitchen.

Meanwhile, in the family room, Sally began a new piece, something simpler and paired down from the full orchestral version.

Mildred heard the first few notes of the 'Blue Danube Waltz' and looked off in the distance trying to hold back the tears.

"I'm sorry, dear," Gregory said. "I know this day is difficult for you." He grabbed a crutch and came to Mildred where he wiped away a tear from her cheek and put her head into his chest.

Mildred's tears trickled down as Sally's precise piano-playing intensified.

"He saved your life then sacrificed himself going after William. He prevented a fire that would have devastated your father's factory. He didn't have to, but that's the special man he was. It's too bad he blurred his past, but that's what happens with a blow to the head, I suppose."

Mildred nodded and dabbed away the few remaining tears. "Thank you, I'll be fine." She sniffed and offered him a weak smile.

"I should clean up before dinner," Gregory said. He grabbed his crutches and went off to freshen up.

Mildred went into the family room where Sally played the last few bars of the waltz. She looked up on the mantle to the jewelry box Marko repaired decades ago. She closed her eyes and drifted back to that hot, hot day at her parent's mansion over twenty years ago. She felt content and satisfied with how her life had turned out, but she would have ran away with Marko then and there.

Acknowledgements

Thank you to the team at Sands Press for recognizing the potential of my story. Of course, were it not for the Digiwriting's CanLitPit event, our paths may have never have crossed.

Writers in Residence at the University of Winnipeg and the Millennium Library including Joan Thomas, Debbie Paterson and Ivan Coyote. All three provided wisdom and advice when I began this project. Bethany Gibson for her exact, sharp and pointed criticism and structural editing support. Jim Blanchard from the Manitoba Historical Society for providing invaluable knowledge into the nuances of society and culture in Winnipeg during the World War I era. Danny Schur for his detailed insight and perspective into Winnipeg's General Strike. Corrine Sidon for providing background on Mike Sokolowski's family.

Manitoba Archives for helping me research information related to the Influenza epidemic and details regarding the General Strike. The Manitoba's Writers' Guild and the Writers' Collective of Manitoba for providing me with support, advice and access to programs that improved my skills and abilities as a writer. Also thanks to Chris Adams and Jim Ingebrigtsen for their advice and support.

A special thank you goes to my writing group, the Cattywampuses (Bob Armstrong, Sue Sorensen, Byron Rempel-Burkholder, Brenda Sawatzky, Josiah Neufeld), for critiquing various chapters of the novel over the past several years. (You too, Linda). They provided valuable tips and insights to improve my writing and to help navigate the wacky literary world. All are better writers than I.

The road was long and hard. My novel could not have been completed without the support and encouragement of family and friends. Thanks to those who endured earlier, bloated, crappier versions and provided comments and suggestions. My children, Arden, Zeke, Zora and Esme, who kept me to task ("When's it gonna be done, Dad?"). But especially my wife, June, who, even during the darkest hours, provided steadfast support through the entire journey and never once wavered in her optimism that this story would see the light of day.

Thanks to many others who have helped me since January 2011 when I started working on this novel. Your advice, criticism, and encouragement is much appreciated.

Richard Zaric, October 2017

Notes

I consulted a variety of sources to help ensure *Hiding Scars* is factually accurate. This research also provided me with an understanding of the mood and sentiment of the era.

The best and most enjoyable book regarding the era has to be *The Boy from Winnipeg* by James Gray. The memoir provides a multitude of facts and observations about life in Winnipeg. It should be required reading for anyone interested in 1910s Winnipeg. I also studied two other books he wrote on the era, *Red Lights on the Prairies* and *Booze*. Both provide insight into the seedier aspects of society including details on Prohibition.

Under the Ribs of Death, a 1957 novel by John Marlyn examines the discrimination faced by Eastern European immigrants. To better understand the Spanish Flu Epidemic of 1918, I consulted with *The Silent Enemy* by Eileen Pettigrew and *Influenza: 1918* by Esyllt Jones. *Winnipeg's Great War* by Jim Blanchard provides detailed insight into the role World War I had on the psyche of Winnipeg.

To gain a general understanding of the look and feel of Winnipeg during the era I studied a variety of books including *Winnipeg First Century* by Ruben Bellon, *Winnipeg in Maps* by Alan Artibise and *Winnipeg: An Illustrated History* also by Artibise.

Of course, the infamous Winnipeg General Strike of 1919 is prominent in my novel. The first book I picked up when I started my research was *Winnipeg General Strike of 1919: An Illustrated History* by J.M. Bumstead. I augmented this with conversation with Danny Schur including his short film *Winnipeg's Bloody Saturday* and a Strike Walking Tour he held one day.

The *Winnipeg Free Press* on-line archives proved to be a fantastic source of information (then called the *Manitoba Free Press*). Pages and pages of my notebooks are filled with notes from the exhaustive and detailed articles from that era. Although I had to be cautious of the reporting, especially regarding the General Strike, I was able to glean important facts regarding the notorious John Krafchenko, the Manitoba Legislative building debacle, the effects of the influenza epidemic (including day by day body counts) and other assorted tidbits.

I found the Manitoba Historical Society's website to be helpful when researching particular aspects of Manitoba's history. Details regarding internment camps during World War I came from *Without Just Cause* by Lubomyr Luciuk. I also gained knowledge by experiencing a Jane's Walk through North Point Douglas and attending the *Titanic* exhibit at the old, short-lived MTS Exhibition Hall here in Winnipeg.

About The Author

Richard Zaric has had a passion for writing as far back as high school when he won the Nan Shipley Award for creative writing. Richard has been a researcher for over 25 years. His research skills helped uncover Winnipeg's storied past. He graduated from the University of Manitoba (Bachelor of Commerce (Honours)) in 1989 and lives in Winnipeg. *Hiding Scars* is his first novel.